Natural Causes

Michael Palmer is the international bestselling author of nine previous novels, including, most recently, *The Patient*. His novels have been translated into twenty-six languages and have been adapted for film and television. He trained in internal medicine at Boston City and Massachusetts General Hospitals, spent twenty years as a full-time practitioner of internal and emergency medicine, and is now involved in the treatment of alcoholism and chemical dependence. He lives in Massachusetts.

NATURAL CAUSES

Michael Palmer

ARROW

First published in the United Kingdom in 1994 by
Piatkus Books

Arrow Books Limited
The Random House Group Limited
20 Vauxhall Bridge Road, London, SW1V 2SA

Random House Australia (Pty) Limited
20 Alfred Street, Milsons Point, Sydney
New South Wales 2061, Australia

Random House New Zealand Limited
18 Poland Road, Glenfield, Auckland 10, New Zealand

Random House (Pty) Limited
Endulini, 5a Jubilee Road, Parktown 2193, South Africa

The Random House Group Limited Reg. No. 954009

www.randomhouse.co.uk

A CIP catalogue record for this book
is available from the British Library

Papers used by Random House Limited are natural,
recyclable products made from wood grown in sustainable
forests. The manufacturing processes conform to the
environmental regulations of the country of origin

Printed and bound in Great Britain by
Bookmarque Ltd, Croydon, Surrey

ISBN 0 09 972711 0

Dedicated to
Luke Harrison Palmer
Welcome, big guy

Acknowledgments

If you read the "About the Author" page, please read this page as well. The people listed below are very much about the author, and share my deepest thanks.

Beverly Lewis, my editor and friend, defines the word *Godsend*.

Linda Grey and Irwyn Applebaum, my publishers at Bantam, have been supportive, insightful, and encouraging.

Jane Rotrosen, Don Cleary, Stephanie Laidman, Meg Ruley, and Andrea Cirillo of the Rotrosen Agency have been major influences on each of my books and on my career as a writer.

Dr. Rick Abisla of Falmouth, Massachusetts, and Dr. Dolores Emspak of Swampscott, Massachusetts, gave me invaluable technical advice in their specialty.

Attorneys Marcia Divoll and Joanne Colombani Smith of Boston, and Ms. Ginni Ward did the same for me in their areas of the law.

Nurses Jeanne Jackson and Carolyn Moulton of Falmouth gave me books to read and helped me appreciate the power and potential of alternative healing. Dr. Bud Waisbren of Ipswich, Massachusetts, provided information and encouragement that nudged me through a particularly resistant block.

Dr. Richard Dugas dragged me off to play bridge from time to time, and so may have preserved my sanity. John

Saul and Michael Sack had just the right words at just the right times.

And finally, my love and thanks to my wife, who once again bore the brunt of my writing maelstrom with remarkable class and an understanding patience.

M.S.P.
Swampscott, Massachusetts

NATURAL CAUSES

Prologue

CONNIE HIDALGO'S CONTRACTIONS HAD BEEN LITTLE
more than twinges for the first two hours of the
drive; but as she and her fiancé passed the New
London exits on I-95, the tightening within her
began to intensify.

"Billy, I think something's happening," she
said.

"Gimme a break. You been sayin' that for a goddamn
month, and you still got a month to go."

"I should have stayed home."

"You should have done exactly what you're doin',
which is to make this trip to New York and help me
make this buy."

"Well, at least you couldda taken the Mercedes. This
seat is killing me."

Connie knew that taking the slick 500SL had been out
of the question. The last thing Billy Molinaro wanted
was to attract attention—or car thieves. Besides, he
never was one to change his routine, especially when
things were going well. The battered Ford wagon had
always been their way into and out of Manhattan. There
wasn't a chance in the world he would have agreed to

doing anything differently this night. He hadn't told her how much money they were carrying in the two gym bags stuffed in the tire well, but she knew it was plenty —more than ever before.

She squirmed as another contraction built and stared out the window, trying to lose herself in the lights and signs as they flashed past. She was a slight woman—all belly, Billy kept saying—with wide, dark eyes and a fine, smooth face that she had learned made most men want her. At fourteen, she had delivered a baby girl and had given it away without so much as looking at it. Now, ten years later, God had blessed her with a second chance. And nothing was going to go wrong. Nothing.

"Billy, I love you," she said softly.

"In that case, light this for me."

He slipped a fat joint from beneath his seat, licked it expertly, and leaned toward her.

"Billy, no. It's bad for the baby."

"*Crack* is bad for the baby," he corrected. "That's why I haven't let you do any since we found out you were pregnant. But no one has ever shown nothing wrong with weed. Trust me on that one."

"Well, at least open the window."

Connie lit the joint and, in spite of herself, breathed in deeply as he exhaled. As always, Billy was right. She had smoked daily during her first pregnancy—cigarettes and marijuana—and the baby had been born plump and perfect.

"Now listen," Billy said. "Manny Diaz is a slime, but after all the deals him and me've done together, I pretty much trust him—especially with you around to translate when he won't talk English. But this is bigger than any of those other deals, so we gotta take extra precautions. I'm gonna have you stay out in front with the motor running. You keep the doors locked until I come out and tell you it's okay. If anything doesn't seem right—anything at all—just get the hell away and call my cousin Richie in Newark. Got that?"

"I got it. I got it."

Another contraction hit. Connie clenched her teeth and pressed her slender fingers against her womb. She had had two bouts of false labor in the past two weeks, and felt more certain than not that this was the same deal. She checked Billy's watch. If the contractions continued to be this bad, she would begin to time them.

But as she worked at convincing herself that there was nothing happening for her to worry about, Connie began to experience another kind of pain—this one in the tips of her fingers. At first she couldn't really call it a pain. It was more of a numbness—an unpleasant lack of feeling. By Stamford, the numbness had given way to a persistent, electric discomfort—worse when she pressed down, but not completely gone when she didn't. Huddled in the darkness, she tested her fingertips one by one. All of them ached.

It was nerves, just nerves, she thought. Billy had relit the joint. One toke wouldn't hurt, and it would probably help a great deal. Connie pulled his hand over, pressed her lips to the moist paper, and breathed in until she couldn't hold any more. It had been nearly six months since she had been even a little bit stoned. Surely one toke wasn't going to hurt the baby. In fact, she reasoned, with what it had in store, the little thing probably needed a buzz even more than she did.

By New Rochelle, Connie had smoked all of one joint herself. The pain in her fingers was no less, and the contractions were still coming every five minutes or so, but neither bothered her as much.

"Billy, I feel better," she said.

"I knew you would, Sugar."

Within just a few miles, though, she sensed the buzzing pain beginning in her toes. Frightened, she tried another joint.

"Hey, back off that stuff," Billy said.

"I think the baby's coming."

"Well, I hope he knows enough to stay put until we

get this deal done. I need you behind this wheel to do it right. Besides, if we blow it, the kid'd be better off not coming out at all."

"Billy, I'm serious."

"And what do you think I am—the Good Humor man?" He glanced nervously at his watch. "Right on schedule. We pull this buy off, Sugar, and we're in the big leagues. Believe me. This is the test Dominic has been waiting to give me. And nothing's gonna fuck it up."

Connie heard the intensity in her lover's voice and clenched her teeth against the throbbing in her hands and feet. Billy was right. It wasn't just their money at stake, it was their future. When she was younger and fat and unattractive, the only thing men ever wanted from her was sex. When she changed and became beautiful, the men who hit on her had more going for them—took her nicer places. But what they wanted was still the same. Only Billy had been different. He had made her his girl. And from the very beginning he had treated her with respect. Now they were about to have a child. And as soon as this deal was done, he had promised they would be married.

Whatever she had to do to help Billy Molinaro to-night, she would do. If only the aching would let up . . . just a little.

With a discomfort that nearly brought tears, she reached up and flicked on the overhead light.

"Hey, what're you doing?" Billy asked.

"Just . . . just looking for a tape to play."

She glanced at her hands, and then quickly switched off the light and pulled them from his line of sight. Her fingers and thumbs from the first knuckle to the tip had turned almost black. The rest of her hands was a dusky gray.

"Well?"

"Well what?"

"'Well, what tape did you pick?"

"Oh, I—I decided I'd rather rest."

Please, God, she thought, *just let me get through one more hour. Just one.*

It was after midnight when they rolled down the Harlem River Drive and turned off onto 116th Street. The fierce contractions in Connie's womb no longer concerned her as much as the fear that when they reached the meeting place, she would be unable to grasp the wheel, much less drive. Her left hand, now fixed in a semiclaw, was nearly useless. And although she could work her right hand and fingers, even slight movements of them sent intense pain shooting up her arm.

Please, God. . . .

"Well, this is it, Sugar," Billy said, stopping beneath a streetlight in front of a dilapidated tenement. "These guys are scared shitless of Dominic, so I don't expect any problems. It never hurts to cut the cards, though, especially with this size deal. So you stay here, doors locked, motor running. I'll go up and check their shit. If it's okay, we'll make the exchange right here on the street. Okay? Connie, I said 'Okay?' "

Connie Hidalgo, her hands and feet throbbing, bit at the inside of her lip while the pain from a particularly fierce contraction lanced through her. As the tightening subsided, she felt warmth begin to pool between her legs. Her water was breaking.

"P-please hurry," she managed. "The baby's going to come soon. I—I think we need to go to a hospital."

Billy snatched up his test kit and adjusted the holster beneath his left arm.

"You just goddamn keep it together until we're done," he snapped. "Understand?" He noticed the pain in her face, and his expression softened. "Connie, honey, everything will be all right. I promise. I'll finish this business with Diaz as quick as I can. And then if you want, I'll get you the best damn doctor in New York."

"But . . ."

"Remember, now, keep your door locked, and keep your eye out for trouble. I love you."

"I love you, too," Connie said. But he was already gone.

With great effort, she slid behind the wheel and locked the driver's side door. Having your water break was no great cause for alarm, she thought desperately. The birthing class nurse had stressed that over and over again. Five minutes passed. Then five more. The contractions were hell.

Anxious to distract herself, to check her fingers, Connie again turned on the interior light. The gray, cold hands with their blackened fingertips looked like some sort of Halloween prop. She glanced at herself in the rearview mirror. *Something was wrong with her face*. It took several seconds for her mind to understand the dark ribbons of blood that had begun winding down from her nostrils, across the top of her lip, and alongside the corners of her mouth.

"Please, Billy. Please hurry," she whimpered.

She was clumsily searching her purse for a tissue when she noticed the deep crimson stain expanding over the groin and legs of her beige maternity slacks. This wasn't the clear or slightly tinged fluid the nurse had spoken of. It was blood! Connie felt dizzy, confused. She tried to dab at the flow from her nose, which now was entering her mouth and spattering down onto her blouse. Her left arm felt leaden.

"Please! Please someone help me," she cried. Then she realized that the words were in her mind, but she could not speak them. Her vision seemed blurred, the left side of her body paralyzed. Terror beyond any she had ever known took hold.

At that moment, the windshield of the Ford exploded inward, showering her with glass. Instantly, from across her brow, blood cascaded into her eyes. She pawed at it with the back of her right hand, managing to clear her vision briefly. Billy's body was stretched across the hood of the car, his shattered head and one arm dangling lifelessly over the passenger seat beside her. Soundlessly Connie screamed and screamed again.

Through the shattered windshield, she could see several men approaching. With no conscious purpose other than to get away, she dropped her hand onto the gear shift, knocking it from park to drive. The Ford shot forward, striking at least one of the men and glancing off several parked cars. As the wagon careened onto Third Avenue, Billy's body fell away. Connie, now more dead than alive, looked to her left in time to see the headlights and grillwork of a bus.

For one brief instant, there was a horrible, grinding noise, accompanied by pain unlike any Connie had ever known. Then, just as suddenly, there was blackness . . . and peace.

Chapter 1

JULY 1, CHANGEOVER DAY

IT WAS EXACTLY SEVEN POINT TWO MILES FROM SARAH Baldwin's North End apartment to the Medical Center of Boston. Today—a Monday—the roads were dry, the humidity low, and at six A.M., the traffic virtually nonexistent.

Sarah squinted up at the early-morning glare, getting a sense of the day. "Nineteen minutes forty-five seconds," she predicted.

She straddled her Fuji twelve-speed, adjusted her safety helmet, and set her stopwatch to zero. Just fifteen seconds either way had become the allowable margin in the contest. More often than not, she won. Over the two years she had been commuting by bike to MCB, she had honed her accuracy by factoring into her average time as many arcane variables as she could remember on any given day. *Tuesday or Thursday?* . . . Add thirty seconds. *Regular coffee at breakfast instead of decaf?* . . . Deduct forty-five. *Two nights in a row off call?* . . . A full minute or more to the good. Today she also factored in the need to pedal hard enough to feel she had exercised, but not so hard as to break much of a sweat.

She glanced along the quaint row houses lining her

narrow street, keyed her stopwatch, and shoved off. Once a near fanatic about fitness, she had now all but given up on formal workouts. Instead, she would push herself to the limit on the ride to work, shower at the hospital, and then change into her scrubs for rounds. But today nothing would be usual. At the Medical Center of Boston, as at most of the teaching hospitals around the country, this was July 1—Changeover Day.

For every physician in training in every specialty, Changeover Day marked a major rite of passage. Brand-new M.D.s stepping into hospitals as first-year residents. First-year residents one minute becoming second-year residents the next. For Sarah, the changeover would be from second-year resident in obstetrics and gynecology to third year. Suddenly more responsibility. Literally overnight, less supervision, especially in the operating room. It helped put some perspective on the tension she was feeling, to reflect on the fears she had dealt with on Changeover Day a year ago, or worse, the year before that.

Now, all things being equal, in another year Changeover Day would usher in Sarah's tenure as the chief resident of her department. On that day, in most situations, her decisions, her clinical judgment, would become the final word. It was a sobering thought. And although being a chief at a modest facility like MCB was hardly like being one at White Memorial or the other huge university hospitals, it was still impressive—especially considering that less than seven years ago, becoming a physician had been the farthest thing from her mind.

She dropped into third gear for the ride over Beacon Hill and then cruised into the Back Bay. Just a few blocks away was the huge, corner brownstone that had once housed the Ettinger Institute of Holistic Healing. As usual when she passed near that building, she wondered about Peter Ettinger—why had he never answered any of her calls or letters? Was he married? Was he happy? And what of Annalee, the West African girl he had adopted as an infant? She had been fifteen when Sarah left. Sarah had felt very close to her. It was still a source of sadness that their relationship had not survived.

Three years before, when she returned from Italy with her M.D. degree, Sarah had stopped by the institute. The place that had once been her home and the focus of her life was now six luxury condominiums. Peter's name was not among the residents. Months later she had learned of Xanadu, Peter's holistic community set in the rolling hills west of the city. She would drive out there sometime, she thought. Perhaps face-to-face they could set some things straight.

But she never did.

Distracted, Sarah cruised through a yellow light, drawing an obscene gesture from a cabby who was preparing to jump the green.

Be careful, she warned herself. *Be very careful.* The last place anyone should end up was in an emergency room on Changeover Day.

As she turned off Veteran's Highway onto the MCB access road, Sarah checked the time. More than twenty minutes already. She dismounted and decided to walk the final few hundred yards. Her little contest had no predictive significance that she had ever discerned. Nevertheless, she did make a passing mental note that this Changeover Day had begun with a loss.

Up ahead of her, picketers lined both sides of the drive, jeering those entering to work and occasionally joining in a ragged chant. MCB had gone a week or more without a demonstration—the longest span Sarah could remember. Now some group or other was on the warpath again. Sarah tried to guess which one. Nurses—RNs and LPNs—maintenance, transportation, security, dietary, clerical, physical therapy, nurse's aides, even house staff—at one time or another, each had run some

sort of job action at the beleaguered institution. Today it
was maintenance.

> Down with Glenn Paris . . . MCB = More Cock
> and Bull . . . Better Management, Not Better
> Promises . . . MCB Nay HMO Yea . . .

The placards were, in the main, professionally done.
The messages on them ranged from snide to malicious.

> Is Paris Burning? Well Why Not? . . . Pay Us
> or Fix It Yourself . . . You Trust This Place
> With Your Life?!!!

Whatever their beef with MCB, Sarah noted, the maintenance workers had some money behind them.

"Nice day for a demonstration, eh?"

Andrew Truscott, a senior resident in vascular surgery
as of today, fell into step beside her. Originally from
Australia, Truscott had an acerbic wit, made even dead-
lier by an outback accent he could fine-tune from trace
to dense. Now thirty-six, he was the only other resident
Sarah's age. He was a difficult person to warm up to—
rigidly traditional, opinionated, and too often facetious.
But he was also a damn fine surgeon. The two of them
had met the day she arrived at MCB and had quickly
connected. At first Sarah expected that rapport—that
sense of comrades-in-arms—to grow into a true friend-
ship. But comrade-in-arms turned out to be as close as
Andrew ever allowed anyone at MCB to get.

Still, Sarah enjoyed her contacts with the man, and
had certainly benefited from his teaching. She also acknowledged to herself that had Andrew Truscott not
been married, she would gladly have dusted off her fem-
inine wiles to try and break down his reserve. As things
stood, she was still without the solution to the nagging
problem of how she was to become a competent surgeon
herself without totally suppressing the need for love,

companionship, sex, and whatever else of merit went with life beyond the hospital.

"What would Changeover Day at MCB be like without a few pickets, Andrew?" she said.

"Ah, yes. Changeover Day at the Medical Center of Boston. At the east wing we have a lineup of professional drug-seekers, duping the new residents with textbook performances of the passing of a kidney stone or the slipping of a lumbar disk. At the west wing, we have a lineup of disgruntled maintenance workers, looking to squeeze a few more bucks from this stone of a hospital. Ain't medicine grand?"

"MCB nay, HMO yea," Sarah said. "Since when are the maintenance workers into hospital politics?"

"Probably since someone told them they might actually get those bucks if Everwell took the place over."

"It's not going to happen."

Truscott smiled. "Try telling them."

For several years, the ambitious—some said avaricious—Everwell Health Maintenance Organization had been waiting and watching like a predatory cat as MCB staggered beneath a crippling weight of fiscal problems, labor unrest, and the controversy surrounding its emphasis on blending nontraditional healing with traditional medicine and surgery. By charter, a vote of the hospital trustees, if approved by the state Public Health Commission, would turn the hospital over to the definitely for-profit operation. And each job action, each piece of negative publicity, brought the unique institution closer to its knees.

"It's not going to happen, Andrew," Sarah said again. "Things have gotten better every year since Paris took over. You know that as well as I do. MCB has become one of a kind. People from all over the world come here for care because of the way we do things. We can't let Everwell or anyone else ruin that."

"Look, mate," Truscott said, his accent deepening, "if you're going to become impassioned about anything, you've got to turn in your surgeon's merit badge. That's the rule."

"You get just as impassioned about things as I do," Sarah said. "You're just too macho to let it show." She glanced past the demonstrators at the bicycle rack, which was empty save two rusted three-speeds, whose tires appeared to have been slashed. "I think the nurse's aides were a bit less physical during their strike," she observed. "It looks like my bike gets chained to the bed in the on-call room. Andrew, don't you have the feeling that someone other than the maintenance men has helped organize all this?"

"You mean Everwell?"

Sarah shrugged. "Possibly. But they're not the only candidate. Thanks to Axel Devlin, there are more than a few people who have the wrong impression about the way we do things here."

Devlin, a *Herald* columnist with an unabashedly conservative slant, had dubbed MCB Crunchy Granola General. He made it a frequent target of "Axel's Axe" in his popular Take It or Leave It column. As an M.D. with extensive training and expertise in acupuncture and herbal therapy, Sarah herself had been mentioned in the column on two occasions, not at all flatteringly. She never had figured out how Devlin learned of her.

"Who knows?" Andrew responded with no great interest. He nodded toward the dozen or so picketers. "They are a gnarly group, I'll say that for them. Not a tattooless deltoid in the bunch." He paused at the door marked *Staff Only* and turned to her. "Well, Dr. Baldwin, are you ready to pop up a level?"

Sarah stroked her chin thoughtfully, then took Truscott's arm.

"What options exist for me are either unacceptable or illegal, Dr. Truscott," she said. "Let's do it."

Fifty feet above the pristine mountain pool, Lisa Summer poised on the cliff's edge. But for the garlands of white lilies around her neck and her head, she was naked. The sun glinted off her long, perfect body and sparkled in her straw-gold hair. All around her, wildflowers billowed, blanketing the cliffs and cascading down the rocks beside the shimmering falls. High overhead a solitary hawk glided effortlessly against the cloudless, azure sky.

Lisa tilted her head back and let the sun warm her face. She closed her eyes and listened to the churning water below. Then, arms spread, she tightened her toes over the edge, took a final, deep breath, and pushed off. Wind and spray caressed her face as she floated more than fell past the falls, twisting and tumbling through the crystal air . . . downward . . . downward . . . downward . . .

"Hang in there, Lisa. Beautiful. Hang in there. The contraction's almost over. A minute ten . . . a minute twenty. That's it. That's it. Oh, you did great. You did just great."

Slowly Lisa opened her eyes. She was propped on the futon in her cluttered room, bathed in the rays of the early-morning sun. Heidi Glassman, her housemate, friend, and birthing coach, sat beside her, stroking her hand. Across from her, waiting, were the crib and changing table she had found at Goodwill and meticulously refinished.

The weeks of practice in class and at home were paying off. Lisa was now in her third hour of active labor, but thanks to the series of sensual images she had developed, the pain of every contraction so far had been easily subverted.

Dr. Baldwin called the process internal and external visualization. It was, she had told Lisa, a modest form of self-hypnosis—a technique that, if practiced diligently, would enable Lisa to make it through even difficult labor and delivery without any anesthesia or other drugs. For some contractions, Lisa used external visualization to send herself soaring off her mountain cliff or for a wondrous undersea ride on the back of a dolphin. For others, she used internal visualization to see the actual muscles of her womb and the baby boy within, and to mentally buffer them both with thick cotton batting.

"How're you doing?" Heidi asked.

"Fine. Just fine," Lisa said dreamily.

"You look very peaceful."

"I feel wonderful."

Unaware she was doing so, Lisa slowly opened and closed her hands.

"Five minutes apart for nearly an hour. I think it may be time to call."

"There's time," Lisa said. She closed her eyes for a few seconds. "I don't think I've even started to dilate yet."

Her mind's eye saw her cervix clearly. It was just beginning to open.

"Want me to check?" Heidi asked.

Heidi was a nurse who had spent several years on an OB floor. Now she was poised to assist Dr. Baldwin with the home birth.

"I don't think there's any need," Lisa said, rubbing her fingers now.

"Something the matter?"

"No. My hands feel a little stiff, that's all—"

"Might be retained water. Let me check your blood pressure."

Heidi slipped a blood pressure cuff around Lisa's arm and set her stethoscope over Lisa's brachial artery. The pressure, ninety over sixty-five, was a bit lower than it had been, although still in the normal range for early labor. Heidi mulled over the change, then decided it was of no significance. She wrote the pressure down in her notebook and made a mental note to check it again in ten or fifteen minutes.

"Who's going to win the pool?" Lisa asked.

"Assuming it's today?"

"Oh, it's going to be today. You can count on it."

"In that case, Kevin will be thirty dollars richer."

Kevin Dow, a painter, was another of the residents of 313 Knowlton Street. There were ten of them in all. Most were artists or writers, and none of them made much money. They called their living arrangement a commune, and in that light shared almost everything. Lisa, who sold her pottery and occasionally refinished old furniture, had lived in the massive, gabled house for almost three years. And although she had twice slept with one of the men in the commune, she felt certain the child within her was not his and had made that clear to him from the outset, much to his relief.

In fact, who the father was, or was not, did not matter to Lisa one bit. The baby would be raised by her and her alone. He would be raised in simplicity, with love and patience and understanding, and without the pressure of expectations.

With Heidi's assistance, she stood and walked over to the window. Her right arm felt tired and heavy.

"Can I get you anything?" Heidi asked.

Lisa absently rubbed at her shoulder as she stared out at a squirrel that was leaping deftly along a series of branches that seemed far too pliant to hold it.

"Maybe some cocoa," she said.

"Coming up. . . . Lisa, are you okay?"

"I—I'm fine. I think another one's about to hit. How long has it been?"

"Five minutes, three seconds."

"I think I'll do this one standing."

Lisa leaned forward and braced herself against the sill. Then she breathed deeply, closed her eyes, and tried to send her mind inside her body. But nothing happened—no images, no sense of peace, nothing—nothing except pain. She was trying too hard, she thought. She had to be centered—that's what Dr. Baldwin had taught her—centered and prepared for each contraction. For the first time she felt a nugget of fear. Maybe she didn't know how bad it was going to get. Maybe she didn't have what it takes.

She gritted her teeth and stretched her arms and legs tightly.

"How long?" she asked.

"Forty seconds . . . fifty . . . a minute . . . a minute ten. . . ."

The intensity of the contraction began to lessen.

"A minute twenty. You okay?"

"I am now," Lisa said, backing away from the window and settling down on the futon. Her forehead was dotted with sweat. "That one was a bear. I wasn't ready."

Lisa swallowed and tasted blood. She probed with her tongue and found the small rent she had made by accidentally biting down on the inside of her cheek. The pain of the contraction was now completely gone, but the weird ache in her arm and shoulder persisted.

Heidi left the room and returned just in time for the next contraction. With Heidi's help and better preparation, Lisa found this contraction was much more manageable. Heidi slipped on the blood pressure cuff and once again took a reading. Eighty-eight over fifty, and even harder to hear than before.

"I think we should call," she said.

"Is everything okay?"

"Everything is fine. Your pressure's fine. I just think it's time."

"I want this to be perfect."

"It will be, Lisa. It will be."

Heidi stroked Lisa's forehead and then went to the phone in the hall. The drop in pressure was minimal, but if it was the start of a trend, she wanted Dr. Baldwin on hand.

Across the street, in front of 316 Knowlton, Richard Pulasky crouched behind his car as he disengaged the high-powered telephoto lens from his Nikon. He had gotten at least two good face shots of the girl, he felt certain. Maybe more. He pulled the frayed photo of Lisa Grayson from his pocket. The girl in the picture didn't look exactly like the woman in the window, but close enough. It was her, and that was that. Six months of work had just paid off big-time. Half the private dicks in town had taken a crack at finding the girl, but Dickie Pulasky had actually pulled it off.

Grinning to himself, Pulasky slid into his car through the passenger-side door. With any luck, he would be pocketing a fifteen-grand payoff within the week.

Chapter 2

SARAH SECURED HER BIKE TO THE METAL-FRAME BED IN the obstetrics on-call room. Over her first two years of residency she had spent nearly as many nights in the narrow cubicle as she had in her own apartment—and none of them very restfully.

After changing from her Spandex into the maroon scrubs favored by her department, she paused by the chipped bureau mirror. She rarely wore makeup of any kind, but in honor of Changeover Day, she smoothed on a bit of pale-pink lipstick. Then, as she often did just before starting her workday, she studied herself for a few quiet moments. Using sun block religiously during her years in Thailand had been worth the effort. Her skin still had good tone, and just a few freckles at the tops of her cheeks. There were some faint creases at the corners of her eyes, but nothing drastic. Her dark hair—mid-back length for most of her life—was short now, and sprinkled ever so lightly with gray. On balance, she decided—especially considering two years of low-paying, hundred-hour work weeks, with no financial or emotional support from the outside world—the woman in the mirror was holding up pretty damn well.

As in past years, the kickoff for Changeover Day at MCB was a continental breakfast and a presentation to the staff and residents by hospital president Glenn Paris, several department heads, and a member or two from the board of trustees. What made this year's kickoff different were the security guards checking photo IDs at each entrance to the auditorium. Sarah caught up with Andrew Truscott just as he was being cleared.

"Planning to watch the show from the last row?" she asked. For years Truscott had staked himself a seat there at most conferences.

"Having seen ol' Paris's slides from that vantage for four years running, I thought I might try something a bit closer."

"Fine by me," she said as they made their way down the steeply banked aisle of the amphitheater to the second row. "At our age we might as well begin learning how to deal with presbyopia and otosclerosis anyhow. Do you happen to know why the security check?"

Truscott thought for a moment.

"I'll bet they're searching for lunatics," he said.

"Lunatics?"

"Anyone who would come to this affair who didn't absolutely have to."

"Very funny."

"Thank you. I have no doubt our fearless leader will address the heightened security—either before or after his yearly recounting of the history of our august institution." He thrust his jaw out in a caricature of Glenn Paris. " 'In 1951, at age fifty, Medical Center of Boston moved from the midcity to the outskirts in order to occupy the nine buildings which once comprised the Suffolk State Hospital, better known as the nut house. And although that transition was completed decades ago, it is still rumored that late at night, the ghost of

Freddy Krueger scrubs up and stalks our operating rooms. . . .' "

"Andrew, what is with you today? Is it the chief residency? Are you just angry at not getting it?"

"Hardly." Truscott's sardonic laugh was unconvincing. "I'm angry about having my all-too-meager paycheck signed by a man who raffles off elective plastic surgical procedures, sends his residents on well-publicized house calls, and has closed-circuit TV put in delivery rooms."

"He's raised thousands of dollars with those raffles and contests—probably hundreds of thousands. And most families love the chance to be part of a birth. We've become the second busiest OB service in the city."

Before Truscott could respond, Glenn Paris stepped forward and tapped on the microphone. Immediately 120 staff physicians, residents, nurses, and trustees fell silent.

Glenn McD. Paris, the president of Medical Center of Boston, exuded confidence and success. He was only five feet eight, but many described him as tall. His jaw was as square as any Boston Brahmin's, and the intensity in his gaze was arresting. He had been described by one supporter as a mix of equal parts Vince Lombardi, Albert Schweitzer, and P.T. Barnum, with a dash of Donald Trump thrown in. Axel Devlin, on the other hand, had once called him the most distasteful and dangerous affliction to descend on Boston since the British.

Six years before, a desperate board of trustees had lured Paris away from a major hospital in San Diego that he had turned around in a remarkably short time. The deal they struck with him included the promise of a free hand in fund-raising and all hospital affairs, generous financial incentives, bonuses tied to any hospital profit, and the rent-free use of a Back Bay penthouse, donated to the institution some years before by a grateful patient. Paris had responded with a vigorous campaign to give the hospital a positive, easily definable image and to turn its red ink to black at all costs.

In some ways, the man had succeeded. The hospital's staggering debt had leveled off, if not lessened. At the same time, its increasing emphasis on whole-body medicine and personalized treatment had led to a growing reputation as a caring medical center.

But there was still a lack of respect for the institution in many quarters, both public and academic, and the feeling among some trustees that before long, the hospital would simply have to move in other directions.

"Good morning, troops," Paris began. "I want to welcome you to the official beginning of MCB's ninetieth year. The purpose of this annual kickoff is to introduce our new house staff and to help them feel at home." He motioned for the new residents to stand and led a round of applause. "You should know," he said to them, "that your group represents the best MCB has ever been matched up with in the national resident matching program."

Again applause. Several of the residents shifted uncomfortably, obviously wishing they could sit down. Paris, beaming as if he were showing off his children, kept them standing. The news of the high match—hospitals make their preferential list, prospective residents make theirs, and a computer does the rest—had been well publicized. But he was not one to miss the chance to milk such a success for all it was worth.

Truscott leaned over toward Sarah. "Note how carefully fearless leader neglects to add that although the match is the highest in MCB history, it still ranks below any of the other Boston teaching hospitals."

"For true?"

"Blankenship let that one slip out at lunch last week."

Dr. Eli Blankenship, the chief of staff, was also the head of the MCB resident training program. It was his impressive knowledge of alternative healing and his enlightened attitude toward Sarah's desire to blend her techniques that had convinced her to rank MCB number one on her match list. At the time, largely because of her unique background and high scores on the National Medical Boards, several more prestigious hospitals had already expressed interest in her.

"Please sit down," Paris said finally.

"In 1951, at age fifty . . ." Truscott murmured.

"Before going any further," the CEO continued, "I want to address the heightened security to which you were all subjected this morning. Over the past year, too much of this hospital's business has been finding its way to certain reporters and other special interests, who have gone out of their way to paint an unfavorable and damaging picture of the Medical Center of Boston. Some of these leaks involve the minor day-to-day errors—no, most are too trivial to be called errors—I should say *problems* in patient care which plague any hospital, and which are never shared with the public. Others involve exchanges at our staff meetings and conferences."

Sarah's beeper went off, the readout summoning her to an outside call. Wishing she could have crawled to the end of the row rather than stand up directly in front of Paris, she made her way to the nearest auditorium phone.

"All hospitals," Paris continued, "are in competition to maintain their allotment of beds and to keep a reasonable percentage of those beds filled. And as you know, that competition is often intense. Hospitals as large and prestigious as White Memorial now advertise in the yellow pages. Negative publicity for MCB, especially *groundless* negative publicity, hurts every one of us. From now on, no unauthorized personnel will be allowed in our medical rounds or staff meetings. Further, anyone other than our public relations office who speaks about hospital business with the press will be asked to leave our employ . . ."

Sarah listened for a minute to her call, gave some instructions, and returned to her seat.

"One of my home birth patients is in active labor," she whispered. "She's still got a ways to go, but her bp's a little low. I hope this program doesn't run over."

"You're doing home births yourself?" Truscott looked at her incredulously.

"No, Andrew. I assure you, I only look dumb. Dr. Snyder will be coming out with me. This will be our second one."

Randall Snyder, the OB/Gyn chief, was one of those seated on the stage behind Glenn Paris. As Sarah nodded up toward him, she realized that Paris had stopped speaking and was glowering down at her.

"Sorry," she mouthed, color rushing to her cheeks.

"Thank you," Paris mouthed in return.

He cleared his throat and took a sip of water. The silence in the hall was dramatic.

"Believe me," he went on finally, "this subversion from within is serious, serious business. As you know, outside interests and some more financially secure institutions have been just waiting for us to go under. Ours is an attractive facility with a wonderful location. But those folks are in for a rude awakening, my friends. *A rude awakening.* For some time now, I have been negotiating with a very well-endowed philanthropic group whose primary aim is the improvement of health care. We are currently on the home stretch of an extensive grant application. If that grant comes through—and at present all the signs are right—MCB will have financial stability and a vast capability to grow. That was the goal I set with you six years ago, and today I am pleased to state that it is a goal well within our reach."

There was a smattering of applause, which gradually spread until all in the auditorium—including Andrew—had joined in.

"That's the spirit," Sarah said to him.

"My hands were getting cold," Truscott replied.

Behind the podium, Glenn Paris again was beaming.

"Please don't stop on my account," he said as the response died down.

"He's a crafty one," Truscott whispered beneath the laughter that followed Paris's comment. "I'll say that for him."

"He's working a miracle."

"He's hyping himself."

"Before I introduce those seated behind me," Paris went on, "and while we are on the subject of outside interference in hospital business, I want to say just a few words about the gauntlet of demonstrators some of you were forced to traverse to get here this morning. Some on our maintenance staff are currently conducting an illegal job action which we have good reason to believe has been instigated and is being abetted by one of those operations committed to our demise. Mark me well. We shall not allow them to interfere one iota with patient care or any other business of this institution." He pounded his fist on the podium for emphasis. "And that you can take to the bank!"

The word "bank" was still reverberating throughout the amphitheater when a set of power lines was crossed, causing the main electrical generator at MCB to short out. The backup system, supplying electricity to the operating rooms, ICUs, and part of the emergency ward, kicked in immediately. But the amphitheater, which was windowless, was thrown into instant, stygian darkness.

The kickoff program for Changeover Day was over.

Chapter 3

I F SARAH HAD A ROLE MODEL IN HER PRACTICE OF OB-
stetrics and gynecology, it was her chief, Dr. Randall
Snyder. From his soft-spoken manner to his gray
Volvo sedan, everything about the man was fatherly
and reassuring. Now in his mid-fifties, he still approached his solo practice with exuberance and
compassion. When a new technique or treatment in
his field was announced, he would be one of the first in
line to learn it. If an uninsured clinic patient had a problem pregnancy, he would accept her as his private patient without a word about payment.

Today Randall Snyder was taking time from his busy
schedule to drive Sarah to the Jamaica Plains section of
the city. There he would assist her in performing a home
delivery on a twenty-three-year-old unwed woman with
no health insurance and an inordinate fear of doctors
and hospitals.

"How do you do it?" Sarah asked as they drove.

"Do what?" Snyder turned down the volume on the
Bach cantata he was playing on the tape deck.

"Keep on doing medicine the way you do without
letting it get to you?"

Snyder stifled most of a smile. "Do you want to define 'it'?"

"Oh, you know—the peer reviews and the lawyers, and the insurance companies and government telling you what you can and can't charge for your work; the mountains of paperwork, and the constant threat that you'll offend some vindictive or imbalanced patient who'll lodge a complaint about you or sue you."

"Oh, *that* 'it,' " Snyder said. "Sarah, as far as I'm concerned, you're not even talking about the *real* stress on this job: the cases that don't come out right, the people with untreatable illness, the people who die in spite of everything we do."

"But that's medicine. The other stuff is . . . is . . ."

"Is medicine, too. It's part of the package. Believe me, I'm not the serene machine a lot of people make me out to be. But neither do I go home after a day's work and beat my wife because I haven't hit the lottery or written the best-seller that will enable me to get out of the profession. I can handle the things you're talking about because by and large I still love what I do, and feel damn lucky to have been given the chance to do it. Why are you asking about all this? Are you having trouble?"

"Not trouble exactly. Oh, turn right at the next corner."

"Got it. Knowlton Street, you said, right?"

"Yes."

"I know the way. Now go on."

"You know that before I went to med school I worked in a holistic healing center."

"Of course. I've been to some of your presentations. Interesting stuff. Very interesting."

"My training was in herbal medicine and acupuncture. But some things happened that made me feel I needed to broaden the skills I had."

Some things happened. The understatement of the week, Sarah thought. She debated going into the details of her final clash with Peter Ettinger, but quickly realized that this was hardly the time or place to unearth that worm.

"Well, our techniques in the holistic center had their limitations," she went on. "I don't question that. But there was a certain, I don't know, call it innocence about our goals and the way we did things—most of us, anyway. Each day we went to work and were able to concentrate almost exclusively on doing what we could for our patients."

"And?"

"Well, as far as I can tell, medicine as I'm being trained to practice it now is often as much about money and liability as it is about patients. We order millions and millions of dollars in marginal or unnecessary tests so that our backsides will be covered if we end up in court. Meanwhile, government agencies, thinking they're saving money, are telling us how long we're allowed to keep patients with a given illness in the hospital. So what if an elderly lady here or there gets sent home too soon after a hysterectomy and falls and breaks her hip? We're talking statistics here—actuarial tables and percentages. Not flesh and blood."

"Sarah, you are too young to be so jaded."

"Dr. Snyder, I wish there *was* something I was still too young to be—anything at all; and you know I'm not jaded. I feel I've made the right decision in becoming an M.D. And I love being a doctor. Sometimes I just wish it all was a little more, I don't know, pure."

Randall Snyder chuckled.

"Ivory Soap is ninety-nine and forty-four one-hundredths percent pure," he said, turning onto Knowlton. "Nothing involving human beings even comes close to that—especially not in our racket. But, listen, I *do* understand what's troubling you, and I promise we'll continue this discussion sometime soon, perhaps over dinner at our place. For now, you should know that you're on your way to being a heck of a doctor—exactly the sort of person I would like to have as a partner in my practice."

"Why, thank you." Sarah could not mask her surprise —or pleasure. It was the first time she had heard Randall Snyder even intimate he might be considering bringing in an associate, let alone her.

"File that one away for the time being," Snyder said. "Sometime later this year, if you want, we'll sit down and talk business. It's okay to take a hard look at the less appealing sides of our profession, as long as you don't get paralyzed by what you see. And for God's sake, don't go putting *anyone* on a pedestal—especially me." He pulled to the curb in front of number 313. "Now, before we go in, how about giving me a thumbnail on our patient."

The concise, highly stylized presentation of a medical case was emphasized more, perhaps, than any other skill during Sarah's training. As a student, she would often lie in the bathtub, oblivious to the progressively cooling water, as she used a stopwatch and a dozen or more repetitions to perfect her next morning's case presentation. Now the technique was second nature.

"Lisa Summer is a twenty-three-year-old unmarried artist, gravida two, para zero, spontaneous a.b. three years ago. LMP ten-two."

Second pregnancy, no deliveries prior to this one, a miscarriage, last menstrual period nine months before. Randall Snyder nodded for Sarah to proceed.

"This pregnancy has been unremarkable in every respect. There has been a thirty-pound weight gain from a base weight of one oh six. At exam one week ago, fetus was in vertex position—head was engaged, probably left occiput anterior.

"Except for the usual childhood diseases, Lisa has a negative medical history. She is a nonsmoker and drinks occasionally. No other meds except for the natural prenatal supplement I prescribe."

"Ah, yes," Snyder said. "The mysterious Baldwin

mix. I was at the departmental conference last year when you spoke of it. Sometime soon I would like to learn more. Please continue."

"Family history is scant. No relationship with her parents at present; no relationship with the father of the child."

"Oh, my."

"Her coach is a woman friend who's a nurse. Apparently, as a child, Lisa had a bad experience of some sort in a hospital. Now she's terrified of them."

"*Ergo* the home birth."

"That's one of the reasons. Lisa's sort of—I don't know—she's very secretive about herself, and very mistrustful of people."

"Even you?"

"Not as much as at first, but yes, even me."

"Well, then, supposing we go on in and try to turn that around."

Sarah gathered up the covered tray of equipment and obstetrical instruments.

"One more thing," she said. "Heidi, the birth coach, said that Lisa's pressure has been dropping slightly and that it's become harder to hear in her right arm than her left. The last systolic I know of was eighty-five, just as Glenn was starting his talk. The highest, a few hours before that, was one ten."

"And what do you make of that?" Snyder asked.

"Low-normal for this stage of labor, I would say. When she called me, Heidi reported that Lisa looked fine. So it's probably nothing."

Sarah saw concern in Snyder's eyes and immediately sensed that she had not taken the report seriously enough.

"The actual number may be low-normal," he said, "but in my experience, not many labor patients have that sort of pressure drop at this stage."

"I—I should have told you sooner, I guess," Sarah responded.

"Nonsense. I'm just a natural-born alarmist. I would suspect that you're right—the low pressure will probably turn out to be due to a little dehydration. You bring the OB tray. I'll bring the pedi one."

As they stepped from the car, they heard a siren, probably a block or so away. They were still on the tree belt when a police cruiser, strobes flashing, screeched around the corner and skidded to a halt behind the Volvo. A uniformed officer jumped out and, ignoring them, sprinted up toward the front door.

"Excuse me," Snyder called out as they hurried after the policeman, "I'm Dr. Randall Snyder from the Medical Center of Boston. What's going on?"

"I don't know, Doc," the officer said, panting. "But I'm glad you're here. We got a nine-one-one call that a woman was in serious trouble here and needed an ambulance. One should be arriving any minute."

"The woman's name?" Sarah asked, aware of a sudden knot in her chest.

The policeman rang the bell several times and then began rapping on the glass panel of the front door.

"Summer," he said. "Lisa Summer."

. . . *The* real *stress on this job: the cases that don't come out right, the people with untreatable illness, the people who die in spite of everything we do* . . .

Randall Snyder's words echoed in her thoughts as Sarah followed the policeman and Heidi Glassman up the broad staircase. From above, she could hear Lisa's sputtering cough and cries of pain. And even before she entered the bedroom, she could smell the blood.

Lisa, sitting splay-legged on her futon, was hemorrhaging from her nostrils and mouth. Fresh and drying blood covered the front of her nightgown and was spattered on the futon, floor, and wall. But even more disturbing to Sarah was the glazed fear in the girl's eyes. It was a look she had seen only a few times before in her medical career, most recently in a fifty-year-old postoperative woman who was about to have a massive coronary. Within minutes that woman was in full, irreversible cardiac arrest.

"It started shortly after I called you," Heidi said as Sarah and Randall Snyder gloved, then knelt beside Lisa to begin their evaluation. "I would have called you back, but I was sure you were on your way. Everything was going fine—except for that blood pressure thing I told you about. Then all of a sudden Lisa began complaining of severe pain in her right arm and hand. During one of her contractions, she had bitten the inside of her cheek. At first there was just a little bleeding from the cut; then suddenly there was a lot. Just before you arrived she threw up, and it was all bright-red blood. I think what she threw up may have come from the back of her nose, but how do you tell?"

"Her pressure holding?" Sarah asked as she locked Lisa's left arm in hers and adjusted the cuff to take another reading.

"It's down a little more. About eighty systolic. I can't hear it in her right arm at all."

Sarah glanced at Lisa's right arm and immediately knew the reason why. She could tell that Snyder, who was feeling for a pulse over the radial artery at the wrist and the brachial artery in the crook of the elbow, knew as well. The arm, from at least the elbow to the hand, was dusky and mottled. The fingers were a deeper gray, the fingertips almost black. For whatever reason, the arteries and smaller arterioles supplying blood to that limb had become blocked. To a lesser extent, the blood flow to Lisa's left arm and both legs seemed compromised as well.

"Still eighty," Sarah said. "Lisa, I know this is scary for you. But please, just do your best to stay as calm as you can while we figure things out. This is the man I told you about, Dr. Snyder. He's my chief."

From a distance, they could hear the *whoop* of the approaching ambulance.

"Wh—what's happening to me?" Lisa asked, as bewildered as she was frightened.

Sarah and her chief exchanged glances. Though the diagnosis needed laboratory confirmation, she knew he suspected, as did she, that they were witnessing the rapid evolution of DIC—disseminated intravascular coagulopathy—the most dramatic and horrifying of all blood-clotting emergencies.

Sarah asked for a washcloth and handed it to Lisa.

"Here, Lisa, blow your nose in this as hard as you can. Once we get the big clots out, the pressure you put on your nose will be more effective in stopping the bleeding."

Lisa, still spitting crimson into a bucket, did as she was asked. Immediately the center of the washcloth was soaked with blood. But there were no clots. None at all. The diagnosis of DIC was now even more likely. For whatever reason, large numbers of tiny clots had begun forming within Lisa's bloodstream. Those circulating microclots were beginning to join together and obstruct the arteries supplying blood to her arms and legs, placing the limbs in great jeopardy.

Even more frightening than the circulatory blockage was the speed with which the abnormal clots were using up the factors necessary for normal blood coagulation. With those factors badly depleted, bleeding from any source was now life-threatening. And a fatal stroke caused by a cerebral hemorrhage was a terrifying possibility.

"Lisa, I'll explain what we think is going on in just a second," Sarah said. "Has your water broken?"

Lisa shook her head.

"I'm very frightened," she managed. "My hand is killing me."

"I understand. Just give us a moment."

Sarah looked over at her chief.

"We need that ambulance to get here, we need an IV,

and we need a hematologist or an internist—preferably both—waiting for us at MCB," Snyder said.

There was still the typical calmness in his voice, but his expression was grim. This would be the second case of DIC in a Medical Center of Boston active labor patient in less than three months. The previous case—not one of Snyder's or Sarah's—had died on the operating table as her physicians desperately tried to deliver her child by cesarean section. With hemorrhaging into the placenta, the infant was severely brain damaged by the time it could be extracted and was pronounced dead before its first week of life was through. The cause of the DIC had never been determined.

"Lisa, please listen," Snyder went on. "And please try not to be too frightened. We believe that something has caused your blood-clotting system to stop working properly. We need to get you to MCB for diagnosis and treatment as soon as possible."

"What *something*? What caused this?" she asked. "Will my baby be all right?"

"We'll know better about your baby as soon as we get a monitor on," Snyder said. "At this moment I can hear its heartbeat clearly."

"His," Lisa said hoarsely.

"Pardon?"

"His. Dr. Baldwin sent me for an ultrasound. His name's going to be Brian."

They heard the ambulance siren cut off as it pulled up in front of the house.

"Lisa," Snyder said, "I know it's not easy, but the more relaxed you can be, the slower your blood will flow, and the better chance we'll have of stopping the bleeding. Is there someone you want us to call? Your parents? A brother or sister?"

Lisa thought for a moment and then resolutely shook her head.

"Heidi's my family," she said.

"Okay. Sarah, do you want to go and call MCB? . . . Sarah?"

Eyes closed, Sarah had placed her second, third, and fourth fingertips over Lisa's left radial artery, trying to assess the six pulses located there, which were used only by acupuncturists and practitioners of traditional Chinese medicine. The left pulses reflected the condition of the heart, liver, kidney, small intestine, gallbladder, and bladder. Many times, especially in patients with vague, nonspecific complaints, careful palpation of the three superficial and three deep pulses at each wrist gave a clue as to the source of the symptom and helped direct placement of the acupuncture needles.

"Oh, sorry," she said. Her exam, influenced by Lisa's agitated state and the profound disturbance in blood flow, was not revealing. And with no circulation at all on the right, there was little point in checking that side. "I'll call Dr. Blankenship and have him waiting for us with someone from heme."

"Thank you."

The rescue squad raced into the crowded room. After a brief explanation from Randall Snyder, they hoisted Lisa onto their litter and set about establishing an IV in her left arm. Sarah started for the hallway phone.

"Dr. Baldwin, don't leave me," Lisa begged.

"I'll be right back."

"Then please just tell me: *Am I going to die?*"

Sarah hoped there would be more conviction in her voice than she was feeling at that moment.

"Lisa, this is not the time for you to be thinking like that at all," she said. "It's very important that you stay centered and focused. You've got to be able to use that internal visualization stuff we've been working on. Do you think you can do that?"

"I—I was doing it before all this started. Once I actually saw my cervix. I really did."

"I believe you. That's great. Well, now you've got to start doing it again. Concentrate on seeing your bloodstream and the structures within your hands. It's very important. I'll help you once we reach MCB. Dr. Blankenship, the internist who will be treating you, is a wonderful doctor. I'm going to call him now. He and a hematologist will be waiting for us. Together we'll get on top of this thing."

"Promise?"

Sarah swept some errant wisps of hair from Lisa's damp forehead.

"I promise," she said.

"IV's in," one of the rescue squad announced. "Ringer's lactate at two-fifty. You want her sitting up like this, Doc?"

Snyder nodded. "Sarah, why don't you let me make that call, and you ride to MCB in the ambulance with Lisa. I'll bring Heidi with me."

As she accompanied the rescue squad out of the house, doing what she could to stem the flow of blood from Lisa Summer's nose and mouth, Sarah tried to remember what she could of the other woman who had developed DIC. Normal pregnancy, normal labor right up to the final stage, then a sudden, catastrophic alteration of her body's coagulation system. Just the way it was happening today.

And as she helped load Lisa into the ambulance, the question that had confounded *that* woman's doctors burned in Sarah's mind: *Why?*

Chapter 4

IX OF THE NINE SUFFOLK STATE HOSPITAL BUILDINGS originally purchased by the Medical Center of Boston were still in use. Two of the others had been razed and replaced with parking facilities. The third, a crumbling six-story brick structure with the name CHILTON etched in concrete over its entrance, had been abandoned and boarded up when Sarah began her training, and remained so—a mute reminder of the hospital's ongoing financial difficulties.

The Chilton Building and garages were separated from the rest of the hospital by a broad, circular drive. Enclosed within the loop was an expansive, grassy courtyard, dotted by some shrubbery and half a dozen molded plastic picnic tables. Vehicle access to "The Campus," as Glenn Paris had named the area, was restricted to those administrators and department heads with parking slots, and to emergency room traffic.

The ride from Knowlton Street to MCB, spearheaded by the sirens of the police cruiser and rescue squad, took fifteen minutes. Seated beside Lisa Summer in the back of the lurching ambulance, Sarah heard the driver radio ahead that a Priority One patient was on the way. She pictured the guard, suddenly puffed with importance, scurrying to open the security gate and move all traffic aside.

Lisa's contractions, now occurring every four minutes or so, were forceful and prolonged. However, Sarah's gentle exam had disclosed a cervix that was still only four centimeters dilated—far from being ready for delivery. The bleeding from her nose and mouth was, if anything, more brisk. And although her left hand and both feet still had some warmth and capillary blood flow, her right arm was now pallid and lifeless from the elbow down.

"Hang on, Lisa," Sarah urged. "We're almost there."

As they turned onto the MCB access road, Sarah reviewed her knowledge of DIC. Having never encountered a severe case of it during her training, her understanding was essentially what she had gleaned from a lecture or two in med school, some reading, and an occasional conference. Rather than being a single, specific disease, the condition was an uncommon complication of many different sorts of injuries or illnesses. Surgery, shock, overwhelming infection, massive trauma, drug overdose, toxins, abrupt separation of the placenta—any of a number of insults to the human body could result in DIC. And in part because of the severity of the predisposing condition, full-blown DIC was, more often than not, fatal.

But Lisa Summer was neither injured nor ill. She was a healthy young woman at the end of a totally uncomplicated pregnancy. Perhaps this wasn't DIC after all, Sarah thought.

The siren cut off as they neared the hospital. Sarah did a quick blood pressure check and exam and began mentally preparing the presentation she would give to Dr. Eli Blankenship. It was her job to present the facts in a totally unbiased manner, carefully avoiding her own diagnostic impression or any other leading statements.

Until a diagnosis was proven, assuming one to the exclusion of others was foolish and potentially very dangerous. *Assume makes an ass of u and me* was the way one professor had stressed that principle.

Eli Blankenship, perhaps the sharpest medical mind in the hospital, would combine her information with his observations. He would then come up with an approach to diagnosis and treatment. Meanwhile, if therapy could not be held off until a definite diagnosis could be made, they would simply have to say a quiet prayer and forge ahead with what measures seemed likeliest to help.

In this case, with two lives already hanging by a thread, it was unlikely they could wait for any laboratory results before instituting treatment. And the treatment for DIC was, itself, life-threatening. All in all, Sarah knew, it was going to be one hellish day for Lisa Summer and the dozens of physicians, nurses, and technologists who would be battling to save her and her baby.

And all the while, swirling about that struggle would be the persistent, gnawing question of *why?*

As they backed up to the emergency room's receiving platform, Sarah could see Eli Blankenship waiting by the ER door. As always, she was struck by the man's appearance. Had she, without knowing, been challenged to name his vocation, her first guesses might well have included tavern bouncer, stevedore, or heavy machine operator. MCB's chief of staff was a bull of a man, less than six feet tall but with a massive chest and head that were separated by a token neck. He was bald save for a dark monk's fringe. But beneath his expansive forehead, his eyebrows were thickets, and his muscular arms were like Esau's. Even clean shaven at the outset of a day, he seemed to have a persistent five o'clock shadow.

Of the man's physical attributes, only his eyes—a pale, penetrating blue—gave hint to his genius. He was board certified in infectious disease and critical care as well as internal medicine. But he was also respected as a humanist, expert at chess and contract bridge, and well versed in the arts. As a teacher, no one at MCB was more open and respectful of the views and approaches of students and residents, and no one taught them more effectively.

Blankenship, already gowned and gloved, met the stretcher as the rescue squad pulled it from the ambulance, and immediately took Lisa's hand and introduced himself to her. From the other side of the litter, where she was keeping pressure on Lisa's nose, Sarah could see that with that first touch, the medical chief had already begun his examination and assessment.

By the time they reached Room A, one of three major medical/trauma rooms, Sarah had nearly completed her case presentation. Blankenship had the phlebotomist from the laboratory waiting to draw blood for them as well as an OB nurse with a fetal monitor. With a nod, he motioned them both into action. At that moment, blood began to ooze through the gauze wrap protecting Lisa's intravenous line. Blankenship noted the development with no change in his expression.

"Now, Lisa," he said evenly, "I'm going to ask you to be patient with us and to forgive us if it seems we're not keeping you abreast of what's going on. You've got several different things going on here at once, involving several different systems of your body. In a few more seconds, you aren't going to be able to tell all the doctors working on you without a scorecard. The main ones besides me will be Dr. Helen Stoddard, who's a blood specialist, and Dr. Andrew Truscott, who's a surgeon. Her job will be to help us stop this bleeding, and his will be to get in another intravenous line and tend to your arm, which right now is not getting enough blood. And of course, we'll have Dr. Baldwin and Dr. Snyder standing by to deliver your baby as soon as we can get you stabilized."

"Is the baby all right?" Lisa asked.

Blankenship looked over at the OB nurse, who nodded toward the fetal monitor. The fetal heart rate was higher than optimum, often an early sign of trouble.

"The baby's under some stress," he said. "We're watching that very closely."

At that moment, the hematologist swept into the room. Helen Stoddard, also a full professor, was a department chief at another hospital and a sometime consultant at MCB. Unabashedly from "the old school," as she liked to say, she had been openly critical of MCB's coddling up to "fringe players"—her term for practitioners of alternative medicine. During one hospital-sponsored seminar, she had been one of the panelists arguing against incorporating any techniques unproven by scientific methods. Blankenship and Sarah were part of the opposition, advocating the use of certain empirically proven treatments such as acupuncture and chiropractic, and careful scientific evaluation of those and others.

"Where do we stand, Eli?" Stoddard asked without so much as a glance at Sarah.

"Studies are off, ten units ordered."

"Platelets and plasma as well?"

"As many of each as we can get."

Helen Stoddard completed a rapid exam of Lisa's skin, mouth, and nail beds. The gauze surrounding the IV was now saturated. Blood dripped from it onto the stretcher sheet and floor. The venapuncture site from which blood had been drawn was also oozing.

"No prior history of bleeding problems?" she asked Blankenship.

"Absolutely none."

Stoddard thought for a few seconds. "We can't wait for the lab. I think we hang up what platelets, blood, and plasma we can and heparinize her."

Randall Snyder and Heidi Glassman entered the room, both a bit breathless. Moments later Andrew Truscott arrived as well. Heidi took Sarah's place at the bedside, while Truscott, Sarah, and Snyder stepped back to the doorway.

"She's in real trouble," Sarah said.

Snyder glanced at the fetal monitor.

"So's the baby," he said. "Have you started Pitocin?"

"In the ambulance. She's still only five centimeters dilated."

"Jesus."

Truscott took a minute to examine Lisa's arms, hands, and feet. Then, with impressive skill and speed, he injected some anesthetic into the skin at the side of her neck, located two bony landmarks with his fingertips, and slid a large-bore needle through the numbed spot directly into her internal jugular vein. Next he threaded a catheter through the needle and sutured it in place. A critical second IV route had been established.

"One way or the other, I think we're going to have to take her to the OR for that arm," he said after returning to the doorway. "I still can't tell about the left or her feet. Can you C-section her?"

Snyder crossed to Helen Stoddard, held a brief, whispered conversation, and then came back shaking his head.

"We may already be down to a mother versus fetus situation," he whispered. "Helen and Eli have decided they can't wait for laboratory confirmation of DIC. They've gone ahead with heparin. As things stand, they feel the girl has no chance of surviving a C-section."

Heparin for DIC. To Sarah, whose practice as a surgeon was built on a bedrock of meticulous attention to the control of hemorrhage, the treatment was a terrifying paradox: the intravenous injection of a powerful anticoagulant to a patient who was already in danger of bleeding to death. The theory was to administer the drug to break up the pathological clots and restore blood flow to the compromised extremities and vital organs. At the same time, continuous transfusions would be used to chase lost blood volume and replace clotting factors. It was a therapeutic balancing act of circus proportions, and one that too often was doomed to fail.

Sarah looked at the woman she had cared for over the past seven months, now barely visible within the clutch of nurses, physicians, and technologists. In just minutes, Andrew had contributed greatly to everyone's efforts. She had yet to contribute anything. True, she acknowledged, he and the other medical players in this drama were all senior to her. But Lisa Summer was still her patient, and there were things the two of them had worked on, things they could try, that might help as well —provided, of course, that Helen Stoddard and Eli Blankenship allowed them the chance.

She excused herself and raced down to the subbasement where a series of rather dimly lit tunnels connected all of the MCB buildings. Her locker was on the fourth floor of the Thayer Building, which housed the administration offices on the first three floors and the house staff sleeping quarters on the top two. Sarah took the elevator up. Minutes later she bounded down the six flights and sprinted back through the tunnels toward the ER. Cradled in her arm was the mahogany box containing her acupuncture needles. The box had been a gift from Dr. Louis Han. She had first encountered Han, a Chinese-born Christian missionary, while teaching with the Peace Corps in the Meo villages north of Chiang Mai, Thailand. Until his death nearly three years later, he was her mentor in the healing arts. The inscription on the box, elegantly carved in Chinese by Han himself, read: THE HEALING POWER OF GOD IS WITHIN US ALL.

The moment Sarah stepped back into Room A, she sensed things had changed for the worse. A tube inserted into Lisa's stomach through her nose was carrying a steady stream of blood into the suction bottle on the wall. Her urinary catheter was also draining crimson. Randall Snyder, his face ashen, stood by the fetal monitor, where the heartbeat of Lisa's unborn child had dropped below the rate necessary to sustain life.

"What's happening?" Sarah asked, moving beside him.

"I think we've lost him," Snyder whispered. "We could go for a section right here and now, and maybe we'd still be in time for the baby. But Lisa would never survive."

"Is she going to anyhow?"

"I don't know. It looks bad."

Sarah hesitated for a moment, and then worked her way to where Helen Stoddard and Eli Blankenship were standing.

"Can I please speak with you both?" she asked.

For an instant, she thought Stoddard was going to dismiss her. Then, perhaps remembering Sarah was one of Blankenship's hand-picked residents, the hematologist moved to one side of the room. Blankenship followed.

"I'd like to try to stop Lisa's bleeding," Sarah said.

"And exactly what do you think we're trying to do?" Stoddard asked.

Sarah felt the muscles in her jaw tighten. She had never forced her abilities and techniques on any resident or faculty member who didn't request them. But Lisa was her patient, and conventional therapy did not seem to be working.

"Dr. Stoddard, I know you don't have a great deal of regard for alternative healing," she said, struggling to keep her voice steady. "But I only want the same thing you do. I want Lisa to make it. For the last four or five months, while we were getting ready for her home birth, Lisa and I have been working on some self-hypnosis and internal visualization. I think she's really gotten quite good at both."

"And?" Stoddard's expression was ice.

"Well, combined with acupuncture, we might be able to use Lisa's own power to slow her bleeding down. Provided, that is, you are willing to give her enough protamine to neutralize the heparin."

"What?"

"If we succeed in slowing her bleeding enough to be able to C-section her, you can start the heparin again to work on dissolving her clots."

"This is ridiculous."

Sarah took a calming breath. Over four years of medical school and two years of training, she had never had a clash of this sort with a professor. But there could be no backing down. "Dr. Stoddard, Lisa's pressure is dropping, her bleeding is getting worse, and it may already be too late for the baby."

"Why, you arrogant, ignorant—"

"Just a minute, Helen," Blankenship cut in. "You can say anything you want when this is over, but right now we have a girl who is going down the tubes, and we've got to focus on her. Dr. Baldwin is right. The heparin's not doing anything for the clots yet, and it's sped the bleeding up to the point where we're falling behind in our transfusions."

"Do this and I'm off this case," Stoddard said.

"Helen, you're one of the best hematologists I've ever known, and one of the most dedicated doctors. I can't imagine you ever allowing anything to get in the way of what's best for a patient."

"But—"

"And deep down, you know that the few minutes it will take Sarah, here, to try what she knows will make little difference to the outcome."

"But . . . all right, dammit. But after this is over, regardless of what happens, this hospital had better clarify its policy on medical quackery, or I am off the staff."

"We'll do that, Helen. I promise. We'll do that. Sarah, how can we help?"

"Well, first give Lisa the protamine."

"Helen?"

"Damn you, Eli. Okay, okay. . . . This is ridiculous," she muttered as she headed back to administer the heparin antidote. "Absolutely ridiculous."

"Now," Sarah continued, sensing her pulse beginning to race, "please just leave Heidi with me, pull as many people away from the bedside as possible, and keep all noise to a minimum."

"Done. Anything else?"

"Just one. Please turn off the overhead lights."

Lisa cried out as another contraction took hold. Sarah stroked her forehead, then knelt beside her.

"Lisa, close your eyes and listen to me," she said softly. "We've got work to do. This is the moment we practiced for in all those sessions. Do you understand? . . . Good. Let's just start with the easy things, the scenes, okay? Use them during your contractions. I'll help you, and Heidi is here to help you, too. In between contractions, I want you to concentrate on my voice and start trying to visualize what is happening in your bloodstream and your heart. Everything's moving too fast . . . too fast. There may be blood clots forming there, too, clogging your arteries. Try to relax and see them, too. Just relax. . . . Just relax. . . ."

Heidi continued whispering in Lisa's ear as Sarah briefly consulted a thin, frayed booklet. Having assured herself of the acupuncture points she wanted to stimulate, she set her first needle by twisting it in just below Lisa's left collarbone. Then, one at a time, she set five more of the steel needles in various points, trying to compensate for the limitations placed on the technique by Lisa's bandages and supine position.

An eerie silence had taken over the room, broken only by the muted churning of the suction apparatus and the soft beep of the cardiac monitor.

"Look," Sarah heard someone whisper. "I think the bleeding's letting up already."

Sarah glanced at the suction bottle. In fact, the drainage did seem to have significantly lessened.

"Lisa, relax," Sarah said again, pleasantly but firmly. "Slow your heart . . . slow your blood . . . and just relax. You have the power. . . ."

One minute passed. Then another. Lisa lay motionless now, her eyes closed. A contraction hit, visibly knotting her abdomen. She remained motionless and serene.

"Her heart rate's down from ninety to fifty, Sarah," Blankenship said. "The oozing from her IV and venapuncture sites may have stopped altogether. Randall, do you want to get ready?"

"Everything's set," Snyder said. "Anesthesia's standing by upstairs. Just say the word."

The nasogastric tube was now draining only small amounts. All oozing had stopped. Carefully Sarah twisted out the six acupuncture needles. For ten seconds, fifteen, all was quiet.

"Go for it," she said.

Chapter 5

JULY 2

SARAH ORDERED THE OPERATING TABLE UP TWO INCHES and screwed sterile handles into the parabolic overhead lights. Her eyes burned a bit; she'd been up and running for twenty-four hours without so much as a catnap. But her concentration, as always when she was in the OR, was as sharp as her scalpel. After centering the focused beams, she cradled the blade in her right hand, minutely adjusting its position until it felt a part of her. With her left, she tensed the skin along what had been the upper margin of the pubic hair escutcheon. Then, with a single, steady stroke, she opened the abdominal wall and separated the thin saffron layer of subcutaneous fat. She next handled what few bleeders there were by snapping each with a hemostat and touching the steel instrument with an electrocauterizer. Finally she cut the peritoneal membrane, exposing the bulging, gravid uterus.

"Everything all right?" she asked the anesthesiologist.

"Stable."

"Okay, here we go."

Sarah scored the surface of the uterus with her scalpel, then made a small opening in it. Inserting her index fingers, she pulled the beefy muscle fibers apart. Then, with the touch of her blade, she opened the amniotic membrane.

"We're in," she said at the first gush of amniotic fluid. "Suction, please."

Time now was critical. The powerful uterus could clamp down at any moment, making the delivery of the baby within it anything but routine. For ten seconds Sarah's breathing, and it seemed her heart as well, stopped as she felt deep in the pelvis for the baby's legs, trying at the same time to assess the position of the umbilical cord. Gently her fingers closed about the spindly legs and drew them up through the incision. Next the torso and gently, ever so gently, the shoulders and arms. Finally she cradled the eggshell skull in her palm and guided it up through the incision. And just like that, the infant was born.

Quickly Sarah cleared its nose and mouth with a suction bulb. Moments later the expectant hush of the delivery room was pierced by the newborn's bleating cry. And instantly the tension in the room evaporated.

"It's a girl, Kathy," Sarah said too flatly. "A beautiful girl. Congratulations. Dad, if you'll step around over here, you can cut the cord."

The father, just out of high school, sidled over nervously, did as she instructed, and then hurried back to the head of the bed where his young wife was alternately crying and laughing for joy. Swallowing at the sudden, unpleasant fullness in her throat, Sarah handed the perfect newborn over to the pediatrician. She hoped no one in the room could tell how close she was to tears herself —tears not of joy but of sorrow for the stillborn death of Brian Summer some seventeen hours before.

It was six o'clock in the morning, following an incredibly stressful, roller-coaster day and night during which Sarah had presided at two normal vaginal births and now this breech-presentation cesarean. But shortly after one o'clock the previous afternoon, the exhilaration of playing a major role in slowing Lisa Summer's bleeding had given way to the inestimable sadness of assisting in the extraction of her baby—dead before they had even reached the delivery room.

Like the infant of the previous DIC patient, Brian Summer had succumbed to massive bleeding within the placenta and premature separation of the placenta from the uterine wall. Had he been delivered even half an hour earlier, he *might* have survived. The agonizing choice, though, had been to channel all efforts toward saving Lisa, who almost certainly would have bled to death had the procedure not been delayed.

With an unfamiliar sense of distraction and detachment, Sarah watched her hands deliver the young woman's placenta, then begin closing the incisions she had made. The decision to try to save Lisa's life had been the correct one. Nevertheless, acceptance of the outcome was not coming at all easily. Sarah was preparing to place the skin clips when the circulating nurse from surgery came up behind her.

"Sarah, Dr. Truscott wanted me to tell you that they've taken Lisa Summer back into the OR," he whispered.

Oh, no, she thought. "Do you know what's going on?"

"Well, apparently the anticoagulation and the heparin flush haven't cleared the blockages in her arm. I'm not sure what Dr. Truscott plans to do now."

"Thank you, Win. I'll be over as soon as I can. Kathy, we're almost done. The pediatrician just signaled to me that your baby's perfect. Her Apgar score is nine. Ten is tops, but we only give that to babies who come out playing a violin. He'll bring her over to you in just a moment."

"Thank you, Doctor. Oh, thank you so much."

Sarah taped a bandage over the incision and stripped her gloves off as she backed away from the table.

"We're all very happy for you," she said.

She left the delivery floor and headed toward the surgical building. Twice during the short walk she was stopped—first by a nurse, then by a medical resident—and congratulated for the job she had done on Lisa.

"The whole hospital's talking about it," the resident said. "You really opened a lot of eyes to the potential of alternative healing. My medical degree's a D.O. from the school of osteopathy in Philly. All of a sudden, for the first time, really, the other medical residents are asking me about my education—about what sorts of things we study that the people in traditional medical schools don't. People who only paid lip service to nontraditional methods are suddenly very interested in them."

The man's words should have been a tonic. But today they did little to alleviate Sarah's sense of impotence. All of her training plus hundreds of thousands of dollars' worth of equipment and personnel had been unable to save Lisa Summer's baby. This was not the first time she had agonized through the loss of patients' pregnancies and newborns. That people die was the most basic tenet of medicine, and on a purely intellectual level, it was a truth she understood. But for whatever reason, her emotional response to this loss seemed impervious to knowledge or logic.

She pictured her old office/treatment room on the second floor of the Ettinger Institute. She had been no less involved in caring for people in those days than she was now. But that world—that serene, uncomplicated, highly personal interaction with patients—seemed light-years away.

The difference, purely and simply, was the degree to which technology and science—whatever *that* really was—dominated western medicine. At times, and this was certainly one of them, it felt as if she had traded in flying on a hang glider for piloting a jet.

Her reason for leaving the Ettinger Institute was the inflexibility and eventually the intolerable behavior of Peter Ettinger. But her decision to obtain an M.D. degree went far deeper than that. She had felt that when she became a physician, many of the limitations and resulting frustrations of her professional life would disappear. Instead, despite all the equipment and her newly acquired technical skill, her limitations seemed just as frustrating, and those frustrations just as limiting.

There were four women now on the hospital's surgical staff and three female surgical residents. Still, there was only one surgeons' locker room, and it remained for men only.

Sarah discarded her maroon OB scrubs in the nurses' locker room, slipped on a sea green pair, and replaced her shoe covers, hair guard, and mask. Twelve hours had passed since she had watched Andrew Truscott probe and irrigate the main arteries supplying Lisa's right arm. Their goal was to remove as much clot as possible and to hope that anticoagulant irrigation took care of the rest. Now, apparently, they needed to do more—perhaps a major dissection of the blocked vessels.

Sarah entered the OR through the scrub room. Lisa, now in an operating room for the third time in less than twenty-four hours, was already anesthetized and intubated. Her face was deceptively peaceful. A low drape across her neck separated her head and the anesthesiologist from the surgical team. On the other side of the drape, Andrew and another surgeon, both on the same side of the table, were focused on Lisa's arm.

For a moment, Sarah thought the second surgeon was the same vascular man who had assisted Andrew on the earlier procedure. But as she pulled the small metal footstool over and stood on it to get a better view, she realized that the other doctor was not a vascular surgeon at all. He was Ken Browne, the chief of orthopedics. It was only then that Sarah saw the severed forearm and clawed hand resting on the metal tray beside the scrub nurse and realized that Browne and Andrew were not doing any delicate vascular procedure at all. They were aggressively paring down what remained of Lisa's radius and ulna—the bones of her forearm—in preparation for the completion of a below-the-elbow amputation.

Sarah felt her muscles go limp and, for just a moment, thought that for the first time in her life she was going to faint. *Oh, Jesus, no. First the baby . . . now this* was all she could think.

Andrew glanced up and saw her.

"You okay?" he asked.

"Andrew, she was an artist. A potter. Her hands were . . . Hey, listen, I'm sorry. It's just that I thought she was going to be all right."

"She probably will be . . . now," Andrew responded somewhat wearily. "I'm sorry about having to do this, too. But impending gangrene is impending gangrene. There was really no choice."

"I understand."

But even as she said the words, Sarah knew that there was precious little of what had happened to Lisa Summer that she understood at all.

Chapter 6

THE SURGICAL INTENSIVE CARE UNIT WAS A TWELVE-bed ward with one-to-one or one-to-two nurse coverage throughout the day and night. Rarely was there an entire unit shift without at least one patient in crisis. And although, except in times of the most extreme urgency, the atmosphere in the SICU was subdued and quiet, it was never silent. Every minute of every day, the monitoring equipment, suction and infusion systems, and respirators droned white noise like the surge of ocean waves. It was here, even more than in the operating rooms, that the true life-and-death battles were waged.

Sarah much preferred the OR to the day-to-day grind of caring for critically ill patients in the unit. But she did enjoy the camaraderie she had with the SICU staff.

At seven-thirty the morning of July 2, six of the SICU bays were occupied. All twelve would be filled by the time the morning OR schedule was completed. Her eyes now gritty from lack of sleep, Sarah sat on the edge of the bed in bay eight, waiting for Lisa Summer to be brought up from the recovery room. The news from there, except for the obvious, was excellent. Lisa had sailed through her surgery with no excessive bleeding. In fact, her DIC was rapidly resolving, and circulation to her kidneys and legs as well as to her remaining arm now seemed unimpeded. It was as if, in some strange way, the performance of the cesarean section had relieved her hematologic crisis.

Lisa's life had been saved. Her womb, her senses, and her nervous system were intact, and she could walk. In time, she would learn to use her left hand better and to control whatever prosthesis was placed on her right. She might even find a way to continue expressing herself as an artist. She would begin to deal with her grief, and someday, perhaps, she would once again bear a child. In a purely clinical way, Sarah knew all these things were true. Still, she could not shake the reality that Lisa was her patient, and that not twenty-four hours before, she had excitedly been preparing to give birth.

"You all right?"

Sarah was sifting through a printout of the already substantial number of lab tests run on Lisa, searching for a clue—any clue—as to what might have caused the catastrophe. Startled, she looked up to see Alma Young, a seasoned SICU nurse, standing at the foot of the bed.

"Oh, yeah, I'm okay, thanks. Just a little tired is all."

"That's understandable. Well, your girl'll be up in a few minutes. Recovery just called. Apparently she's doing reasonably well, all things considered."

"That's great," Sarah said, with little enthusiasm. "I keep staring at these numbers, hoping that something I missed will suddenly leap off the page and explain what's going on."

"Maybe you should just close your eyes and nap for a few minutes."

"I'm afraid that if I do that, my body will figure out it doesn't have to feel the way it does right now, and I'll be finished for the day."

"You know, the whole hospital's talking about what you did yesterday. The ER nurses are saying that girl would have died for sure if you hadn't stepped in and then held your ground against that hematologist."

"Then why don't I feel better than I do about all that, Alma?"

The older woman sat down on the end of the bed.

"Because you're a good doctor," she said. "That's why. You're sensitive. You care about people's suffering and pain—I mean really care."

"Thank you."

"But may I say something?"

"Sure."

"Sometimes I think you care too much. You take it all too personally. Sitting here poring through those lab reports when you could be resting is a perfect example. That's taking sensitivity one step too far. I've seen all kinds of residents—and nurses, too—come through here. One thing I've noticed that the really good ones all have in common is this little switch they can throw that lets them become totally objective when they need to be that way. You have everything it takes to be one of the really good ones, but I think sometimes you let all this get you down too much."

"You see that in me?"

"I do. So do some of the other nurses. Our favorite sport is dissecting the residents, you know. We all really like you, Sarah; and we love working with you. But we worry about you, too. It's as if you always think there's something more you should be doing instead of just accepting that you can only do what you can do."

The nurse's observations triggered a rush of images and emotions, most of them unpleasant, and all of them centering on Peter Ettinger.

"Alma," Sarah said, "I've never been much good at accepting my limitations. In fact, if I didn't always think there was more I could do for a patient, there's a good chance I'd never have ended up as an M.D."

"What do you mean?"

Sarah laughed uncomfortably. "Do you have a few hours?"

There was concern in Alma Young's eyes.

"Actually," she said, "I'm completely caught up until our friend Lisa arrives."

Sarah thought for a time before responding. She had always been a private person. And the compartmental- ization of her life—high school in upstate New York, college in a Boston suburb, the Peace Corps in Thailand, Peter and the Ettinger Institute, medical school in It- aly, and now this residency—had made it easy for her to stay private. In each place she had begun to develop friendships, but none of those relationships, except with her mentor, Dr. Louis Han, was strong enough to sur- vive the next move. And gradually she began to find that when asked to talk about herself—even when she felt inclined to do so—she simply didn't. Or couldn't.

Now, a woman with whom she had worked for more than two years seemed genuinely interested in who she was and how she was reacting to this most difficult case. Perhaps it was time to open up a bit.

"A number of years ago," she said finally, "—ten, actually—I was living in the mountains in northern Thailand, building a clinic while I was teaching and studying acupuncture and herbal medicine. An older man became my friend and my mentor. It was—you know—the father-I-never-had sort of thing. Well, he died rather suddenly. And soon after, a man quite like him, although much younger, passed through our vil- lage. He was brilliant and dashing, and interested in the same things I was. At the time, he was already world renowned in many areas of alternative healing.

"Well, within a month, I was back in the States, living with him and his daughter, and working at his insti- tute. . . ."

Sarah debated sharing Peter's name, but decided there was no reason to do so. "For almost three years I lived with him and the teenage daughter he had brought back from Africa when she was a baby and adopted. For those three years I was the closest thing she had to a mother. Although, as I said, this man and I worked together at his institute, as far as he was concerned, I always worked *for* him, not *with* him. When the event I'll tell you about happened, he had actually asked me to marry him. But this dark side of him—an enormous, insatiable ego, and an inflexibility that frightened me—had begun to surface more and more in our life."

"Go on, please," Alma said.

"He had a patient, a sculptor, whom he had quite literally cured of a case of rheumatoid arthritis that the man's doctors had labeled incurable."

"How did he do it?"

"Oh, dietary changes and herbs, plus some of the same sort of techniques I used yesterday with Lisa. The man went from being a cripple to playing racquetball every day."

"Amazing."

"Not to us it wasn't. Alternative healing cures many, many patients that western physicians have given up on. We M.D.s still don't have much of a handle on the mechanism of disease, you know. Our microscopes get bigger and bigger, and the things we can look at get smaller and smaller. We prescribe penicillin without giving it much thought. But we still don't know why Person A got the strep throat we're treating, or why Person B didn't.

"Anyhow, my friend went away for a month and left me in charge of his patients. He was treating the sculptor for headaches with herbs, acupuncture, and chiropractic adjustments. I saw the man several times and felt more concerned about him each time. He said his headaches were better, or at least no worse, but he seemed to me to be walking funny. And believe it or not, his smile seemed off center as well."

"That sounds like trouble."

"That's what I thought. I called White Memorial and spoke to a neurologist who wanted to see him at eleven the next morning. My friend was due home from Nepal that night, but I decided his patient needed to be seen no matter what. So I made the arrangements. That may sound like an easy decision, Alma, but it wasn't. There was still the matter of explaining why I would go against everything my friend believed in—"

Sarah could not remember the last time she had shared with anyone that final, horrid day with Peter. But Alma Young was such a wonderful listener that the story came with surprising ease. And although Sarah told it rather quickly, the pieces she actually voiced were only snippets of what she was remembering. . . .

The night that resulted in so much torment had actually felt magical. Peter listened quietly and attentively to her account of the referral of the sculptor, Henry McAllister. Peter's response—the response she had so dreaded—was, in essence: *Hey, listen. I left you responsible for the institute because you are a responsible person. You saw what you saw, made a decision, and went with it. What could possibly be wrong with doing that?*

Later that evening they made love—consuming, passionate love, the way it had been in the beginning.

Peter had come through—for her and their sputtering relationship. She knew it wasn't easy for him. He honestly believed that, on balance, traditional western medicine had become so lost in science, competitive pharmacology, and dehumanizing technology that it now did more harm than good. In fact, above his desk was a placard engraved:

IATROGENIC: ILLNESS OR INJURY CAUSED BY THE
WORDS OR ACTIONS OF A PHYSICIAN

Now the chance was right there for him to belittle her judgment—to once again force his famous views on M.D.s and their methods down her throat. But he hadn't taken it.

Like Peter, she understood the miraculous potential in

the relationship between healer and patient. She had great faith in the power of holistic methods to diagnose and treat. But unlike him, she had never viewed traditional medicine as a court of last—or no—resort. After all, she had once survived a nearly fatal ruptured appendix by getting airlifted to a U.S. military hospital and having emergency surgery.

Peter was forty—a dozen years older than she. That age difference, along with his imposing size—he was six feet four—his immense drive and material successes made holding her own in their relationship a challenge and asserting herself in it almost a pipe dream. But at last Peter had chosen to listen rather than to react: to understand that his way of doing things might not be the only way.

They took the following morning off from work and spent a good deal of it making love. By the time Sarah arrived at the institute to begin seeing a full afternoon of appointments, she was feeling more centered and positive about her life than she had in some time.

By three o'clock, though, she began wondering why she hadn't heard from the neurologist at White Memorial. At least some of his evaluation of Henry McAllister should have been completed by then. If her observations of the artist's motor problems were correct, an emergency CT scan and several other tests were in order. The physician had promised to call Sarah at her office as soon as he had anything to report.

Three-thirty . . . four . . . four-thirty . . .

She checked the time again and again as she worked her way through her clients. Finally, after the last of them had left, she called White Memorial.

"Miss Baldwin, I assumed you knew," the neurologist said.

"Knew what?" She felt a sudden, unpleasant tightness in her throat.

"When I arrived at the office this morning, there was a message waiting with my answering service from your

Mr. McAllister. He called at, oh, ten o'clock last night to say that he had spoken with his own medical advisor and would not be keeping his appointment with me. I thought that by medical advisor he meant you."

"No," she said. "No, I'm afraid he meant someone else. Thank you, Doctor."

"Well, I'm sorry I couldn't have been of more—"

She was already lowering the receiver to its cradle. She stalked down the hall to Peter's office. He was leaning back in his chair, his feet up on the corner of his desk.

"Peter, why didn't you tell me last night that you called Henry McAllister?"

"I didn't think it was that important."

"Important? I probably gave myself an ulcer agonizing over the decision to refer him."

"Well, now you don't have to worry about it anymore." He lowered his feet to the floor.

"But you said I did the right thing."

"And you did. The right thing for you. But not necessarily the right thing for Henry."

"But how do you know? How could you tell him to cancel that appointment without even seeing him?"

"First of all, I don't believe there's much an M.D. can do that our people can't do as well or better. You know that. And second, I didn't tell him to cancel his appointment. I told him that he should use his judgment, and that no matter what he decided, I would be available to see him all day today. He need only call and set up a time to come in."

"And did he call?" She felt her pulse begin pounding in her temples. Her cheeks were burning. She wanted to leap over the man's desk and pummel the self-assuredness off his face. "Well, did he!"

Peter's expression tightened.

"I—I guess in all the excitement going on here today I forgot to check." He glanced at his message spindle and then called the receptionist. "It seems he didn't feel the need to call," he said as he hung up.

"Peter, you are really a son of a bitch. Do you know that?"

She whirled and hurried back into her office.

"Hey, easy does it, babe," he called after her. "Easy does it."

Henry McAllister's clinic record was on her desk. She dialed his number and let the phone ring a dozen or more times. Then she dialed 911. If she was wrong, she'd look like a fool. But there was no way she could let matters drop. For the first time in three years, she felt as if she were reacting to a challenging situation like Sarah Baldwin, and not like Peter Ettinger's flunky.

Peter was just coming out of his office as she raced past him, down the stairs, and out of the institute. He called to her, but she never even looked back.

McAllister lived in a South End loft about ten blocks away. She thought briefly about looking for a cab. Then she just gritted her teeth, clenched her fists, and sprinted off. . . .

"So?" Alma Young asked.

"Pardon?"

"So what happened to the sculptor? You can't leave me hanging like that!"

"Oh, sorry," Sarah said, uncertain of precisely how much of her thoughts she had actually shared. "Well, in that particular situation, if I had accepted that what I had already done was everything I could do, the man would probably have died. The police ended up breaking into his apartment. We found him unconscious on the floor. Two hours later he was in the operating room at White Memorial. He had a slowly growing malignancy—a meningioma, actually—on the right side of his brain. And as sometimes happens, he had begun bleeding into the tumor. Pressure was building inside his skull."

"Thank God you reached him in time." Alma gasped, genuinely relieved at the fate of a man whose crisis had occurred seven years before.

Sarah smiled at the nurse's reaction.

"I was allowed into the operating room to watch them take the tumor out. It was really incredible. That's when I decided I wanted to be a surgeon of some sort. Eventually I settled on OB/Gyn."

"And the other man? Your . . . um . . . friend?"

Sarah shrugged. "I moved out the next day, and we haven't spoken since."

"That's quite a story."

"And part of the reason that I'm never comfortable accepting that I've done all I can for a patient."

"Maybe. But I still say you'll be better off when you admit you're only human. Doctors today have remarkable capabilities, but they still aren't God. Never were, never will be. If you can't come to grips with the fact that in spite of your best efforts, some of your patients are going to lose their baby, or lose their arm, or both, or worse, then sooner or later this racket's going to eat you alive."

"I understand."

"Do you?"

"Yes. Yes, I do."

Alma Young reached over and gave Sarah a reassuring hug. "In that case, Dr. Baldwin, I don't want to see you beating up on yourself because a horrible condition you had nothing to do with took that girl's baby and arm. I want to hear you bragging from the rooftops about what you did yesterday to help save her life. It was big, big stuff for this hospital. And everyone who cares about MCB will be crowing right alongside of you. Got that?"

Sarah managed a smile.

"Cock-a-doodle doo," she said.

The doors to the SICU glided open, and Lisa was wheeled in by a transportation worker and a nurse. Andrew Truscott followed moments later. The night he had just spent in the OR showed in the faint shadows enveloping his eyes, but no one would have guessed that he was into his second straight day without sleep. It was a phenomenon Sarah had noticed in herself as well. With each passing year of surgical training, sleep deprivation had fewer biologic effects—as far as she could tell.

"How's she doing?" she asked.

"Not the most elegant of surgeries, those amputations. Sorry we couldn't pull off the alternative."

"You and me both. But I'll bet she's going to do all right from here on out."

"Well, what do you expect? You cured her with those spiffy little pins of yours."

"Nonsense." As often happened, Sarah was uncertain whether Andrew's sarcastic tone reflected his real opinion.

"Sarah, Dr. Truscott," Alma Young called out, "could one of you M. Deities please come help us transfer this girl?"

"I'll be right there," Sarah responded.

"That's grand, old shoe," Truscott said, "because I've got a consult I must do on Med Five. Why don't we plan to meet for coffee in the caf in, say, an hour. I have some questions to ask you about yesterday's magic show. Alma, the postop orders for our young charge are tucked under the mattress. Dr. Muscles, here, is coming to assist you straightaway."

With Sarah's help, Lisa was transferred from the recovery room stretcher to Bed 8. Then Sarah stepped aside as Alma and another nurse quickly hooked up Lisa's IV infusion pumps, cardiac monitor, and urinary catheter.

"She's all yours," Alma said, moving out of earshot. "It's going to be a long haul for her—especially with no money and no family support."

"I'll get social services on her case as soon as possible."

"You might consider a psych consult, too. She hasn't spoken a word to anyone since she heard about the baby."

"I know. Thanks, Alma. That's an excellent suggestion."

She moved over to the bedside. Lisa lay motionless, staring up at the ceiling. Her lips, still dotted by a few obstinate flecks of dried blood, were cracked and puffy. Her bandaged, shortened right arm protruded from beneath the starched sheet. As she talked, Sarah examined the site of the cesarean. Not once did Lisa respond.

"Hi, Lisa, welcome to the ICU. . . . Are you having much pain? . . . Well, just be sure to tell the nurses if you do. You don't have to talk to me or anyone else until you're ready. . . . I'll just say a few things for now, then I'll leave. The bleeding and clotting problems seem to be gone. That means no more transfusions. . . ." Sarah looked for some spark of understanding in the woman's eyes but saw none. "Lisa," she went on finally, "you know we all feel terrible about what's happened to you and . . ." She took a calming breath. ". . . and to Brian. We're going to do everything in the world to help you deal with all this, and to find out why it happened. Please try to be strong. . . ."

Sarah waited half a minute for a response. Then she brushed Lisa's cheek with the back of her hand. "I'll be back to check on you a little later."

She turned away, thinking that somewhere there had to be an explanation for all of this. *Two such similar cases in one hospital in just a few months.* Somewhere there was an answer. And, she promised herself, whatever she had to do to find that answer, she would do.

She glanced back at the young artist lying in bay eight and tried, with little success, to fathom what it must be like to endure such sudden, inexplicable tragedy. Then she headed out of the SICU. There were forty-five minutes remaining before she was to meet Andrew, and she had a dozen patients to see on morning rounds.

. . .

"Where are you going?"
"Just out."

"Just out has never been an acceptable answer to that question, and it is not an acceptable answer tonight."

"Daddy, I'm eighteen years old. The other kids don't—"

"You are not like the other kids. You are not supposed to be like the other kids."

"But—"

"You are an eighteen-year-old who plays polo, vacations in Europe, and will be attending Harvard in the fall and, most of all, who has a twenty-million-dollar trust fund waiting for her when she turns twenty-five. That is not like the other kids, and it never will be. Now, who were you going to see tonight?"

"Daddy, please. . . ."

"Who? That . . . that greaseball, low-life Chuck you think likes you for your spirit and your soul? He was voted best-looking boy in his high school class, he expects to make it as a model and isn't even planning on going to college. Did you ever stop to wonder why such a boy would suddenly become attracted to a Stanhope Academy girl who not only has absolutely nothing in common with him but is forty pounds overweight to boot?"

"Daddy, stop. Please stop."

"I will not. These are things you've got to hear. Things you've got to know. Your wonderful Chuckie is dirt. He spends almost every night when you're not sneaking off to be with him shacked up with a cheerleader named Marcie Kunkle. The pictures my man took of the happy couple are right upstairs in my desk. Would you like to see them?"

"You had someone follow him?"

"Of course I did. I'm your father. It's my job to protect you until you have enough sense and experience in the world to be able to protect yourself."

"How could you?"

"Honey, listen. You know that I love you. That man is interested in one thing and one thing only. Money. That's the name of the game. And the sooner you learn *that, the better. You are who you are. And the only way you're ever going to be sure a man really cares for you is when he has more money than you do."*

"You bastard."

"Don't you dare speak to me like that!"

"You bastard! You fucking bastard! You ruin everything for me. Everything! . . . Don't touch me. . . . You touch me, and I swear you'll never see me again."

"Go to your room."

"Go to hell."

"Come back here. Right now."

"Go to hell. . . . Let me go! I told you not to touch me! Dammit, let me go! . . . I hate you! . . . I hate you!"

"Lisa, wake up. It's the nurse. Lisa, you're all right. You've got to stop screaming. . . . That's it. That's better now. Much better."

Lisa Summer's eyes fluttered open. Everything was blurred. Gradually the concerned face of the nurse came into focus.

"You were having a nightmare," Alma Young said. "Anesthesia does that to some people."

Lisa averted her eyes and once again stared at the ceiling.

"Can I get you anything? Some ice chips? Something for pain? . . . Okay. I'll be here if you need me."

Alma Young partially closed the curtains on each side of the bed and returned to the nurses' station.

Behind her, softly, Lisa began to cry.

"Daddy," she said. "Oh, Daddy."

Chapter 7

SARAH BOUGHT A STICKY BUN AND COFFEE AND TOOK them to the corner of the expansive cafeteria reserved for physicians. Two staff internists were chatting at one Formica-topped table, but the other four tables were unoccupied—no surprise, given that this was the busiest time of day in the hospital. Andrew was already five minutes late, but Sarah had long ago learned that most surgeons showed up late for everything, assuming they showed up at all.

She had been able to make rounds on three of her patients, one of whom had already heard about her performance the previous day. And as Alma Young had predicted, her dramatic and successful use of nontraditional therapy did seem to be the talk of the hospital. In the few minutes she'd spent on the OB/Gyn floor, she had gotten calls from the director of medical education asking her to present grand rounds and from Glenn Paris's secretary, requesting that she stop by his office later in the afternoon. Nurses shook her hand or pumped their fists as she came by, and the chief resident on the OB/Gyn service asked her to lunch so that he might hear the details of the "save" firsthand.

Just as Sarah was wondering whether it would be gauche to sit somewhere other than with the two internists, they gathered their things and stood up. One of them, a scholarly endocrinologist named Wittenberg, came over and shook her hand.

"George Wittenberg," he said.

"I know. We met at Glenn Paris's reception last year. Calcium metabolism and parathyroid disease, yes?"

"You have an excellent memory."

"I read some of your papers for a research project when I was in medical school. They were very interesting."

"Why, thank you. I came over to congratulate *you*, but I'll take the compliment just the same. From what I hear, you pulled off a miracle yesterday."

"Lisa had a number of people working on her. What I did was only one of the reasons she made it."

Sarah felt relieved that she sensed only a passing urge to point out the negative aspects of the "miracle."

"Well put," Wittenberg said. "But if what the hospital drums are pounding out is true, you were a most significant reason. The story made both the *Globe* and the *Herald*. And whoever has been leaking all those negative MCB stories to Axel Devlin really blew it this time. Devlin happened to have written another of his Down with MCB columns for today. So page three has this glowing article about East meets West to save a life at the Medical Center of Boston, and Devlin sounds like a fool for not at least acknowledging the event. Have you seen the paper?"

"No. No, I haven't."

"Here," Wittenberg said, handing over his copy. "I'm done reading this, and I just changed my parakeet's cage, so I have no further use for it."

"Thanks."

"No problem. You know, I'm not exactly on *Devlin's*

wavelength, but I am one of those who's been skeptical of being associated with a place that tenures an Indian Ayurvedic physician and has a chiropractor working in the orthopedic clinic. But after what you accomplished yesterday, I've resolved to keep a more open mind and to learn more about alternative medicine."

He shook her hand warmly and headed off. Sarah spread the paper on her table and skimmed the sensationalized, but reasonably factual, account on page three. A pro-MCB article in the *Herald*—maybe there had been a miracle after all. Then she folded the paper open to Axel Devlin's column.

TAKE IT OR LEAVE IT

by Axel Devlin

July 2

. . . And finally, I give you Axel's Axe, absent from this column for a few days, but always poised to take a good chop at the tires of those who would try to take us all for a ride.

Today, the ol' blade swishes through the air and once again thwacks into your favorite hospital and mine, Crunchy Granola General, otherwise known as the Medical Center of Boston. Hospital president Glenn Paris, a.k.a. California Glenn, presented his state-of-the-hospital message yesterday at the annual residents' change day assembly. That's when the new residents start their training and the old ones move up a notch.

And although the hospital shogun didn't come up with any innovations as spectacular (or embarrassing) as his breast implant raffle or his free crystallography clinic, he did pledge that nothing was going to stop the resurgence of his hospital back to the topmost ranks of academia. "And," he blustered, "you can take that to the bank!"

Well, at that moment, at that very moment, the power—and all the lights—went out in the entire hospital. Get the message, Glenn? Your approach might have worked in San Diego. But here in Boston we like our doctors to do it by the book, not by the alignment of the planets.

"I don't believe it."

"Don't believe what?" Andrew Truscott slid a plate of watery scrambled eggs and suspect hash browns onto the table and took a seat catty-cornered from Sarah.

"This—this vicious, unprincipled . . . crap."

"I gather that's a copy of the *Herald* there before you."

"Why's Devlin got it in for this place so badly?"

"You don't know?"

"I guess not."

"Five years ago—I know because it was right after I started here—his wife needed gallbladder surgery. Devlin wanted her to go to White Memorial, but she liked Bill Gardner and the newly ordained, touchy-feely atmosphere here. Two days after Gardner did the operation, she had a massive pulmonary embolism and croaked on the spot."

"That's terrible, but it could happen to anyone at any hospital."

"Apparently that's what the malpractice lawyers told Devlin. So he set about getting retribution his own way."

"How sad."

"Maybe not. For some people vendettas of one kind or another are therapeutic. *Don't get mad—get even.* Lashing out at MCB like he does probably helps to keep him going."

"And how do you think he gets his information? This article sounds almost as if he was sitting in that amphitheater when the lights went out."

"Sarah, I hope this doesn't come as too much of a

shock, but not everybody is as gung ho about this place as you are. But enough about Devlin. I thirst for knowledge."

"Knowledge about what?"

"Don't be coy now. You are currently the doc of the hour around here, and I want to know exactly what you did in there yesterday."

Sarah smiled.

"Just what you saw," she said. "The only way I could think of to stop her bleeding was to slow Lisa's heart rate and circulatory speed while she was mentally doing what she could to seal off the bleeding points in her body."

"Excuse me for saying so, but Lisa Summer mentally stopping an arterial pumper is a bit hard for this swagman to swallow."

"Except that you saw her do it, Andrew. Listen, a good hypnotist can tell a hypnotized subject that he is going to be touched on the arm by a hot poker. When the subject is touched with a pencil eraser instead, he raises a welt, then a blister on that spot. How do you explain that? You know, the real problem is that western physicians are taught about the autonomic nervous system by physiologists and anatomists. If we were taught by yogis or acupuncturists as well, our concepts of what humans can and cannot control in their bodies would be quite different."

"Believe in your limitations and they are yours, huh? Well, I for one am certainly impressed. Maybe you can ask young Miss Summer to look inside her body and tell us exactly what in the hell happened—how she got into this pickle to begin with. Does she know she's not the first?"

"I don't think so."

"Well, she ought to. Maybe if she knew how lucky she was to survive this at all, she'd perk up a bit."

"There's plenty of time for her to perk up. She just lost her baby and her arm. Andrew, do *you* have any idea what might be going on? Did you ever see that other girl as a patient?"

"No. *Et tu?*"

"I haven't a clue as to what's going on, and I was on vacation when the other woman came in and died. But I did see her in the clinic."

"And?"

"And she was a healthy young woman with an uncomplicated pregnancy. Just like Lisa. I put her on the herbal supplement I like to use and wished her well with her delivery. That was the only time I saw her."

"Herbal supplement?"

"Yes. Almost all pregnant women are given some kind of prenatal vitamins by their doctors. In our OB clinic, it's standard fare. Well, in the mountain villages where I worked in Thailand, the women all took prenatal supplements as well—a combination of roots and herbs, crushed and taken as a tea twice a week. The only study done of these women showed higher birthweights and better infant survival than in women who delivered in the teaching hospital in Chiang Mai. And believe me, the nutrition in the Meo villages was not very good, and the hygiene even worse. I helped conduct that study with an M.D. from the public health service and the herbalist who taught me most of what I know."

"Remarkable."

"It was, actually."

Sarah was excited to have the chance to talk about the Thai study and her work with the Meo and Akha tribes. It had been a wondrously happy and peaceful time in her life. She might still be working and studying there had it not been for the sudden death of Louis Han and the subsequent entry into her life of Peter Ettinger.

"So you use this herbal mix instead of prenatal vitamins?"

"Ever since I found a herbalist in town who could put it together, I have. I give every woman I see in the OB clinic the choice of taking whatever vitamin samples we happen to have on hand or the tea. Some pick one, some pick the other. I've been keeping some notes on birthweights and infant health, but the numbers are still too small to see any difference."

"Fascinating. What sort of herbs and roots are we talking about here?"

"Do you know about herbal medicine?"

"Not unless you consider having an assortment of Celestial Seasonings teas as being knowledgeable. I am interested in being enlightened, though."

"In that case, here's the handout I give to all the women I see in the clinic. It lists the nine ingredients in the supplement, and what each does."

"Angelica, dong quai, comfrey," Andrew said, scanning the list. "This is exotic-sounding stuff."

"Not really. If we were in Beijing, folic acid, beta-carotene, cupric oxide, and many of the other components of our standard prenatal vitamins would be considered just as far out."

"Point taken. This hospital is certainly tailor-made for you, isn't it."

"I know you have some misgivings, but I think we deliver the best patient care of any hospital in the city."

"Maybe so. We're certainly becoming the leading hospital for treating active labor complicated by DIC, I'll say that much for us."

Sarah's beeper sounded, ordering her to call extension 2350.

"That's the birthing room," she said. "I've got to go."

"Don't worry about your trash. I'll take care of it."

"Thanks. Andrew, do you think we should form some sort of committee to begin investigating these cases?"

"I think that's a splendid idea. If there's one thing this hospital could use more of, it's committees."

"I'm serious. I mean, it's not like an epidemic or anything. But two such similar and unusual cases. It certainly makes you wonder. Well, as they say in the postal service, I've got a delivery to make. We'll talk about all this more later, won't we?"

"You bet," Andrew said.

He watched until Sarah had left the cafeteria. Then he took an envelope from his lab coat pocket and tapped it thoughtfully against his palm.

"Not two cases, m'dear," he muttered. "Make that three."

Chapter 8

THE SURGICAL SENIOR RESIDENTS' OFFICE WAS AN eight-foot square, windowless box that had once served the Suffolk State Hospital as a storage closet. To Andrew Truscott, occupying the office at all, let alone sharing it with two others, was an indignity quite in keeping with those he already had to endure for being associated with the Medical Center of Boston. This should have been his year. He should have been chief resident and after that a staff surgeon on a tenure track. There was no justification for the flake who had been chosen over him. At any *normal* hospital it just wouldn't have happened.

After a year of postgraduate medical training in western Australia, he had met and married an American tourist and elected to move to the States. He expected the research and practice opportunities for a surgeon—and the income—would be much greater there. The Medical Center of Boston was not his first choice for a residency, but he was not disappointed to accept Eli Blankenship's offer of a position. After all, he reasoned, it was still a Boston teaching hospital.

Three months into his first year of surgical training at

MCB, Truscott began discreetly searching for vacancies in the residency programs at other hospitals. But the only available slots were at borderline facilities with even less prestige than MCB. So he stayed.

He detested Glenn Paris and the carnival-like atmosphere that surrounded the place. He disliked working at a hospital that so deemphasized clinical research that it was considered by many academicians to be something of a joke. And most of all, after investing five years of his life, he resented being passed over because he was, in the words of his department head, "too inflexible and intolerant." He was then informed that there was neither the money nor the research/office space to keep him on staff when his residency was over. Cut loose by Crunchy Granola General: the final ignominy.

Now Andrew Truscott sat in the tiny office, sipping orange juice from a Styrofoam cup and rereading a letter that had been routed to him by the head of the surgical service. Dated June 23, the letter was from the medical examiner's office in New York City. It was the department head's request that Andrew, as chairman of the surgical morbidity/mortality committee, look into the matter and recommend what departmental action, if any, was indicated.

DEAR DOCTOR:
First, let me apologize for the delay in getting this letter off to you. Budget cutbacks have hit our agency and greatly slowed the laboratory, cytologic, and clerical work necessary to complete a case. And unfortunately, our caseload continues to grow.

The case I write you about is a twenty-four-year-old woman, Constanza Hidalgo, who was killed when the car she was driving was struck by a bus in November of last year. The details surrounding this case, and the findings of my department, are presented in the enclosed documents. As you will note, the woman appears to have been in active labor at the time of her death. Our laboratory and microscopic studies also indicate that she was suffering from an acute hemorrhagic disorder, most likely disseminated intravascular coagulopathy.

A couple of months ago, one of my staff pathologists was attending a national meeting at which he heard another pathologist mention a case of fatal DIC complicating active labor. Quite incidentally, he returned to work and mentioned the case to me. The hospital at which that woman died was yours. I have been able to learn from contacting her family that Miss Hidalgo was also from Boston and was being followed in your outpatient department. Whether this is coincidence or not, I do not know.

Please use the enclosed information in any way you wish, and do keep me posted of any developments. Certainly DIC occurs in some pregnancies, but in my experience not without a very obvious cause.

Best regards,
MARVIN SILVERMAN, M.D.
Associate Medical Examiner

Andrew opened the copy of Constanza Hidalgo's MCB chart. The record dated back to the woman's childhood, but contained no medical history of particular interest. Her prenatal appointments were kept without exception, and nothing in the clinic notes gave a hint as to the disaster awaiting her and her fetus.

Truscott had already reviewed the chart several times since receiving Silverman's letter. Now, though, he read even more carefully, running his finger down each page until he found a brief outpatient note dated August 10. The note read:

Patient doing well and continuing part-time work as a waitress. Some complaints of fatigue, but no ankle edema, abdominal pain, urinary frequency, headaches, blurred vision, or unusual bleeding.

P.E.—normal vital signs, unremarkable cardiac exam, no edema, 22 wk. uterine fundus. Fetal heart heard easily at 140/min.

Impression: 22-week intrauterine pregnancy

Plan: Ptnt. elects to switch from prenatal multivits to herbal supplements. Three month supply and instructions given.

Return to Clinic: 4 wks.

The note was signed: S. Baldwin, M.D.

Truscott opened his briefcase and withdrew copies of the outpatient records of Lisa Summer and Alethea Worthington, the twenty-two-year-old woman who had gone into labor on the morning of April 4, had developed horrible DIC, and had essentially bled to death in the delivery room. Like Constanza Hidalgo, Alethea Worthington had been seen once in the obstetrics clinic by Sarah. And like both Lisa and Constanza Hidalgo, she had elected to take Sarah's herbal prenatal supplements.

Setting his feet on the corner of his desk, Truscott mulled over the situation. No doubt, the fact that each of the three DIC victims had taken Sarah's herbal supplement was coincidence. She had seen dozens of patients—possibly hundreds—in the clinic during her two years at MCB, and most of them had gone on to perfectly normal deliveries.

Still, he thought, until the actual cause of the DIC could be determined, the possibility of using the coincidence to further undermine the public confidence in MCB was most intriguing—especially in the hands of Jeremy Mallon. Truscott had almost not even bothered telling Mallon about the lights going out on Glenn Paris.

But he had, and through Mallon, the attorney who represented the Everwell HMO, the information had found its way to Axel Devlin. The acid-penned reporter had done the rest.

Truscott opened the *Herald*. He did not know how much Mallon would be paying him for the Changeover Day story, but the equivalent of two weeks' salary was a decent guess. The money was certainly welcome. But more important was the matter of a letter from Everwell guaranteeing Andrew a surgical staff position should the HMO acquire the Medical Center of Boston. Mallon had been generous enough with his payments, but he had yet to deliver on that promise. Perhaps this DIC business was just the lever Andrew needed to pry that letter loose.

Truscott slid a Gaulois from the sterling cigarette case a former lover had given him, lit up, and then dialed Jeremy Mallon's private line.

"Greetings, Mallon, Truscott here," he said. "I'm glad to see you made such quick use of the Changeover Day tape. Listen though. I have something more for you. Something quite good, actually. . . . No, I don't want to discuss it over the phone. . . . That will be fine. Just fine. Oh, one more thing. A letter that was promised me. . . . Yes, precisely that letter. Have it with you when we meet, will you? . . . That's splendid. Just splendid."

Truscott hung up, gathered the Xeroxed records together, and locked them in his briefcase. Of all the payoffs from Mallon, this promised to be the sweetest. That his disclosures might cause problems for Sarah Baldwin troubled him very little. As a surgeon, she was as capable and self-assured as any woman he had known in medicine. But she also represented everything he found distasteful about the Medical Center of Boston. And now, with this Lisa Summer thing, there would be no living with her or the rest of the oddball element at the hospital. She and her cronies were basking in the sunlight of her success like a herd of overfed sheep. The timing was perfect to seed the clouds for a little rain.

Besides, Sarah's ego had survived the other tidbits about her he had fed to Mallon. It would survive this batch as well. The real prizes at stake were Glenn Paris and his hospital sideshow. Already wounded and weakened, their survival was not nearly so certain.

As he headed out to check on his service, Andrew Truscott was singing softly to himself "Oh, MCB is falling down, my fair lady . . ."

Chapter 9

JULY 5

SARAH HAD NEVER MUCH LIKED GETTING DRESSED UP. As far as she could tell, that displeasure dated back to Sunday mornings in Ryerton, the rural New York town where she was raised. Her mother, perhaps responding to the stigma of having had a daughter out of wedlock, spent at least an hour each Sunday getting her ready for church. Sarah's dresses were pressed and perfect, her shoes spotless. Her hair was often braided half a dozen times before every strand was deemed in place. And always—at least until the early symptoms of her mother's Alzheimer's disease began to appear—the outfit was topped with a large, white bow.

Now Sarah twisted and turned before her bedroom mirror, trying to assess the third—or fourth—in the series of outfits she had tried on. It was eight o'clock in the morning. In fifteen minutes her cab to the hospital was due. Two days before, instigated no doubt by Glenn Paris and his PR department, the story had broken in both Boston papers about how eastern and western medicine had joined forces at the Medical Center of

Boston to save the life of a young woman. However, the positive publicity for MCB was short-lived.

A day later, a small article, under no byline, had appeared in the *Herald.* Unnamed but reliable sources had reported that the unusual and cataclysmic obstetrical bleeding complication was not the first but the third such to occur in an MCB patient within the past eight months. And unlike Lisa Summer, the source further related, both of the previous cases had died.

Glenn Paris's rapid response to the story had been to schedule a press conference for nine o'clock on the morning of July 5. With Independence Day being relatively slow for news, his carefully prepared statement was carried by every Boston radio and television station. Presenting at the session, he announced, would be Drs. Randall Snyder and Eli Blankenship, chiefs of the departments of obstetrics and internal medicine at MCB, and Dr. Sarah Baldwin, the resident who had contributed so uniquely to saving the life of Lisa Summer.

At eight-fifteen, when the doorbell rang, Sarah was wearing leather flats, a gathered madras skirt, a beige cotton blouse, and a hand-embroidered Burmese belt, topped by a loose-fitting turquoise blazer. Her major concession to the formality of the occasion was wearing panty hose—not comfortable in any month, but even less so in July.

"Coming," she shouted into the intercom.

She snatched up the ornate brass earrings fashioned for her by an Akha craftsman and slipped them in place as she hurried down the stairs. Though she admired Glenn Paris, being a performer in one of his extravaganzas was not Sarah's style. But the report of a third DIC case in an MCB patient did demand a quick, reassuring-but-informative response from the hospital. And Paris felt she could help accomplish that. What had been a curiosity with the first patient, then a serious concern with the second, had suddenly become a terrifying priority.

The cabbie let her off on the street side of the Thayer Building. Glenn Paris met her in his outer office and greeted her warmly. As always, he was noticeably well dressed. Today, his tan suit, sky-blue shirt, and red power tie seemed tailor-made for television. He appeared somewhat tense, but there was a confident, dedicated energy about him that Sarah found disarming and attractive. It was the same sort of aura that had initially drawn her to Peter Ettinger.

"Sarah, do you have any idea who might have leaked this information to the *Herald*?" Paris asked.

"No, sir."

"Neither does anyone else I've talked to. A letter about the Hidalgo case comes in from the New York City Medical Examiner to our chief of surgery. He sends copies to pathology, obstetrics, hematology, internal medicine, the morbidity and mortality committee, and then, almost as an afterthought, to me. No sooner do I read about the case in my copy of the letter, than I read it in the damn paper. Now, isn't that just something! Each of the people I have spoken with gave a Xerox of the letter to one or more others. At last count, any of twenty-five or thirty people could have leaked it. They all say they had no idea it was that important. Not important! Well, I'm going to get him, Sarah. This time whoever it is has gone too far. Mark my words, I'm going to get him."

"I'm sure you will," Sarah said softly.

Although she understood his anger, she was not comfortable with it. She came close to reminding him that, regardless of the source of the news leak, regardless of the negative publicity, something very serious and frightening *was* going on. And the Medical Center of Boston *did* seem to be right in the middle of it.

When they left the building on the campus side, they saw a fairly large number of people—hospital staff, reporters, and one television camera crew—streaming across toward the auditorium.

"Looks like we're going to have quite a turnout," Paris said. "That's good. We've got to let the public know we're on top of this thing. Our foundation grant is looking very good, but it's not a lock. Negative publicity can still hurt us."

"Have you met with any members of the medical staff yet?" she asked, hoping to bring him back to the real issue at hand.

"Dr. Blankenship and I have been huddled almost continually since this article broke. I have an old friend who's an administrator at the Centers for Disease Control in Atlanta. I put Eli in touch with him, and he tells me they're trying to get someone up here in time for—"

Paris stopped short, his hand raised to keep her silent. He motioned her into the shadow of the outpatient building. Ahead of them, just at the corner of the building, a well-dressed man with a briefcase in one hand was engrossed in intimate conversation with one of the hospital's maintenance workers. Two days before, the maintenance staff's wildcat job action had crumbled before Paris's threat to fire everyone involved. Fliers damning his action were subsequently posted throughout the hospital. And although they were all back at work, none of the maintenance staff had moved to take them down.

"You know that guy in the suit?" Paris whispered.

Sarah shook her head. The man, perhaps in his early forties, had a slight build, blow-dried hair, and a distinctively aquiline profile. The diamond in the ring on the small finger of his left hand was easily noticeable from where they were standing, some fifty feet away.

"I would say he's either a car salesman or a lawyer," Sarah said.

"What he is, is scum," Paris responded. "But he is a lawyer. And as a matter of fact, he's also an M.D."

"I'm impressed."

"Don't be. His name's Mallon. Jeremy Mallon. Ever heard of him? . . . No? Good. He's a bigtime ambulance chaser who is also on retainer for Everwell. I think he even owns a piece of their action. For months now, I've suspected he's been behind some, if not all, of the trouble we've been having. This little *tête-à-tête* we're watching goes a long way toward proving me right."

Suddenly Mallon caught sight of them. A word from him sent the maintenance worker scurrying off in the other direction. Paris moved in quickly, with Sarah a few feet behind.

"You son of a bitch," Paris snapped. "I knew it was you."

"I have no idea what you're talking about," Mallon said unctuously. "And I would caution you to watch what you call *anyone* in public."

Even if Paris had not prejudiced her, Sarah knew she would have instantly disliked the man.

"That power failure was no damn accident," Paris raged. "Neither was that bogus strike. I thought it, now I know it. I hope you paid that worm well, shyster, because as of now, he's out of a job."

Paris had raised his voice enough so that several of those headed toward the auditorium stopped to watch. Two MCB administrators, one of whom Sarah recognized as Colin Smith, the hospital's chief financial officer, hurried toward them.

"Paris, you're way out of line," Mallon said. "I don't need to make any trouble for you. You do a perfectly good job of that all by yourself."

"Get out of here right now."

"Nonsense. There's a publicly announced press conference that I want to attend. It will be fascinating to see how you plan to tiptoe around the fact that this place is becoming a death house."

"Why, you filthy—"

The two administrators stepped in front of Paris before he could lunge at the man.

"Easy, Glenn," Colin Smith said. "He's not worth it."

"I want you away from my hospital!" Paris shouted.

"You're looking and sounding more and more like a drowning man, Paris," said Mallon, who suddenly appeared to Sarah as some sort of serpent. "And as for its being *your* hospital, enjoy it while you can, because I don't believe that will be the case for much longer."

"Get out of here!"

This time Colin Smith had to physically restrain his boss.

"I *do* actually have more important things to do than to watch you gun yourself in the foot again, Paris. I can catch the highlights of that on the evening news." Mallon turned without waiting for a response and left through the outpatient building.

"Scum," Paris muttered.

"Easy does it," Smith urged.

"They're not going to get us, Colin. The day Everwell and that creep take over MCB will be the day they have to bury me."

"It'll never happen, Glenn," Smith said. "We've got the ace up our sleeve. You know that, and I know that."

His words had a remarkably calming effect on Paris. Sarah could see the muscles in his face relax. His fists unclenched. And finally he smiled.

"Right you are, Colin," he said. "Right you are. You're a good man."

He apologized to Sarah for his loss of composure, and introduced her to Smith and the other man, whose title had something to do with overseeing the hospital's physical plant. Then he sent them on ahead.

"Sarah, in case you hadn't guessed," he said, "the ace Colin was talking about is our grant. It's coming from the McGrath Foundation, and we've been courting them for almost three years now. But please, not a word to anyone. As I said before, this is not yet signed, sealed, and delivered. And I have no doubt that if he knew the magnitude of the grant and who it was coming from, that sleaze Mallon would do whatever he could to keep it from happening."

"It'll happen," Sarah said.

"Well, it's down to the wire now. We get the money, we win; we don't, Mallon and Everwell win. It's about as simple as that."

As they reached the building that housed the auditorium, they heard, then spotted a sleek helicopter, which swooped over the campus and then made a neat landing on the helipad Paris had insisted be built atop the surgical building.

"The person from the CDC?" Sarah asked.

"Doubtful. I don't even know if they're sending anyone yet. More likely it's some network VIP coming to the press conference."

"Or else one of our patients has some well-off family or friends."

"Doubtful again. I have every admission checked over by our PR staff. If somebody worth knowing about was a patient here, I promise you I'd be aware of it. Now, then, let's go in and give them a show."

"I'll do what I can," Sarah said.

. . .

Belted in the copilot's seat of his Sikorsky S76 jet helicopter, Willis Grayson watched the Medical Center of Boston expand below. What excitement he felt at the prospect of seeing his only child for the first time in five years was virtually consumed by his rage at those who had led her to such a place and such a condition.

Upon his return from restructuring a Silicon Valley company, he had found a detective named Pulasky camped outside the gate to his Long Island estate. The detective had the first new photos Grayson had seen of his daughter since well before she disappeared. The man also had with him copies of both Boston papers. And although the stories in them contained no pictures of Lisa Summer, Pulasky assured him the patient in the Medical Center of Boston and his daughter were one and the same person.

A visit by some of Grayson's Boston people to Lisa's Jamaica Plains address confirmed Pulasky's claim. After paying the man off, Grayson had made two calls. The first was to summon his pilot; the second was to order Ben Harris, his personal physician, to cancel his office patients and clear his schedule for an immediate flight. Within two hours they had touched down on the roof-top heliport of the Medical Center of Boston.

"Keep her warm, Tim," Grayson said, stepping out onto the tarmac. "If Lisa's in any condition to travel, we're getting her the hell out of here and down to our hospital." He helped his internist out onto the roof. "Now don't hold anything back from me, Ben," he ordered. "Remember, your allegiance is to me, not to that inbred medical fraternity I keep reading about. If someone's fucked up with Lisa's care, I want to know."

For nearly all of his fifty-four years, the driving force in Willis Grayson's life had been anger. As a child, he had drawn strength from the helpless rage of being strapped down on hospital beds while doctors wrestled with his life-threatening attacks of asthma. In his teens, fury at the prolonged absences of his industrialist father and the emotional unavailability of his socialite mother became manifest in repeated aggressive acts, leading to his expulsion from several private schools.

And years later, when he was finally admitted to the inner sanctum of his father's company, it was his desperate, unbridled need for retribution that drove him to maneuver the man out of power and to rechart the course of the business from manufacturing to corporate raiding. In just over two decades, his personal worth had grown to nearly half a billion dollars. But within him, little had changed.

Lisa's room was on the fifth floor of the building on which the chopper had landed. While the helipad was state of the art, the fifth floor was in need of refurbishing. In less than a minute, Grayson had made mental notes of an unemptied wastebasket, walls in need of paint, an unattended elderly patient strapped to his chair in the hall, and a pervasive smell that he suspected was a mix of grime, sweat, and excrement.

"This place is a pit, Ben," he said. "I just don't understand it. She could buy her own goddamn hospital, and she ends up in a place like this."

Grayson's people had reported Lisa's room as 515. With his physician several paces behind, Grayson hurried past the nurses' station, oblivious to the woman who was seated there, writing notes.

The stocky young nurse, whose name tag identified her as Janine Curtis, R.N., M.Sc.N., called out to them. "Excuse me. May I help you?"

"No," Grayson growled over his shoulder. "We're going to room five fifteen."

"Please stop," she demanded.

Grayson stiffened. Then, his fists slowly opening and closing at his sides, he did as she requested. Behind him, Dr. Ben Harris breathed an audible sigh of relief.

"Lisa Summer's real name is Lisa Grayson," Grayson said with exaggerated patience. "I'm her father, Willis Grayson, and this is her private physician, Dr. Benjamin Harris. Now may we proceed?"

Confusion darkened the nurse's face and then just as quickly vanished.

"Our visitors' hours don't begin until two," she said. "But if Lisa approves, I'll make an exception just this once."

Grayson's fists again clenched. But this time they remained so.

"Do you know who I am?" he asked.

"I know who you say you are. Look, Mr. Grayson, I don't want to be—"

"Ben, I just don't have time for this," Grayson snapped. "You stay here and explain to this woman who I am and why we're here. If she gives you any problem, call the goddamn director of this excuse for a hospital and get him up here. I'm going to see Lisa."

He stalked off without waiting for a reply.

One of the slide-in labels on the door of room 515 read "L. Summer." The other was blank. Willis Grayson hesitated. Had he done the right thing by not sending flowers or calling first? If, as he suspected, others had poisoned her against him, there was no telling what she was thinking. No, he decided, it was better to make this visit unannounced.

After she had been coerced into leaving home by Charlie or Chuck, or whatever the hell his name was, Grayson had spent tens of thousands of dollars trying to find her. The trail went cold in Miami. Then suddenly the boy showed up at home without her and with no idea where she had gone. For months afterward Grayson had him followed and his mail screened. But nothing came of it. Eventually the boy had just drifted away, with no clue as to how close he had come to having both his legs broken—or worse.

No, Grayson thought angrily, *it will take more than a few flowers.*

He tapped lightly on the door, waited, and then tapped again. Finally he eased it open. The olio of powder and lotion, starch and antiseptic was familiar and unpleasant. He had not been in a hospital room since the evening nearly eight years ago when he and Lisa sat together, holding his wife's hand as she surrendered to the malignancy she had battled for over a year.

Now his daughter sat motionless in a padded, high-backed chair, staring out the window. The sight of the bandages covering what remained of her right arm brought bile to Grayson's throat. He stepped around and sat down on the marble sill. Lisa glanced at him momentarily, then closed her eyes and looked away.

"Hi, honey," he said. "I'm so glad I found you. I've missed you so much."

He waited for a response, but knew from her expression and the set of her shoulders that there would be none.

Damn them, he thought, lumping her friends, room-mates, lovers, and doctors—real and imagined—into an ill-defined object of molten hate. *Damn them all to hell for bringing you to this.*

"I'm sorry for what you've been through." He tried again. "Please, Lisa. Please talk to me. . . . I want to get you out of here. Dr. Harris flew up with me. You remember him. He's right outside. His staff is waiting for you at the medical center back home. He'll check you over, and if he says it's safe, we'll have you there in ninety minutes. Tim's on the roof with the helicopter. He's missed you, too, hon. Everybody's missed you. Lisa?"

Lisa continued looking away. Grayson stood and paced about the room, searching for the words that would begin to open her heart to him.

If only you had listened to me in the first place, he wanted to scream. *If only you had listened to me, none of this would have happened.*

"I know you're angry with me," he said instead, "but everything can be all right now. You're all I have, and I'll do anything to have you with me again. . . . Please, Lisa. I know you're hurting. I want to help you fight back. I want to help you find out why this horrible thing happened to you and . . . and to my grandson. And if anyone is responsible, I want more than anything to be the hammer that helps you strike them down. . . . All right, all right." He took a calming breath and moved back to the window. "I understand that it might not be easy for you after all this time. Listen, I'll be staying at the Bostonian. The number will be right by your phone. I'm going to arrange for a private nurse to take care of you, and I'm going to have Ben Harris get in touch with your doctors. Please, baby. I—I love you. Please let me back in your life."

He hesitated, and then turned and headed for the door.

"Come back later, Daddy," she said suddenly.

Grayson stopped. *Were the words only in his mind?*

"This afternoon," she said. "Three o'clock. I promise to talk with you then."

Her soft monotone held neither anger nor forgiveness.

Willis Grayson turned back and stared at her. Lisa was again sitting motionless, gazing out the window.

"Okay," he said finally. "Three o'clock."

He gently kissed his daughter on the top of her head. She reacted not at all.

"I'll be here at three," he whispered. "Thank you, baby. Thank you."

He paused by the door and looked back once again at the stump that had been her hand and arm.

Someone was going to pay.

Chapter 10

SARAH FOLLOWED GLENN PARIS THROUGH THE FRONT entrance to the amphitheater and up onto the stage. Only the last few rows of the hall were empty, and people were still trickling in. The three Boston television stations, representing the big three networks, each had a pod of lights, a video man, and a reporter set between the low stage and first row of seats. Although Sarah rarely watched television, she recognized two of the newspeople. Clearly, the possibility of the outbreak of some rare disease held more than a little public allure.

The podium, covered with wine-color velvet, was festooned with microphones, a dozen or more. Behind it were five folding chairs, three to one side and two to the other. Eli Blankenship and Randall Snyder were already seated, with one empty chair between them. Paris motioned Sarah to that seat.

If Paris was nervous about the event or the absence of a representative from the Centers for Disease Control, it did not show in his face or manner. He measured the hall for a time, then buttoned his jacket and crossed over to the three physicians.

"Well, we certainly can't cry apathy about this one," he said softly. "This whole show would have been a bit tighter if the CDC could have gotten someone up here, but we'll just have to make do. I'll make a few introductory remarks, then you Eli, you Randall, and finally you, Sarah. I would suggest keeping your statements brief and filling in as questions are asked. The only advice I would give you is to remember that the less you say, the harder it will be for them to misquote you. I'm going to limit each of you to ten minutes, including questions. If it seems appropriate at the end, I'll allow a few more. And don't worry, you'll all do fine."

Sarah knew the "all" was aimed directly at her.

"He really loves this stuff, doesn't he," she said as Paris approached the podium.

"He should," Blankenship responded. "He's very good at it. You, on the other hand, look a little peaked. Are you going to make it?"

"I thought I'd be fine until I got up here. Look at that mob."

Blankenship reached over a meaty hand and gave her a fatherly pat on the shoulder.

"Just remember the old medical adage," he said. "All bleeding eventually stops."

"That's very reassuring. Thank you."

Paris's introductory remarks, made without notes and delivered without a hitch, painted the picture of an institution devoted to the health and welfare of the citizens of Boston, and fearless about stepping forward to confront problems of public concern.

"We have been in close contact with the epidemiology division of the Centers for Disease Control in Atlanta," he said, "and they have promised to send us one of their top people to augment our own intensive investigation. I had hoped he would be here in time to participate in this news conference—" He gestured to the empty chair beside his. "—but unfortunately that wasn't possible."

The three cases of DIC, he stressed, might add up to

nothing more than coincidence. However, the approach decided upon by the Medical Center of Boston was to take the bull by the horns and begin an immediate investigation, while keeping the public aware in an ongoing manner.

Sarah was disturbed that Paris would tout the imminent arrival of a CDC epidemiologist, when he had just told her he did not know if one was even coming at all. But she reasoned that the exaggeration was harmless enough, and given the circumstances, understandable. He was simply trying to diffuse as many issues as possible. And in fact, by the time he introduced Eli Blankenship, it was as if the *Herald* item had not forced his hand at all.

Buoyed by the CEO's performance, Sarah felt some of her tension abate. Still, it was not until Blankenship was finishing his formal remarks that she felt comfortable enough to look out at the audience. If, as she remembered once hearing, the amphitheater held 250, at least 200 were there. Many of those attending were residents and medical school faculty, including Andrew, who was back in his traditional last-row center seat. But a significant number, judging from their appearance and dress, seemed simply to be from the community. Among them, Sarah recognized one woman with whom she was training to do home birth, just as she had with Lisa. It wasn't difficult to imagine her thoughts and concerns.

But it was another woman, seated not far from Andrew, whom Sarah found the most interesting. She was African in her skin color, hairstyle, dress, and jewelry. And even through the lights and distance, her uncommon beauty was obvious. Sarah was scanning the audience when she realized the striking young woman was looking straight at her, smiling.

I know you from someplace, don't I? Sarah thought. *But from where?*

Blankenship lumbered back to his seat to a smattering

of applause. Sarah whispered congratulations, even though she realized that she had been preoccupied with the woman in the last row and had missed his final answer.

As Sarah expected, Randall Snyder was down-to-earth and reassuring in his presentation and responses to questions. The three DIC cases were certainly a cause for concern, he said. But without a careful review, especially of the way the diagnoses were made, it was still too soon even to link them. Meanwhile, he concluded, the public should rest assured that his department would be carefully screening all obstetrical patients for any abnormality suggesting an increased susceptibility.

The applause for Snyder was measurably louder than it had been for Eli, even though his presentation had not been nearly as substantive. The power of the fatherly image, Sarah acknowledged, recalling at the same time that she had voted for substance over fatherly image in almost every presidential election since she turned eighteen and had only once backed the winner.

Finally it was her turn. In an effort to keep reasonably organized, she had printed the points she wanted to make on a set of three-by-five file cards. By the time her five-minute presentation was over, she had covered most of what was on them. Throughout her remarks, though, she felt a gulf separating her from the audience. She knew that, in spite of herself, she was sounding stilted, and far more proselytizing and pompous than she had intended.

Hey, everyone, this isn't me! she wanted to scream out. *These are issues I really care about. I would love to talk about them—but with you, not at you. How about we all go to the Arnold Arboretum, throw some blankets on the grass, and really get into why people become ill, what it means to be sick, and what it takes to get well?*

Concluding her formal remarks, she thanked everyone for their concern and involvement and invited questions. In an instant the audience, which had seemed indifferent and half asleep, became a kelp forest of waving arms and hands. Sarah glanced over at Paris to see if he wanted to step up beside her and choose. But the CEO just smiled and winked. She shrugged, turned back to the forest, and pointed.

"Do you honestly think your acupuncture and Lisa Summer's imaging of her blood cells stopped her bleeding?"

Of course I do, you idiot!

"I believe strongly that they were two of the factors. As I said, there were other efforts going on at the same time."

"Have you ever stopped someone's bleeding with your techniques before?"

Perhaps if you tried your very hardest, ma'am, you could sound even more *patronizing.*

"Not specifically. But I have assisted on several operations in which only acupuncture anesthesia was used. Each time, the amount of bleeding was impressively minimal."

"Tell us more about your background. You mentioned working in a holistic healing center. Where was that?"

Glenn, is it time yet?

"Right here in Boston. It was called the Ettinger Institute."

Annalee! In disbelief, Sarah stared across the audience at the woman in the last row. Annalee Ettinger smiled and waved. It had been seven years since Sarah had seen the girl Peter had brought home from Mali as a child and subsequently adopted. But time was hardly the reason that recognition had come so slowly. When Sarah moved out of their Back Bay condominium, Annalee had been a dear and interesting fifteen-year-old. But she was also painfully shy and markedly overweight. Her transformation was miraculous. Her face, with its wonderfully high cheekbones, seemed almost sculpted.

Sarah's gaze shifted to her long enough to confirm

that the connection had been made. Annalee smiled and nodded.

"Ettinger," the questioner went on. "Is that the same Ettinger who does those programs on TV for that diet powder?"

"I—I really don't know," Sarah said. "Outside of catching *Jeopardy!* once in a while in the on call room, I almost never have time to watch television. And I haven't been in touch with Mr. Ettinger in many years."

"It is," a woman called out. "It is the same man. I'm taking that stuff of his and I've already dropped thirty pounds. It's fantastic."

The audience laughed roundly, and Sarah knew that she had lost control of the session. Glenn Paris quickly stepped to the podium.

"Dr. Baldwin, thank you very much," he said.

He motioned her to her seat and led the audience in applause. Perhaps it was the somewhat controversial nature of her presentation, perhaps the lack of a crisp, definitive closing; whatever the reason, Sarah felt that the audience reaction to her was polite but hardly enthusiastic. If Snyder got the tens of thousands of dollars in prize money and the chance to return tomorrow to defend his championship, and Blankenship got the home entertainment center, she had just won best wishes and a *Jeopardy!* board game.

Oblivious to the supportive whispers from Blankenship and Snyder, Sarah focused on a spot of floor next to Glenn Paris's shoes, waiting for the words that would send everyone home. Her performance had been far from stunning, but not a disaster. Best of all, it was over. Now there were questions—seven years' worth—occupying her thoughts. And the answers to them all were as close as Annalee Ettinger.

Glenn Paris ended the session with the promise to keep the public informed of any developments. Immediately, a number of reporters rushed onto the stage, rudely jostling one another as they jockeyed for position around the speakers. Concerned about the delay, Sarah made eye contact with Annalee, who assured her with a dismissive gesture that she was in no hurry.

Finally the gaggle of questioners began to disperse. Sarah accepted a pat on the back from Paris and was about to leave him when an older woman approached, a leather portfolio tucked beneath one arm. Sarah had noticed her standing at the back of the auditorium throughout the conference. She was quite unimposing— five feet four or so—conservatively dressed in a straight, dark skirt and blazer. Her short, carefully permed hair was an equal mix of brown and gray. And although her face had a pleasant, peaceful quality, her features were nearly lost behind round, oversized tortoiseshell spectacles. In her survey of the crowd, Sarah had cast the woman as a grandmother from the community, too self-conscious to work her way past people and into a seat.

"Dr. Baldwin, Mr. Paris," she said, "my name is Rosa Suarez."

Her pronunciation of her name was distinctly Latin.

"Yes, Mrs. Suarez," Paris said, unable to cull the hint of impatience from his voice. "What can we do for you?"

The woman smiled patiently. "That man from the Centers for Disease Control about whom you spoke— the top-notch epidemiologist you were promised?"

"Yes," Paris said. "Yes, what about him?"

"Well, I am he."

Chapter 11

THE PARK, A SANDY OASIS WITH A FEW SLATTED BENCHES and some well-worn playground equipment, was located several blocks from the MCB. Sarah signed out to one of the other residents and walked there with the woman who had once very nearly become her stepdaughter. But this Annalee Ettinger—slender, self-assured, and surprisingly worldly—bore little resemblance to the shy, rotund girl Sarah had once tried so hard to befriend. From the first tentative minutes of their conversation, Sarah felt a stronger connection between them than at any time when Peter was part of the equation.

"I wrote you from med school," Sarah said, as they settled on one of the benches. "Two or three times. You never answered."

Annalee nodded.

"I know," she said. "About a year or so after you left, I was looking for something in my father's desk, and I found one of your letters. It didn't have an envelope or a return address. I made a copy of it and kept that. But I never confronted my father about it. I was a self-centered little tub back then, and pretty wrapped up in myself and my problems. Perhaps I should have pushed things and tried to get back to you. But whatever your reasons, you *had* left us. I guess it really didn't matter enough to me at that time to pursue it."

Her voice was deep and melodic, her nails perfectly manicured and polished a high-gloss crimson. If as a teen she was often silly, self-absorbed, and immature, she now projected a maturity well beyond her years.

"I'm sorry for leaving the way I did," Sarah said. "I was so angry. Still, I can't imagine Peter doing something like keeping my letters from you."

"He was very hurt and angry when you walked out on us. So was I for that matter—at least until I found that letter." She slid a pack of Virginia Slims from her purse. Her gold and silver bangles—eight or ten on each wrist—jangled as she tapped one out. "I don't suppose you smoke."

"Not for years."

"Good. Good for you." She lit up and inhaled deeply through her nose and mouth.

"I tried to explain the reasons I left in one of my letters to you," Sarah said. "God, I shudder to think what version of the story you must have gotten."

"My father's a marvelous man, but he does have his faults. Holding grudges is one of them. Did you know that he got married a year or so after you left? A revenge marriage if ever there was one. She was quite a looker in a WASPy kind of way, and from a big-bucks family that probably came over on the *Mayflower*. I'm surprised he didn't send you an invitation."

"Very funny. Listen, Annalee, things happen the way they're supposed to happen. I really believe that. Ninety-five percent of what your father was I loved. But the other five percent involved big-league stuff that I just couldn't see having to live with for the rest of my life. And I didn't believe there was much chance that those particular things would change. I think it's terrific that he got married."

"Well, I don't believe he shares your opinion, Doc. The marriage only lasted a year."

"Oh, I see. Did *you* get along with her?"

"Considering that I was probably the first black woman Carole had ever been near who didn't work for her, I guess we did okay. I didn't see her much, really. A short time after you left, Peter shipped me off to boarding school. That was another reason I never got around to trying to find you. I was so messed up. Sending me off to school may have been the right idea, but his timing was lousy. I think when he brought me home with him from Mali, he expected I'd become someone other than what I was turning out to be—a college professor or concert musician or something. Anyhow, being away at Miss Whatzername's the way I was, it seemed to me like one minute ol' Carole was there, the next, poof."

"And when did he close the institute?"

"Not too long after all that. We lived in Boston for a while longer, then his Xanadu thing actually began to happen."

"Ah, Peter's dream," Sarah said. "I knew he'd pull it off someday."

Xanadu—the first of what would eventually be a chain of upscale residential communities centered about the principles of living a long and healthy life through diet, exercise, seasonal routines, stress management, and holistic medicine. Peter had spoken about his ambitious concept the day they first met, and they had spent countless hours discussing and dissecting it during their years together.

At the time of their breakup, he had begun looking for available land and investors and even had a glass-enclosed architect's model of the prototype complex prominently displayed in the institute's conference hall. The design of the homes, he insisted, would be strictly controlled. All construction would be in accordance with the ancient laws of health and harmony subscribed to by the Indian Ayurvedic healers.

"It's beginning to happen in a pretty big way now," Annalee said. "But the whole thing was touch and go for a while. At one point, Peter was even talking bankruptcy."

"Well, what happened?"

"That powder happened, that's what."

"Powder?"

"The powder they were talking about at your conference. From what I can tell, it really saved his behind." She laughed exuberantly. "Hey, that's great, now that I think about it. That powder saves Peter's ass and gets rid of mine. What a product."

"I don't understand."

"The Xanadu Ayurvedic Herbal Weight Loss System," she said. "Why, woman, surely you have heard of it."

"Not until today I haven't. I was very confused when they started talking about it at the press conference and everyone in the place seemed to know what was going on except me."

"That's because everyone in the place except you *did* know what was going on. Most folks in the country for that matter. Why, Peter's been on TV so much lately pushing that ol' system of his, it's a wonder he hasn't been nominated for an Emmy. You don't watch TV?"

"I don't have time."

Annalee stubbed out her cigarette and seconds later lit up another.

"Well," she said, "he does these things called infomercials. They're set up to look like real programs, half an hour long with guest stars and film clips and all— but what they really are is commercials. They run mostly in the off-hours—you know, late nights and Sunday mornings. And damn, are they beginning to bring in some bucks. Peter's got charts all over the wall in his office showing the constant rise in sales. Since he started this campaign just a few months ago, it's been phenomenal. And all of a sudden, the big bad wolf has backed away from the Xanadu door."

"Does the powder actually work?" Sarah asked. "I'd be fascinated to know what herbs are in it."

"Hell, yes, it works," Annalee said. "Peter didn't invent the mixture, though. This Indian doctor, Dr. Singh, did. He's not an M.D., he's an Ayurvedic doctor. I guess you know what that's all about."

"Ayurvedic medicine was being taught in India centuries before Hippocrates or Galen were born. There are some pretty solid reasons why it's survived over all this time."

"Well, Dr. Singh brought his powder to Peter a few years ago and offered him some sort of a partnership, I think. I'm not sure of the details, but I'm sure they included Peter's acting as the spokesperson for the company. Dr. Singh seems very bright, but he isn't exactly the most dynamic, photogenic critter I've ever seen. Have you heard of him?"

"No. No, I haven't."

"I don't know much about him either. Anyhow, seeing as I had only tried one or two hundred different diets without much success, Peter asked me if I wanted to be his guinea pig and try the stuff out before he invested in it. The result?" She rose and spun around to give Sarah a look.

"Bravo. And you don't have trouble staying on your diet?"

"What diet? Why, those of us who are into infomercials know that the Xanadu Ayurvedic Herbal Weight Loss System preaches no dieting, only moderation and avoidance of a few forbidden foods."

"Let's hear it for moderation," Sarah cheered, delighting more every minute in the once-sullen girl.

"Here's the best part," Annalee went on. "In the beginning, when I first started the powder, I tried moderation and I lost weight. After a month or two, just because I am who I am, I tried eating like a piglet. And I *still* lost weight. That's what really sold Peter. Now isn't that something?"

Sarah rose and hugged her lovingly.

"It is that," she said. She held Annalee by the shoulders and moved her back enough to focus on her face. "Annalee, I always thought you were pretty special and that problems or no problems, you had tremendous potential. I want you to know that I underestimated you. You have really become a wonderful, beautiful person."

"Hey, thanks. You're pretty special yourself. But you left a word out when you were describing me."

"Let's see, *wonderful . . . beautiful.*"

"And pregnant." Annalee read the shadow that crossed Sarah's face. "And happy," she added quickly. "Very happy. This baby's being born come hell or high water, and if I have my way, you're gonna deliver it."

"Hey, that's great. Thanks for asking me. I'll have the chief of the department be our backup. Annalee, I'm really, really excited for you. Are you sure about the pregnancy?"

"Planned Parenthood did the test. Goodness, but those people are some of the best on earth. They guessed maybe four or five months more, but they couldn't be certain without more tests. My periods have always been screwed up. That's why I waited so long before even considering I might be pregnant."

"Well, congratulations. I'll check you over and maybe even get an ultrasound. Annalee, this is going to be fun."

"I know it will. I was in the middle of deciding who to go and see when I read about you in the papers. Then I heard about the press conference on TV and I said to my boyfriend, 'Taylor, the first hands to touch this baby are going to be Sarah Baldwin's.' "

"Taylor, huh. I like the name. So, give me the lowdown. What does he look like? What does he do?"

"Let's see . . . he's got a face like Denzel Washington, an ass like Wesley Snipes, and he moves like Michael Jordan."

"Lord."

"And he's a musician—a damn good one. Bass, guitar, horns even."

"Rock and roll?"

"Hell no. Jazz. I sang with his group for a while. That's how we met. You see, Dr. Singh's powder kind of backfired on Peter—on me, too, I think. I was in college at U Mass, doing reasonably well as a psych major, but not enjoying it or my miserable social life very much. Then all of a sudden, the woman beneath the flab emerged, and I guess I sort of got, well, out of control, you might say."

"That's understandable."

"I ended up on the West Coast, running with a fast crowd, singing with this group and that, and trying to make it in films. I had some nibbles from a few producers, but more often than not, they were nibbles on my earlobes and breasts. Finally I met Taylor. His last name's West. Right then and there I began to mend my ways. He's on the road a lot, and we aren't exactly rolling in dough. So a few months ago, I took Peter's offer to come home and help him at Xanadu."

"And what does he think about becoming a grandpa?"

"He . . . um . . . he doesn't know. He's only now getting to know Taylor. And he still believes I'm going to start school again in January."

Sarah took time to ponder that news.

"I certainly hope you *will* get your degree at some point," she said finally. "But you know, I'm thinking that you ought to tell him. Give him the benefit of the doubt."

"I'll consider it."

"Well, speaking from a purely biological standpoint, Annalee, pretty soon he's going to start wondering why his fabulous Xanadu Ayurvedic powder has failed in such a specific, low-belly way."

"You *do* have a point there."

"Thanks. It's good to know I've mastered some of the basics over my years in obstetrics. And you know, as long as you're giving him the benefit of the doubt, I think I'd feel more comfortable if you'd tell him about your seeing me as well. Seven years is long enough for most wounds to heal—even Peter's. Besides, just like your belly, sooner or later, that's going to come out, too."

"If you wish it, it shall be done."

"I wish it. But you should certainly do what feels right to you. It just seems as though if you're living with him, and he's helping to support you—"

"I understand."

"On the other hand, I don't think anything would be served by getting on his case about the vanishing letters from me."

"Ancient history."

"Exactly. God, I'm blabbering on and on. Do you think I could be nervous about dealing with your father after all this time?"

"Let's just say that you better be a damn sight more relaxed when you're delivering our baby." Annalee laughed again. Her smile made her remarkable face even more appealing.

"I'll work on it," Sarah said. "One last thing, though."

"Name it."

"If I'm going to be your obstetrician, and you want to give that kid of yours the best chance to be healthy, those cigarettes have got to go."

The younger woman's almond eyes narrowed.

"Couldn't I find something else to give up instead?" she asked.

Sarah shook her head. "I'm afraid it's a big deal."

"All right, okay. The smokes are history."

"Excellent." Sarah checked the time. "Listen," she said, "I'm due back at the hospital. But if you'll walk me back, I'd like to tell you at least a little bit of my version of what happened—why I left."

"You don't need to."

Sarah slipped her arm inside Annalee's. "I know," she said.

By the time they arrived at the gate to the MCB campus, Annalee, shaking her head sadly, had *her* arm draped around Sarah's shoulders.

"Nothing you've told me comes as much of a surprise," she said. "He's really not a bad guy, just difficult sometimes. And speaking of surprises, it probably won't surprise you much to know that Henry McAllister is as devoted to Peter as ever. He's been to Xanadu for dinner, and he's designing a big fountain for the front lawn."

"You're right," Sarah said. "I'm not surprised. . . ."

Her voice trailed away. Although she had visited McAllister once in the hospital after his operation, he never indicated that he knew the role she had played in saving his life. And she had chosen not to be the one to tell him. *She* knew, and that was all that mattered—or at least so she had thought at the time.

"Well, now," Annalee said, quite obviously changing the subject, "I for one and this baby in here for two are gonna have the time of our lives over these next few months. I'm gonna stop smoking, and stop drinking, and stop staying up to all hours, and stop eating Twinkies, and—say, do I have to stop . . . ?"

"No," Sarah said. "No, you can keep doing that right up to almost the end."

"In that case, what you see before you is the start of the perfect pregnancy."

"A textbook case. Listen, as long as you're here, I'll tell you what. Why don't you come by the clinic right now. You can register as an outpatient afterward, and have the routine blood and urine tests done before you go home. I have enough time to do a quick exam just to make sure everything's okay. After that, we'll stop by my locker. I have a supply of the natural prenatal supplement that many of my patients take. You ought to get started on it now. That is, assuming you prefer the organic to the stuff from the drug houses."

"I'm still my father's daughter," Annalee said. "Besides, if you recommend something, I'm doing it. After all, you're the doctor."

. . .

Rosa Suarez placed the last of her clothes into the maple highboy, and then set framed photographs of her husband, Alberto, three daughters, and four grandchildren on the doily-covered bedside table. The bed and breakfast she had chosen from the list supplied by her department was hardly elegant, but it was comfortable enough and within easy walking distance of the Medical Center of Boston.

After nearly twenty-five years on the job and dozens of extended field investigations, the routine of unpacking was as familiar as her robe. But there was something special about this assignment. Long term or short, significant findings or not, this investigation would be her last. She had left her letter of resignation on the section chief's desk and had promised Alberto that *this time* she meant it.

Now everybody would be happy. Her husband, at seventy nearly a decade older than she, would have some reasonably healthy years to enjoy retirement with her. Her department would be able to bring in some new blood. And more important, they would be able to wash their hands of a colleague who had become something of an embarrassment to them—the old lady who many of them believed had botched a major investigation.

"Mrs. Suarez, there's two packages here for you. Heavy ones," her landlady called out from just outside her door.

"Just sign for them, Mrs. Frumanian. But don't try to

lift them. They're books. I'll be down for them in a minute."

Following her assignment to the Boston case, Rosa had spent hours in the library. She set her portfolio on the bed and took out the notes she had made. Diligent preparation and obsessive attention to details. Those had always been her trademark—the keys to what had once been an unbroken string of successes. They had never failed her, not even in San Francisco. And, she vowed, they would not fail her now.

She knew there was nothing her section chief wanted less than to turn this investigation over to her. The BART fiasco had probably cost him a promotion. And since then, he had gone out of his way to keep her shuffling papers, making out bibliographies, and sorting through miles of computer printouts. But at the moment of the call from Boston, she was the only field epidemiologist available. And people were dying.

She changed into the gray Champion sweatsuit her daughters had given her for Christmas and padded down the narrow stairway. Mrs. Frumanian was standing guard over the two boxes, waiting, it was clear, to check on their contents. She was a pleasant, ample woman with a deeply etched face that Rosa found interesting.

"I can manage all right, Mrs. Frumanian, thank you," she said.

"Nonsense, I am twice your size, and you are my guest. If you have books to carry, I have books to carry."

Her dense accent was Eastern European, but Rosa could pinpoint it no closer than that. Frumanian sliced open the boxes with a paring knife she conveniently produced from her apron pocket.

"Hematology . . . Advanced Computer Programming . . . Differential Calculus . . . Coagulation." The older woman read the titles off as she stacked each volume on her arm. Her pronunciation was surprisingly good. "Two of my boys finished college," she said. "They brought home books like this on their vacations all the time, but they never read them."

"Well, I expect to spend a good deal of time reading these, Mrs. Frumanian."

Rosa ushered the woman out the door as gently as she could. Limits had to be set if she was to get work done. She had been given this one chance—this one last chance —to go out a winner. This time she would trust nobody. Nobody at all.

Chapter 12

WILLIS GRAYSON, CRADLING A $150 BUNDLE OF exotic flowers, trotted up the stairs to the fifth floor of the Surgical Building. A slight cold had kept him out of his pool since his return from the coast, and even this bit of exercise was welcome.

He had left the hospital that morning ecstatic over Lisa's decision to talk with him. Later he and Ben Harris had spent an hour with Dr. Randall Snyder. The obstetrician seemed a decent enough sort, though certainly no intellectual giant. Still, Ben was impressed with him, and that was sufficient to soften much of Willis's knee-jerk anger toward the physicians who had cared for his daughter. It also alleviated some of his misgivings about the Medical Center of Boston. The care Lisa had received seemed to have been adequate, especially considering that Snyder and the hospital had believed all along that she was without any means to pay for it.

It was disappointing to learn that Snyder and the others on the medical team had no clue as to what might have caused Lisa's blood problem. Still, it did appear that an effort was being made to get to the bottom of things. Grayson charged Ben Harris with obtaining the names of the leading experts in the field so that they could be put on the case.

Next on Grayson's agenda would be a visit later that afternoon to the head of physical therapy and rehabilitation. He would tactfully inform her that, while he appreciated the efforts of her department, the people at the Rusk Rehabilitation Institute in New York would be overseeing the selection and implementation of Lisa's prosthesis. And then finally, perhaps in the morning, he would try to meet with the obstetrics resident who was said to have done more than anyone else to save Lisa's life. If, in fact, Sarah Baldwin had played such a role, his people would be instructed to learn about the woman and her needs, and to come up with an appropriate reward.

Energized at regaining the control that had eluded him for nearly five years, Grayson strode down the corridor to room 515. Both of the slide-ins on the door were empty. He knocked once and then eased the door open. Both beds were newly made, and the room unoccupied.

"What in the hell?"

Battling anxiety, confusion, and anger, Grayson checked the two metal armoires and then the bathroom. All were clean and empty. After leaving Lisa that morning, he had tried to get her transferred to a single room. When informed that every room on the floor was a double, he had left strict instructions with the head nurse on the floor to notify admissions that he would pay whatever was necessary to keep the other bed in room 515 empty. *What in the hell could have happened?*

He threw the flowers onto one of the beds and raced to the nurses' station. Janine Curtis, the nurse to whom he had spoken earlier, appeared prepared for a confrontation.

"Miss Curtis," he demanded, "what's become of my daughter?"

She held his gaze evenly.

"Nothing's *become* of her, sir," she said with exaggerated patience. "She's doing fine. She's been moved to another room."

"But we agreed this morning she would stay where she was, and that no one would be moved in."

"I know what *you* requested, sir. But Lisa asked to be moved to another room, and we obliged her."

"Well then, where is she now?" he snapped.

"I'm afraid I can't tell you that, sir," the nurse said.

"Miss Curtis, I'm not in the mood for games."

"It's *Mrs.* Curtis, and this is no game. Your daughter told us quite emphatically that she does not wish to see you."

"What?"

"She said that if you want to speak with her, you might try coming back tomorrow morning. She'll see how she feels then."

"Dammit, she told me just a few hours ago to come back at three this afternoon. Now where is she?"

"Mr. Grayson, please keep your voice down. Our patient has given us a clear and specific order, and we fully intend to honor it. I would suggest you do as she asks and return tomorrow."

"And *I* would suggest you be very careful whom you talk to like that."

"Mr. Grayson, you made it perfectly clear who you were this morning. In all honesty, it makes no difference to me. Lisa is an adult with control over the decisions involving her life. She is also my patient. She's been through a great deal, and I intend to do whatever I can to honor any wishes she might have."

She smiled at him coolly and then returned to her work.

Glowering at her, Grayson gave brief thought to searching every room on the floor. Then he stormed off.

. . .

The initial meeting between Andrew Truscott and attorney Jeremy Mallon, some two and a half years before, had actually taken place at a Red Sox–Yankees game. Before Glenn Paris canceled the Everwell HMO's contract with MCB, the organization had used the hospital for a modest percentage of its inpatient cases. Each year, as a "thank you" to the residents, the HMO would rent a bus, load it with beer, and take the entire house staff to a clambake and then to Fenway Park.

Having heard rumors of Andrew Truscott's profound disenchantment with MCB, Mallon had carefully arranged the seating so that he was next to Truscott. By the end of the third inning, they had evolved makeshift code words for the hospital and key personnel, and had established their mutual distaste for Glenn Paris and his offbeat antics. By the bottom of the fifth, Truscott had made it clear that he was not unwilling to provide inside information on hospital goings-on in exchange for certain considerations. And by the seventh-inning stretch, they had exchanged numbers and agreed to meet again in the near future.

Now, some $30,000 later, Andrew scribbled a fictitious name in the log book of the office building at One Hundred Federal Plaza and rode the elevator to the twenty-ninth-floor law offices of Wasserman and Mallon. His relationship with the attorney was a shaky one. Andrew neither trusted nor liked the man, and although Mallon was too slick to get a decent handle on, Andrew suspected those feelings were reciprocated. However, there was no denying that each had profited from the other. And with the information he had tucked in his briefcase tonight, their collaboration seemed destined to continue.

The brass plaques on the mahogany doors to the firm's suite listed four partners and about twenty associates. Jeremy Mallon was the only one with an M.D. in addition to his law degree. The spacious interior, with its glass-enclosed library and multiple secretary's desks, had an array of original oils on the walls that included a Sargent, an O'Keeffe, and a small Wyeth. Truscott wondered in passing how many physicians' malpractice victories and settlements it had taken to develop such a collection.

As soon as he entered the reception area, Andrew caught the aroma of Chinese food. And after brief stops before the Sargent and a striking piece by the contemporary realist Scott Pryor, he followed the scent down the hall to Mallon's office. Although the number of white cartons spread across the teak table suggested a small banquet, only Mallon was there.

"Come in, Andy. Come in." Mallon motioned Andrew to a seat with his chopsticks. "I didn't know what you liked, so I ordered a little of everything."

Andrew winced at the use of his nickname, which he had never liked. *Andy.* Despite the hefty payments, he felt wary around Mallon, a gladhander who always seemed to have a hidden agenda. If it served his purposes, Andrew suspected, the attorney would devour him with the same dispassionate enthusiasm he exhibited toward the Peking duck.

"There's beer, wine, or whatever else you want in the fridge beneath the wet bar," Mallon said. "Forgive me if I seem to be rushing, but Axel's holding up writing his column until he hears from me, and there's a reception at my club that my wife has made mandatory."

"No problem."

My club. Although Andrew was uncomfortable with the man personally, he did admire his power and style. More than once in their dealings, thoughts of what a law career would be like crossed his mind. Somewhere down the road, a brass plaque might read Wasserman, Truscott, and Mallon.

"Did you watch the news tonight?" Mallon asked.

"No, I just got out of work."

"Goddamn Paris made it onto all three stations. I'm really sick of seeing that Bozo's face on TV."

"What goes around comes around," Andrew said, tapping his briefcase.

"Well, I hope whatever it is you have is good, because we are running out of time."

"What do you mean?"

"Just that. Competition in the managed health care business is getting more intense every day. It's already big fish eats little fish. No one is safe, and everyone is justifiably paranoid. Right now, Everwell's in a pretty decent position. But they're so strapped for beds and office space that they've decided they can't wait much longer for MCB to go up on the block. They're looking at other options, the best of which will cost millions more than it would to make a fire-sale buy of MCB. *Millions.* And ultimately, anything else they acquire will deliver much less in terms of space and equipment. We need that hospital."

"I've heard rumors of massive layoffs pending at MCB. Doesn't that suggest the financial problems are getting worse?"

"There's a big difference between rumors and done deeds, Andy. People may be talking about layoffs, but my sources say that MCB has actually begun some *hiring*. And there's more. For several years now I've had a pipeline into some of the really big creditors of the hospital, including the bank that holds one of its mortgages. They tell me that recently Paris and his financial advisor, Colin Smith, have stopped scrambling for money. They've even started paying off some bills. I think it's got to be that foundation Paris talked about in the speech you recorded."

"That was the first time I ever heard him mention it," Truscott said.

"And you're sure he never gave the name?"

"You heard the tape."

"I want that name, Andy, and quickly. If we know

what we're up against, chances are we can come up with some sort of countermeasure. If Paris and Smith manage to get that place out of the hole, we'll probably never get another shot at it. Remember how much I said is at stake for us."

"Assuming I get you the name," Andrew heard himself say, "I expect a small portion of those millions will find its way in my direction."

Mallon's eyes flashed.

"Do yourself a favor, Andy," he said with chilling calm, "and don't try and put the screws to me. Okay? Just come up with that name. Let me choose the reward. We both know you have no future at Crunchy Granola General. Zip. And need I remind you that except for a few hospitals way out in the boonies, the market is already glutted with general surgeons? It's a safe bet that those few who *are* getting hired for decent jobs were chief residents in their training programs. That's something you're never going to be putting on your résumé. Your future is with us, Andy. You know it, and we know it. So just help us out where you can, and get me that name."

Truscott reddened. Clearly he was out of his league. Mallon was a pro at manipulation and control. All Andrew could do was hang in there and learn from the man. His own day would come.

"Point made," he said.

"Excellent. Now, what have you got for me in that briefcase?"

Andrew handed over the sheet Sarah had given him, along with Xeroxes of the three hospital records and also some notes he had made.

"This involves Sarah Baldwin," he said.

"Ah, yes. Another major thorn in our side. The woman has certainly become a media darling."

Andrew remembered Sarah, the next chief resident in obstetrics, seated across from him in the cafeteria, smugly lecturing him on the power of alternative healing.

"Well, your friend Devlin may be in a position to change that," he said.

Mallon scanned Sarah's prenatal information sheet. "Bloodroot . . . moondragon leaves . . . elephant sleeper. These are all herbs of some sort?"

"They are. They're boiled and drunk as some sort of tea. As you can see, each item has several names. Baldwin recommends them over the standard supplements pregnant women are required to take. She claims a study done in the jungle somewhere proved the herbs are superior to what she calls 'processed vitamins.' "

"Fascinating. Go on, Andy."

"Well, most everyone at MCB thought the Summer girl was the second DIC case at our hospital. She wasn't. She was the third." He slid across the letter from the New York medical examiner. "As you will see from studying the hospital records I've copied, all three women who got DIC—the two who died, and the one who is still in the hospital—have one definite thing in common besides the fact that they all were MCB patients. All three opted to take Baldwin's herbal porridge."

It was clear from Mallon's expression that no further explanation was necessary.

"Does any other obstetrician prescribe these?" he asked.

"No."

"Where does she get them?"

"From some herbalist in Chinatown. Do you want me to find out who?"

"Absolutely. There's no time tonight, though. As soon as we're done, I'm going to fax these over to Devlin. And don't worry. No one else will lay hands on those records. Tell me, do you think taking these herbs could have caused that blood problem?"

"Not by themselves, I don't. But there are examples—

many examples, actually—of an allergy to one substance sensitizing patients to the action of something else."

"Give me an example," Mallon said, scratching notes on a pad.

"Well, let's see. A number of antibiotics—tetracycline is probably the best known—cause extreme sensitivity to sunlight in certain patients. The reaction is not completely understood and can be very, very severe. We have no idea which tetracycline users are going to get it. Many don't. So we just tell everyone who gets put on the drug to stay covered up."

"Yes, I remember that now. Have you had a chance to study this list?"

"I've looked it over. None of it makes much sense to me. I tried looking up some of the herbs."

"And?"

"It's going to take someone with more time than I have, and access to a better library. The various names—scientific, western, Asian—make the whole thing pretty complicated."

"The more complicated the better," Mallon said. "There are potential problems of miscommunication all over the place. Language problems, fouled-up shipping orders . . ."

"Lack of consistent dosage control," Andrew added. "Contamination with other herbs or pesticides."

"Scary stuff—especially if any of these herbs has potential effects on blood clotting." Mallon spent half a minute absently tapping his eraser on the table. "Well, the whole thing would pack more punch if we knew more of the biology," he said finally. "But until we do, I suspect Devlin will be able to get a few miles out of what we have here. This material has potential, Andy. Big potential."

"I agree."

"Tell me. What's your relationship with this Sarah Baldwin?"

Truscott thought a bit, then said simply, "I don't have one."

"Well, then, do what you can to dig up anything else on her, Andy. Anything at all." Mallon took two envelopes from his desk. "A reward for your loyalty and for this information," he said, passing one of them over. "And here's the letter you requested from the medical director at Everwell. The position it promises assumes that Everwell will be taking over MCB. No takeover, no position. Clear?"

"Clear."

"Good. I like clear. You're doing fine, Andy. Just fine." Mallon slipped the material into his briefcase and snapped it shut. "Rather than try to fax all this to Devlin, I'm going to drop it off myself. Sorry to seem as though I'm rushing you out, but my wife is waiting for me."

"No problem," Truscott said as they headed out. "I'm about a week behind in sleep, and I ought to try to get at least a little caught up—especially seeing as how I'm scheduled to meet with Willis Grayson tomorrow morning."

"*The* Willis Grayson?"

"Yes. Didn't I mention that? God, that was dumb of me. I meant to tell you about that when I got here, and I got so involved with—"

"Tell me about what?" Mallon had stopped walking.

"The girl who survived the DIC, the one who's still in the hospital—"

"Yes?"

"She turns out to be Grayson's daughter."

"What?"

"I don't know the whole story, but apparently she's been living this hippie existence for years as Lisa Summer. Grayson showed up by helicopter this morning. He's made appointments with every doc who had anything to do with her case."

"Why?"

"I don't really know. I guess he wants to find out exactly what happened. I'm scheduled to meet with him at eleven."

Mallon rubbed at his chin.

"Do you know where he's staying?" he asked.

"Grayson? Nope. No idea."

"It doesn't matter. I can find that out. What kind of shape is his daughter in?"

"She's depressed as hell. But medically she's doing pretty well. Her arm—what's left of it—is healing nicely."

"And she lost her baby?"

"That's right."

"Willis Grayson's grandchild. . . ."

"Pardon?"

"Nothing. Nothing." Suddenly oblivious to Andrew, Mallon snatched up the phone from a nearby desk, called Axel Devlin, and alerted him that a messenger would be by shortly with a special package for him. Then he dialed another number. "Who's this, Brigitte? . . . Oh, Luanne, how're you doing? This is Jeremy Mallon speaking. . . . Fine, I'm just fine, thank you. Listen, you know the reception? . . . Yes, well, Mrs. Mallon is there right now, and she's expecting me. Would you find her please and tell her I'm going to be late. In fact, tell her that if I'm not there by ten I won't be there at all. Do you have that? . . . Thank you, Luanne. Thanks very much. I'll catch up with you later in the week." He set the receiver down. "I don't think Mary Ellen would trash seventeen years of marriage over one missed reception," he said as much to himself as to Truscott. "Listen, Andy, I'm going to stay here and make some calls. You know the way out, yes?"

"Sure. Are you going to try to contact Grayson?"

"The man's got a ton of lawyers, I'm sure. But I doubt any of them are M.D.'s. Men like Grayson want the best. I've just got to find a way of educating him as to who, in this type of legal business, the best is. You take care now."

Without waiting for Truscott to leave, he hurried back into his office.

TAKE IT OR LEAVE IT

by Axel Devlin

July 6

Dateline: Crunchy Granola General, a.k.a. the Medical Center of Boston (MCB). At a news conference attended by just about everybody in the city with a microphone, Glenn Paris, a.k.a. **California Dreamin'**, let the public in on the latest tribulation to befall his once-august institution of healing. It seems MCB obstetrics patients, THREE OF THEM that we know of, have developed a horrible bleeding disorder called DIC. One of those poor souls lost her arm. The other two lost their lives. And all three of their unborn children died before they could be birthed. **FIVE DEAD; ONE MAIMED.** This is serious stuff, my friends. Serious and terrifying as hell.

Always image conscious, Paris yesterday staged a smooth and appealing show, the purpose of which was to assuage public concern over this sudden lethal epidemic. M.D.'s gave medical explanations. Paris promised an immediate investigation by the epidemiology section of the Centers for Disease Control in Atlanta. And last but far from least, herbalist, acupuncturist, and obstetrician **Sarah Baldwin, M.D.,** explained how she had leapt into the breech with her trusty acupuncture needles to save the life of the latest DIC victim.

Well, it turns out that there was one fact that neither Dr. Baldwin nor Mr. Paris chose to share with the public—one potentially crucial thing that all three afflicted women had in common. They had all taken a special **HERBAL PRENATAL SUPPLEMENT** concocted by Dr. Baldwin herself. It's made up of nine different herbs and roots with names like **elephant sleeper** and **moon-dragon**. The good doctor recommends it to all her clinic patients in place of tried and true (and FDA controlled) prenatal vitamins. Now two of those **HERBAL PRENATAL SUPPLEMENT** patients are dead and a third is maimed. Coincidence???

Well, I ran all this past a pharmacist friend of mine. We are still trying to wipe the astonished look off his face. He now has the list of the roots and herbs in Dr. Baldwin's potion and has promised to do some research for us all. Meanwhile, even he will not be able to answer such questions as: Where do these herbs and roots come from? Who checks them for **contamination**? Who checks them for composition?

Incredible, isn't it, what can happen when a health institution is allowed to slip farther and farther out of the mainstream of accepted medical care. Well, stay tuned. . . . And don't say the old Axeman didn't warn you.

Chapter 13

JULY 6

SARAH STOOD IN THE OPERATING ROOM BENEATH AN icy, blue-white light. She was delivering an infant by cesarean section before a gallery of observers that included, it seemed, every person with whom she had had any contact over the eventful week just past.

"Too bad, your baby's dead," she said to the patient, whose face was covered with a sheet. She turned to the gallery and bowed. "Too bad, everyone, her baby's dead. Too bad."

Glenn Paris smiled down at her approvingly, as did Randall Snyder and Annalee Ettinger. Alma Young, in uniform, applauded and blew her kisses. Several reporters from the press conference gave her A-okay signs. Others photographed her. Then, with a flourish, she whisked the sheet aside only to see herself. Her eyes were bloody hollows; her mouth was agape in a silent scream of death.

Sarah awoke shrieking, bathed in a chilling sweat. It was four-thirty in the morning.

Trembling, she pushed herself out of bed and pulled on her robe. Then she put on some tea and drew a hot bath. She was terrified, she knew, not only by the disturbing content of her dream, but by the fact that she had experienced it at all. For much of her early life, she had been a slave to all manner of nightmares. The most consistent scenario, often recurring as many as two or three times a week, revolved around her being bound, gagged, and totally helpless. From there, on any given night, she would be stabbed repeatedly, beaten, smothered, thrown from a great height, or hurled into the sea. Never in the horrible dreams did she actually see the face of her assailant. On rare occasions, the man—she never doubted it was a man—would burn her with cigarettes. At times the vivid nightmares so haunted her, so dominated her life, that she would simply refuse to go to sleep.

In her mid-teens, at the suggestion of a concerned teacher, she began seeing a psychologist. It seemed obvious to the woman that some event in Sarah's past—isolated or recurrent—was at the core of her terror. The therapist did what she could to get at that source. But Sarah's mother, already drifting deeper and deeper into her dementia, could supply little useful information.

The psychologist then sent Sarah for a number of sessions of hypnosis, and once even took a day off to drive her to Syracuse for a consultation at the university medical center. Nothing helped. Sarah simply could not connect with any event in her childhood that could have sparked such bizarre and debilitating fantasies.

During college, the disturbing dreams seemed to come less frequently, but they were no less terrifying. She tried another course of psychotherapy and hypnosis, and even consented to take some sort of pill designed, her physician said, to alter the neurologic pattern of her sleep. What the drug altered instead was her grade point average, which dropped that semester from a 3.8 to a 2.9.

Eventually peace did come for her. The answer lay in the simple mountain people whom she had traveled halfway around the world to help. In a village in the foothills of Luang Chiang Dao, just a few miles from the Burmese border, Dr. Louis Han, placed her in the hands of a healer—a wizened, stoop-shouldered man, who was, Han said, over 110 years old.

The healer, speaking a dialect of Mandarin that Sarah could not understand, communicated with her through Han. Whether her nightmares were grounded in a past event, or perhaps even a future event, was of no consequence, he said. What mattered was that at the time of sleep, she was not at ease. The spirit that guided her throughout each day remained locked within her. The devastating dreams were nothing more than that day spirit, expressing anger at being detained and demanding a clean separation from her so that it, too, might rest and renew.

All Sarah need do to end the nightmares, the old man promised, was to spend some quiet, contemplative time at the end of each day, first embracing her guiding spirit and then releasing it.

Not even Louis Han knew the exact nature of the tea the healer brewed for her that night. But Sarah drank it willingly and soon drifted off to sleep. When she awoke, two days later, she knew the day spirit within her, an elegant, pure white swan.

Each night from then on, she meditated before going to bed, often actually seeing her swan take flight. Her days, even the most trying ones, began ending peacefully. And the vivid nightmares that had defied her and so many physicians had never recurred—not until tonight.

The hot water supply in Sarah's building, which later in the morning would be inadequate even for a decent shower, was plentiful at such an early hour. Sarah kept the tub filled with a slow, hot stream until she trusted her shivering was gone for good. *Things happen for a reason,* she reminded herself. The belief was one of the pillars on which she had built her life. *Things happen to teach us or to send us off in other, more important direc-*

tions. By the time she toweled off and slipped into her robe, the message in her nightmare—two of them, actually—seemed quite clear.

Understandably, but quite unacceptably, she had begun allowing the demands of work to override her life. Her periods of meditation and reflection had grown brief and generally ineffectual. The connection with her spiritual self was all but gone. She was paying less and less attention to Sarah, trusting more and more that her work on behalf of others was enough to provide her with the strength to deal with each day. The nightmare was telling her otherwise.

It was telling her something else as well: She had made more than enough appearances on center stage. Lecturing to educate medical students and other residents was one thing; providing news footage was quite another. From this morning on, she resolved, it would be back to basics and back to business. No more cameras, no more interviews.

She padded over to the window. The first streaks of dawn glowed against a dull, slate sky and shimmered off a misty rain. One other positive thing her nightmare had given her was some extra time before work. Time to get centered, to regain perspective. Beginning tomorrow, she resolved, when she wasn't at the hospital, she would set her alarm to awaken her twenty minutes earlier. She put on a tape of ocean sounds, set a large pillow on the floor, and eased down into a lotus position.

Please let me do the right thing today, she thought, settling herself with a few deep breaths. *For my patients and myself, let me do the right thing.*

Her breathing slowed and grew shallow. The tightness in her muscles began to disappear. Her thoughts grew more diffuse and less distracting.

Then the telephone rang.

The fifth ring told her that her answering machine was not turned on; the tenth, that the caller was determined —or in trouble. Betting a hundred to one that it would be a wrong number, or worse, a crank, Sarah crawled over to the phone by her couch.

"Hello," she said, clearing some residual sleep from her throat.

"Dr. Baldwin?"

"Yes?"

"Dr. Baldwin, this is Rick Hochkiss. I'm a stringer with the Associated Press, and I was at the news conference you gave yesterday."

"You are extremely thoughtless and rude to be calling at this hour." She debated simply hanging up. "What do you want?" she asked finally.

"Well, for starters, I'd like your comments on the accusations made about you in Axel Devlin's column this morning. . . ."

. . .

Lisa Grayson sat before the pop-up mirror in her tray table, trying as best she could to do something with her hair. In minutes her father would be making his third visit to the hospital. This time she was ready to see him. She had made the decision the night before. But not an hour ago, a messenger had delivered a gold necklace bearing her name in elegant script, with a diamond chip dotting the "i."

Had that been all—had her father continued to show no insight into who she was or what was important to her—she might well have decided to send him away once again. But with the gift was a note. It was written on stationery her mother had commissioned years before, featuring an etching of Stony Hill, their home. Lisa set her brush aside and studied the picture, wondering if her room had been changed at all. Then she reread her father's words.

DEAR LISA,

I know that you are angry with me for things I did that hurt you. I'm sorry, very sorry that I did not take the time to understand you better. I need you. Please forgive me, and come back into my life. I promise this time it will be on your terms.

I love you,
DADDY

I'm sorry. Five years. Five years gone from their lives together. If only he had understood that those were the only words she needed to hear. *I'm sorry. . . . I need you.* Lisa touched the bandage covering what remained of her arm. Now she needed him as well. Perhaps she always had.

The telephone interrupted her thoughts.

"Hello?"

"Lisa, it's Janine at the nurses' station. Your father's here again."

"Good. It's time. Could you please send him back?"

When Willis Grayson knocked and entered her room, Lisa was on her feet, facing him. He held a rose in one hand and a newspaper in the other. He stood in the doorway for a time, getting a sense of her; then he tossed the paper and flower on the bed and rushed to embrace her.

"You have no idea how much I've suffered without you," he said.

"Daddy, you wrote you were sorry for the way you treated me—for driving me away from you. That's all you ever had to say."

"I want you home with me. Today."

"I think they're not going to discharge me until to-morrow."

"They'll do it today if you say the word. I've already spoken with Dr. Snyder and Dr. Blankenship. Your blood is back to normal, and we can have your stitches taken out at our hospital."

"How's my room?"

"At Stony Hill?"

"Yes."

"Why, it's . . . it's the same. The same as the day you—the same as it ever was. You'll come?"

"I have some things to pack at home, and I want to say good-bye to my housemates."

"Tim and I will help you," Grayson said excitedly. "Your friend Heidi is welcome to come anytime and stay with us for as long as she wants. I've spoken with her several times. She's a very fine person."

"Can we leave here now?"

"We notify the nurses, and as soon as your doctors stop by and write the order, we're out of here."

"I'd like to see Dr. Baldwin before I go."

Grayson's expression tightened. "Lisa, could you sit down for a few minutes? There's something we need to talk about."

He handed her the *Herald*, folded to Axel Devlin's column.

"Two women died? Is this true?"

"I'm afraid so. Did you take those herbs?"

"Every week. Twice a week toward the end. Both of the other women did that, too?"

Grayson nodded. "Lisa, I have two men outside I'd like you to speak with. They're attorneys. I want them to represent us."

"Represent us?"

Grayson gestured toward her bandage. "If someone, *anyone*, is responsible for this, and . . . and for what happened to my grandson, your son, I want them to pay as dearly as you have."

"But Dr. Baldwin—"

"Lisa, I'm not saying she was responsible, or anyone else for that matter. I only want you to talk with these men."

"But—"

"Honey, two other women and their babies have already died from this thing. We need to get to the bottom of it. For their sake, for your sake, and especially for the sake of whoever may be next."

"As long as you promise me that nothing will be done without my approval," she said tentatively.

"I promise."

"Daddy, I mean it."

"Nothing will be done without your approval. Now, will you speak with these people?"

"If you really, really want me to."

"I do."

Grayson stepped to the doorway and motioned. Moments later two men entered carrying briefcases. One was overweight. The other was thin and sharp-featured, with hard, gray eyes.

"Miss Lisa Grayson," her father said proudly, motioning to the heavier of the men, "this is Gabe Priest. His firm handles much of our business on Long Island."

The lawyer stepped forward, about to offer Lisa his right hand. At the last moment, he realized what he was doing, stepped back, and nodded.

"And this man will be handling matters for us in Boston," Grayson went on, motioning the other one forward. "Lisa, I'd like you to meet Jeremy Mallon."

Chapter 14

AT ONE-FIFTEEN IN THE AFTERNOON, FOR THE FIRST time in her professional life, Sarah asked to be replaced in the operating room. The case, a tubal ligation by laparoscope, was straightforward enough, and one she had looked forward to doing. But the morning had been a blur of conferences, explanations, phone calls and more phone calls. And no matter how she tried, she simply could not get focused enough to feel at ease in the operating room.

For a physician with distracting problems—personal or professional—there is no more difficult or dangerous place to be than in a hospital. Sarah had heard that statement more than once in required courses on risk management and liability. But she had never experienced it personally. Under the best of circumstances, one lecturer had warned, the possibility of committing a serious error was like a raven, perched constantly on the shoulder of every doctor, feeding on fatigue, time constraints, routine, and loss of concentration. A collapsing marriage, financial strain, alcohol, drugs, or accusations of any sort of impropriety only heightened already disconcerting odds.

A momentary distraction, the omission of a decimal point in a medication order, the failure to notice a change in one of dozens of laboratory test results—the possibilities for disaster in an acute care facility were endless, and frequently well camouflaged.

Make the physician in question a surgeon, Sarah thought now, *and add the pressure of having her problems become public knowledge, and the lecturer's spectral raven turns into a vulture.* She took a cup of tea to an empty room in the residents' sleeping quarters and lay down, trying to will her dull headache into submission.

The 5:30 A.M. call from the AP stringer had been quickly followed by three others, all reporters, all wanting her thoughts on Axel Devlin's column. After her tenth "No comment" and her fourth "Please don't call me again," she unplugged her phone.

A brief try at returning to her meditation was fruitless. Finally she pulled her yellow slicker over her Spandex and walked her bike through the soft rain to the small market at the end of her street. There were three other people in the store. Sarah felt conspicuous and ill at ease as she paid for a coffee and muffin and then, as casually as she could, a copy of the *Herald*. Huddled in a deserted shop doorway down the street from the market, she first scanned, then carefully picked through Axel Devlin's prose.

The column did disturb her greatly, but more for its bald-faced bias and obvious intent to harm than for its content. What Devlin had written was, in essence, factual. All three of the DIC victims *had* seen Sarah in the outpatient department. And all three *had* opted to take the herbal supplement over the synthetic. But whatever had caused their bleeding problem had nothing to do with that choice. The herbs she prescribed were the precise mix that a scientifically designed study had proven superior to synthetics. She had reprints of the article, published in English in one of the most prestigious medical journals in Asia, and would have provided a copy had she only been asked.

The content and purity of her herbal mix was the province of Kwong Tian-Wen, one of the oldest, most experienced, and most respected herbalists in the Northeast. The purity of his products, she could easily argue, rivaled or exceeded that of most pharmaceuticals, especially the generics. Time and again since government regulations had begun requiring the use of generic substitution wherever possible, one or another of the many fly-by-night manufacturing companies had been cited for peddling substandard medicine. And many times the drugs involved had life-or-death potential. Still, the punishment meted out to the companies was, more often than not, an admonition and a slap-on-the-wrist fine.

It would have been a pleasure, Sarah felt, to air such issues. If only Devlin had done his job fairly. If only he had asked for her side. Now she was faced with the prospect of having to hold a press conference of her own, just to be certain her responses to his allegations were laid out clearly and completely.

Throughout the morning just past, the atmosphere surrounding her had been a striking contrast to the cheers and back-slapping that had followed her treatment of Lisa Summer. By the time she arrived on the OB/Gyn floor for rounds, copies of the *Herald* were everywhere—at the nurses' station, on the bedstands in patients' rooms, even in the bathroom of the staff lounge.

There was an almost palpable coolness from many of the nurses, along with whispers behind her back and gestures she caught out of the corner of her eye. But virtually no one mentioned the column to her—no one except her department chief, the chief of staff, the CEO of the hospital, and the head of public relations.

At noon she managed to break away from the madness to visit Lisa. If anyone deserved a personal rebuttal of Devlin's implications, it was she. The empty room, scrubbed and waiting for its next patient, was unsettling, but no more so than the news that Lisa had left the hospital with her father not fifteen minutes before with no attempt made to call Sarah. No message left. Just a discharge order from Randall Snyder, and she was gone. An hour later Sarah had asked someone to take over for her in her laparoscopy case.

By two-thirty, a brief nap and three aspirins had eased the pressure in Sarah's head. She set her copy of the *Herald* on the small metal desk and pulled a pad of lined progress note sheets from the drawer. She had always been a fighter. But twice in the past she had decided not to dignify Axel Devlin's jibes at her with a response. This time there was no way she was going to turn her back on his bullying. She would state and restate her position and qualifications. And she would not stop until his destructive, irresponsible reporting techniques were exposed.

At Wellesley, her anthropology honors thesis had been highly praised, both for its content and for her writing style. There was no reason she could not draft a press release that would put Devlin in his place and make strong points for certain herbal therapies as well.

Carefully she read through the column again, this time underlining key words and phrases. Although it was not essential, it would help to know the source of Devlin's information. Glenn Paris had spoken of the constant, damaging leaks of hospital goings-on and had even threatened termination for anyone found responsible. Was this particular column the result of just another in that series of leaks, or was someone specifically trying to bring her down?

Herbal Prenatal Supplement . . . nine different roots and herbs . . . elephant sleeper . . . moon-dragon . . .

Was there any chance a patient of hers had gone to Devlin with the clinic handout? That made no sense. She had never kept secret the supplement or its contents.

And no one—not even Devlin—had shown any particular interest in it. Not until now.

Now two of those . . . patients are dead and a third is maimed. . . .

Sarah scratched her pen absently along one edge of the pad. Who knew that she had at one time or another seen all three victims in the clinic? Who would have had access to their records? Would Devlin have trusted a source other than a doctor?

Where do these herbs and roots come from? Who checks them for contamination? . . . For composition? . . .

Even the tone of Devlin's questions sounded professional. Someone had fed him the words. Furthermore, that someone almost certainly had to have been a physician. For a few suspended minutes, Sarah closed her eyes, searching her memory, sorting through the facts and possibilities.

"No," she whispered suddenly. "Oh, no."

She hurled her pen against the wall. Then she snatched up her clinic coat and stormed from the room.

"Why, Andrew?" she cried as she raced down the stairs. "For God's sake, why?"

"Money, of course," Truscott said simply.

Sarah slammed her fist down on the *Herald*, landing dead center on Axel Devlin's sketched likeness. "Andrew, I know you don't like Glenn, and you don't like this place. But we've been friends for over two years. You would do this to me for money?"

"Not for money, luv. For lots of money. And as for our being friends—the last friend I remember having stole my bike in the fourth grade and gave it to a girl he liked."

"Oh, Andrew."

"You can handle it, kid. You are possibly the most competent woman I know. And just remember, there's no such thing as bad publicity. There is only publicity. The article will raise public awareness of your cause."

"That's bullshit, and you know it. Who paid you? Devlin? Everwell?" Sarah glared across the desk at the surgeon.

"It's really none of your business who paid me," Truscott said. "You know, Sarah, I didn't make up any lies—about this place or about you. You *did* see all three of those women, and you *did* give them your little potion."

"Andrew, before turning bits and pieces of information over to a person like Devlin, you could at least have taken the time to speak with me, or to read the studies on the supplement. You know what you did—the way you did it—was wrong. Can't you at least admit that?"

"I'll tell you what," Truscott said with sudden vehemence, "I'll admit that what I did was wrong as soon as you admit that ever since you arrived at this place, you've annoyed people with your holier-than-thou attitude regarding the inadequacies and callousness of the way we poor, limited M.D.'s do things. You walk around with this smug if-only-you-all-knew-the-great-secrets-I-know,   if-only-you-all-were-as-complete-a-doctor-as-I-am attitude that just about everyone in this place finds threatening."

"But—"

"Let me finish! You may think you're helping to make all of us more complete doctors. But even in this place, even in Crunchy Granola General where almost anything goes, you're looked on as a kook. The women on the staff think you're not professional enough, and the men are so intimidated by you that they avoid you like sea captains avoid icebergs. So before you start attacking me, you might take a look at yourself."

Sarah felt perilously close to tears. She had been wronged, clearly wronged by this man. Yet here he was, putting *her* on the defensive. Over her years at MCB, she had felt almost universal respect and acceptance from the staff, male and female. Many, like Alma Young, had gone out of their way to tell her so. Her performance evaluations were consistently among the highest of the residents. After two decades of solo practice, Randall Snyder was considering *her* for a partnership. Why was she letting this, this *clone* of Peter Ettinger, get to her so?

She bit at the inside of her lip until she felt certain her tears were contained. Then she snatched up the *Herald* and turned toward the door.

"Where are you going?" Truscott demanded.

"I'm going back to work."

"What are you going to do about all this?"

"If you mean am I going to Glenn, the answer is I don't know yet."

"They won't fire me. Not without hard proof."

"Andrew," she said without turning back, "right now, thanks to what you've done, I have more important things to worry about than whether or not they fire you."

Chapter 15

JULY 7

THE EXERCISE ROOM, AN EXPANSIVE SOLARIUM AT THE rear of the Great House, was as well equipped as most health clubs. Annalee Ettinger, while not nearly as fanatical about exercise as her father, did work out most days. There was a Universal, free weights, a StairMaster, treadmill, and Nordic-Track, as well as a continuous-current lap pool, ballet bar, tumbling mats, and a sauna. Today Peter had just finished a session with his trainer and was putting in some extra time with the weights. Annalee was feigning a workout on the Universal, waiting for the right moment for conversation.

Although she was no longer in as much awe and fear of the man as she had been for so many years, neither was she particularly comfortable around him. And although she understood him well enough to predict his reaction to most situations, she was completely in the dark as to how he would respond to what she was about to disclose.

She glanced over at him and couldn't help but be impressed. At forty-eight, he had the body of a thirty-year-old. He worked obsessively on his strength and flexibility and did forty minutes of Tai Chi a day for balance and centering. In his professional and personal life, he was unaccustomed to weakness or failure. *How would he view the decisions his daughter had made?*

Annalee was not yet two when he brought her home from Mali. In his accounts of the adoption, Peter left no doubt that he had saved her life. Her mother had died from dysentery, and the chances for her own survival were poor.

"I wanted to bring every orphaned child in the village home with me," he had told her more than once. "But that wasn't possible. So I carefully evaluated dozens of factors in dozens of children, and I finally picked you because you wouldn't let go of my leg."

From the beginning, the standards of achievement and success he set for himself were those he set for her. It might not have been fair, but it was the only way he knew. Throughout her school years, her persistent weight problems and ennui were a source of constant concern for him. Still, though she always felt judged, and often inadequate, she never doubted that he cared.

Over their twenty years together he had dated many women, lived with two, and married one. But he had never made her feel secondary to any of them. And now, despite her years of rebellion and insensitivity toward him, he had welcomed her home, provided for her, and made her a part of Xanadu—a part of his dream.

The Xanadu Holistic Health Community was being constructed on 150 acres of mixed farmland and forest, crisscrossed by centuries-old fieldstone walls. The Great House, a rambling, thirteen-room structure, had been built in 1837. At the time Peter purchased the property, the house had decayed to the point that several architects felt there was no possibility of restoring it. He had proven them wrong. And now the house, complete with nine-foot ceilings and reconstruction that was true to the original, was a showplace—the centerpiece of Xanadu. Peter had given Annalee a small office on the ground floor and made her the assistant director of marketing and public relations. It was their decision—his, really—that she would switch her major to business when she resumed full-time studies in January. Eighteen months later, she would be ready to go for an MBA. Meanwhile, summers and vacations, she would continue to expand her role at Xanadu.

Now, one way or the other, those carefully designed plans were about to change.

"Hey, Dad, lookin' good. Lookin' *good*," she said.

Peter was doing situps with a five-pound dumbbell in each hand. His forehead and razor-cut, silver hair glistened with what seemed to Annalee to be just the right amount of sweat. *Perfect perspiration*, she thought. *That's it. That's Peter Ettinger in a nutshell.*

"Enjoy your youth while you have it," he responded without slowing. "This gets harder and harder. You quitting?"

"Yeah, I—I'm not feeling so hot today."

The comment put an abrupt end to Peter's workout.

"Now that you mention it, I've been noticing that you haven't looked well the last couple of days," he said, toweling off.

Nonsense, she thought. It was doubtful that they had seen each other for five minutes over the preceding week. *You don't have to impress me, Peter. Believe me, I'm already impressed.*

"A little peaked, huh?" she said.

"Yes, yes. Exactly." He glanced over at her fine, ebony face. "Oh, very funny."

Annalee reminded herself that her father's sense of humor was far less developed than most of his other attributes. She would do well during this session to keep hers in check. She stretched her long, slender body to the maximum and wondered if he noticed the smooth, low mound beneath her leotard.

"I've been feeling a little sick to my stomach," she said.

"Perhaps some ginseng tea."

He stared out at a backhoe, rumbling down the hill toward the lakeside amphitheater construction site.

"And a little bloated."

"In that case, perhaps we should brew it with a bit of apple bark and saffron."

"And—and I haven't had a period in five months."

Peter tensed visibly and turned to her slowly. "How long?"

"Five months."

His eyes narrowed. "Am I to assume, then, that you are pregnant?"

Annalee managed a thin smile.

"That would be a safe assumption," she said.

"West? The musician?"

"Yes. His first name's Taylor, Dad, in case you forgot."

"You're certain?"

"About it being Taylor?"

"No, about the pregnancy."

Annalee searched her father's face and voice for clues as to what he was thinking and feeling. At first reading, the signs weren't encouraging.

"I'm certain. I had the test. And, Peter, before you ask the next obvious question, I want you to know that I'm very happy and excited about the whole thing."

"That's nice."

"Please, don't be flippant."

Peter pulled on a loose, terry-cloth T-shirt. Annalee could see him processing the implications of her news. His displeasure was clear. But that was no surprise. Little pleased him that he did not initiate or control.

"And Taylor?" he asked.

"He'll still be on the road a lot with the band. But sooner or later we'll be getting married."

Peter snatched up a ten-pound dumbbell and absently did half a dozen curls, first with one arm, then the other.

"You love him?" he asked suddenly.

The question startled Annalee—especially coming, as it had, before any inquiries about Taylor's income or earning potential.

"Yes . . . yes, I love him very much."

"And he's serious about his music?"

"He is. Very serious."

Annalee could barely believe what she was hearing. This was a side of her father that for years she had thought was reserved for paying customers only.

"I have a friend—a patient, actually—who's a vice president at Blue Note Records. Do you know that company?"

"Only the best jazz production people in the business."

"I can get Taylor's band a recording audition."

"Peter, that would be wonderful."

"After the marriage."

"That's sort of up to—"

"And if my friend says they're good enough, I will back the production of their album."

"I see."

"Provided the two of you and the child choose to make your home here at Xanadu—at least until you are on your feet financially."

"That's a very generous offer."

"Annalee, you are my only child. I want you to have a good life."

"I understand," she said, still surprised and a bit bewildered by his reaction. "I can't say for sure that Taylor will go along with your conditions. But I think he will."

"So do I," Peter said. "And of course, I would like the child to be delivered here at Xanadu. We'll get the finest midwives in the world to attend you."

"Peter, I—I had kind of decided that I wanted to have the baby born in a hospital and delivered by an obstetrician."

"Oh?"

Annalee strongly sensed that her father already knew

what was to come next. "I've already been to see one. She's agreed to take me on as a patient."

"She?"

Annalee sighed. "Sarah. Sarah Baldwin. I went to see her at her hospital."

The explosion she expected did not happen.

"I know," Peter said simply.

"What?"

"I saw you in the audience on the evening news. To say you stood out in the crowd would not be doing you justice."

"Why didn't you say something?"

"I am saying something. Now that I know what your visit there was all about, I'm saying a great deal. I will not have my grandchild brought into this world in some germ-infested, antiseptic-reeking, mistake-prone hospital. And especially not by Sarah Baldwin."

"But—"

"Annalee, there's a copy of yesterday's *Herald* and this morning's *Globe* on the bench over there. Both of them contain stories about Sarah. I assume you haven't read them or heard the news last night. Otherwise, you would surely have mentioned it."

He waited patiently as she scanned the papers.

"Did she put you on those herbs?" he asked.

"Yes. I—I thought that was something you would approve of."

"There is nothing Sarah Baldwin could ever do that I would approve of, except maybe to abandon altogether her destructive efforts to combine medicine and healing."

"But—"

"Annalee, there are some men coming to see me at two o'clock this afternoon. I think you should be present at that meeting."

"Who are they?"

"Two o'clock. My office. And please, not a word to

Sarah Baldwin—at least not until you hear what these men have to say. Agreed?"

Annalee studied the pain and anger in her father's face. She knew Sarah had hurt him by leaving. But until now she really hadn't appreciated how much.

"Agreed," she said finally.

Chapter 16

JULY 8

LYDIA PENDERGAST BENT AT THE WAIST AND SLOWLY, ever so slowly, stretched her hands downward toward the floor. To one side of the small examining room, Sarah, chiropractor Zachary Rimmer, and one of the pain unit nurses watched expectantly.

"Down and down she goes," Lydia said, "and where she stops nobody knows."

She was a sprightly woman in her early seventies who had become virtually bedridden by low back pain and stiffness. A number of orthopedists and neurosurgeons had pegged degenerative arthritic spurs as the cause of her disability. They cited the uncertainty of the corrective surgical procedure, as well as her age and the advanced condition of the spurs, as reasons why they could not operate. Finally, one of them had referred her to the MCB pain unit, a multidisciplinary clinic that was rapidly becoming known and respected throughout the Northeast.

Shortly after arriving at the hospital, Sarah had begun volunteering her acupuncture skills at the clinic. She usually managed half a day a week.

Lydia's fingertips touched the tile.

"Ta da," she sang, without straightening out. "Okay, now, Dr. Baldwin. This one's for you."

She shifted her feet slightly, continued down until her palms were flat on the floor, and waited until Sarah snapped a picture with the clinic's ancient Polaroid. Then, to the applause of her small gallery, she straightened up and curtsied.

"God bless you. God bless you all. . . ."

Lydia Pendergast's words were echoing in her mind as Sarah carried her box of acupuncture needles up the stairs to the lockers on Thayer Four. A treatment success; a grateful patient; work to do. The day seemed almost normal—especially when measured against the two that had preceded it. There was still a coolness from many on the hospital staff that Sarah found unpleasant, but certainly not unbearable. And several times, just as she sensed she might be breaking down, someone would say something kind or encouraging. The annoying, persistent, and unconscionably rude press was another problem altogether. She had stopped answering her phone at home and had gotten the hospital operator to screen calls to her carefully.

It wasn't fun. But she knew that like all things, it would pass.

Sarah had opened her locker, and so was partially screened when the elevator doors glided open and Andrew Truscott stepped out. He hurried down the corridor and into 421, one of the sleeping rooms that Sarah frequently used. It was odd that Andrew would be taking a break at this hour, she mused, although it was close enough to lunchtime. Perhaps he was hoping to sleep off a headache or something.

She smiled at the thought.

One headache he would *not* be needing to sleep off was Sarah's reporting him to Glenn Paris. She had opted not to do so a few hours after their confrontation in

Andrew's office, and had told him of her decision the following day. She had not expected him to thank her, and in that regard, she was not disappointed.

"You do whatever you want," he had said testily. "Without proof and with your current status in this hospital, I doubt Paris or anyone else would pay much attention to what you have to say."

Truscott was absolutely right, she knew. She had enough problems without getting into a his-word-against-hers battle with the impeccably proper senior surgical resident. Even so, she would have gone ahead and reported him if she'd thought it would help. If the leaks continued, she would no longer have a choice.

Sarah was about to close her locker when the elevator doors opened again. This time Margie Yates, a pediatric resident, stepped out. Yates, the mother of two, was married to a sweet guy who ran the hospital's social service office. She was bright and attractive, but she was also insecure and a terrible flirt. From behind her locker door, Sarah could not help but watch as Margie straightened her white clinic skirt, checked herself in a compact mirror, knocked softly on the door to room 421, and slipped inside.

Andrew and Margie Yates! Not really that much of a surprise, Sarah decided, as she gently closed her locker door and headed down the nearby stairs. Andrew seldom spoke of his wife or child. And Margie, from time to time, had been linked by rumor to other physicians at MCB. Both had huge egos and massive need for approval. Their tryst, unpleasant as it was to observe, made perfect sense.

Sarah picked up a tuna sandwich, chips, and pineapple juice in the cafeteria, and carried the lunch outside to one of the campus tables. *First the admission of betraying his hospital, and now Margie Yates.* Over the past few days, Andrew's stock had plummeted. She ate quickly and reentered the hospital through the surgical building. Andrew's name was being called out via the overhead page. He was wanted in room 227 *stat*. A first-year surgical resident named Bruce Lonegan raced past her and up the stairs toward the second floor.

"Hey, Bruce, what's going on?" she called.

"Don't know," he yelled back excitedly. "A ruptured triple A, maybe."

Triple A—an abdominal aortic aneurysm. Rupture of one was, perhaps, the ultimate surgical emergency. Even if she had pressing obligations on her service, which she did not for at least another hour, Sarah would have responded to any such call for help. *Besides*, she thought cattily, *at this moment Andrew Truscott might not be in the greatest shape to perform emergency vascular surgery.*

Room 227 was in the early stages of the organized chaos that accompanied crisis in a teaching hospital. Bruce Lonegan and another surgical resident were scurrying about an elderly gentleman who was in obvious, severe distress. He was unconscious or barely conscious, twitching about, and moaning.

"Get ten units crossmatched *stat* and be sure the OR is ready," Lonegan called out. "Art, get an arterial line in him. Somebody try and get a pressure! Dammit, where the hell is Andrew?"

"How can I help?" Sarah asked as the overhead page again urged Andrew to the room.

"This guy's Andrew's patient," Lonegan said. "He came in about three or four days ago for an elective aneurysm repair. He was in some heart failure, so the medical people had us delay his surgery while they got that under control. He was scheduled for the OR tomorrow. A nurse just walked in and found him like this. His pressure's way down. He's out of it. His belly seems tense. It's got to be the triple A leaking. Dammit, are they beeping Andrew as well as voice paging him?"

At that moment, Sarah remembered that there was no overhead page on the Thayer sleeping floors. Andrew obviously hadn't given the room number to the operator. If his beeper was turned off, no one would know how to reach him. *No one except me.* She picked up the bedside phone and suggested the operator try ringing Thayer 421.

"If Dr. Truscott doesn't answer, please call me back immediately," she instructed.

Lonegan and the other resident had been joined by someone from internal medicine. It was clear the patient was losing ground. Lonegan had been a practicing M.D. for exactly one week. Without the senior vascular surgery resident, he was lost. And he looked it.

"Andrew's pager may not be working," Sarah said, realizing that she had to take over until someone more senior or surgically specialized arrived. "I've given the operator some instructions on reaching him. Meanwhile, be sure of your lines, get some fluids into him, use a Doppler stethoscope to check what pulses you can, catheterize him, and have everything ready in the OR. Why is he twitching like that?"

"His blood pressure's only about sixty," the medical resident said. "That's why."

Although she admitted to herself that the internist might be right, Sarah did not feel comfortable with that explanation. She had seen many patients in shock, some of them in full-blown seizure because of it. But something here was different from those cases. Without making any show of it, she carefully checked the old man's acupuncture pulses. Several of them felt weak and thready. She was not experienced enough to know the exact significance of her findings, but she sensed that whatever was happening was more generalized than a leaking artery—perhaps some sort of metabolic derangement.

The phlebotomist had just finished drawing the man's blood. Sarah pulled the woman aside.

"Have them run a complete chem screen, please," she said. "As absolutely fast as they can. Especially electrolytes, sugar, calcium, phosphorus, and magnesium."

The bedside phone rang. Sarah snatched it up, listened for a moment, and then set the receiver back down.

"Dr. Truscott will be here in just a minute," she said.

It was almost five minutes before Andrew charged into the room. By that time the anesthesiologist was at the bedside, some incompletely crossmatched blood was being pumped in, and transportation was standing by outside the room, awaiting the dash to the OR. The patient's family had also been called and told about his turn for the worse. Emergency as opposed to elective repair of the aneurysm lowered his chances of survival considerably.

"Sorry, everyone," Truscott said, immediately taking control. "My damn beeper went belly up."

Ignoring Sarah completely, he rapidly assessed the old man's physical status and then ordered transportation into the room. Next he turned to his intern, who gave a nervous, somewhat garbled account of what had transpired.

"I have the OR on standby," Lonegan concluded. "Blood is off for chemistries and crossmatch."

"That's good, old boy," Truscott snapped, listening once again to the man's abdomen with his stethoscope. "Because we're going to be cutting skin before you can say 'Tie me kangaroo down.'"

Transportation rushed into the room and began transferring the patient to a litter. Only then did Truscott turn to Sarah.

"So, what brings you down here, Doctor?" he asked. "Is this man having some gynecological problems on top of everything else?"

One nurse laughed out loud. Sarah kept her cool by reminding herself that she cared too little for the man to allow him to upset her in any way.

"I thought you might be a little tired and in need of a little extra help," she said. "I knew you were, um, *rest-*

ing in room 421. I was at my locker when you went in. That's how the page operator knew where to find you."

Truscott's face paled. The corners of his mouth twitched.

"Thank you for that," he managed. "You certainly have been kind to me lately."

"Think nothing of it," Sarah responded, her eyes fixed steadily on his.

The team had finished loading the old man onto the litter. Truscott motioned them to the OR with a flick of one hand. In seconds the room was empty, save for Sarah and one nurse. The floor, littered with bloody pads and gauze wrap, needle guards, rubber gloves, IV tubing boxes, and the like, looked like a war zone. Sarah gloved and began picking up some of the litter.

"I'll take care of this," the nurse said.

"Why, are you more trained for this job than I am?"

The nurse smiled. "Thanks," she said.

At that moment, the phlebotomist raced into the room carrying a computer printout.

"Where is everyone?" she asked breathlessly.

"Gone to the OR. Why?"

The technician handed over the printout.

"His magnesium level is zero point four," she said. "The supervisor said to tell you they've run it twice and—"

Sarah was no longer paying attention. She glanced at the phone, thought better of it, and then raced from the room. A magnesium level of 0.4, far below normal, would explain the clinical picture entirely. It was life-threatening in any circumstance, but would be fatal if not corrected before surgery. The cause, she guessed, might be the old man's intolerance to the vigorous diuretic treatment that was being used to correct his heart failure.

IATROGENIC: ILLNESS OR INJURY CAUSED BY THE WORDS OR ACTIONS OF A PHYSICIAN.

Sarah flashed on the sign that once hung over Peter

Ettinger's desk. There was every reason to believe that the patient's striking turn for the worse was due to his *treatment,* not his disease—to the diuretics, not the aneurysm. She reached the operating suite doors just as the litter was being wheeled into one of the ORs.

"Andrew, wait!" she cried out.

It took less than half an hour for the old man to respond to his magnesium infusion and wake up. Until his retirement a year before, Terence Cooper had been a boatbuilder of some note. He had a cackling laugh and a wonderful, toothless smile. And upon meeting Sarah, he immediately asked her out on a date, assuring her that his wife wouldn't mind all that much.

"Mrs. Cooper keeps telling me to try out new things," he said.

Sarah let him squeeze her hand and then turned to leave. Until that moment, Andrew had said very little to her. Now he stepped between her and the door.

"I can explain about room four twenty-one," he said softly.

"I couldn't care less," she responded. "Except that you should have been more alert after you got down here. If you hadn't been . . . sleeping, I suspect you would have checked those chems before you took him to the OR."

"I suspect you're right."

"Good," Sarah said, easing past him and into the hallway. "I love being right."

"Thanks for saving my bacon," he called out after her. "You're a hell of a doctor."

Sarah considered some sort of response, then just shook her head and continued on. Her pager sounded just as she reached the OB/Gyn floor. She responded, expecting to hear Andrew, anxious to continue mending fences. Instead, the voice on the line was Annalee Ettinger's.

Sarah sat on the edge of the bed in the small resident's call room, listening sadly to Annalee's account of what had transpired with her father.

"I couldn't tell what upset him more," Annalee said, "my going to see any M.D. at all, or my going to see you in particular."

"I'm the least important factor in this equation. I know an obstetrician in Worcester who would be happy to do a home birth for you."

"Peter's insisting on no M.D.s. Midwives only. He's even talking about flying some in from Mali."

"How do you feel about all this?"

"I feel sorry for you for what's being written in the papers. But that stuff hasn't influenced me one way or the other."

"Good."

"And even the things Peter promised—the money, and the recording chance for Taylor and all. But no matter how hard I try, I can't get past all the things Peter's done for me—from the very beginning."

"I understand."

"I know he's not perfect, but—"

"Annalee, you don't have to explain. I understand. Besides, you're a healthy young woman in great shape. I have no reason to think there'll be any problems. I'll send you the name of the obstetrician in Worcester, just in case you want his help in any way."

"Thanks for not making this any harder for me, Sarah."

"Nonsense."

There was a prolonged, uncomfortable silence.

"Sarah, there's something else," Annalee said finally. "Peter insisted I sit in on part of a meeting in his office."

"Go on."

"Four men and Peter. They want to hire him to check into the composition of that herbal supplement of yours and to check up on someone named Kwang or Kwok or something. Do you know who that is?"

Sarah was beginning to feel queasy.

"Yes, I know who that is," she said. "Who were the men?"

"Two were suits from New York—lawyers. They were there with this guy, Willis Grayson, the father of the girl you saved. The dude must be big stuff, because Peter was like a puppy around him. He acted as if I was supposed to know who he was, too, but I didn't."

"Who was the other man?" Sarah asked. Her hands felt like ice around the receiver.

"Another lawyer. Oilier than the others, if you know what I mean. His name's Mallon."

"Unfortunately, I know him, too."

"Sarah, Peter said some pretty unkind things about you. I think that's what he wanted me to hear. He said you were never as good an herbalist or acupuncturist as you liked to believe. I was on the edge of telling him to stop, or just walking out, but I just couldn't do either one. I'm—I'm sorry."

"Annalee, don't be sorry," Sarah said. "Just do what feels right, and don't lose touch with me. I appreciate your calling me like this."

"I'm sorry," Annalee said again.

Sarah hung up without another reply. She felt there was a chance that if she tried to speak, she would begin to cry. And Annalee did not deserve that sort of additional stress. *How crazy.* When they were together—at work and as lovers—Peter had told her and anyone else who would listen that she was one of the finest American herbal therapists and acupuncturists he had ever known. Now, suddenly, she was an inept fraud.

Sarah bunched the pillow beneath her head and stared wearily at the ceiling. The truth was that in becoming an M.D., in trying to blend the best of eastern and western medicine, she had become a threat to practitioners on both sides. That Andrew and Peter, the two practitioners attacking her now, both happened to be male may or may not have had significance. But she suspected it did.

For a time, blanketed by a pall of loneliness and isolation, she wept. Soon, though, she felt her spirit begin to regroup within a nidus of anger. Beyond tweaking two bulbous egos, she had done nothing wrong. If it was a fight they wanted, it was a fight they would get. She picked up the phone and paged Eli Blankenship. Within a minute he returned her call.

"Dr. Blankenship," she said. "I don't know exactly who I'm supposed to talk to, or what I'm supposed to do, but I'd like to meet with you as soon as possible. I think I'm about to be sued."

Chapter 17

JULY 20

SARAH WAS CERTAIN THAT AT TIMES IN HER LIFE SHE must have felt as conspicuous and ill-at-ease as she did tonight, but she could not remember when. The Milsap Board Room at MCB was long and fairly narrow, with a plush Oriental carpet, floor-to-ceiling windows that overlooked the city, and a massive walnut table surrounded by twenty high-backed oxblood leather chairs. Although Sarah had never actually seen the room before, she had heard about it, mostly through doctors' litanies of the medical equipment that Glenn Paris elected *not* to purchase so that it might be built.

Five men—Paris, Drs. Snyder and Blankenship, chief financial officer Colin Smith, and a prissy attorney named Arnold Hayden—sat at one end of the table, sipping drinks from a mirrored wet bar and chatting amicably. Sarah paced at the other end, alternately gazing out at the sheets of windblown rain and checking her watch.

Several days before, a letter from attorney Jeremy Mallon to Sarah's insurance carrier, the Mutual Medical Protective Organization, had made it official. Sarah was being sued for malpractice by Lisa Grayson. Two days after that, the claims adjuster at the MMPO assigned an attorney named Matthew Daniels to her case. The meeting tonight had been requested by him.

Sarah had spoken with her new attorney by phone for almost an hour, but had come away from that conversation with little sense of the man other than that he was southern and most economical with his words. The hazy image she had formed of him sprang more, she suspected, from the balding, potbellied, perspiring Hollywood stereotype than from anything Daniels actually said.

"Sarah," Paris called out, "come on down here and have a glass of this Chablis. We're all getting nervous just watching you stalk around over there."

Sarah hesitated, then took the path of least resistance and accepted the offer. Paris, like the two department heads, had been cordial enough toward her since the news of her suit, but she could tell that each of them had doubts.

"I wonder why this Daniels wanted us to get together here at the hospital and not at his office," Arnold Hayden blustered. "Irregular. Highly irregular."

"Arnold, have you ever heard of him?" Smith asked.

"No. I started doing some checking, but I haven't gotten too far. He's an Essex Law grad."

"Not exactly Harvard."

"Not exactly law school," Hayden corrected snidely. "His firm is Daniels, Hannigan and Goldstein. I've never heard of them, but I have someone making inquiries."

"I'm certain the insurance company wouldn't assign someone to my case who wasn't good," Sarah said. "It's their money. Besides, I don't think it will take any Clarence Darrow to prove that I'm not guilty of malpractice. All Mallon has to base his case on is that the three women happened to have taken my supplement. We can produce many others who also took it and had perfectly normal deliveries."

"True," Blankenship said. "What we really need to close the circle, though, is a case of DIC like the others, but in a woman who never took anything other than standard prenatal vitamins."

"I'd rather be found guilty than have another woman go through that," Sarah said.

"Of course. Of course. It goes without saying that we all feel that way. But if such a case does occur—or has occurred somewhere—it would certainly take you and your mixture right out of the loop, as it were."

Sarah checked the time and began pacing again. Matthew Daniels was already five minutes late. His arrival would bring the group to two attorneys, two medical professors, two hospital executives, and her. Being the only woman in the group was more or less neutralized by her status as an M.D. But nothing offset her dismay at being the accused. In truth, she couldn't have been more out of place had she accidentally crashed an exclusive fraternity induction ceremony. The whole evening would have been significantly easier to handle had Rosa Suarez agreed to come. But the epidemiologist had begged off, stating that it would be best for her to stay removed from hospital politics and personalities.

Since her arrival on the scene, Suarez seemed to have been living at MCB. Sarah had seen her at all hours, measuring off corridors with blueprints in her hand, lost behind a wall of tomes in the library, making notes in the record room, or talking to staff. She had interviewed Sarah at length early in her investigation and briefly a number of times since. Although Suarez was reluctant to speak of anything not germane to her mission, she did share that she had a husband, Alberto, back in Georgia, and that she had no family or friends in Boston. Sarah had responded with an invitation to dinner, but the woman politely declined. Her manner was soft-spoken and certainly not aggressive, but Sarah had no difficulty discerning her intelligence and determination.

"Sarah," Paris said, "did you put together this list of the ingredients in your vitamins?"

"The list yes, the explanation of each component, no. Rosa Suarez did that. She plans to expand on the information when she has a chance to do the research."

"Does she now. What a little beaver that woman is. I only wish she would keep me better informed about what's going on. I have the feeling she doesn't like me very much, although I'll be damned if I know why. I gave her essentially free run of the hospital. Do we know if she's gotten anywhere?"

"She's borrowed one of my technicians and is setting up a spare lab of mine to do some cultures," Blankenship said. "Sarah, I agree with Glenn. Mrs. Suarez is exceedingly capable. But she's also very secretive. I do suspect, though, that somehow or other she is going to get to the bottom of all this."

"Which would make both this meeting and your tardy attorney moot," Paris added.

"Late to his own meeting." Arnold Hayden clucked. "Irregular. Highly irreg—"

As if on cue, the door to the Milsap Room opened and Matt Daniels backed in, shaking off his umbrella and his trench coat in the hallway. The moment he turned around, Sarah was pleased to acknowledge that her projection of him could not have been much farther off target. He was tall and well built, with a rugged, weathered face. He was also soaked.

"Daniels, Matt Daniels," he said, pawing at his forehead and dark hair with a handkerchief even more sodden than he was. "Sorry I'm late. I had a flat. My own damn fault, too. I did enough dumb things today to bring a curse on the Pope."

His drawl was unmistakable, though not nearly as pronounced as Sarah remembered. The initial vibrations she was receiving were all positive, especially those that were telling her he was ingenuous enough to be almost as out of place in this gathering as she was. He moved to shake hands with the man closest to him, who happened to be Randall Snyder. But then, when it was apparent that the OB chief preferred to stay dry, he backed off and simply nodded.

Irregular, Sarah thought, pleased. *Highly irregular.*

Daniels circled to an empty seat, slid his briefcase onto the table, and wiped it dry with the sleeve of his sport coat. If he was aware of the expressions of amusement and disbelief on the faces of the other five men, he certainly did not show it.

"Mr. Daniels, I'm Sarah Baldwin," she said, extending her hand, which felt lost in his.

"Matt," he said. "Matt'll do fine."

She introduced the five to him, but blanked out on Arnold Hayden's name.

"Well, I'd like to apologize again, and thank you all for coming out on such a night," Daniels began, after Hayden had somewhat irritably filled in Sarah's blank. "Our adversary in this case is a lawyer named Jeremy Mallon. I decided to set up this meeting after I spoke with him earlier today. As you'll hear, he certainly seems intent on moving things along."

No comment at all on his opponent. Sarah noted the MCB men exchanging glances and had no trouble reading their thoughts. In malpractice circles, according to what she had been told by Glenn Paris, Mallon was something of a legend.

"Mr. Daniels, do you know who Jeremy Mallon is?" asked Arnold Hayden.

Uh-oh, Sarah thought. *Here we go.*

"Well, actually sir, I don't."

"Well, Mr. Daniels," the attorney went on, clearing his throat, "I—um—I think before we begin, it might help us some if we knew a little of your background in the area of medical malpractice. The hospital hasn't been sued yet, but there's every reason to believe we will be if it looks like Sarah's going to lose—and not just by the Graysons, but by the families of those other women as well. Even worse, we stand to take a pounding in the press. So I hope you won't think it presumptuous of me to ask."

"Not at all, Mr. Hayden," Daniels said evenly. "Why, you hardly seem like the presumptuous type. Let's see, the answer to your question is: I've only defended one doctor for malpractice. He was a dentist, actually. A woman claimed her headaches were caused by his pulling out an extra molar and messing up her bite. For what it's worth, we did go to trial, and I did win the case."

"That's very reassuring," Hayden said not kindly. "Do you have any idea how the MMPO came to choose you for this case?"

"To tell you the truth, I've kind of wondered some about that myself, although I'm very pleased they did. I've been on their roll of available attorneys for a couple of years now, and this is the first time they've sent me a case."

"Well, that's great, just great!" Paris erupted. "Mr. Daniels, I don't mean to sound rude, but you must understand that there is a great deal at stake here. Your adversary, as you call Jeremy Mallon, is totally dedicated to bringing this hospital to its knees. And he is damn good at what he does, which in the main is to sue doctors. Don't you think we ought to call the MMPO and have them assign some other firm to the case?"

Sarah studied Daniels as he thought over the question. If he was disturbed by the two-pronged attack from Hayden and now Paris, it did not show in his face, which at that moment reminded her of Fess Parker as Davy Crockett, debating whether or not to stay on and defend the Alamo. His expression was severe enough, but there was a spark in his azure eyes—a defiance—that Sarah felt certain only she was appreciating.

"Well," he said finally, "for any number of reasons, I'd sure hate to see that happen. But since you've brought it up, I guess we ought to consider it."

"Good," Paris said.

"However," Matt went on, "there are a couple of points I'd like to make. For one, Dr. Baldwin here is my client. Whether I stay or go is really up to her. For another, since speaking with her the other day, I've done some reading and some talking to people. Mallon or no Mallon, I think I can do a good job representing her."

"How can you say that, with almost no experience in this area?" Hayden demanded.

"Because the law's the law, Mr. Hayden. And I'm still just naive enough to equate the legal process with getting at the truth. And getting at the truth is something I always liked doing."

Glenn Paris turned to Sarah. "Sarah, it is our opinion that you can get better counsel and a better defense from someone more, how should I say, experienced than Mr. Daniels here. But he is right. You are his client. And it is for you to decide."

Sarah looked over at Daniels, who held her gaze coolly. *Bring on Santa Ana, Mr. Travis. I ain't plannin' on goin' nowhere.*

"Well, Mr. Paris," she said, "provided my job isn't on the line over this, I guess I feel that if Mr. Daniels handles himself in court the way he has here, I'm in pretty good hands. Mr. Daniels—Matt—I'm sure that if you needed to involve Mr. Hayden or any of the other MCB lawyers, you'd do it, wouldn't you?"

"Anytime."

"In that case, Mr. Paris," Sarah said, "I'm comfortable being represented by this man."

"Good Lord," Eli Blankenship suddenly exclaimed, "I think I just figured out who our Mr. Daniels is. Let's see if I get this right, Matt. Bottom of the ninth, no outs, bases loaded, three and nothing on the Toronto batter—"

"Yes, yes," Matt said, a bit impatiently, "that *was* me. Thank you for remembering. But that's ancient history now."

"Remembering what?" Sarah asked.

"Nine pitches, nine strikes, three outs, ball game over," Blankenship went on. "One of the greatest short relief performances ever. I thought the name sounded familiar when I first heard it."

"I'm sure the 'Matt' part threw you off," Daniels said more kindly. "Not many remember that I actually had a real first name."

"Hey, do I get clued in here? I *am* the defendant."

"I'm afraid I'm in the dark, too," Paris chimed in.

"Black Cat Daniels," Blankenship explained. "Ten years as a relief pitcher for the Red Sox."

"Actually twelve," Daniels said. "Now, if you all wouldn't mind getting back to the business at—"

"Why Black Cat?" Paris asked.

Daniels sighed.

"Dr. Baldwin—Sarah—I'm really sorry about this," he said. "I would imagine that what you're going through is not pleasant, and is probably more than a little scary for you. Having to sit there while my qualifications get called into question, and now all this baseball talk, certainly can't be helping."

"I'm fine, actually," Sarah said. "Besides, I want to know, too."

"Okay. Mr. Paris, my nickname came from my having a fair number of superstitions back when I played the game."

"Always stepped on first base coming into a game," Blankenship said. "Never sat down in the bullpen. Never pitched without a piece of red ribbon tied around his belt."

"Blue," Matt corrected. "You know your baseball."

"Yes, of course, it was blue. Are you still like that? Superstitious, I mean."

"I—um—still have an interest in ritual and luck if that's what you're asking. But trust me, Dr. Blankenship, it doesn't get in the way. When I'm in the courtroom, I keep that ribbon tied on my belt in the back where my suit coat hides it. Now, I think maybe we ought to get down to business. As Mr. Paris so eloquently put it, we have a lot at stake here. And unfortunately, it seems that our esteemed adversary has gotten a bit of a jump on us."

"What do you mean?" Paris asked.

Daniels took some notes from his briefcase. "Sarah, the man who provides you with your herbs and roots, his name is Mr. Kwong?"

"That's right. Kwong Tian-Wen."

"Well, this afternoon Mr. Mallon obtained an *ex parte* discovery order to seal off Mr. Kwong's shop. At eight tomorrow morning he'll be there with a chemist, someone from the sheriff's office, and God only knows who else. He plans to get samples from the place and follow chain-of-evidence procedures to have those samples analyzed."

"Can't you do something about that?" Paris asked.

"I'll defer to Mr. Hayden to answer that question, sir."

"Not at this point, Glenn," Hayden said. "It's just a case of being outmaneuvered. Dr. Baldwin, do you have any idea how Mallon could have gotten the name of this man so quickly?"

"A couple of possibilities come to mind," she said.

"And?" Paris asked.

"I think I ought to do some checking before throwing out any names. Besides, I have implicit faith in Mr. Kwong. He is one of the very best at what he does. The sooner Mallon gets this thing done, the sooner he'll learn that he doesn't have a case."

"I think someone from the hospital should be there," Daniels said. "We'll be meeting tomorrow morning at this address." He slid the court order over to Hayden.

"Can't do it," the lawyer said. "I'll be in court."

"Eli, how about you?" Paris asked. "You'd be a perfect representative."

"I think I can be there," Blankenship said.

"Perfect. Extra dessert for you, Eli. We must hope

Sarah is right about all this, Daniels. But do you see what we mean about Mallon? He has handled dozens—probably hundreds—of malpractice cases. He's got a huge staff, and he won't leave any stone unturned."

"He doesn't seem like someone you can just hook and reel in," Daniels acknowledged. "I'll give you that."

"Perhaps," Hayden offered, "you can involve your partners in this case. Do either Mr. Hannigan or Mr. Goldstein have any expertise in this arena?"

Damn, Sarah thought. *Are they ever going to let up?*

"Actually," Daniels said, "I'm glad you mentioned that."

"Then they *do* have some malpractice experience," Hayden said. "That's excellent. Collaboration is the key in this business."

"Well, sir, not exactly. You see, Billy Hannigan never did like being a lawyer, but his wife wouldn't let him quit. Then last year, after she ran away with another attorney, he just took off. Last I heard he was working as a disc jockey on a radio station in Lake Placid."

"And Goldstein?"

Daniels rubbed at his chin and then sighed.

"Well," he said, "the truth is, Goldstein was someone Billy made up. Before I joined him, he was in solo practice, but he called his firm Hannigan and Goldstein. Something about Billy's wanting to attract Jewish clients. I just got around to having new stationery printed up with only my name, but I keep forgetting to have our little yellow pages ad changed."

"This is highly irregular," Hayden blustered. "*Highly* irregular."

"Sarah," Paris said, "I think this deception allows you to reconsider your decision."

"Mr. Paris, deception seems a bit strong a word," she countered. "Clearly, there's been no attempt to hide the truth. I think we'll do just fine with Mr. Daniels, even without Mr. Goldstein."

"Much appreciated," Matt Daniels said. "Now, if we're all in the same corner, I think we ought to start putting together our case. Tomorrow morning at eight, round one begins. So let's have at it."

"Highly irregular," Sarah heard someone mutter.

Chapter 18

EXCEPT FOR THE NIGHT CLERK, ROSA SUAREZ WAS alone in the medical record room. It was nearing ten-thirty and she had not eaten since noon. Her back and neck ached from hunching over her work table. But in some ways, the discomfort was pleasurable. It had been over two years since she had put in these kinds of hours on a project, two years since she felt challenged.

The initial phase of her investigation would be done tonight, and both Alberto and her department head were anxiously awaiting her return to Atlanta. Neither stood to be very pleased with what she had to tell them. As yet she had no explanation for the bizarre DIC cases. However, two things were clear. From a purely statistical standpoint, there was virtually no possibility that the three cases were coincidental. And almost as certainly, unless the underlying cause of the tragedies was determined and dealt with, there would be more.

There were several integrations and many combinations she needed to run through the data banks at the CDC, and some preliminary culture results to be checked. Then, in all likelihood, it would be back to

Boston. To date, she had unearthed dozens of demo-
graphic and physical commonalities among the three
stricken women—some quite possibly significant, some
too obscure to take seriously. Their blood types were all
A positive and their primary residences within three
miles of the hospital. All had been associated as patients
with the Medical Center of Boston for at least four
years, and each had been pregnant once before. On the
more obscure side of the ledger, all were born in April,
although in different years; all were firstborn; and none
had been educated past high school. In addition, all were
right-handed and brown-eyed.

There were still more data to be gathered, but by far
the most persistently troublesome aspect of her research
to this point was the prenatal supplements given each
woman by Sarah Baldwin. A botanist at the Smithsonian
and a friend on the faculty of Emory University had
provided some preliminary data on the nine components. But much more detailed biochemical information
was needed. Rosa's instincts were telling her that although the components of the mix might serve as some
sort of cofactor in a lethal biological reaction, they were,
in and of themselves, harmless. But the tools of her trade
were numbers and probabilities, not instincts.

"Excuse me, Ramona," she called out to the night
clerk whose desk was on the other side of a broad bank
of files. "I just want to be sure there are no more records
in the group we're working on."

"Seven years of women who delivered here and required transfusions during or after their deliveries—
you've gotten them all. Mrs. Suarez, do you know that
since you came to MCB you've spent more time down
here than the whole medical staff combined?"

"I'll bet I have. Well, this will be my last night for a
while. Tomorrow I'm heading back to—"

Rosa stopped in midsentence and stared down at the
chart in front of her. It belonged to Alethea Worthington, the second of the DIC cases. She had dissected the

record word by word, just as she had the records of Constanza Hidalgo and Lisa Summer. What caught her eye at this moment, though, wasn't something *on* the page, but *between* it and the previous one. She picked up the chart and stared at it from several angles.

"Mrs. Suarez, is everything all right?" the clerk called out.

"Oh. Yes. Everything's fine, dear. Ramona, would you happen to have a pocket knife or a nail file?"

"I have a Swiss Army knife in my bag, so I guess that means I have both."

"Perfect. And could you please bring me back those two charts of—"

"Summer and Hidalgo. I know. I know."

"Thank you, dear."

Using the lenses of her bifocals as magnifiers, Rosa peered along the cleft where the pages of the chart were held together by a flexible metal binder. At the spot where the arms of the binder passed through the pages, small, jagged edges of paper protruded. Rosa marked the pages on either side of the fragments and then carefully loosened the binder just a bit. Next she slid the largest blade of the Swiss Army knife along the space beside one of the arms. Two minute scraps of paper dropped out onto the table.

Rosa gently brushed the fragments into an envelope and then convinced herself that similar pieces were tucked behind the other arm. She left those in place and tightened the binder back as it had been. Pages—probably two of them—had almost definitely been torn out of the record. It took most of ten minutes to find identical fragments in Constanza Hidalgo's chart. The tiny bits of progress notepaper represented at least two and possibly three missing pages.

Lisa Summer's chart was by far the thickest of the three. By the time Rosa convinced herself that there was no physical evidence of missing pages, it was nearly eleven. She piled the record on the others and, for the first time in two hours, stood and stretched. The meaning of her discovery was not at all clear. But even though the Summer chart seemed untouched, the finding that at least two of the three DIC records had been tampered with was significant. Of that she had little doubt.

Outside, the rainstorm had ended. A few faint stars were visible in the black velvet sky. Rosa felt energized by the sudden new twist. Part of her wanted to stay up all night as she had so often done, studying and working through puzzles until the answers came. But she was sixty now, and the cost of that sort of exuberance was just too unpredictable. Facing a busy day in Atlanta, she needed to pack and get at least a few hours of sleep before her early-morning flight.

She wanted desperately to share what she had found with someone—almost anyone who could be a sounding board and give her feedback. Verbalizing her ideas and streams of consciousness with colleagues had once been an invaluable tool. But the wounds from BART, though now more than two years old, were still painful. And that refractory pain reminded her over and over to trust as little as necessary.

Rosa gathered her things, thanked the clerk, and promised to be back before too long. Then she left the building on the campus side. Two women dead of a mysterious medical complication, and both of their charts altered. Rosa searched her imagination for some sort of innocent explanation but could conjure up none. What had been a fascinating epidemiological puzzle had suddenly turned sinister.

.   .   .

Sarah shook hands with the five MCB representatives and thanked each for his willingness to help in her defense. The meeting, which had gotten off to such a tense and confrontational beginning, had actually ended up accomplishing a good deal. All concurred that the key to a quick resolution of the Grayson suit lay in finding an

identical case of DIC in an end-stage labor patient—
whether at MCB or any other hospital—who had never
had contact with Sarah.

At Matt Daniels's suggestion, Paris and Snyder agreed
to contact their associates around the country, and
Blankenship to institute an in-depth search of the medical literature. Arnold Hayden vowed to stay in close
contact with Daniels, and Colin Smith gave assurances
that any expenses incurred by Hayden or his staff would
be covered by the hospital. Finally, the group pledged to
present a unified front to Jeremy Mallon and the press.
Unless and until she was proven responsible beyond
reasonable doubt, Sarah Baldwin was innocent of any
wrongdoing. Tomorrow morning, in a show of support,
Eli Blankenship would accompany Sarah and Matt to
the shop of her Chinese herbalist.

"Nice going tonight," Sarah said as Matt retrieved his
coat and umbrella. "I think you handled a very difficult
situation with a lot of restraint and class."

"Nonsense. If you hadn't gone to bat for me, I would
have been out of the game."

"I'm not much of a baseball aficionado," Sarah said,
"but isn't it true that if someone goes to bat for you, you
are out of the game?"

Matt's grin was, for the first time, spontaneous and
unstrained. And Sarah added it to the growing list of
things she liked about the man.

"I still don't know why the claims adjuster at MMPO
selected me for this case," he said, "but I'm glad he did.
I'm not as slick as most of the attorneys I oppose, but I
promise you, I'm a fighter and a survivor. I do my
homework, and fortunately, I'm smarter than I look."

"I'm not worried. Believe me I'm not. Besides, after
tomorrow, I'm hoping we'll be able to go out and celebrate the end of your shortest case ever. Tell me, how
did you ever manage to play baseball *and* get through
law school?"

"Well," Matt said, "I was a relief pitcher. I always had

good control, but I was never that flashy to watch. From about my second year in the majors on, the press began writing about how I didn't have good stuff—that's speed or movement on my pitches, and about how the Red Sox had no plans to keep me, and how I wouldn't last another year. Finally I had read enough of my own derogatory press clippings to decide that I ought to have something to fall back on. So I started law school in the off seasons. Eight off seasons later I was done. I had been with the Red Sox several times, as well as the Expos in the National League, and Pawtucket in the International League, and I still had a year of major league pitching left in me."

"That's amazing."

"Correction, that's two rabbits' feet, a two-thousand-year-old Egyptian amulet, and that infamous blue ribbon Dr. Blankenship talked about. Plus about a dozen other little rituals."

"You really believe in that stuff?"

"To paraphrase something Mark Twain once said about God, I choose to believe in that stuff just in case there's something to it."

"A superstitious attorney who quotes Mark Twain and pitched major league baseball," Sarah said. "You certainly can't be called middle of the road."

"Neither can you," Matt said. "God, it's nearly eleven. I promised to have the sitter home by then."

"Sitter?"

Although their relationship was strictly professional, and Sarah knew Matt was ethically bound to keep it that way, she found the news that he was married disappointing.

"I have a twelve-year-old son, Harry. He lives with his mother most of the year."

"Oh, I see."

"Well, then, shall we meet tomorrow morning at Mr. Kwong's?"

"If you think you can find it."

"I've already driven past it. Like I said, I try to do my homework. I'm going over to Brookline. Do you need a ride?"

"Thanks, but I live in the North End, and I have my bike. Besides, the rain's stopped now, and riding just after a storm is something I really enjoy."

Matt reached across to shake her hand. Their gazes met and, for the briefest moment, connected. But just as quickly, he looked away.

"Don't you worry," he said. "We're going to do fine."

"I know. One last question, though. Before you arrived, that lawyer, Arnold Hayden, implied that most attorneys would have scheduled a preliminary meeting like this one in their office. Why didn't you?"

Matt slipped on his coat, took his briefcase in one hand and his umbrella in the other.

"Well, the truth is, I wanted to make a good impression—on Glenn Paris and his crew, but especially on you. And my current office is hardly the largest, most opulent in the city."

"I see," she said again.

"And to make matters even worse, that damn partner of mine, Mr. Goldstein, can't seem to keep the place neat. Next time maybe I'll chance letting you see it. Meanwhile, get some sleep. We have a big day ahead of us."

Sarah watched Matt shamble down the hall to the elevator. What apprehension she had about the next morning's gathering at Kwong Tian-Wen's shop was more than offset by the notion that in just nine and a half hours, she would be seeing her lawyer again.

"Are you all done in there?"

The stoop-shouldered cleaning lady had been patiently vacuuming and dusting in the corridor for most of an hour, waiting for the Milsap Room to empty.

"Oh, yes, I'm sorry," Sarah said.

"No problem, no problem. He's a fine-looking man,

that one. A *fine*-looking man." The old woman's eyes were sparkling.

"You know," Sarah said, "I was thinking the very same thing myself. But I have a feeling you could tell that."

"Well, chile, I wasn't jes' watchin' him," the woman chided. "I was watchin' *you*."

.   .   .

Savoring the sweet, scrubbed summer air, Sarah left the medical building on the campus side and crossed to where she had chained her bicycle. The campus was fairly well lighted and patrolled. And although there were, from time to time, reports of women being harassed at night, and in one case mugged, Sarah did not find the broad mall particularly menacing.

The groundskeepers periodically posted notices requesting that bicycles be left only in designated areas. But since those areas were outside the campus, house officers and nurses who planned to be at the hospital after dark continued to secure their bikes to the wrought-iron railings leading up to the entrances of many of the buildings.

Sarah had chained her Fuji to a low, steel-pipe railing by the side entrance of the surgical building. It was a convenient site, and one she had used frequently with no problem. Now, as she rounded the corner, she was struck by the darkness of the spot. The light over the entrance was out, although she could never remember its being so before. She peered through the gloom and took one tentative step forward . . . then another. The man was pressed tightly against the wall to her left.

Sensing a presence, Sarah froze. She squinted and blinked, but her vision had not yet adjusted enough to pierce the blackness. The night was soundless. She strained to hear breathing or movement of any kind. Someone was there . . . close. She shifted her weight to her right foot, preparing to push off and sprint away.

"I know you're there. What do you want?" she suddenly heard herself saying.

Five endless seconds passed . . . ten.

"P-p-please d-don't r-r-run," the man said in a whispered stutter.

Sarah reflexively moved away from the voice even as she was turning toward it. The man, now a silhouette, stepped from the shielding darkness. He was not much taller than she, and very slightly built. Sarah could just make out the narrow contours of his face.

"Doctor B-B-Baldwin. I've been f-following you f-for days. I must s-speak with—"

"Sarah, is that you?"

Sarah whirled. Rosa Suarez was standing not ten feet away, angled so that she could see Sarah but not the man. At the sound of the intruder's voice, he bolted. Head down, he charged past Rosa, shoving her off balance and very nearly to the ground.

"Stop, please!" Sarah cried.

But the man was already crossing the lawn of the campus, heading full bore toward the front gate. Her pulse jackhammering, Sarah rushed to Rosa's side.

"Are you all right?"

"I'm fine, I think." Rosa was breathing heavily as she stared across the deserted campus in the direction the man had run. She patted her chest. "Who was he?"

"I don't know. He called me by name and said he had to speak with me. Then when you called out, he ran."

"How strange."

"He stuttered terribly—worse than almost anyone I can remember. And he said that he had been following me. You know, now that I think about it, I believe I've noticed him, too. He drives a blue foreign car—maybe a Honda. God, was that weird just now. I can't believe I just stood there and didn't run. Now I can't stop shaking."

Rosa took Sarah's hands in hers. Almost instantly the shaking began to lessen. Sarah unlocked her bike.

Slowly, the two women walked together toward the main gate, Sarah wheeling her bike along.

"I'm sorry I couldn't support you at that meeting tonight," Rosa said. "How did it go?"

"Pretty well, I think. Lisa's lawyer has a court order to inspect my herbalist's shop tomorrow morning and take samples."

"Are you worried about that?"

"Actually, I'm relieved it's happening. The sooner they check the samples, the sooner this lawyer will see I couldn't have been responsible."

Rosa stopped and looked at her. It was quite apparent to Sarah there was something on her mind—something she wanted to talk about.

"Sarah, I—I'd like it very much if you could walk me home," she said finally. "My bed and breakfast is just a few blocks from here. I'd like to explain why I chose not to discuss my findings and opinions at your meeting."

"There's no need to."

"The fact that you're being followed bothers me. I think that what I've discovered may be very important —especially if what just happened to you has something to do with this case."

"Go on."

"To begin with, in my native country, Cuba, I was a physician. . . ."

Sarah listened, rapt, to Rosa Suarez's concise, eloquent sketch of her life. A political exile from Cuba, she found herself in a series of refugee camps with only minimal English, and the painful realization that there was no way she would ever be able to document her education or medical degree. Following a series of rather menial jobs, she managed to gain an entry-level, clerical position at the CDC. Her husband, a poet and educator in his homeland, worked in a book bindery, where he remained until his retirement a few years before.

Within a few years, Rosa's quick mind and medical expertise had landed her a place as a field epidemiologist.

Some of her successes—a major role tracking down the source of the Legionnaire's disease outbreak in Philadelphia and tying a regional increase in leukemia deaths in one Texas county to a nuclear-contaminated stream— Sarah had actually heard of. Then, at the peak of what had been a valuable career, Rosa was sent to investigate reports of an unusual bacterial infection that had begun cropping up in geographic pockets throughout San Francisco. Already the uncommon germ had killed a number of immune-compromised and otherwise medically debilitated patients.

Her data, amassed over nearly a year, and involving thousands of interviews and cultures, pointed the finger of responsibility directly at the U.S. military. The army, she maintained, was using what they thought was a biologically inactive bacterial marker to test germ warfare/ air current theories in the tunnels of the BART—the Bay Area Rapid Transit system. Because of the sensitive nature of her accusation, Rosa did not reveal her findings until her case was, to all intents, airtight. But somewhere along the line, she had spoken of them to the wrong person.

A blue-ribbon commission of the country's foremost epidemiologists and infectious disease specialists was appointed by Congress to validate her conclusions. What they found, instead, were critical pieces of data missing all along the line. Computer programs that Rosa herself had designed functioned poorly or not at all. Probability calculations failed to support hypotheses. Laboratory technicians denied ever having received specimens that she swore to having sent. Finally, and most ignominiously, one expert on the commission quite easily traced the source of the bacteria to a dump site on the edge of the city. The directors of the private laboratory responsible for the disposal error readily admitted it. They were fined but soon after, Rosa learned, were the beneficiaries of a hefty military contract.

"So," she said, "the dumping site was cleaned up, and

of course, the rate of infection began to drop. I was put into mothballs, so to speak, and was brought out for this investigation only when no one else was available to do it."

"They sabotaged your work. I don't believe it," Sarah said. "Correction. Actually, I *do* believe it."

"Well, at least now you may understand why I have maintained some distance from everyone involved in this case—including you."

"Please, Rosa, don't worry about it. Just do your work."

"Tomorrow morning I am returning to Atlanta for a while. My investigation is still in a most preliminary phase. But I have come across some things that disturb me, and I wanted to warn you."

"Warn me?"

"It's not what you think," Rosa said, patting her reassuringly on the arm. "In fact, I've wanted for several days to tell you that my initial studies are pointing toward some sort of infection, not a toxin or poison. But I—I've just been reluctant to speak of my work with anybody."

They had reached the doorway of the old stucco Victorian where Rosa was staying.

"Then what is there to warn me about?"

"Sarah, you are a kind and caring person—a credit to your profession. I can see the pain the charges against you have caused. I don't want to go into details just yet, but I have reason to believe someone may be trying to keep me from getting at the truth in these cases. Assuming that person is not you—and that is an assumption I have chosen to make—you must be careful whom you talk to and whom you trust."

"But—"

"Please, Sarah. Sharing this much has been difficult for me. I'll tell you more when it seems right to do so. Meanwhile, I have a great deal of work yet to do, and you have a defense to put together."

Sarah sighed. "Your assumption is right, you know. I'm not that person."

Again, Rosa patted her arm. "I *do* know, dear. Just be patient with me, and be very, very careful."

Sarah waited until the epidemiologist was inside. Then she pedaled slowly toward the inner city. For a time, she worked at clearing her mind entirely. Failing that, she tried to focus on her new lawyer and the strange, stuttering little man. But always, her thoughts drifted back to Rosa Suarez's cryptic warning.

Just be patient with me, and be very, very careful.

If the woman's intention was to frighten her, Sarah acknowledged finally, she had done a pretty damn good job.

Chapter 19

JULY 21

THE SHOP OF THE HERBALIST KWONG TIAN-WEN occupied the ground floor and basement of a dilapidated, four-story brick tenement. Sarah paid more than customary attention to her appearance and to selecting an outfit, then left her apartment at seven-fifteen and walked the few miles from the North End to Chinatown. She sensed some apprehension at having to deal with Jeremy Mallon, and was still bewildered by the frightened, stuttering man and by Rosa Suarez's strange warning. But the morning was bright and unusually clear, and she felt upbeat—about taking this step to eliminate her herbal supplement from suspicion *and* about seeing Matt Daniels again.

She had known Kwong from her days at the Ettinger Institute, and following her return from medical school, she had checked him out with several members of the Boston holistic community. He was still highly regarded. Nevertheless, she interviewed him twice before selecting him as her supplier. He spoke almost no English, but Sarah's once-decent Chinese was still good enough to conduct business with him. When she needed a translator, Kwong would rap his cane on the ceiling or strike it against a certain steam pipe. And within a minute or two, one of his American-born grandchildren would appear.

Sarah was impressed with the man's knowledge and drawn to his consistently optimistic outlook. And of course, there were the striking similarities—physical *and* metaphysical—between him and Louis Han. She could not help but believe that in Kwong, she was getting a glimpse of her mentor had he lived into his seventies.

Initially Sarah picked up her herbal orders herself. But as the pressures of her medical training mounted, she had begun having the mixture delivered. Now, perhaps for the first time, she realized how much she missed her visits to the shop. The frayed connection with Kwong was, she thought sadly, just another item on the list of casualties exacted by her residency.

The shop was on a narrow street, barely more than an alley, off Kneeland. As Sarah rounded the corner, she saw the old man and Debbie, one of his granddaughters, standing by the building. She was wondering why the two weren't inside when she noticed the yellow vinyl ribbon crisscrossing the doorway and windows. It pained her to think of Kwong's humiliation and confusion when some sheriff's deputy or constable showed up with a court order to seal off the place.

"Hello, Mr. Kwong," Sarah said in Cantonese. "Hello, Debbie. I'm sorry for this." She gestured toward the ribbons.

Kwong brushed off the apology with a gnarled hand, but Sarah could tell he was agitated. She suddenly realized that it had been perhaps a year since they had actually seen one another. His gray-white goatee was unkempt and stained with nicotine below his lip. His blue silk robe—possibly the only outfit she had ever seen him wear—was threadbare and frayed. Had he aged so? Or had she simply been viewing him through younger, more naive eyes?

"A man has been guarding the shop ever since they put up those ribbons," Debbie said. "He goes from the alley back around to here, and then to the alley again. He said he wants to make sure no one tampers with anything inside. What does he mean?"

"Nothing, Debbie," Sarah said. "Things will be back to normal for you before you know it. I'm just so sorry that you and your grandfather have to go through this at all."

The old man's frailty was striking. Sarah prayed that Mallon and his people would simply take whatever samples they wanted and leave. If they tried intimidating Kwong in any way, it would be up to Matt to protect him at all costs. She was about to try to explain the situation to Kwong through Debbie when Matt entered the street from the far end. Eli Blankenship was lumbering along beside him, gesticulating forcefully, as if to get across a difficult point. Sarah was relieved to have him along. There was no finer intellect at MCB, nor any more imposing physical presence, either. Matt was reasonably tall and well built, but next to the professor, he looked slight.

With Debbie's help, she introduced the men to Kwong. It seemed clear the herbalist had no interest in any of them beyond having them leave him alone.

Matt immediately excused Sarah, Blankenship, and himself and led them to the other side of the street.

"Does the old guy know what's happening?" he whispered.

Sarah shrugged.

"He's not addled by any stretch," she said. "I suspect he has a pretty good idea of what's going on. But I'm not sure he understands that it all has to do with me, and not with him."

"He looks like he's spent more than his share of time with his lips curled around the stem of an opium pipe."

"So what? Opium is part of his culture. Any idea where Mallon is?"

"Nope. I expected him to be late, though. It's an old legal ploy to unnerve and annoy the other side. It's survived in the law game over the ages mostly because it works." He motioned them back to Kwong and the girl. "Debbie," he said kindly, "please apologize to your grandfather for our imposing on him, and promise that we will compensate him for the trouble and inconvenience."

The girl, dressed in baggy jeans and a sweatshirt, was perhaps thirteen. She had a plain face and short, jet hair. Sarah was about to suggest that Matt choose words she was more likely to understand than *impose* and *compensate*, when the teen rattled off a translation to Kwong. The old man responded with no more than a grunt and a dismissive wave of his hand.

"He says that it is his pleasure to serve you, and that you need not think about paying him," Debbie said.

At that moment, a Lincoln Town Car pulled up at the end of the street. Sarah turned to Kwong to reassure him about the new arrivals.

"The pudgy guy's Sheriff Mooney," she heard Matt say to Eli, "and that tall guy—isn't he the one from the weight loss shows on TV?"

She groaned softly and looked back at the Lincoln. Peter Ettinger, ramrod straight, towering above Mallon and the sheriff, was staring down the narrow street, straight at her. Even in the pale, indirect morning sun, his silver hair looked almost phosphorescent.

"You bastard," she muttered to herself. This must be Mallon's expert witness.

She gave Kwong, who now looked somewhat confused, a gentle touch. Then she stood back and watched as the two groups of men, like combatants in some macabre sport, approached one another for introductions. She took the moment when Matt reached across to shake Peter's hand and froze it in her mind for future reference.

The county sheriff, the MCB chief of medicine, Peter,

Matt, a bewildered old Chinese man, a precocious teen. The whole affair was suddenly taking on a carnival atmosphere. In just a few minutes, when the eight of them worked their way inside, things were bound to get even more bizarre. Kwong's shop was an impressive hodgepodge, with no clearly defined aisles. Eight people would be well beyond its critical mass.

Matt led the opposition back to where she was standing. Peter allowed himself to be introduced to her. He reached out his hand, but Sarah refused to take it.

"So," he said. "It appears we've gotten ourselves in a wee bit o' trouble." His smug expression was close to the one Sarah remembered from that last horrid day in his office.

"And it appears *we've* become even more overbearing and unpleasant than *we* used to be," she replied.

This isn't the wide-eyed earth child you brought back from the jungle, Peter, she was thinking. *If it's a fight you're spoiling for, you're not going to be disappointed.*

"You two know each other?" Matt said.

"Dr. Baldwin once did some work for me," Ettinger said quickly.

"*Hard labor* would be a more descriptive term, Matt. I'm not proud of it, but we lived together for three years before I woke up and jumped the wall."

"Lived together!" Matt exclaimed. "Mallon, what in the hell?"

In the second or two before Mallon responded, Sarah could see the confusion in his eyes. *Peter hadn't told him!* The bastard wanted to get back at her so badly, he hadn't said a word about their past.

"He—um—Mr. Ettinger is being used to help us organize our case," Mallon said, blustering. "We—we certainly never intended having him appear in court. He is serving us strictly in an advisory capacity."

"Well, I would certainly hope you can do better than a rebuffed suitor for your expert witness," Matt said.

"I'd hate to have my job made that easy. Shall we go in and get this over with?"

Mallon said nothing. But it was clear from his stony expression that Matt had drawn blood, if only a drop or two.

"Nice going," Sarah whispered. "Now please, just make sure Mallon doesn't take it out on Mr. Kwong."

The vinyl ribbons were cut away, and the combatants, led by Kwong Tian-Wen and his granddaughter, filed into the herbalist's shop. *Carnivale de Baldwina*, Sarah mused. Sheriff Mooney, the ringmaster, in his white seersucker suit. Jeremy Mallon, snake and charmer in one. Eli Blankenship sans leopard skin, nearly spanning the narrow doorway. Peter Ettinger, the Human Stilt, ducking to enter. *Carnivale de Baldwina*. Once inside, Sarah noted with some pleasure that the protruding rafters kept The Stilt in a persistent hunch.

The shop was more cluttered and more fragrant than Sarah remembered. Stalks of wild reeds and dried flowers were everywhere, interspersed with barrels of roots, various ground flours, rice, and leaves. The old glassfront counter and the shelves behind it were packed with jars of widely varying sizes, shapes, and contents. One contained desiccated scorpions; another, huge beetles; still another, an eel in preservative. A few of the jars had labels handwritten in Chinese, but many of them had none.

Two somewhat mangy, long-haired cats, one pure white, the other black as chimney soot, huddled sleepily in one corner. And standing like a totem, or perhaps an exclamation point, in the center of the disarray, was a well-stocked wire display rack of Dr. Scholl's foot products.

"I don't think parading a jury into this place will help our cause too much," Blankenship whispered.

"Let's hope it never comes to that," Sarah said.

"Well, Counselor, how do you want to proceed?" Matt asked.

Mallon, apparently unaware that his Armani suit was backed up against a thick, dusty crop of dried sunflower stalks, made a visual survey of the shop that was theatrically slow and disparaging. Clearly, he was back on track.

"We have a list of the ingredients in Dr. Baldwin's supplement," he said finally. "One at a time, we'll ask for them. Mr. Kwong's granddaughter may translate if necessary. The sample will then be placed in two labeled evidence bags. The first will be sealed by Sheriff Mooney and the seal initialed by you or Dr. Baldwin. The second will be inspected by Mr. Ettinger, who will make what notes he wishes. Beginning later today, he will be working with a team of botanists and chemists to identify each component scientifically. Does that approach meet with your approval, Counselor?"

"Sarah, Eli, is that all right with you?" Matt asked.

"As a representative of the Medical Center of Boston, I would like to examine the specimens as well," Blankenship said.

"Do you know herbal medicine?" Sarah asked.

"Oh, a bit."

His half smile suggested that, as in many areas, what he considered a "bit" of knowledge made others experts.

She motioned Blankenship and Matt into a huddle.

"There's something I ought to explain," she whispered.

"To us or to everyone?"

"To everyone." She cleared some nervousness from her throat.

"Just be very careful," Blankenship warned. "Remember, they're the enemy."

"I understand. Mr. Mallon, before you start this process, I want to explain that I brought the composition of the mixture I use back with me from Southeast Asia. It was written out in Chinese by a brilliant herbalist and healer. I have a copy of that version here. It is this list Mr. Kwong has used to prepare the tea which I dispense.

Some of the names on the list you have—the one I give to my patients—are my best guesses at the English equivalent of the roots and herbs he uses."

"As long as the two lists are in the same order, and you and Mr. Kwong concur that what he puts in these bags is what you gave to Lisa Grayson, I have no problem with what names you call things. In due time, Mr. Ettinger and his team will be providing us with scientific names and chemical compositions. I'd like a copy of that Chinese list, though."

Debbie translated what had been decided to Kwong and handed him the list. Sarah felt certain that the old man had the components of the mixture memorized. But sharing that information with Mallon would not serve their cause at all.

"Okay, then," Mallon said. "Number one is Oriental ginseng."

"*Panax pseudoginseng*," Sarah heard Blankenship whisper to himself.

Debbie told her grandfather to proceed. The herbalist nodded somewhat impatiently and, with only the briefest glance at the list, pulled a large jar of brown plant fragments from beneath the counter. Using a worn metal scoop, he filled a pair of plastic bags. Sarah authenticated the seal on one and gave it to Matt, who gave it to the sheriff. The other was passed first to Blankenship and then to Peter. Blankenship took only moments to assess the contents. Peter sniffed it, tasted it, and rolled a bit between his fingers. Then, after a few hmms, which Sarah felt certain were to irritate her, he placed specimen one in his briefcase.

The second item on the list, a gnarled root, was handled the same way, as was the third, which Sarah's list called moondragon.

"It's actually shavings of bark from the medarah tree," Sarah explained. "Endemic to Java, but also found in southern China. Wonderful for intestinal and stomach disorders. Great for morning sickness."

As she spoke, Sarah noticed that at the far right end of the counter, Sheriff Mooney had begun peering intently into one of the glass containers. It was on the topmost shelf, behind several larger jars. Sarah strained to see what the lawman was finding so interesting and was about to inform Matt, when Kwong began waving his arms wildly about and yelling.

"No, no, no!" he shouted, his expression a disconcerting mix of anger and bewilderment. "No, no, no!"

He was nearly hysterical as he railed at his granddaughter, gesticulating toward the five-gallon jar holding the sample he had just meted out—the fourth component on the list. Sarah had never before heard the man so much as raise his voice. But the frightened, frustrated look in his eyes was one she knew well. She had seen it often in the eyes of her mother as the woman's Alzheimer's disease inexorably progressed. Something had gone wrong—very wrong.

Chapter 20

DEBBIE, WHAT'S GOING ON?"

The teen, who was trying with no success to calm her grandfather, just shook her head.

Sarah grabbed a small, cane-back chair and helped induce the old man to sit down. Kwong continued, though hoarsely now, to rattle at Debbie and everyone else in machine-gun Cantonese. Sarah knelt beside him and stroked his hand until he finally began to quiet down.

"I don't know what happened," Debbie said. "He scooped out the herbs and put them in the Baggies, and everything seemed fine. Then all of a sudden, he took a bit from the jar, smelled it, and started shouting. I'm very frightened for him. He's not been well."

Kwong's complexion, sallow to begin with, did seem even paler to Sarah. Reflexively she checked the radial pulse at his wrist. For a moment she thought his heart was beating wildly. Then she realized that it was her own pulse she was feeling, hammering in her fingertips. Clearly the significance of this turn of events had registered in her autonomic nervous system, if not yet completely in her mind. *The confusion . . . the apparent error . . . the hysterical reaction.* These were the last things she would have ever expected from her herbalist. But then again, Kwong Tian-Wen was not the man she remembered.

"Dr. Blankenship, do you think he's okay?" she asked.

"Are you?" he whispered.

Sarah bit at her lower lip and nodded. "I just can't believe this is happening."

"Just what is going on here?" Mallon demanded.

Sarah turned on him like a startled cat.

"He's getting sick, that's what's going on!" she snapped. She took a deep breath to calm herself. "I'm sorry. I didn't mean to jump all over you. Listen, I need to speak to Mr. Daniels, and I think Dr. Blankenship should check Mr. Kwong over."

Mallon backed away while Sarah held a whispered conversation with her lawyer. Meanwhile, Eli Blankenship tested Kwong's carotid pulses and cardiac impulse, checked his pupils and fingernail beds, and assessed his respiratory excursions.

"Okay," Matt said, after hearing Sarah out. "The situation is this. The fourth herb on the list is supposed to be a type of chamomile. Apparently Mr. Kwong is upset because the herb in this jar is not what he expected."

"Well, what is it?" Mallon asked with sharklike eagerness. "Is it on the list at all? Debbie, ask him what that stuff is. Ask him whether he put it in the mixture he gave to Dr. Baldwin."

"Debbie, do nothing of the sort," Matt ordered. "God, Mallon. What is with you? Eli, how does he seem to you?"

"I wish I had my stethoscope," Blankenship said. "I think he's okay, but I can't say for sure."

Kwong was much calmer now, though clearly no less bewildered. He sat, hands on knees, staring at the offending jar, shaking his head.

"Debbie, is your mother home?" Sarah asked. "I

think we should get him upstairs and have him lie down."

"No one's home," the girl said. "I could watch him, though. Maybe give him some Chinese wine. He loves that."

"Just a moment," Mallon said. "I'd like to have my questions answered."

"Stuff it, Counselor," Matt snapped. "This session is over."

Peter, who had been conducting an examination of the herb, cleared his throat for attention.

"I might be wrong," he said, his tone suggesting that he knew very well that he wasn't, "but I believe this is a herb called noni. *Morinda citrifolia* is its scientific name. It's used throughout the Pacific Islands as a poultice to stop bleeding, and as a brew to regulate menstrual flow and abnormal internal hemorrhaging. Very effective. Very potent."

The implications of Ettinger's declaration, if correct, were lost on no one. A powerful herb that affected blood clotting, erroneously dispensed by Kwong Tian-Wen as chamomile. For a time, everyone seemed to be talking at once, Mallon urging Peter to get a biological and chemical report prepared on the herb as soon as possible; Matt telling Mallon to back off; Blankenship reassuring Kwong and asking if he was feeling strong enough to continue; Sarah inquiring if Debbie could fetch her grandfather's medicines so that they might get a sense of his medical problems.

The confusion and noise were brought to an abrupt halt by Sheriff Mooney.

"Excuse me, everyone," he said loudly. "I have a meeting I need to get back to my office for. However, before I go, I'm afraid Mr. Kwong, here, might have another little situation to explain." He turned to Blankenship. "Doctor, is Mr. Kwong okay to reach up there and get that jar down for me? The one with the brownish powder. Way in the back, there. At the very end of the shelf."

"I suppose if it's important, there's—"

"Hold it," Matt cut in. "Sheriff Mooney, what are you doing? You have no right to harass this man."

Mooney, with an inch or so of gut overhanging his belt, bobbed a stubby index finger at the lawyer.

"We never met before today, Matt," he said, "but I sort of feel like I know you. I enjoyed watching you pitch. In fact, I was at that famous Toronto game. However, I don't much take to you telling me what I do or do not have the right to do."

"But—"

"*Especially* when you're wrong." He withdrew a paper from his inside suit coat pocket and passed it over to Matt. "This warrant was issued by Judge John O'Brien yesterday afternoon. It gives me the right to enter this shop and to take whatever samples I wish."

"Issued on what basis?" Matt asked.

"On the basis of a call regarding this man, made to our drug hot line. I obtained the warrant just in case. I hadn't intended to use it until I had had some time to check up on him. But I used to work for the DEA, and I know opium when I see it. And I think that is precisely what is in that jar back there."

Kwong's English, though limited, clearly included "opium." His agitation immediately began to crescendo again.

"Opium no! No mine!" he shouted between staccato bursts of Cantonese.

Sarah could see not only confusion in his face, but sheer terror.

"Dammit, Mooney," Matt exclaimed. "Can't you see the old guy is in no shape for something like this?"

"Young lady, would you ask your grandfather to get that jar for me?" the sheriff persisted.

Matt snatched the jar from the shelf and banged it down on the counter. "You want the bottle so damn bad? Here, take it. What kind of policeman are you, doing this to an old man in front of his grandchild?"

"One who doesn't like dope pushers no matter what age they are."

At that moment, Kwong, who had been screaming and waving his sticklike arms about, stopped abruptly. His breathing became suddenly labored and grunting, and his color immediately darkened.

"Grandpa!" the girl cried.

Sarah and Eli grasped what was happening almost simultaneously. *Acute pulmonary edema*—heart failure— almost certainly from a coronary. Quickly they lowered Kwong onto the floor. He was battling for air now, wheezing audibly, breathing at a rate at least twice normal, and fighting any attempt to lay him on his back.

"Get an ambulance," Blankenship ordered to no one in particular. "Sarah, can you communicate with him?"

"Some."

"Come on down here beside him then, and do your best to calm him down. We've got to buy some time until the rescue squad gets here with some oxygen and morphine."

Sarah toweled off the old man's forehead and face, both of which were drenched with sweat. She whispered in his ear and rubbed his back. *Oxygen and morphine*, she was thinking. *Oxygen and morphine* . . .

"Dr. Blankenship," she said suddenly. "The opium."

The professor understood immediately. Acute heart failure—even if caused by a coronary—often responded dramatically to narcotic sedation. Morphine was one of the treatments of choice for the condition. And morphine was a chemical derivative of opium.

"Are we sure of what's in that jar?" he asked.

Sarah mopped Kwong's brow again. His color now was truly ghastly. It was quite possible his pulmonary edema would result in full cardiac arrest before the rescue squad arrived.

"Debbie, come quickly, please," she said. "Please

don't be frightened. We need your help. . . . Ask your grandfather if that really is opium in that jar. Tell him it's very, very important."

The girl stayed where she was.

"Debbie, please," Sarah begged. "It may save his life. We need to know. Please ask him."

"I don't have to," the teen said suddenly. "It is opium. It's *his* opium. Everyone in the family knows— he smokes it with his friends. But he hardly does it anymore. And he always keeps it locked up downstairs. I don't know how it got onto that shelf."

"Thank you, Debbie," Sarah said. "You did the right thing telling us. Don't worry."

Eli Blankenship was already working some of the crystals beneath the old man's tongue. Sarah returned her attention to Kwong, reassuring him, and drying him off. After a minute, Blankenship dosed him again.

"You practiced in the jungle," he said. "For an old hospital man like me, medicating this way is a bit scary."

But already Kwong's respirations had begun to slow and his color to improve. He was still laboring for every bit of air, but the mortal fear in his eyes was clearly abating.

"His pulse rate is coming down, and it's stronger," Sarah said excitedly.

For the first time during the crisis, she looked over at Matt.

"Nice going," he mouthed.

By the time the rescue squad arrived, Eli had administered a third pinch of opium, and Kwong was no longer *in extremis*. In minutes, with the two legal sides watching in silent fascination, the paramedic and EMTs had their new charge strapped onto a stretcher with oxygen in place, an IV running, and medications given. As treating physician, Eli Blankenship had ordered the meds. Now, although the situation seemed under control, he insisted on riding with Kwong. They loaded the old man into the ambulance, and Blankenship, with surprising grace, hopped up behind the stretcher. Then with a final nod from him and a thumb's-up to Sarah, they were gone.

Jeremy Mallon mumbled something to Matt about being in touch and led his two stunned associates from the shop. Debbie ran upstairs to leave a note instructing her mother to meet them at White Memorial.

Sarah, suddenly only marginally less pale than Kwong had been, sank onto the cane-back chair. Matt brought her a glass of water.

"You did an amazing job there," he said.

"I'm grateful Dr. Blankenship was here. He's the best."

"You're the one who thought of using the opium, remember? Is the old guy going to be okay?"

"I don't know. He—he's so frail. It's as if he's turned old just since the last time I saw him."

"Not like he was then?"

"Not at all. Matt, I'm in trouble, aren't I?"

"Well, that depends. Do you believe Kwong was giving you the wrong stuff all this time?"

"I don't know. I don't know what to believe."

"Well I, for one, smell a rat. What was that opium doing on the shelf like that?"

"Tian-Wen may be getting senile. He could have put it in the front window if that's the case."

"I don't buy it. At least not yet. An anonymous call to the drug hot line? Give me a break."

"What about the noni herbs? If Peter's right, and I think he is, how do you explain that?"

"I don't know. Maybe the old guy *has* messed up there. Maybe that part's legit. The opium part seems too neat, though. Too packaged."

"But you have no idea how to prove that Tian-Wen was set up—if in fact he was?"

"Not a clue."

"So I'm in trouble either way."

"Well, I will allow as how we've got some hard work

ahead of us," he said grimly. "But hard work never scared me. We'll be all right."

At that moment, Kwong's black, long-haired cat stretched to its feet, padded over to where Matt stood, and settled down on his shoes.

Chapter 21

THE BALL STARTED RIGHT, RUMBLING DOWN THE ALLEY not an inch from the gutter, much closer than Leo Durbansky would have liked. Ten men—the five on his perennial doormat Precinct Four team and five from Dorchester, the perennial Police and Fire League champions—held their collective breath as the English on the ball began to draw it back toward the one-three pocket. It was taking forever to reach the pins.

"Go, baby," Leo heard Mack Peebles whisper. "Go, baby. Go, baby."

The whole thing was straight out of *Wide World of Sports*, Leo kept thinking. The last ball of the last match of the season. The championship on the line, the Never-Won-Anythings versus the Always-Win-Everythings. And up steps Leo Durbansky, with his one-fifty average, to roll the three-game series of his life. Two forty-five, two sixty-eight, and now, maybe—just maybe, a—

Leo's maroon Brunswick slammed into the pocket with authority, exploding through nine of the pins like a howitzer shell. But the ten-pin remained standing, ticking from side to side like a metronome. Several team-mates groaned. One reached over and patted Leo on the shoulder. Then suddenly, from out of nowhere, one pin clattered back onto the alley and began spinning across it in excruciating slow motion.

The teams froze. The renegade pin, as if pulled by an invisible string, clicked against the tenner. The moment was right. The stars were right. The ten, slightly on one edge at impact, tilted past its center of gravity, teased for an interminable second, and then toppled over.

The screaming and cheering were unlike anything Leo had ever experienced. He was a twenty-year veteran pa-trolman who had done nothing to disgrace himself over those two decades, but little to distinguish himself either. Now his name and his heroics tonight would be immortalized. Mack Peebles promised to submit the story to *Sports Illustrated* for their "Faces in the Crowd" segment. Joey Kerrigan spoke about calling his cousin, who wrote sports for the *Herald*. Even the Dor-chester team bought him a beer.

It was after eleven when Leo decided it was time to head home. He had already called Jo and told her about the incredible evening and that she shouldn't wait up. But maybe, just maybe she had. The night was cool and moonless. Knowing he had had a couple of beers, Leo was driving with even more care than usual. Had he been going faster, he might have missed the movement in the darkened basement doorway just ahead of him and to his right.

Leo tapped the brakes on his Taurus and instinctively cut the lights. One man, being pushed by another, stum-bled up the short stairway. The second man, blond, was half a head or so taller than his victim. He had his hand in the pocket of his windbreaker, angled in such a way that Leo had no doubt he held a gun. Leo cut the engine, unlocked his glove compartment, and withdrew his ser-vice revolver.

Had he been in the cruiser, protocol would have de-

manded an immediate call for backup. But his own car
had no C.B. Protocol in *this* situation called for him to
take whatever cautious action seemed appropriate.
Other nights, there was no telling what he might have
decided to do. But for him, this night was charmed. He
checked the cylinder of his revolver and watched as the
shorter man was pushed, head to the floor, knees on the
seat, into the passenger side of a black or dark-blue late-
model Olds. It was a position in which the victim was
virtually helpless and easy to control. Using it suggested
that the taller man might well be a professional. Leo
moistened his lips.

He recited the license number of the Olds to himself
as he followed it through the South End and onto the
expressway. His mouth was dry, his palms damp. Still,
in spite of himself and the situation, he kept reliving his
moment of triumph at the Beantown Lanes. In his mind,
the approaching ball sounded like a timpani crescendo,
its impact on the pins like a landmine explosion.

As they crossed the Neponset Bridge, he saw some
movement through the rear window of the car ahead
and wondered if, perhaps, the guy on the floor had just
bought it. He shrugged at the notion. If it had happened,
there wasn't a damn thing he could do about it. But if it
hadn't, then this magical night held in store more than
just a bowling trophy for Leo Durbansky.

Leo was imagining how proud his wife would be of
his departmental citation, when the Olds pulled off the
bridge and down a dark, sparsely settled street. He
slowed and dropped back. This would not have been the
first corpse to be dumped in this particular area. But
now, fate had decreed that it just wasn't going to happen. His uniform was folded on the backseat. Without
taking his eyes off his quarry, Leo felt around for his
cuffs and slipped them into his pocket.

The lights on the Olds had already been cut, but Leo
could still easily make out its silhouette against the glow
from the city. It was parked by the wall of a burned-out

building. Leo spotted a couple of ways he could get close without being seen. The interior light flicked on for several seconds as the hitman opened the passenger door, shoved his captive onto the ground, and followed him out.

Perhaps not such a professional after all, Leo thought. A real pro never would have allowed the automatic interior light to go on. He reached up and flicked his to the "off" position. Then he eased his door open, slid out, and quickly dropped to one knee. He could hear the voices of the two men but was too far away to pick up any words.

With no idea how soon the hit was going to be completed, he had to get close in a hurry. His stomach was churning. An unpleasant jet of beer and bile washed up into his throat.

Be careful, he warned himself. *Just keep your cool like you did on alley nine, and you'll nail this sucker to the wall.*

He cradled his revolver, finger on the trigger, and quickly closed to within thirty yards.

"P-p-please, d-don't d-do this. I'm n-no danger t-to anyb-body."

"You've got just one minute to tell me who you've talked to about this. That's only sixty seconds. . . . Make that fifty."

"P-p-please. P-please."

The victim, stuttering almost every word, was on his knees, moaning and sobbing. Leo moved to the corner of a decaying wooden fence. He was no more than fifteen yards from the pair now. He wished to hell he had kept a flashlight in the Taurus. As it was, he had a more than decent advantage. Add a powerful flashlight beam in the blond man's eyes, and the whole thing would be a lock. He moved five feet closer. Then another five.

"Time's up," the gunman said.

"Freeze," Leo barked, his heart pounding mercilessly. "Not one move. Not one fucking—"

The blond man turned his head just a fraction. But somehow Leo knew in that moment that there was no way he was going to give up without a fight. Leo's finger was tightening on the trigger when the gunman dove to one side, spinning in the air. Leo fired a moment before he saw a pop of flame from the hurtling shadow. He heard the firecracker snap of his adversary's gun almost on top of the man's screech of pain.

Gotcha! Leo thought. *Gotcha!*

The gunman had fallen heavily and was clutching his leg, writhing from one side to the other. His stuttering victim had scrambled away and was now on his feet, sprinting off. *Probably some smalltime punk,* Leo reasoned as the man disappeared into the darkness. The prize he wanted—the headlines and the departmental citation—was rolling about on the ground in front of him. *Probably wanted,* he thought. *Maybe on the big list.*

"Okay now, asshole. Stay right where you are and don't move. I'm the police!"

Leo barked out the words. But strangely, he didn't hear any sound. He felt suddenly dizzy . . . detached . . . nauseous. . . . Only then did he become aware of the stinging on the right side of his neck, just beneath his ear. Awkwardly he reached up to touch the spot. Warm, sticky blood spewed over his hand and arm. The dizziness and nausea intensified. He sank to one knee. Then, ever so slowly, he toppled over onto his side.

The last sound Leo Durbansky heard was the enormous rumble of a thousand Brunswick bowling balls, thundering down a thousand alleys, spinning right into a thousand one-three pockets.

Chapter 22

AUGUST 29

JUST AFTER TWELVE NOON, SARAH CROSSED THROUGH the Public Garden and headed onto the Boston Common toward the spot where she was to meet Matt. The day, which had dawned hot, was sultry now. Businessmen in short-sleeved dress shirts, their ties loosened, ate their lunches beneath broad shade trees, their suit coats carefully folded on the ground beside them. All across the field where Minutemen had once trained for the Revolution, pockets of mothers in shorts and tank tops chatted languidly, their children racing about them on the rich summer grass.

Sarah wished she could just stretch out and relax. She wished that she and Matt were meeting for a picnic of pesto turkey sandwiches from Nicole's and then a leisurely stroll along the Charles. Almost anything at all, in fact, would have been preferable to what lay ahead of her. At one o'clock, she and Matt would be in a room on the second floor of the Suffolk Superior Court Building, facing a medical malpractice tribunal.

Matt, who had served on three such tribunals over the past few years, had explained the process to her in some detail, including the option that she not attend at all. He emphasized that physicians being sued seldom chose to be present at this proceeding, especially when, as was the case today, the decision was likely to go against them. But with a flexible outpatient rotation at the hospital and an almost morbid need to experience her legal battle firsthand, there was no way she could stay away.

The tribunal system, begun in Indiana and eventually adopted by Massachusetts, was an attempt to do away with frivolous litigation against physicians. It was hoped that the screening procedure would one day lower the horrific insurance premiums that continued to drive many doctors out of clinical practice. The premiums and retroactive surcharges, totaling over $100,000 annually for some specialists, were a major cause of spiraling health care costs. And adequate coverage was mandatory in the state for licensure. Those physicians who wished to continue practicing in Massachusetts had no choice but to increase their patient load and order more and more "defensive" laboratory tests.

The tribunal, made up of a judge, an attorney, and a physician of the same specialty as the defendant, was not set up to determine guilt or innocence, Matt explained. The only question to be answered today was: Assuming Lisa Grayson's allegations are true, has malpractice occurred?—or in legal terms: Do she and her attorneys have a *prima facie* case?

"The tribunals find in favor of the plaintiff much more often than not," Matt had explained. "But even in cases where they lose in tribunal, plaintiffs can proceed to trial if they are willing to post a bond—in Massachusetts it's six thousand dollars—to cover court costs and the defendant's legal fees. And even then, the judge can waive the bond if he doesn't believe the plaintiff can afford it. That's obviously not an issue with the Graysons."

A scuffed, grass-stained baseball bounced off the lawn and rolled over the sidewalk, just in front of where Sarah was walking. She picked it up and threw it overhand to the teen who was chasing it. The youth, possibly Hispanic, gloved the toss with reflexive ease and smiled shyly at her from beneath a Red Sox cap.

"Not a bad arm for a girl, huh, Ricky?" she heard Matt call out.

He waved to her from across an expanse of grass and then left the group of boys he had been playing with and loped over. He had on sneakers, a Greenpeace T-shirt, and the trousers to his suit. As he spoke, he gestured with his well-worn mitt as if it were part of his hand.

"Ricky, thanks for the catch," he said as he passed the youth. "That fork-ball of yours is really starting to move. Hey, maybe I'll see you guys tomorrow."

"He's cute," Sarah said.

"He's a felon," Matt replied. "Just kidding . . . sort of. Those kids out there are a gang. *Los Muchachos*. A couple of years ago, the court assigned the defense of two of them to me. Nothing too serious, fortunately. Anyhow, I showed them some of my press clippings— only the good ones, of course—and we sort of got to be pals. Now the whole gang is playing ball, and a number of them are working with younger kids. Ricky, there, actually made his high school team. He's got some talent."

"You made all that happen?"

"Hell, no. *They* made it happen. I just let them know there was nothing uncool about beating up on a baseball instead of someone's head. Next week will mark the end of Ricky's probation. I got a couple of box seat tickets to a Sox–Baltimore game. I originally got them for me and Harry—that's my son. But he had to go back home for some summer school. So I'm taking Ricky instead. It was supposed to be a surprise, but I've already told him. I'm not much good at surprises."

"Where does Harry live?" Sarah asked.

A shadow of sadness darkened Matt's face. "California," he said.

His tone discouraged further questions on the subject.

After a few uncomfortably silent moments, he smiled thinly and nodded toward the far side of the Common. "My office is that way."

Sarah was relieved to turn away from his pain and just walk.

Matt's work clothes were in his office, which was on the fifth floor of a converted brownstone. The three-room suite was not nearly as dismal or disorganized as he had painted it to be, Sarah pointed out.

"Everything's relative," he said. "Unfortunately, in this law business, with more attorneys around here than scrod, image counts. Sometime, just for the hell of it, I'll take you to visit Jeremy Mallon's place."

"Spare me," Sarah said.

He introduced her to his secretary, a pleasant, motherly woman named Ruth. Sarah could tell she was eager for conversation even before a word between them was spoken.

"Mr. Daniels is a wonderful man," Ruth began, moments after Matt had gone into the inner office to change.

"He seems that way."

"A good lawyer, too. And a great father. He says you're the most important client he's ever had. He always works hard, but I've never seen him put in hours like he has on your case."

"That's reassuring."

Sarah smiled a little uncomfortably and scanned the narrow coffee table for a magazine of any remote interest to her. She ended up with a dog-eared, four-month-old copy of *Consumer Reports*. The message she had hoped to deliver to Ruth went unreceived.

"He's here when I leave at night," she prattled on, "and he's here when I arrive in the morning. That lady he was seeing just couldn't understand how important building up this practice is to him, after what's happened with Harry and all. I think that's why she broke it off, because he wasn't paying enough attention to her. I never liked her much anyway. Too snobby, if you know what I mean. Mr. Daniels can do better."

Suddenly Sarah felt torn between asking the woman to stop sharing such personal information about her boss and grilling her for every bit of data she could deliver. She settled on a middle-of-the-road approach.

"What's happened with Harry?" she asked, reflecting on the sadness in Matt's face and thinking the worst.

"Oh, it's not Harry. It's that ex of his. A few years ago, she as much as kidnapped the boy and up and moved to California. Los Angeles, no less. Mr. Daniels fought her in court, but he got no place—even though everybody knows that she drinks too much, and he'd be a much better parent for him."

"That's very sad."

"You said it. And he cares too much about Harry to refuse anything that *woman* asks. Private school. Summer school. Extra money for clothes. Plus the cost of flying him here and back whenever she *permits* it. I write a lot of the checks, so I know how much *he* pays for those trips. I think that's why this case of yours is so important to him. If he does well with it, the medical insurance company will probably send more business his way. Am . . . am I talking too much? Mr. Daniels keeps scolding me for talking too much to the clients. But the truth is, if there were more clients, I'd probably do less talking, if you know what I mean."

Sarah wondered how long she would have to know her laconic attorney, and how well, before learning as much about him as she had in just two or three minutes with his secretary. At that moment, the ancient intercom on Ruth's desk crackled.

"Sarah, I'm sorry to be taking so long," Matt said. "I called a client about a small matter, and he's had me on hold forever. I won't be much longer. Ruth, take a break from whatever you're doing and entertain her. We don't want her to think we're one of those stuffy, aloof firms."

• • •

The Suffolk Superior Court Building, a granite relic, was a five-minute walk from Matt's office.

"I want to be sure you're not expecting something out of Perry Mason," he said as they waited at a light to cross Washington Street. "Today Mallon gets to put on the gloves and hammer us as mercilessly as he wants—affidavits, letters from experts, the works. After he's done, we get to regale the tribunal with arguments that are roughly equivalent to alleging that Mallon's mother wears army boots. This is the first fire fight we'll be in, only they get to have guns and we don't. So it's not going to be very pleasant. But just remember, it's only a skirmish."

"It sounds awful."

"Don't worry, we'll have our chance. Just don't get rattled by what you hear. As you were told that day in Mr. Kwong's shop, these people are not your friends. I saw him yesterday, by the way."

"Tian-Wen?"

"Yes. I've been over there a few times. I dropped him as a client because of conflict of interest with your case, but I got him Angela Cord. She's an excellent attorney. I really like the old guy. By the way, he says you haven't been by to see him since he got out of the hospital."

"With all that's happening to me I—I just haven't wanted to go. He's a sweet old man. I feel sorry about his getting sick, and then being charged for having that opium. But the truth is, I'm angry, too. That *was* his opium. He doesn't deny it."

"Yes," Matt said. "But as I recall, you're the one who reminded me that his smoking opium was cultural, not criminal. Besides, he keeps denying ever having opium in his shop. And he still maintains that even if he had smoked fifty times his customary pipeful, he could never have confused that noni herb with chamomile—"

"But he did. Denying responsibility doesn't alter reality. Matt, I've smoked opium. A number of times when I was in Thailand. I know what it can do. And it's quite possible that because of carelessness, or old age, or opium, or some combination of the three, Tian-Wen screwed up. And because of his errors—his mistakes in preparing my supplement—people have died."

"I don't buy it."

"Well, I certainly hope not. You're my lawyer. But until you can prove someone set him up, including *who*, and *why*, I've got to believe that he might have been responsible for what happened to those women. And that makes me just as responsible for using him."

They rounded the corner of the concrete and granite mall that fronted the Superior Court Building. Ahead of them, a small group of demonstrators—perhaps twenty —milled about. A single, uniformed policeman kept them back from the steps. Off to one side, a camera crew from Channel 7 was interviewing one of the demonstrators, a gaunt, bearded man who was wearing a full-length, hooded, crimson robe.

"I don't like the looks of this," Matt muttered, stopping some distance away to assess the situation.

"What's it all about?"

"Unless I miss my guess, it's about you. Did you see the *Herald* this morning?"

Sarah shook her head. "I was in the clinic working at seven. I barely had time for a cup of coffee. Don't tell me I made it again."

"You *and* your hospital, actually. On page four there's an article about some grant that MCB has just received to build a huge new center to scientifically study certain areas of alternative healing. Is there a Charlton Building?"

"It's the Chilton Building," Sarah said. "It's deserted and boarded up now. In a few months they're going to demolish it to begin work on the center. But that's old hat. Everyone at MCB's known about that for weeks."

"Well, it's news to the *Herald*. And right across from

that item, on page five, is the announcement that you're going before a malpractice tribunal today. Axel Devlin mentioned it as well. 'The beginning of the end for Dr. Flake' is the way I think he put it. Something like that. My office got several calls wanting to know details. I didn't speak to anyone, but Ruth told me it sounded like somebody was organizing a demonstration on your behalf. And I think this must be it."

"Oh, no," she moaned.

"There's no back way into this place unless prior arrangements are made. I don't think we have any choice but to run the gauntlet. So, as your attorney, I'm suggesting you limit your vocabulary for the next minute to four words: 'Thank you' and 'No comment.' Okay?"

"No comment . . . thank you," Sarah said.

The small demonstration was made up primarily of practitioners of various forms of alternative healing. Sarah recognized some of them, including a very talented chiropractor and an acupuncturist who was once a full professor in Beijing. There were also three women who had taken Sarah's supplement, had normal labor, and delivered without incident. Two of them carried their infants with them in backpacks.

As Sarah and Matt approached, the group fell back and applauded.

"Hang in there," one called out.

"Good luck, Doctor," a woman said. "We're behind you."

She carried a handmade sign that read:

ALTERNATIVE HEALERS REALLY CARE

The specter in the red robe broke off his interview with Channel 7 and rushed over, extending a bony hand.

"Dr. Misha Korkopovitch, energy healing and shamanism," he said. "We're with you all the way, Dr. Baldwin. You're bringing us all together like nothing else ever has."

"Thank you," Sarah managed, as Matt whisked her up the stairs. "Matt, this is very strange and a little hard to take. Some of those people I revere as healers. Some, like that Misha, are probably kooks."

Matt glanced back as they entered the building. "Not much different than if they were a group of M.D.'s, right?" he said.

". . . Let's look at what we have here, and how we intend to prove our case. . . ."

Jeremy Mallon consulted his notes briefly and then began a slow strut before the tribunal. He was closely observed from the plaintiff's table by two other attorneys, one about his age and one quite a bit older.

"Grayson's lawyers," Matt whispered.

He nodded toward the courtroom, which had been nearly empty when they arrived. Several of the demonstrators had taken seats. And now Willis Grayson and an entourage of four were making their way down a row. Before Sarah could look away, Grayson's cool gray eyes found hers. The power and anger in them made her shudder. As she returned her attention to Mallon, she wondered about Lisa—how she was doing, and whether she had been given the option of attending today.

The physician on the tribunal, an obstetrician from Harvard named Rita Dunleavy, and the attorney, a balding, rumpled man named Keefe, were squeezed in behind the bench beside Judge Judah Land, according to Matt an implacable veteran of twenty-five years or more on the bench.

Mallon's opening remarks had included the words dangerous, reckless, irresponsible, negligent, arrogant, substandard, flawed, and fatal. Sarah, he alleged, had prescribed a potentially powerful set of drugs to patients who were at their most sensitive and vulnerable—those readying their bodies to give birth.

"Given the lack of control over herbal medicines," Mallon went on, "there are any number of points between the soil in Southeast Asia and the bloodstream of a woman in Boston where something can go awry. Our offer of proof today consists of letters from an obstetrician, Dr. Raymond Gorfinkle, and from a non-M.D. specialist in herbal medicine, Mr. Harold Ling. The letters from these two experts make it clear that Dr. Baldwin acted outside of standard medical practice in prescribing an herbal supplement for her patients in place of prenatal vitamins, and outside of standard holistic practice in the manner in which her supplement was prepared and dispensed. Specifically, Mr. Ling's letter questions the competence of the herbal pharmacist who ordered the herbs and then compounded the medicinals prescribed by Dr. Baldwin."

Mallon then proceeded to read the two condemning letters out loud. Gorfinkle, an obstetrician operating out of West Roxbury, stressed that in thirty plus years of practice, he had seen all manner of rites and rituals used by his patients. Some of those he felt were unhealthy, some innocuous. But never had he seen any broad deviation from the norm *at the request of a physician*. In his opinion, in Boston, Massachusetts, in the 1990s, substituting herbs of any kind for FDA-approved prenatal vitamins constituted substandard medicine.

Ling, an herbalist from New York's Chinatown, was no less damning. Herbal supplements had their place in maintaining health, he wrote, but only in small amounts, and only when provided by an established, responsible herbal pharmacist. It was his opinion that Kwong Tian-Wen, a well-known chronic opium abuser, was neither established nor responsible. He further felt that noni, the herb in the jar that Kwong believed contained chamomile, could well cause problems with blood clotting.

"Ling is one of Peter's oldest friends," Sarah whispered. "And Gorfinkle is just a hired gun. He makes a fortune testifying against other doctors."

"I'm not surprised," Matt said. "I'm sure my ex-wife

would love the chance to do to me what Ettinger is doing to you."

"Mr. Daniels," Judge Land said, with a weariness in his voice that suggested Matt might as well remain mute, "you have about five minutes to present your arguments. You know that no letters from experts or other evidence will be considered from your side at this time."

"I do know that, your Honor, yes. Thank you. . . . Sarah, listen," he whispered. "I don't want to say anything now that will give Mallon a clue as to what part of his case we intend to home in on. As things stand, I can't see how we can win here. So we can only hurt ourselves."

"I understand." But Sarah wasn't at all certain she did.

"Your Honor, Dr. Dunleavy, Mr. Keefe," Matt said, eschewing the pacing tactics of his opponent and allowing just a hint of drawl into his speech. "What we're all looking for today is the presentation of a *prima facie* case from my colleague, Mr. Mallon. But what we have gotten instead is a very impressive smoke screen. What's missing? What void is Mr. Mallon trying to hide behind all that smoke? Well, I suspect you see the answer to those questions as well as I do. He's trying to hide the fact that he has nothing that connects action taken or not taken by Dr. Sarah Baldwin with the development of DIC in Lisa Grayson.

"Frankly, with what little substantive material he has produced today, I'm surprised Mr. Mallon has the gumption even to bring this case before a tribunal. We've heard a *shouldn't have* from Dr. Gorfinkle and a *could possibly have* from Mr. Ling, but those are the weakest speculations. There's no science here, no expert saying that what this caring, dedicated physician did was wrong, and that because—*because*—of her alleged actions, an infant was stillborn and her mother gravely injured. Without such an expert, Mr. Mallon has failed to prove his *prima facie* case. On that basis, I request a dismissal of the charges against my client."

"Bravo," Sarah whispered after Matt sat down. "Bravo."

"Bullshit," he whispered back.

"What?"

"I'm the one whipping up a smoke screen. And you can see by the faces on our panel up there that they know it. Mallon's done more than he had to to win here."

The judge thanked the participants, promised to have a decision within the hour, and dismissed the tribunal.

Matt spoke not at all as they left the courthouse and headed back toward his office.

"Well?" Sarah asked finally.

"Well, what?"

"Well, what do you think?"

"Think about what?" He seemed distracted and perplexed.

"About what just went on in there, of course," she said irritably.

"I think we lost."

"So what? You told me that was going to happen before we even went in."

"That doesn't make me feel any better about it. We were pretty much hammered in there. And Mallon did it without even working up a sweat." He sank down on a curbside bench. "Sarah, listen," he went on. "Dead babies and maimed young women make juries angry. Sometimes very angry. I don't know how solid a link Mallon's going to be able to forge between Mr. Kwong's herbs and Lisa Grayson's DIC, or even if a judge is going to allow him to introduce the two other DIC cases. But my sense is that with Kwong's drug arrest, and frail, pretty, one-armed Lisa coming forward to testify, he'll be able to pluck enough emotional chords to make a jury stick the burden of proof on us. And that's a position the defense never wants to be in."

There was a nervousness about him, a tension in his

eyes and the set of his jaw, that Sarah had never seen before.

"Maybe you should go right to the bottom line," she said.

He looked up, startled that she had read him so quickly and so accurately. "Well, the bottom line is that there's an option available to us that I haven't discussed with you, but that I think we ought to seriously consider."

"Namely."

Black Cat Daniels chewed at his lower lip and scuffed at a cigarette butt with the toe of his shoe.

"Namely, to quit," he said.

Chapter 23

THE THREE-FAMILY CLAPBOARD TENEMENT WAS ON A dead-end street in a decaying section of Dorchester. It was badly in need of new shingles, gutters, and a coat of paint. Lugging a heavy briefcase, Rosa Suarez trudged up the front walk. Her datagathering was well along now, but nothing had yet emerged to explain the three DIC patients at the Medical Center of Boston.

At her urging, the CDC had sent out requests to hundreds of hospitals searching for other, similar cases. But those that had been reported so far all had logical, well-established explanations such as *abruptio placentae*, toxemia, or overwhelming infection.

Now, in hopes of stirring up something that she might have overlooked, Rosa was retracing some steps. She was starting with follow-up interviews with the families of the two deceased victims and later in the week with Lisa Grayson. At the same time, she planned to check and recheck the massive number of cultures she was running.

Although her supervisor had said little to her directly, the first signs of his impatience had already surfaced in the form of a brief memo. Dr. Wayne Werner, senior field epidemiologist, would be finished with his current project and would be available for reassignment in three to four weeks, it read. Anyone in the department needing Werner's help with an ongoing investigation should submit a request in writing within the next two weeks. Rosa knew that the memo was at least a demand for some sort of likely hypothesis from her, and at worst a threat that she was soon to be replaced.

The name crudely painted just above the mail slot of the first-floor flat was BARAHONA. Fredy Barahona, a laborer, was home all day, every day, drawing disability for a back problem. His wife, Maria, was working the night shift in a sneaker factory. Maria's daughter by her previous marriage, and the only child she would ever conceive, was Constanza Hidalgo.

Rosa was feeling the strain of her intensive investigation, now nearly seven weeks along. She had lost weight, quarreled with her husband for the first time in several years, and developed an annoying tic at the corner of one eye. But she was frightened enough and determined enough to keep pushing herself to the limit. She desperately wanted to leave her profession a winner. More important, she wanted to head off what she firmly believed was impending disaster.

Someone had deliberately torn pages from the hospital records of at least two of the three DIC cases she was investigating. Sarah Baldwin was being followed and had been accosted once. And the meticulous research techniques that had served Rosa so faithfully over the years were not delivering. She felt as if she were tiptoeing around a ticking bomb, with no clear idea how to disarm it. The only thing that seemed certain to her at this point was that unless answers were found, and soon, more women and their unborn infants were going to die.

Maria Barahona was a plump, work-weary woman who had almost surely been quite attractive at one time in her life. She kept up a cheery front, but the pain of losing her only child showed in her eyes. Once, during Rosa's initial interview with her, she had begun to weep. But just as quickly she composed herself, apologized, and went on answering questions. Now, with her husband across the room, dozing on a tattered recliner, she served Rosa tea and talked once again of Connie. Although her English was decent enough, she seemed relieved to be conversing in Spanish.

"There were drugs in the car, you know," she said. "They told us Connie had marijuana in her blood, but I don't believe it. She was a happy girl. A good girl, too. And so, so beautiful. Her only crime was falling in love with that bastard, Billy Molinaro. Please, Mrs. Suarez, please. Forgive me for swearing."

"Mrs. Barahona, there is no need for you to apologize."

"She was so beautiful. You should have seen her, Mrs. Suarez. Men would just stop what they were doing and stare when she walked by. We had already picked out her boy's name. Guillermo. Even though he would have been called Billy, Connie was going to spell it the Spanish way."

As she had during their first interview, Maria Barahona was rambling. She was once again nearing tears. Rosa broke in somewhat desperately.

"Mrs. Barahona," she said, "somewhere between three and five years ago your daughter was treated for something at the Medical Center of Boston. Would you have any idea at all what that was?"

Some of the anguish left the woman's face as she focused on Rosa's question.

"I—I don't remember anything. She had some headaches and some stomach trouble—especially with, you know, her monthly. But nothing that didn't get better when she took medicine. She always had great faith in the doctors at the Medical Center. If they said take this pill at three minutes after four, my Constanza sat looking at her watch until three minutes after four."

Another dead end. Rosa stared at the floor, trying to imagine Connie Hidalgo's mounting terror during those last nightmarish hours of her life. Was there anything else? Anything at all she could try?

"Mrs. Barahona, Maria, I know that Connie was living with Billy Molinaro," she said finally. "When did she leave home for good?"

"They were planning a wedding," Maria said, obviously embarrassed. "And she still spent many nights here. Many nights."

"Please, Maria. I'm sorry. I didn't mean to imply anything at all. I just wondered if her room still had her things in it. That's all. If it does, with your permission I'd like to check it over."

"Oh. Well, if you think it might help, certainly you can look at anything you want. It's the room back there on the right. I haven't changed anything. If you don't mind, though, I'd like to get dinner started. I work the night shift, you know."

"I know," Rosa said, glancing over at Fredy Barahona, who was in need of a shave and hadn't so much as stirred since her arrival. She wondered if he had ever prepared a meal on his own, and reflected momentarily on how lucky she was to have spent forty years married to Alberto Suarez. "Thank you, Maria. I'll be fine."

Connie Hidalgo's bedroom spoke of a woman who had never really stopped being a little girl. The bureau and bed, possibly painted by Connie herself, were white with pink accents. The pillow cases, also pink, were frilly, with hand-painted teddy bears and balloons. And there were stuffed animals everywhere—a hundred or more. Zebras and elephants; bears and orangutans; kittens and all manner of dogs. The walls were covered with posters of romantic island getaways and neon-lit cities. Rosa swallowed against the sadness in her throat. Despite the marijuana reported in Connie's bloodstream, Rosa sensed she would have developed into a loving, devoted parent.

Rosa took a framed five-by-seven snapshot from the bureau and raised the window shade to view it in better light. Connie, looking even more vibrant than in the newspaper photo Rosa had in her files, stood arm in arm with a swarthy, handsome, confidently grinning young man, whom Rosa was certain was Billy Molinaro. The snapshot was taken on board a boat of some sort, possibly the sightseeing kind. Behind them was the distinctive skyline of Manhattan. Connie, copper skinned, slender, and full breasted, was absolutely lovely.

Uncertain of what she was after, Rosa first checked the bureau drawers and then the contents of the small bookcase. The books were mostly paperback romances and library books that had never been returned. There were no photo albums or scrapbooks, but there was a yearbook—*The Sword and Rose*—from St. Cecilia's High School. The yearbook was clearly low budget—a far cry from the glossy, full-color productions Rosa had seen from other high schools, including the one her daughters had attended.

She skimmed through the pages of black-and-white photos, searching for some that included Connie. There were, at least on first perusal, none. Nor were there many messages from classmates. The few she read were hardly passionate: *All the best to a terrific kid. . . . We didn't know each other well, but I hope you have a wonderful life. . . . Good luck from your friend in Latin 213. . . .* Rosa glanced again at the radiant, sensuous woman sharing a harbor cruise with the dashing young man who was to become her husband. The tepid comments from Connie's schoolmates did not jibe at all with that woman.

Rosa flipped to the class photos at the back of the book. Where her daughters' yearbooks had four good-sized color portraits per page, *The Sword and Rose* had ten—all black-and-white. Printed in minute type beside each photograph was a summary of that student's activities during her years at St. Cecilia's. Constanza Hidalgo had been a cafeteria aide and a member of the culinary arts club. Nothing else. No music, no drama, no sports. Rosa stared at Connie's photograph. Even allowing for the fact that the portrait was slightly out of focus, Rosa doubted she would have been able to identify its subject without being told.

Once again she held up the framed snapshot. The girl in the yearbook was most certainly the woman with Billy Molinaro . . . yet she wasn't. The mouth was the same, and the eyes, too, although they held none of the spark that Rosa saw in the more recent picture. But the face in the yearbook was much rounder and very much less interesting. It was as if someone had taken a paring knife and carved away the younger Connie's plainness.

Rosa set the yearbook on the bed and completed her inspection of the room. There was nothing else of interest in the bookcase or on the floor. She opened the small closet. Along with two maternity dresses, there were a number of fairly chic outfits and dresses, all size six, and a dozen or more pairs of shoes. If what Rosa was seeing were the clothes Connie had chosen *not* to move to Billy Molinaro's place, the former cafeteria aide and cooking club member had become a legitimate candidate for any best-dressed list.

The floor of the closet, like much of the room, was covered with stuffed animals. Rosa would never know what caught her eye, or what instinct made her bend down and move part of the pile aside. But there beneath the bears, snow leopards, and toucans was a shoe box, bound with rubber bands.

And inside the shoe box was a diary.

* * * *

Matt delighted his secretary by sending her home for the remainder of the afternoon. Then Sarah and he split the corned beef sandwich and fries they had picked up at Gold's and talked for a time about absolutely nothing of any importance.

"Do you have to be back at the hospital soon?" he asked, as he poured coffee for them from the carafe of a well-used Mr. Coffee.

"I have some patients to sign out to the on-call doc, some dictation I need to do, and I have to get my bike. But I'm okay for a little longer."

"Good. There are some things we ought to go over."

"Like quitting?"

"Like understanding what we're up against here, and how malpractice underwriters like the MMPO operate."

The tension that Sarah had seen develop in her lawyer over the course of the past six weeks seemed indelibly etched across his brow. When they had met initially, her innocence—their case—had seemed so clear-cut, so straightforward. *Now?* She sipped at her coffee and asked him to continue.

"First of all," he said, "I want you to know that I think something's screwy with this whole business. I know you're not convinced, but I believe someone set Kwong Tian-Wen up to make him—and you—appear responsible for those three DIC women."

"But as things stand, we have no proof that he and I are not responsible. Only Tian-Wen's word."

"And his family's. We can put together a defense based on the presumption that someone's out to make you look guilty. But without *who* and *why*, it won't hold up."

"Meaning, if we pursue this into court, we'll lose."

"Sarah, we're really up against it." His voice drifted away. His fist was clenched.

"But, hey," she said, "aren't you the one who told me that more often than not, the legal system manages to sort out what's truth and what isn't?"

" 'More often than not' is still not *always*. Things aren't that simple in this case. Tian-Wen's frail. He gets confused a lot. I might be able to get a doctor's excuse to keep him off the stand. But that's a long shot because he's not that bad off anymore. And even if we succeed, Mallon will just depose him at home, maybe use closed circuit TV. One way or another, the jury will get to meet him up close and personal, as they say."

"But how will Mallon explain why so many women who took my supplement had no problem?"

"I suspect you know the answer to that."

"You mean he'll just claim that Tian-Wen messed up with some batches and not with others."

"Or else that the incorrect herb or herbs reacted with some women and, for whatever reason, not with others. In this situation, he just has to have a response that works. It doesn't necessarily have to be right. With Lisa Grayson on their side, and Kwong Tian-Wen on ours, and the penchant of juries to think they're settling claims against megabucks insurance companies, not flesh-and-blood people, I'm afraid it's going to boil down to our having to prove in court that we're *not* at fault. I can just see Mallon now."

He picked up his baseball and mitt, and began pacing, popping the ball into the pocket as he spoke.

"'This lovely young artist, with two good, strong arms and a healthy fetus, puts her faith and trust in Dr. Sarah Baldwin. Dr. Baldwin does something unusual and irregular to the lovely, pregnant young artist with two good strong arms—something well beyond the accepted norm for her medical community. And suddenly, the lovely young artist loses her baby and her right arm. Since nothing else happened during our lovely young artist's pregnancy, Dr. Baldwin must prove to this court that she was not the cause of this tragedy.'"

"That sounds gruesome."

"In legal terms, that little twist at the end is called *res ipse loquitor*—the thing, or deed, speaks for itself. It's a legal gun barrel that no defense lawyer ever wants to find himself staring down. But it happens—especially, from what I've been able to read, in medical malpractice trials."

"I thought I was supposed to be innocent until proven guilty."

"If Mallon gets a judge to accept *res ipse loquitor*, and we can't prove that you are *not* responsible, we're cooked. What's more, if we lose here, two more families are almost certain to go after what insurance you have left, and whatever else you own or *may ever* own." He stopped pacing and sank back into his chair.

"What do you think we should do?" she asked.

"Well, before I answer that, there's one more thing you ought to know. It has to do with Willis Grayson. It's been troubling me almost since the beginning of this case. Finally, today, seeing him and his legal army in that hearing room, I think I know what it is. Sarah, he doesn't want just to see you lose this case. He wants to bury you."

"I—I don't understand," she said, feeling suddenly chilly.

"The way I see it, Grayson's got more money than God, right?"

"I suppose."

"I'm sure he's not adverse to winning sixty percent of a huge jury award. But my guess is it still wouldn't equal the interest he earns on his personal checking account. The way I put it together, Mallon's in it for the money and to stick it to your hospital. But Grayson wants you, or whoever is responsible for Lisa's tragedy, to be put away for a long, long time."

"I can't believe this. Willis Grayson out to destroy *me*. It's crazy, absolutely crazy. But do you want to know what's even crazier, Matt? The absolute craziest thing of all? I don't even know whether he's justified or not."

"I told you how I feel about that."

"I know. What do you think we should do?"

"Well, we can try for some sort of settlement without

admission of guilt. I'm not sure I can get the MMPO, Mallon, or Grayson to buy it, but you never know. It's sort of a Mexican standoff. Our side says we would have won at trial, but the legal fees would have been higher than the settlement. The other side says that even though there's no admission of guilt, the fact that the MMPO paid up implies that they were right to sue. Then the rhetoric dies down and everybody goes back to his life. Before you know it, the ripples go away and the big pond is still again."

"We can do that?"

"We can try."

"And you think we should."

Matt pressed his fingertips into a steeple and stared out the window. The creases traversing his brow deepened.

"If they'd accept, the answer is yes," he said finally. "Yes, I think we should."

"I need to think about it. How long do I have?"

"A week, maybe. A little longer if you need it."

"Thanks."

She felt distracted, ill at ease, and suddenly very tired. *Kwong Tian-Wen . . . Mallon . . . Lisa . . . Willis Grayson . . . the hospital . . . goddamn Peter . . . criminal charges . . . further lawsuits . . . How could the case once have seemed so simple?* She set her cup down and turned to go.

"I'll drive you back to the hospital," Matt said.

"That's okay."

"No. I—I want to. I want to very much."

Sarah turned back to him, but he quickly looked away and began loading papers into his briefcase.

I want to. I want to very much. Had he really just said that?

"Offer accepted," she replied.

Matt fixed his gaze on the rear end of the car ahead of them as he inched his red Legacy away from the city.

Sarah would never have imagined a situation in which she was grateful for heavy traffic, but she was this afternoon. The ride from Matt's downtown office to MCB, which should have taken fifteen minutes, was going to take closer to forty. Except for some small talk unrelated to the case, they rode in silence. She looked at him directly when she was speaking, but continued to study his face out of the corner of her eye when she wasn't. The timing couldn't have been much worse, she told herself. Falling for the attorney representing her in a malpractice case was hardly the wisest thing in the world. But it was happening. And there really wasn't a damn thing she could do about it.

Though he hadn't actually said so, she sensed Matt was attracted to her as well. But there were ethical issues that would be pressuring him neither to act on those feelings nor even to voice them. Perhaps if they could settle her case, those considerations could be set to rest, and they could get on with the business of really getting to know one another and possibly even falling in love.

But before she agreed to try and settle, there was something she had to know. "Matt, tell me. If you could script this whole legal thing exactly the way you wanted —the way that would benefit *you* the most—how would it go?"

He looked at her strangely. "What a funny question. What do you mean the way that would benefit me the most?"

"Financially, career-wise. You know."

She debated, then rejected, the notion of sharing with him what Ruth had told her. The woman was too gabby, and probably a professional liability to him, but it seemed premature to make trouble.

For a moment, she was afraid Matt was about to guess that she knew more about his situation than he had shared with her.

"Well," he said finally, "I suppose if the hypothetical options were placed in order, the number-one most desirable would be a knock-down, drag-out court battle against Jeremy Mallon that generated a ton of publicity and fees for me, followed by a jury verdict of no negligence for you."

"And the number-one *least* desirable?"

"The same exact scenario, I suppose, except that we lose. That would pretty much finish me as far as malpractice cases go, to say nothing of referrals. In this game, everybody knows who wins and who doesn't. And nobody likes to put their life on the line with an established loser."

"Is that why you recommend that we try to settle?"

He slammed on the brakes and glared at her, oblivious to the blaring horn behind him.

"Is that what you think?" he asked.

"I—I'm sorry. No, that's not what I think, and it's not what I meant. Dammit, Matt, I'm not putting things together too clearly. I just want this whole business to be over."

His expression quickly softened. He reached over and squeezed her hand. Then he pulled over to the curb. "Sarah, I'd let someone put bamboo splinters under my fingernails if I thought it would help us win in court. But I've been working like hell on every angle I can think of, and I keep running into dead ends. If I'm pushing too hard to settle, it's probably because today just gave me a firsthand feel for what it's going to be like.

"Still, if it's what you want, or if they refuse our offer, I'm ready to dig in and do battle. You probably don't know much about relief pitchers, but we're notoriously lacking in the part of the brain that tells a person there is legitimate reason to be frightened of something. Suggesting we settle is what I think is best for *you*. It may be best for me, too, but believe me, that's incidental. Think about it, though. This case has already generated more publicity than most, and it hasn't really even started. If we go to trial, you're going to be the featured performer in a three-ring circus like you couldn't imagine. Axel Devlin will be just one of your problems."

"I understand. Matt, I'm sorry for what I said before. I'll let you know as soon as I decide."

He nodded and pulled back into the traffic.

"Don't worry," he said. "One way or the other, things will work out. And no matter what happens . . ."

"Yes?" *Go ahead, Matt, say it,* she urged silently. *Tell me that no matter what happens, we'll face it together. Tell me how happy you are that we've met.*

"I—um—I just want you to know I'm behind you one hundred percent."

Two silent minutes later, he pulled to a stop by the main entrance to MCB. Sarah thanked him and momentarily considered sharing her own feelings. Finally she turned away. He had enough pressure on him as it was. If she was reading him wrong, she would just be adding to it.

She entered the campus through the security gate and headed toward the surgical building where she had left her bicycle. A short ride through the arboretum would be just the ticket before her long-overdue session in the dictation carrel. *To settle or to fight?* Her thoughts were racing. Distracted, she was just a few yards from the surgical building before she realized what had happened.

A bucket of paint—bright red enamel—had been poured over her bike. Tied onto the seat was a rag doll, also drenched in glistening scarlet. One of its arms had been ripped off and dropped on the ground. Its abdomen had been slashed open. Pinned to its chest was a crudely written sign that read

KILLER QUACK

Sarah tried, unsuccessfully, to keep calm. Tears streaming down her cheeks, she raced into the surgical building. Her first call was to hospital security. Her second was to Matt.

"Please call me at the hospital, Matt," she said to his answering machine. "It's very important that I see you as soon as possible. I've decided what I want to do."

Chapter 24

THE TISSUE CULTURES ARE RUINED. ALL OF THEM. This has never happened before. Absolutely never."

The distraught microbiology technician, a bright young man named Chris Hall, shook his head in disbelief. Rosa patted his arm consolingly, although in truth she was probably the more upset of the two of them.

"When did you check them last?" she asked.

"Yesterday afternoon. I go through the incubators each afternoon. It's not just your stuff that's been lost, it's everything. Dozens and dozens of experiments and cultures are gone. God, I just can't believe this. Dr. Wheelock, Dr. Caro, Dr. Blankenship—they're all going to be furious. I changed the growth media yesterday, and the stuff I threw away was perfect—crystal clear. Somehow, the replacement media must have been contaminated with some kind of cytotoxin."

"Easy does it, Chris," Rosa said. "These things happen. Anyone who's ever done any microbiology understands it—especially anyone who's worked with tissue cultures." Unlike bacteria, which were grown in the lab-

oratory on top of solid, nutrient agar, viruses could only
be grown within sheets of living, multiplying cells—tissue cultures. "Show me a lab that's never had any problem with tissue culture contamination," she went on,
"and I'll show you a lab that's not getting any work
done. Do you have any frozen backup specimens?"

"Some."

"Any of the specimens I gave you?"

"I don't think so. Dr. Suarez, I'm sorry. I really am."

"Chris, listen. If you did it on purpose, you may apologize. Otherwise, just go and get your lab back in shape,
and don't worry. We'll do fine."

She was determined not to add to the earnest technician's distress by snapping at him. But a pounding,
fatigue-and-frustration-driven headache was making her
more irritable every second. In fact, although she would
not share the information with Chris Hall no matter
what, the lost cultures were not the disaster they might
have been—at least not yet. Because of BART, she had
become nearly paranoid about backing up even the most
trivial work. She had sent duplicates of everything to
Ken Mulholland, an old friend at the CDC lab in Atlanta. At last check, a week or so ago, he had found
nothing.

"I hope the others are as understanding as you are,"
Chris said.

"Oh, I'm sure they will be. Do you have the log book
of the cultures you were running for me?"

He handed over a standard, cardboard-bound lab
notebook, with R. Suarez written on the cover. Rosa
opened her briefcase and laid the notebook on top of
Connie Hidalgo's diäry. After some Tylenol and a nap,
the diary would be her next project.

"Did I mention that I was just beginning to see something in a couple of your bottles?" Chris asked.

"No. No, you didn't."

"I marked the specimens with stars in the margin of
the log book, so I could check them a little more fre-

quently. It was nothing definite, mind you; just the slight rattiness of the tissue sheet that we sometimes see during early infection. We see the same sort of changes when the tissue cells themselves are running out of gas. That's when we know we need to thaw out a new batch."

"Thank you, Chris. I'll break the code when I get back to my room and see which specimens were in those bottles."

"If those cultures *were* starting to grow something—and I really doubt they were—whatever it was would be the slowest-growing virus I've ever encountered."

"It's probably nothing. I appreciate your telling me, Chris. And also how cooperative you've been. I'll drop a note to Dr. Blankenship and tell him the same thing."

"Thanks. After this disaster, I'll need it."

Rosa fished two Extra-Strength Tylenols from her purse, swallowed them with a drink from one of MCB's ubiquitous tepid-water bubblers, and left the hospital. The steamy afternoon heat radiating up from the pavement and off the tree trunks reminded her of home. It also reminded her that no one—not her boss, not her children, not her husband—had wanted her to return to Boston. No one except Rosa herself. Now, despite the contamination of the tissue cultures, she sensed that maybe, just maybe, her hard work was beginning to pay off.

A previously unexamined diary and a log book containing possibly positive cultures. Not much, but certainly more than she had just a few hours ago.

By the time she reached her bed and breakfast, the underarms and neckline of her dress were soaked. She handled the obligatory conversation and progress report to Mrs. Frumanian with even terser responses than usual. Then she trudged up the stairs to her room, grateful that her landlady hadn't taken the small window fan away.

After changing into shorts and a T-shirt, Rosa

checked the coded cultures Chris Hall had starred. There were two of them—172A and 172B—both grown in fibrocyte cell tissue culture. The code key, which she kept inside one of her textbooks, identified the source of both specimens as serum taken from what little remained of Lisa Grayson's blood work. Rosa skimmed through the rest of the log book and then called Ken Mulholland in Atlanta. The virologist reported no growth of any of the specimens she had sent, in fibrocytes or any other cell type. *Dead end.*

Rosa put her feet up, closed her eyes, and tried to nap as she had planned. Within minutes she gave up. There would be plenty of time to sleep when this whole affair was over. She set a pen and legal pad on the bed beside her, worked her large spectacles back onto the still-reddened bridge of her nose, and opened Constanza Hidalgo's diary.

The journal, a five-year record, had entries nearly every day. Some of them were just a few words long. Some were typed pages stapled to the appropriate date. A few of the names were initials only, or some other kind of shorthand. And throughout the pages there were drawings, faces mostly—small sketches that were really quite good.

The entries began on Connie's seventeenth birthday and ended near her twenty-second. The tone of the first entry made it sound as if a similar volume had preceded this one. Immediately Rosa was immersed in the sad life and painful fantasies of a shy, ill-educated girl, living with a mother who had little time for her and a stepfather who, for years, touched her far too often and much too intimately. As she read along, Rosa vowed to keep the diary from Maria Barahona at all costs. Somehow, Connie had managed to fend off most of Fredy Barahona's advances. And by her twentieth birthday, there was no further mention of them. If Maria had not learned any of this while Connie was alive, there was no reason she should be exposed to such anguish now.

Visits to various clinics at the Medical Center of Boston were mentioned from time to time. There were, as Maria Barahona had related, occasional sore throats and headaches. There was also one episode of gonorrhea at age eighteen. It was treated in the emergency room, and gotten from someone named T.G. who "lied to me when he said he loved me, but I knew he was lying. Oh well," Connie had written at the bottom of that entry, "it was fun while it lasted. And beggars can't be choosers."

Rosa was again beginning to tire, and was about to set the diary aside when she noticed another mention of a visit to MCB. This one occurred when Connie was nineteen.

April 3
At MCB medical clinic today for headaches. Strange little Dr., Dr. S. came up to me . . . an Arab or something, I think. He says I don't have to be fat anymore. I told him diets don't help me, but he said I wouldn't have to diet except just a little. He wants to see me in a week. I don't think I'll go. But maybe I will. He's sort of nice.

Suddenly Rosa was wide awake. Many more visits to the clinic to see Dr. S. followed. Several times there was mention of a diet powder of some kind. And most impressively, there was weight loss. Over just four months, Connie Hidalgo dropped nearly fifty pounds! In all, she lost seventy over about six months, finishing at 108. That remarkable transformation was, in and of itself, impressive. But even more intriguing to Rosa was the realization that the date of Connie's initial visit with Dr. S., and the ones that followed it, fell within the pages missing from her hospital record. There was nothing beyond the missing pages that connected Connie's visits to Dr. S.—whoever he was—with her violent death. But if there was such a connection, Rosa had no doubt she would find it.

She was working her way through the rest of the diary when Ken Mulholland called from Atlanta.

"Rosa, I hope I didn't wake you," he said. "You sounded bushed before."

"I was, Ken, but I'm perking up. Down one minute, up the next. You know how it is with us old ladies."

"We should all be old like you are. Listen, Rosa, after we talked, I went back and ran a quick spectro on a couple of the specimens you mentioned. One of them— just one—has a funny piece of DNA floating around. My tech is checking it again now. I think it might be viral, but the tissue culture seems clean, and there's just not enough of the stuff present to tell. Is there any way you can get me some more specimen?"

"From the same patient, maybe," Rosa said. "But she was sick at the time that serum was obtained, and she's not sick now."

"I see."

"Listen, the best I can do is convalescent serum, so that's what I'll try for. But I'm not at all sure I can get that either. The patient in question is suing one of the doctors at this hospital for malpractice. She may not be too anxious to cooperate at this point."

"What about the other patients with the same problem?"

"They're both dead."

"And there are no other cases?"

"Nope," Rosa said. She hesitated, and then added, "At least not yet there aren't."

• • • •

By the time Matt returned her call, Sarah was home, curled up on the sofa, wearing her most comfortable, torn, unprofessional pair of jeans and working on her second glass of Chardonnay. She had filed reports with hospital security and the police, and left a note for Glenn

Paris, who was away at some sort of meeting. Then she signed out to the resident on call and accepted a ride home from the OB/Gyn unit secretary. The dictation, she decided, could wait.

"Any idea who could have done it?" Matt asked after she had sketched the events of the past few hours.

"Nobody. Everybody. Those three girls have friends and relatives. To say nothing of the everyday, run-of-the-mill nutcakes, who see some thirty-second news clip on TV and become instant crusaders. I'm not a cynic, Matt, but I do know that people can be very ugly."

"Amen to that. You said you've made a decision about the case. Want to tell me over the phone or in person?"

Sarah had hoped the question would be asked and had already decided on her response.

"Would you like to come over here?" she asked. "I enjoy cooking and almost never get to do it anymore. There's enough stuff here to put some sort of meal together provided you're not too picky. And you can do your part by keeping me from finishing this bottle of Chardonnay by myself."

"Deal. I can be there in half an hour. Do you want to give me a hint as to what you've decided?"

"I think I can do better than that," she said. "I can tell you that I've decided that I can't agree to settle this case under any circumstances."

"You know, Matt, I thought I knew what I had to do when I left you this afternoon," Sarah said. "Then, the moment I saw what they'd done to my bike, I was sure."

They sat on her sofa, drinking decaf and eating what remained of a Sara Lee pound cake she had found in the recesses of her freezer. Dinner—mushroom chicken crêpes and some stir-fried vegetables—had gone over reasonably well. Still, she was not nearly as relaxed as she would have liked. The incident at the hospital was one reason, of course. But another was that Matt was the first man she had been alone with in her place in almost two years.

"Listen, whatever you say is what we're going to do," he said.

If he was upset by her decision to go against his recommendation, he hid it well.

"I'm terrified by what might happen in court, Matt," she went on. "But settling with no actual finding won't do anything to stop the red-paint people. And I don't intend to spend my life running from them or being harassed by them. If I'm innocent, they've got to know it. And if I'm guilty, *I've* got to know it. Believe me, I won't fall apart, even if the worst happens, even if Willis Grayson gets his wish and I get sent to prison. I believe in a Higher Power, and I believe She has a plan for me. So there you have it."

"There I have it," he said. "Well, for what it's worth, I suspected you would decide to push forward. In fact, after I dropped you off, I started scheduling depositions —beginning as soon as possible with your old pal Ettinger. I can promise you one thing, Mallon is in for a hell of a fight."

"And I'm glad you're representing me," Sarah said.

"There is one problem, though. Something I need your help with."

"Just name it."

He stirred uncomfortably. Then suddenly he turned to her and took both her hands in his. "Sarah, we can't have anything happen between us—at least not until this case is over. I . . . dammit, I don't even know what I'm trying to say. You've got to stop looking at me like that."

Sarah locked her fingers in his. His face—his kind, wonderful face—was saying everything she needed to know about what he was feeling for her.

"I'd like to help you out," she managed, "but I have no control over how I feel or how I look at someone.

Just like you can't control how you're looking at me now."

She ran her tongue slowly over her lips. Matt loosened his collar.

"Hey, I need you to stop doing that before I melt altogether," he said. "Sarah, listen, I'm working ninety hours a week, I'm lonely as hell, and the truth is, I'm starting to think about you all the time. But if I'm going to continue being your lawyer, this really isn't a good idea. Lawyers are strongly discouraged from getting romantically involved with clients. It tends to wreak havoc with their professional objectivity. In some states it's the law now. It may be in Massachusetts before long."

"I understand."

"Then you'll help me out? At least for now? I don't have a lot of willpower."

"I'll think about it. But, Matt, I'm a big girl now. I can take care of myself pretty well, and I have no intention of reporting you to the bar no matter what. Besides, what more could a client ask for than to be defended by a lawyer who's thinking about her all the time?"

"Sarah, I mean it. There are a lot of choices to be made in a case like yours. A lot of decisions. Tonight's decision you made pretty much on your own. But for others you'll need an objective, unemotional attorney. If it seems like I'm too wrapped up in you to represent you properly, I've got to quit."

"Wrapped up in me," she said. "I like the sound of that. . . . Matt, I'm sorry. Please don't be upset with me. I understand. Really I do. I'm not trying to cause problems for you. If you need another attorney to help you, then I'm sure you'll get one. I trust your judgment on that—and mine. My case is important, sure. But take it from someone who's spent far too much time behind a stethoscope the past few years, so's this stuff."

She took his hands in hers. Their eyes met. This time Matt made only the most fleeting attempt to look away. Sarah felt her mouth grow dry. How long had it been since she had felt like this with a man? Slowly her eyes closed. His hands slid up her arms and drew her toward him. She sensed his head tilt, his lips draw closer. Then her phone began ringing.

Instantly the fragile tension building between them shattered. Matt smiled awkwardly, lowered his hands, and pulled away.

"I have an answering machine," she said, wishing she could rip the phone from the wall.

"That's all right. Go ahead and take it," he replied. "Please. Take it."

The voice on the line was one she hadn't heard in six weeks.

"Sarah, this is Andrew Truscott. If you're about to hang up, please don't."

Damn, Sarah thought. She covered the mouthpiece.

"It's Andrew Truscott," she whispered. "The surgeon I told you about. . . . Yes, Andrew," she said with exaggerated coolness. "What do you want?"

"You've been really decent about not causing me trouble with Paris," he said. "And also with the way you handled that . . . that other business."

"Is that what you called to say?"

"Paris has just offered me a damn good staff appointment at MCB complete with a teaching appointment at the med school, and my own lab in that new center—the one they're going to be constructing where the Chilton Building is. He's setting up some really exciting programs. Apparently his methods have pulled the place out of its financial hole after all."

"No thanks to you."

"Well, if you had complained to him about me, the faculty appointment might never have come through."

"And that's what you called to say?"

"No. No, Sarah. Please listen. I don't know how much longer this guy's going to be here. Something's happening right now that has to do with you. And I want to help you. I really do."

"I don't understand."

"I'm in Chinatown right now. I was having dinner with an old friend from Australia at a place called the Szechuan Terrace, on Hudson Street. My friend had to go back to his hotel. After he left, I decided to stay for one last drink. That's when I heard someone in the next booth mention your name. He was saying something about how you were in court today, and about how easy it was to change the stuff in your herbalist's shop. He said he loved hanging your ass and Kwong's out to dry."

Sarah felt her heart begin pounding. Her body tensed.

"Where is he now?" she asked.

"He's right over there. Right across the room from me. I just paid the cashier twenty bucks, and she told me his name. It's Tommy Sze-to." Andrew spelled the name. "Do you know him?"

"No. I've never heard of him."

"Well, he's with two other guys. The cashier seems a little afraid of them. She said she doesn't know where he lives and— Shit, listen Sarah. I think they're getting ready to leave. I'm going to try and follow them. Meet me here in three-quarters of an hour. Szechuan Terrace. Hudson Street. See you then. Please believe me. Please come—"

Sarah listened to the dial tone for ten seconds or more before she set the receiver down. Nearly two months without so much as a word from Andrew, let alone an apology. Now this. From his spot on the sofa, Matt was looking at her curiously.

There was no reason to believe Andrew Truscott about anything, yet she couldn't come up with any ulterior motive that made sense. If what Andrew had just told her was true, and they could prove it, everything in her life was about to change for the better.

"He says he's calling from a restaurant in Chinatown, and that the man who changed the herbs in Kwong's shop was in the next booth, talking about what he did.

He wants to meet me there in three-quarters of an hour. Will you come?"

"Of course I will. Do you believe him?"

"Does it matter? I want it to be over, Matt. I want it to be over so badly."

He put his arms around her and held her tightly.

"So do I," he said.

Chapter 25

"THIS PLACE MUST SERVE INCREDIBLE FOOD," MATT said, "because it certainly isn't staying open on its atmosphere."

The operative description for the Szechuan Terrace was plastic. Plastic lanterns off the ceilings; plastic coverings on the tables; plastic bas-relief Chinese landscapes on the walls. Even the booths, themselves some sort of red vinyl, were separated by curtains of plastic.

Sarah and Matt had walked to Chinatown from her apartment. The air had cooled considerably, and they could see lightning to the east. But the breeze was pleasant, and the city vibrant.

It was nearing nine-thirty. The Szechuan Terrace was still perhaps a quarter full. Most of the patrons were Asian.

"Do you think that a measure of the goodness of a Chinese restaurant is how many Chinese are eating there?" Sarah whispered.

"Of course. Doesn't everyone think that?"

"I used to before I spent all those years in the Far East. It turns out there are probably as many Asians with a taste for bad Chinese food as there are Americans with a taste for bad western food. It's only a matter of time before someone opens a McEgg Roll in Beijing."

Matt took a place at the long mahogany bar, while Sarah wandered nonchalantly past the booths and then back.

"No Andrew," she said, sliding onto the vinyl-covered bar stool next to his.

"Just going by your description of this Truscott, this turnaround of his is very strange."

"Not really. Andrew knows I could have caused him a great deal of trouble at the hospital and didn't. I also picked up an abnormal lab result he had missed not too long ago. The patient might well have died on the table. Besides, Matt, what choice have we got? This Tommy Sze-to may be the key to everything."

At ten minutes before ten, Sarah approached the cashier. He checked briefly with the waiters and then reported to her that no one of Andrew's description had been in the restaurant. However, he added, the night had been very busy. There was a flicker of recognition in the man's dark eyes at the mention of Tommy Sze-to, but he denied knowing of any such person.

"Nobody here remembers Andrew," Sarah whispered to Matt. "But I think that guy knows who Sze-to is. He says he doesn't, but his expression says otherwise."

"But where in the hell is Andrew?"

"I don't know, but I have this uneasy feeling right here under my sternum. Let's wait ten more minutes."

"I have a better idea."

Matt went to the pay phone just inside the front doorway and consulted the phone book. Sarah noted that from where the phone was situated, Andrew would have been able to see Sze-to leave almost any of the booths. Her intuition was telling her that Truscott had overheard precisely the conversation he reported. *But if so*, she wondered uneasily, *where is he now?*

"S-z-e dash t-o. . . . Is that how you said the guy spells his last name?" Matt asked, returning to the bar.

"That's what Andrew said."

"Well, there are some Sze-tos in the book, but no Tommy."

"I'm not surprised."

"But there's a guy I knew from Chinatown—Benny Hsing. And sure enough, Bennett Hsing is listed."

"And?"

"Benny was a clubhouse man with the Sox before he got fired. He was always into everyone's business, and always telling everyone's business to everyone else. If this Sze-to is anything more than a figment of Truscott's imagination, Benny will know him."

"Where does he live?"

"Regal Street. Just a few blocks from here."

"And will he talk to you?"

"He might. He actually liked me. For one thing, my life was so dull that he never got into trouble by spreading gossip about me. No one would have believed I was into anything out of the ordinary, so he never bothered. And for another, when Steve Matz accused him of stealing his gold necklace and eventually got him fired, I tried to point out that legally, without an eye witness or the actual purloined item, Matz didn't have much of a case."

"Then why did this Benny get fired?"

"Well, I was just a second-year law student back then, and not such a wily one at that. And besides, Matz was leading the team in wins, strikeouts, and earned run average. As long as he kept pitching that way, he could have gotten just about anyone in the organization fired."

"Should we call this Benny first?"

"Benny never was one to stick his neck out for anybody else. I think he might have more trouble coming up with a reason not to deal with us if we just show up on his doorstep."

At ten o'clock, they left the restaurant. But first Sarah called Andrew's home. She had met Andrew's wife,

Claire, several times and had always viewed her as sweet, though painfully shy. Never did she seem a heaven-made match for her flamboyant, acid-tongued husband.

"I . . . um . . . I thought maybe you knew," Claire said. "You and Andrew being friends and all."

"Knew what?"

"We've separated. Andrew left here about six weeks ago. He's been living in an apartment not far from the hospital. I have his phone number if you want it."

"Claire, I'm sorry to hear that."

"Thanks. But we're managing okay. It felt as if he'd been married to the hospital the past few years anyway. Now he tells me he's been involved with someone else for a while. He won't say who. Believe it or not, I actually thought he might have taken up with you."

"Not at all, Claire. In fact, Andrew and I haven't spoken to one another in weeks."

Sarah wrote down Andrew's new number and tried it before returning to Matt. There was no answer.

Regal Street was not far from what remained of the Combat Zone, Boston's once-booming red-light district. They walked the three and a half blocks through a light rain and the rumble of distant thunder. Benny Hsing's address was an uninviting brick apartment building with the odor of urine in the entryway and a column of what seemed like too many doorbells for the size of the place. Benny's name was beside one of them. After two buzzes, he appeared at the top of the hallway stairs, peered down at them, and then rushed to the door.

"The Cat!" he exclaimed. "Are *you* ever a sight for sore eyes." His speech was quick and choppy, in sharp contrast to Matt's drawl.

"Hi, Benny. How're you doing?" Matt said. "Benny, this here's Sarah Baldwin. You got a minute?"

"For you? For Black Cat? Of course. Of course. Come up. Come up."

He was a paunchy, balding man with bad teeth behind

a smile that lacked much sincerity. His chinos and T-shirt were stained, and he smelled of tobacco, sweat, and beer. Sarah acknowledged that he might have changed over the years since he last worked for the Red Sox. But as things stood, she did not have to stretch her imagination far to picture Benny Hsing pilfering someone's gold necklace.

"The wife's asleep," Benny said, pointing at the bedroom door. He motioned them to a couch that was covered with a brown army blanket. "I get you something? A beer? A Coke? Gosh, Cat, what a coincidence. I watch the Sox playing Detroit just a little bit ago, and I was thinkin' about—you know—the old days. This man here was a hell of a pitcher, miss. A hell of a pitcher."

"So I've heard," Sarah said.

"And smart. I tell you, miss, they don't come no smarter. You lawyer now, huh Cat?"

"Yeah. Benny, we need your help," Matt said.

"My help?"

"We're looking for someone. A man named Sze-to. Tommy Sze-to."

Benny whirled and pointed a knobby finger at Sarah.

"The doctor! That's who you are. Kwong Tian-Wen's doctor. God, you excuse me for saying so, miss, but you much better looking than that picture they have of you in the papers."

"Thank you," Sarah managed.

"Kwong claims that somebody set him up," Matt said. "He swears that someone messed around with the herbs in his shop, and then brought his opium up from the basement and planted it on the shelf. Have you heard anything about that?"

"Black Cat Daniels, right here in my apartment. I owe you, Cat. You were only one who went to bat for me against that bastard, Matz. The only one. It's been hard for me since they let me go, Cat. Damn hard."

He gestured around the tiny apartment. Matt responded by pulling out his wallet and laying two twenties on the coffee table.

"It's important, Benny," he said.

Benny eyed the money with disdain.

"I don't know much," he said. "Nothing, really."

"Benny, that's all the cash I have. Believe me. Hey, wait, listen." He reached into his wallet again and slid out the two tickets, handling them as if they were priceless crystal. "Here're two front-row box seats to see the Sox play the Orioles next week. First base line just behind the bag. Tell us what we need to know about Tommy Sze-to, and the forty *and* the tickets are yours."

Sarah started to object to making Ricky pay such a price on her behalf, but Matt stopped her with a quick glance. Benny eyed the tickets avidly.

"You know how long since I been at a game?"

"Next week you're there, Benny. Just tell us what you know about this Sze-to and where we can find him."

"It's only rumors what I know, Cat. Only rumors. Sze-to's no good. No good at all. He hears I talk about him to anyone, he sells my body one part at a time. He's tong. You know what I mean?"

"A gang member, right?"

"Tong tougher than any gang, Cat. Gangs operate around here only if tong tell them okay."

"Go on."

"Rumor—only rumor, remember—is that Sze-to got big bucks to mess Kwong up. Big, big bucks."

"I knew it," Matt whispered.

"From who?" Sarah asked, at once bewildered and frightened at the thought.

Benny Hsing shrugged and shook his head.

"Where can we find him?" Matt asked.

"He come and go. In New York a lot. You know, where the ships come in. Here he's either with some woman, or more often playing poker at Maurice Fang's."

Benny eyed the money and the tickets, but Matt made no move to slide them over.

"Where's this Maurice Fang's place?"

"Please, Cat. Sze-to finds out I told you anything, I'm dead."

"He won't find out anything. Now where is it?"

Benny hesitated, then scribbled an address on the back of an envelope. "Second floor. Green door. Poker game every night until five A.M. Starts up again at ten A.M. Maurice is okay, but he's Sze-to's pal. Sze-to is a snake. You should be careful."

"We will be. How'll we know Sze-to?"

Benny drew an imaginary line from beneath his eye to the corner of his mouth.

"Big-league scar, Cat," he said. "Knife, I think."

Matt backed away from the money and the tickets. Benny snatched them up. Then he hurried into the bedroom and returned with a baseball.

"Here, Cat," he said. "You been good to me. Then and now. This here is ball you threw to clinch division title against Toronto. Remember? I've almost sold it half a dozen times, but I always say, 'No. This is Cat's ball, and someday I'm gonna have the chance to give it to him.'"

"That's very nice, Benny. Thanks."

Matt hefted the ball a couple of times and then dropped it into his jacket pocket.

"You just be careful of Sze-to," Benny said. "Be careful, and keep Benny Hsing's name out of it. Good luck, miss."

Sarah thanked him and then preceded Matt down the dimly lit stairs to the fetid entryway. Outside the glass-front door the rain was heavier now, and more wind-whipped.

"Let's go to that diner at the corner and figure out what we want to do next," Matt said.

Sarah gestured to their surroundings and pinched her nose shut. "Anything that will get us out of this spot.

That was really pretty sweet of Benny, though. Don't you think?"

"What?"

"Giving you that baseball."

"Yeah," Matt said. "That was very sweet except for one thing. I already have the ball from that Toronto game in a case in my den."

The steady rain continued, though it still was something less than a thunderstorm. After coffee and deep dish apple pie, Sarah and Matt left the small diner and darted from doorway to doorway to a Bank of Boston money machine. They had considered and rejected all of the options they could think of, and had finally returned to the first one—find Tommy Sze-to and somehow get him to disclose who had hired him, and why. They would resort to whatever it took: pleading, bribery, threats—if necessary, even some arm twisting.

Sarah no longer harbored any doubt that someone had hired Tommy Sze-to to tamper with the herbs in Kwong Tian-Wen's shop. Someone out there wanted to see the old man ruined or Sarah's career destroyed. Possibly both. But the chances of keeping a gangster like Sze-to around Boston long enough to have him questioned through legal channels were slim—roughly the same as the chances of interesting those legal channels in the whole business to begin with. There really was no good option. They had to confront Sze-to before he learned they were after him and disappeared. It was that simple.

The money machine refused to shell out more than $250, but Matt allowed as how that might be to the machine's credit. They darted and splashed the four blocks to the address Benny had given them for Maurice Fang's all-night poker game. Though unasked, the question of what might have happened to Andrew Truscott continued to gnaw at them both.

Their plan—what little there was of it—was to act as if

they had official legal business with Sze-to, maybe some money due him.

"What if he doesn't bite on that?" Sarah asked.

"Then we move on to Plan B, whatever that is. In the end, everything just might boil down to which one of us is bigger."

"Or more heavily armed. . . ."

The three-story, dilapidated building was tucked on a narrow side street just a block from Kwong's shop. The street door opened on a foyer that was cluttered with junk mail and no better lit than the one on Regal Street. The avocado-green door, painted in high-gloss enamel, was just at the top of the first flight of stairs. Sarah and Matt could hear string music and a woman's high-pitched singing voice from the other side.

"Just remember to look like you know what you're doing," Matt whispered before he knocked.

The door was opened a fraction of an inch—just enough for them to see a sliver of a face and a single, rheumy eye. The singing, louder now, was Chinese, and clearly a recording of some sort.

"What do you want?"

The voice was gravelly and impatient.

"My name's Matt Daniels." Matt flashed a business card, then just as quickly put it away. "I'm an attorney with Hannigan, Daniels, and Chung. If you're Maurice Fang, I need to speak with you."

"About what?"

"Actually, it's about money that is owed to one of your clients. A lot of money. Mr. Fang—please. I know about the card game going on in there, and I couldn't care less. But I don't do business standing in hallways. Now please, could we come in? It's very late, and I'd really like to get this whole thing over and call it a night."

Out of sight of the eye, Sarah nodded that she was impressed with Matt's performance. After a momentary hesitation, the police bar was moved aside and the avocado door opened. Maurice Fang's apartment was considerably better furnished than Benny Hsing's, but it was also a lot smokier. A thin, cirrus cloud wafted out from a room one doorway down the hall.

"Who are you looking for?" Fang asked.

He was a willowy man, perhaps sixty, wearing a black dress shirt and solid white tie. *Someone's grandfather trying to be Nathan Detroit* was Sarah's first impression. Matt immediately maneuvered his way around so that he was between Fang and the smoke-filled room.

"As I said, I'm an attorney. This is my associate, Miss Sharp. There's been an estate settlement. We're trying to find a man named Sze-to. First name, Tommy. I've been authorized to pay up to fifty dollars for information that will help me find him so that we can take care of this matter. We've been looking for him all day. Finally someone suggested we try here."

"Who?"

"Mr. Fang, I'm a lawyer. Everything that's told to me is told in confidence. That way no one has to worry. Including you."

"Let's see the fifty," Maurice Fang said.

He took the bills and ordered Matt and Sarah to wait in the living room. Then he stepped around them and into the card room. Matt remained where he was. Sarah moved up beside him. After a minute, Fang returned and handed back the fifty.

"No one knows where Sze-to is," he said. "Hey! Wait a minute!"

Matt had barged past him to the doorway.

"I want to ask myself," he said. "We've had a long day."

Sarah stepped up behind him and could see immediately that one of the six Chinese men playing cards and smoking was Tommy Sze-to. He was slightly built and pasty, with simian features, a pencil mustache, and a striking scar running exactly as Benny had depicted.

Maurice Fang tried to pull Matt from the room, but Matt easily shook him off.

"I don't know if any of you is Mr. Tommy Sze-to," he lied, "but I need to speak to him about money he's got coming to him—a lot of money."

The men at the table just stared up at him. No one moved.

"You see?" Fang protested. "You see? Now, get the hell out of here!"

Matt glanced back at Sarah. They both knew there might never be a second chance. Sze-to was obviously not buying Matt's story.

"I guess we go to Plan B," Matt whispered over his shoulder.

He gauged the room for a moment, and then stepped forward and grasped a startled Tommy Sze-to's right hand with his.

"Nice to meet you, Mr. Sze-to. Nice to meet you," he gushed.

Before Sze-to could react, Matt pulled him to his feet, twisted his right hand behind his back, and locked his own left arm around the smaller man's neck.

"What the fuck?" Sze-to gurgled.

"I'm not going to hurt you, Tommy," Matt said, pulling him out into the narrow hallway, "but we need to talk." He tightened his grip. "Do you understand?"

Sze-to nodded. Matt kept his firm hold and turned Sze-to around to face Sarah.

"Do you know who she is?" he demanded. "Do you?"

Sze-to struggled briefly, but quickly gave up. He was at least six inches shorter than Matt and fifty pounds lighter.

"Let go," he managed to say.

"Do you know who she is?"

"Yes."

"And why we're here?"

"Yes. Yes. Let go."

Matt loosened his grip. With sudden, surprising speed, Sze-to whipped his hand free, slammed Matt backhand across the face, and then kicked him full force in the groin. Matt grunted in pain and reeled back heavily against the wall. Sze-to moved to follow up, but Matt was already steadying himself. After the briefest hesitation, the gangster cried out something in Chinese to Maurice Fang, sprinted to the window at the end of the hall, and dove through it onto the fire escape. Matt, his eyes glazed and watery, the corner of his mouth bleeding, lurched after him, with Sarah close behind. They saw Sze-to vanish from the platform. Then they heard him cry out in pain from the alley below.

"He's hurt himself," Matt said, peering into the rain-swept darkness through what remained of the window. "We can get him."

Without waiting for Sarah to respond, he stepped out onto the slick, slatted metal platform. In seconds, she was beside him.

"Fuck you, you crazy bastard!" they heard Maurice Fang cry out.

Sze-to, apparently unable to loosen the escape ladder, had jumped. Now he was about twenty yards away, hobbling badly through the heavy rain toward another alleyway.

"We've got to hurry," Matt said, kneeling and releasing the ladder.

"Are you okay?" Sarah asked as he scrambled down to the muddy, ill-paved alley.

"Later!" he shot back. "Come on."

Sarah slid as much as climbed down the ladder and dashed after Matt, sloshing through muddy puddles as she ran. She caught up with him at the corner of the next alley. It was lined with trash cans and overflowing cardboard boxes, and had no working lights. They peered through the darkness and the rain, but could see no one.

"What did Sze-to yell out back there to Maurice?"

Matt asked, taking a few tentative steps down the alley. "Could you tell?"

"I'm not sure. 'Call Guo-Ming.' Something like that."

They made their way carefully down the alley. Ahead there were any number of places where Tommy Sze-to could be hiding, perhaps waiting to ambush them. Suddenly a brilliant spear of lightning flooded the alley with light. Moments later thunder exploded. Then there was another flash.

"There!" Matt cried, pointing ahead.

Sze-to was a shadow, gliding along the building, heading toward the far end of the alley. The moment he heard Matt's voice, he took off. They sprinted after him, across a deserted street, and onto the ribbons of railroad track leading into massive South Station. Ahead of them, Sze-to hobbled toward a row of vacant passenger cars and ducked between two of them. Breathless now in the heavy air, Matt followed, with Sarah, clearly more fit, just a few steps behind. They worked their way between the two cars. Then they froze.

Sze-to was, perhaps, fifteen yards away. But he had ceased running, and turned to face them. Standing alongside him in the downpour were three other men. Two were Asians, one of whom was holding a gun. The third was Andrew Truscott.

"Jesus," Matt murmured.

"Matt, that's Andrew," she whispered, squinting through the gloom.

"I guessed," he said sardonically.

"Andrew, what are you doing?" she called out. "What's going on here?"

"Come here," Sze-to yelled out over the rumble of rain on the steel cars. "Move slowly. Guo-Ming, here, is an excellent shot. Don't make him prove it."

"Andrew, what's going on?" Sarah pleaded.

"Sarah, can't you see?" Matt said in an urgent whisper. "Get behind me and move back toward the cars. Quickly!"

Sarah did not understand what he meant, but she did as he demanded.

"Another step and you're both dead," Sze-to warned. "Just like your friend here."

The men standing on either side of Andrew moved away, and his lifeless body crumpled forward onto the tracks.

"Guo-Ming, please kill them," Sze-to said calmly.

"Sarah, run!" Matt cried out as Sze-to limped forward behind the other two men. "Run!"

Matt's right hand was already in his sport coat pocket, his fingers tight around the baseball. With a continuous, fluid motion, he drew the ball out, stepped forward, and threw. The gunman, now no more than thirty feet away, spent a second trying to comprehend what was happening. For him, that second was far too long. The pitch, a hard rising fastball, caught him squarely in the throat, just above the breastbone. The revolver discharged harmlessly, then clattered to the gravel. The man snapped backward as if kicked by a mule, dropped heavily to the ground, and lay there moaning.

Sarah was already backing through the space between the cars.

"Run, Sarah!" Matt called out again. "Back toward the alley!"

They recrossed the road. As they reached the alley, they turned back in time to see Sze-to and the remaining man climb out from between the cars. The revolver, now in Sze-to's hand, sparked. The brick just to the right of Sarah's head shattered. Matt grabbed her hand and pulled her down. Then together they whirled and sprinted down the alley.

Chapter 26

"DO YOU SEE THEM?" SARAH ASKED.

They were on a dark, deserted street, huddled behind a parked car. It was nearing midnight. The relentless, stinging downpour was continuing. Matt peered through the windows of the car.

"They're across the street," he whispered. "I don't think that other guy wants to go too far without Sze-to, and Sze-to's having trouble moving with that leg so messed up. I think we can beat them out of here."

"Do you know where we are?"

"Not exactly. But downtown is that way."

Sarah inched her way up until she could see the two men. They didn't seem to be moving with any great urgency.

"They're crazy! They killed Andrew. Matt, I'm really scared. I can't stop shaking."

"That means you're going to have to be in charge because I'm worse off than you are. Listen, we can do this. Sze-to can hardly move." He scanned the street. "That alley over there. We break for it, and then try and make it to Stuart Street—or at least to where there are some people. You okay for that?"

"Matt, look!"

Where moments ago there had been two, now there were four. A pair of men had emerged from behind Sze-to, and now stood beside him, scanning the street. One of the new men held a gun. The other was speaking into a cellular phone or radio of some sort. Both of them looked relaxed and athletic.

"Jesus, they're like an army."

"The tong. Remember what Benny said about them?"

"We've got to get out of here."

"Oh, God, Matt. Over there. I think there's more of them."

There were, in fact, three more, sealing off the street from the far end.

"That alley over there is our only way now. We've got to go for it. Just keep low until we reach the corner of that building, then run like hell. Ready?"

"Yeah."

"Sarah, I—I really do care a lot for you. Come on. Let's do it."

Crouched low, they inched backward, keeping their hands on the pavement for balance.

"Now!" Matt said.

They whirled and fled down the alley. Behind them, one of their pursuers cried out. An instant later they heard the snap of two gunshots.

"Stay low!" Matt warned. "Keep running."

The alley was narrow and filled with debris and loose garbage. Matt pulled over one overflowing trash can as he passed, then another.

"Cut to the right!" Sarah cried, pointing ahead of them.

At the far end of the alley, two more men had appeared. Suddenly Chinatown, which was no more than a dozen or so square blocks, seemed endless. Reacting to Sarah's command, Matt spun into the narrow gap between two buildings, slipped and fell, scrambled up, and kept running.

"They're multiplying like rabbits," he said, panting. "Sarah, I'm not sure we can make it out of here. I think we've got to find someplace to hide."

Sarah was now clearly the quicker of the two of them. She was about ten feet ahead as they approached a cross street. She slowed and glanced to her right. The doorway of an old theater was just a few yards away. The theater, boarded up and not in any apparent use, still displayed torn posters advertising Chinese movies, and even one showing Humphrey Bogart and Katharine Hepburn navigating the *African Queen*.

"Matt!" she gasped, pointing at the door. "Can you get us in there?"

He hit it once with his shoulder, then stepped back and, with one vicious kick, slammed it open. They slipped inside and closed the door quickly behind them. The lobby glowed dimly with the outside light from two small windows set high in one of the walls. Except for a worn carpet of some sort, the place was stripped. Still, even after what was probably years of disuse, Sarah could smell the popcorn that had once been made and sold there. Hand in hand, they entered the theater itself. Like the lobby, the space had several narrow windows near the ceiling, which had probably been curtained off during shows. The light from them was enough to make out a stage in front of where the screen once had been. The seats, with a few battered exceptions, had been removed.

"Probably dates back to vaudeville," Matt said. "We've got to find a place to hide, or else a side door out of here, and quickly."

Sarah leapt onto the stage and then called out in a loud whisper, "Matt, up here. Look."

Just offstage was a steel ladder, free-hanging, its base just inches above the floor. It led straight up to a narrow catwalk, which was suspended from the ceiling. The catwalk, perhaps twenty-five feet overhead, was barely visible in the gloom. Without waiting for discussion or agreement, Sarah grabbed a quilted moving blanket from a pile of them near the stage and began to climb.

"It's solid, Matt," she called down. "Come on."

Moments later they heard the lobby door crash open. Then there were voices. Matt peered overhead but could not see Sarah at all. He threw two more of the packing blankets over his shoulder and scrambled quickly up the ladder. The metal catwalk, three feet across and suspended from the ceiling by steel struts, was actually quite sturdy. Matt spread one of the packing quilts out next to hers and folded the other as a makeshift pillow. The blankets were damp and smelled of mold. But terrified and soaked to the skin, the two of them were quite beyond feeling discomfort. Matt lowered himself down next to her and pulled his knees up, just as some men entered the theater.

"Can you see anything?" she whispered, her lips against his ear.

Matt shook his head and then lay back, praying they were both completely screened from the men below. The men—it seemed as if there were two of them—chattered on in Chinese, without any particular urgency in their voices. Then, after only a minute or two, they made one pass around the theater and left. The lobby door opened and closed. Had they both gone?

Sarah started to speak, but Matt silenced her with a finger to his lips and pulled her closer to him. Five minutes passed before the man in the darkness below them cleared his throat and softly coughed.

"I knew it," he murmured.

At that instant the lobby door slammed open once again. Several different voices conversed with the man who had been standing guard. And suddenly the dark, musty air was pierced by spears of bright light.

"Shit."

Matt mouthed more than spoke the word.

Sarah pressed her body even tighter to his. She tried desperately to understand the Chinese being spoken below them, but could only come up with scattered words and, occasionally, a phrase. It was clear that Tommy Sze-to was both frightened and furious. It sounded as if someone—there was never a name spoken that she recognized—wasn't going to like it at all if Sarah and Matt got away and started talking. Whoever found them would be rewarded.

Trying not to move even as they breathed, they watched the beams of light play across the ceiling, the catwalk, and possibly even the underside of the packing quilts on which they were lying. Grabbing them had been sheer genius on Sarah's part, Matt was realizing. He tried to imagine what their nest looked like from below. *Probably like nothing at all.* If they made it out, he would have to find some special way to thank her. *If.*

Below them, the lights and voices moved closer to the stage. A beam flashed through the catwalk . . . then another. The lights panned back and forth. Sarah felt herself beginning to shake. Perhaps sensing her movement, Matt turned his head slightly and pressed his lips against her forehead. The catwalk shook as one of the men below took hold of the ladder. Then it tilted as he stepped onto the first rung. Matt's lips pressed even more tightly against Sarah's skin. Another step. And another. They could see the man's flash playing over the spot where they lay. Another step . . . then suddenly the catwalk heaved and shuddered as he pushed off and jumped back to the floor.

"Nothing," they heard him say.

The flashlight beams—what they could see of them—began moving to other parts of the theater. Huddled on the overhead walk, sodden and exhausted, Matt and Sarah fought the need to move. Their limbs tingled and cramped. Electric pain knifed into their hands and feet. They clung tightly to one another, unable to move or speak; together, yet very much apart.

The search within the theater continued for at least another half hour. Tommy Sze-to left well before that, but the others kept on looking. Twice Sarah and Matt heard the outside door open and close. The theater was quiet.

Sarah started to shift her position, but Matt stopped her.

"They're still down there," he whispered almost soundlessly. "Don't move."

He turned his head slightly, and suddenly his lips were resting on hers. From somewhere in the darkness below them, there was a scuffing bit of movement and the clearing of a throat. Not wanting—or daring—to move her lips away from his, Sarah slid her free arm upward until her fingers touched his neck. For the next two hours they lay that way, their eyes closed, their breathing synchronous. Every fifteen minutes or so, the man stationed beneath the catwalk made some sort of movement or sound. Finally, after a painful eternity, he switched on his radio telephone and spoke in Chinese.

"He wants to leave," Sarah whispered excitedly.

They heard him stretch and groan. He shuffled toward the back of the theater. Again the lobby door opened and shut. Then there was only silence.

"What do you think?" Matt risked asking.

"I think they haven't found us."

"I believe he's gone."

"Matt, I can't stop thinking about Andrew. Please don't move yet."

Matt turned his head so that once again their lips were touching.

"If you insist," he whispered.

    .   .   .

At five-thirty, the hazy light of the new day began to brighten the theater. Huddled on the rusting metal cat-walk above the empty stage, Sarah and Matt had moved enough to keep their limbs from paralysis. But they had not broken their embrace, nor had they spoken. One or possibly both of them had slept for a time, though neither of them was sure. Matt worked his hands up to the sides of her face and kissed her gently on the eyes.

"You've been incredibly brave," he said. "I did a very stupid thing trying to play Green Beret with that bastard."

"Are they really gone?"

Matt sat up slowly and carefully, and peered between the rails of the catwalk.

"I can't vouch for the lobby, but the theater is empty. I think we should wait until nine or ten before we leave, though. The more people out there, the better chance we have of making it home. Although frankly, if I were Tommy Sze-to, I'd already be on my way to someplace far, far away from here."

"Poor Andrew. He really was trying to help me."

"Maybe he did it in time to reclaim his place in heaven," Matt said. "Considering how he ended up, I guess you'd have to say it was a pretty damn noble act. I only wish he had been able to learn who bankrolled Sze-to in the first place. Any ideas?"

"None," Sarah said. "No idea who, and no idea why. Except now we know one important thing."

"Namely, that someone is willing to go to any length to ensure that you look guilty of causing those DIC cases."

"That's not absolute proof that Tian-Wen and I are innocent. But it seems like someone thinks so. When we get out of here, we can begin to focus on who that might be. But the first thing I'm going to do is go and speak with Claire Truscott."

"I thought you said Andrew had left her."

"He's still the father of their child. I intend to help Claire out in any way I can—now and in the future."

Matt glanced at his watch.

"Two hours," he said. "Maybe two and a half. I think we ought to stay up here and keep pretty quiet."

"I agree."

She smiled and kissed him lightly. He slipped his hand up beneath the back of her blouse and rubbed her back.

"You know," he said, "this isn't exactly the under-the-sheet situation with you I had been fantasizing about."

"And here I thought this whole night was an elaborate setup just because you knew that my tastes run to the unusual and the exotic."

"Promise you won't turn me over to the bar association?"

"If you promise not to drop me as a client."

She kissed him again, this time more searchingly. Her tongue explored his mouth. Then she reached down, loosened his trousers, and gently caressed him.

"You were pretty macho last night, Cat," she whispered. "Did that coward hurt you?"

"I don't remember," he said, looking at her wide-eyed. "A little maybe. God, what you're doing right now is really helping. I mean *really helping*."

Again she smiled at him. The horror of the night just passed had largely given way to thoughts of the future and of the man whose gentle eyes were fixed on hers.

"That's just the beginning," she whispered. "I'm a doctor, remember. When I think it's clinically appropriate, I'm going to kiss it and make it all better."

Chapter 27

OCTOBER 9

S CALPEL. . . . SPONGE, PLEASE. . . . SCOPE READY, please. . . . How're you doing, Kristen? Are you feeling any of this? . . . Excellent, that's excellent. . . . Do you still want to watch this procedure on the monitor? . . . All right then. Here we go. . . ."

The young woman on the operating table, a mother of three, had begged for local rather than general anesthesia. Although general was the norm, Sarah had agreed. She had done her first tubal ligation by laparoscopy late in her first year of residency. That procedure had gone without a hitch, as had the twenty or twenty-five she had done since then, three of them utilizing a local anesthetic with heavy sedation. She was a damn good surgeon. Technically and clinically one of the best, if not *the* best, her training program had ever had. Why then had her life in the hospital become such hell?

"Okay, Kristen. What you're looking at are your insides. There's a small but very powerful light at the tip of this laparoscope. Right next to the light source is a fiber optic pickup that can take light and actually make it bend around corners. The fiber optics carry the images back to this eyepiece and also to the television monitor. As of this moment, your left ovary—that little pink thing in the middle of the screen—is a star! Amazing, huh?"

Fiber optics. Sarah found herself momentarily wondering about the scientist responsible for the remarkable, revolutionary discovery. Worldwide communications forever changed. The frontiers of surgery pushed farther back perhaps than with any other single discovery since anesthesia. *Had life rewarded the inventor? Was he rich? Was he at peace? Or had controversy, illness, or the machinations of others made things hard for him?*

Sarah had inserted a bipolar cautery instrument through a small incision just over Kristen's pubis. Now, watching through the laparoscope, she guided the tips of the cautery unit around the narrow fallopian tube. Next she traced along the tube from where it entered the uterus to its fimbriated tip—the fringed end next to the ovary.

"Okay, Kristen, your tube's completely freed up. I'm going to grasp it with the little pincher on the cautery unit and burn it closed. If you still want to watch, you might actually see the fat cells in the tissue sizzle and pop. Then, just to be sure there are no little surprise tax deductions in your future, I'm going to repeat the procedure in a second spot as well, a bit closer to your uterus. The burns we're going to make will deaden the sensory nerves along with the tubal tissue, so there won't be much pain from that area after we're all done—if there's any pain at all. . . ."

We're *going to make* . . . *after* we're *all done* . . . The phrases, used reflexively, now sounded as awkward as Sarah was feeling. She glanced over at the nurses. They used to love working with her; they'd talk and joke with her during cases. Now, whether they intended it or not, there was distance.

She and Matt had reported Andrew's murder to the

police. But the one detective assigned to the case had failed to find Andrew's body or any evidence at all of foul play. He couldn't locate Tommy Sze-to or even turn up a witness willing to corroborate any part of their story. The malpractice case against her was proceeding along and, fueled by her unsubstantiated account of the night in Chinatown, was still receiving a goodly amount of media attention. There were any number of rumors circulating around the hospital grapevine. One of them had Andrew leaving his wife for Sarah, and then leaving for Australia when Sarah jilted him for another man. Another had Sarah killing Andrew after a lovers' quarrel and then making up the Chinese gang tale in case his body was ever found. It was terribly frustrating to know that without concrete proof of some sort, she was powerless to convince any doubter of the truth.

In the press, the publicity about Sarah and the Medical Center of Boston had ranged from disruptive to brutal. A nasty letter from the president of the Chinatown Neighborhood Association had been published in the *Globe*, calling her allegations about tongs and violence damaging to his community. In various publications and broadcasts, her motives had been questioned, as well as her morality, and even her sanity. Worst of all, nothing had changed. Absolutely nothing.

Desperate to clear Sarah's name, and his own suddenly shaky reputation, Matt had hired a private detective. After nearly three weeks and more than $2,000, the man had come up with essentially no more information than that Tommy Sze-to was no longer in Boston and possibly no longer in the country. Nobody in Chinatown to whom he spoke knew anything about Dr. Andrew Truscott.

"That's it, Kristen. A couple of Band-Aids and you're off to recovery," Sarah said. "Thank you all. Thank you very much."

There were a few mumbled replies, but no praise for a job that was, in fact, exceptionally well done. Sarah stripped off her gloves and rushed into the nurses' locker room, feeling quite alone and perilously close to tears. She still felt committed to staying at work and to seeing things through—more so than ever since Andrew's death. But it was doubtful she would ever again feel comfortable at MCB. Being up on pedestals the way most M.D.s were made them easy targets. She would never have believed how fragile a physician's reputation and professional respect could be. It was incredibly painful to realize that more than two years of consistently good work—of always staying the extra hour, of always helping out when help was needed—were no real match for baseless rumor and innuendo.

She changed into fresh scrubs and her clinic coat, and stopped by the mail room to check her cubby. Among the pathology reports and copies of operative dictations, there was a note from Rosa Suarez, dated that morning, asking Sarah to get in touch with her. There was also a letter from the chairman of the hospital board of trustees, sent out via a computer-generated mailing sticker. The envelope was indistinguishable from those she frequently received announcing a staff/trustee tea, or requesting an update on her continuing education activities. The contents of the envelope, however, were hardly routine. The letter, signed by some typist in lieu of the board chairman, politely informed Sarah that due to the confusion and uncertainty surrounding her and her future, the professional conduct subcommittee of the board had requested OB/Gyn department head Dr. Randall Snyder to submit an alternate recommendation for the position of next year's chief resident.

"Damn!" Sarah shoved the letter in her clinic coat pocket and pounded her fist on the counter.

"Damn what?"

Eli Blankenship, his massive pate gleaming beneath the fluorescent light, smiled down at her. The sight of him immediately softened Sarah's anger. Throughout her ordeal, the medical chief had been one of the few constants at the hospital—always upbeat and encouraging; always applying his incredible intellect to her problems. There was no doubt, he had told her, that the story she and Matt told about Tommy Sze-to and Andrew Truscott was perfectly true. Any real student of mysteries would have known that, he said. Their account was simply too far out, too rough around the edges, to be anything other than fact.

"Mornin', Dr. Blankenship," the mail clerk said, handing over a huge stack of announcements, lab reports, journals, and magazines.

"G'morning to you, Tate. How's the Mrs.?"

"Still doin' great, thanks to you."

Blankenship smiled his pleasure and led Sarah away from the window.

"What's going on?" he asked.

She pulled out the letter from the hospital trustees and passed it over.

Blankenship read it in seconds.

"This is ridiculous," he exclaimed. "Rob McCormick and the rest of those fops on the board of trustees spend so much time worrying about appearances that they forget about accomplishments. *Ergo*, they have none. Idiots. Sarah, don't we have a meeting scheduled with you and your lawyer?"

"Yes, sir. Tomorrow evening."

"Well, I promise you I shall have spoken with McCormick by then. I can't guarantee you a reversal of his position, but I can be very persuasive when I must be. I also promise you a lengthy dissertation on DIC. I've become quite an expert on the condition. I feel strongly that some force other than or in addition to your prenatal supplements is at work. And I swear, we're going to find out what it is." He studied the anger and frustration in her eyes. "Sarah, you must keep your chin up through all this. You have a good deal more support around this hospital than you might think, including, as far as I can tell, Dr. Snyder. I'd be surprised if he had anything to do with this letter."

"How could he not?" Sarah asked. "Just a few months ago he was offering me a partnership. Now he's as chilly and formal as can be. I get the feeling that most folks around here, including Dr. Snyder, would be happy if I would just dry up and blow away."

"But you're not going to, right?"

"No, Dr. Blankenship, I'm not. I'm not because regardless of what most people seem to be thinking, I don't believe I've done anything wrong—not to those three women, and not to Andrew."

Blankenship put a reassuring arm around her shoulders.

"We are going to get to the bottom of all this," he said with firm conviction. "We are going to find out what afflicted those women, and we are going to find out who was responsible for Andrew Truscott's death. Something is going to break for us soon, Sarah. I sense it in my gut." He patted his sumo wrestler's midsection. "Which, incidentally, is hardly the most sensitive part of me. And meanwhile, I intend to do what I can to ensure that no one in this hospital takes action against you because of what they believe *might* be true."

"Thank you," Sarah said. "Thank you for everything."

"Okay, then," Blankenship said. "I'll see you tomorrow evening—hopefully with some good news from that damn board of trustees. Where are you headed now?"

"To give Rosa Suarez a call. Apparently she's got something she wants to talk to me about."

"Well, you can report on whatever it is tomorrow night," Blankenship said. "Or better still, perhaps you can talk our secretive epidemiologist into coming and reporting to us herself."

"Perhaps I can," Sarah mused, feeling more centered

and determined than she had in weeks. "Perhaps I can at that."

* * *

"Rosa, what do you mean you've been taken off the investigation?"

Seated on a maple rocker by the foot of the bed in Rosa Suarez's room, Sarah stared at the older woman incredulously.

"I told you before that my supervisor and I don't see eye to eye much of the time."

"That study you did in San Francisco."

"Precisely."

"But your data were altered."

"He doesn't believe that. Anyhow, he's cited my lack of progress and the absence of any further cases of DIC, and he's sent me back to the library until my retirement in four months. For the time being, I will not be replaced on the project."

"That's terrible." Sarah felt a knot of panic in her chest. She had hoped, *believed*, that the impressive, diligent little woman would somehow solve the mystery that was threatening her career. "After the things you told me, I really had high hopes for some sort of breakthrough. Now you're leaving. I just—"

Rosa Suarez stopped her with a raised hand. She then sat down on the edge of the bed, her gaze leveled at Sarah.

"There has been a breakthrough, Sarah," she said. "And I am most assuredly not leaving."

"But—"

"I had about six weeks' worth of unused sick time. So as of today, I am on medical leave, recuperating from a slipped disk. An orthopedic friend of ours who owed me a favor has kindly supplied the official documentation of my plight."

Sarah's emotional roller coaster began another upward swing.

"Thank you," she said hoarsely. "Thank you for not giving up. But I don't understand. How can your department head stop the investigation if there's been a breakthrough?"

"Because," Rosa said grinning, "he doesn't know about it. And he won't know about it until it is airtight and backed up twice over. I sense that while the U.S. military doesn't seem to be involved here as it was in San Francisco, some very powerful and resourceful folks might be."

"Tell me."

"The problem you have faced is two-pronged. First, there have been no DIC cases found that are unrelated to you. And second, the three DIC cases from your hospital have no major risk factors in common other than your herbal supplement."

"Yes, I understand that."

"Well, after many dead ends, I have unearthed another, most significant factor that our three DIC cases had in common."

"Namely?" Sarah asked excitedly.

"Namely, their weight."

It took no more than fifteen minutes for Rosa to describe the efforts that culminated with her discovery of Constanza Hidalgo's diary and the revelation of the girl's incredible weight loss, achieved with some sort of powder from a "foreign" MCB doctor, referred to in the diary only as "Dr. S."

"Armed with that information," she explained, "I retraced my steps through Alethea Worthington's past and finally through Lisa Summer's. It has taken a lot more time than I would have liked, because Alethea's family is just about nonexistent. And Lisa and her father have been out of the country for much of the past month. But what I've learned is more than intriguing. Alethea once had a horrific weight problem. Two hundred and forty pounds, one of her neighbors told me. Here are a couple of photocopies I made from her high school yearbook.

This is Alethea, here. As you can see, she was quite large."

"Do we know if she took the same diet powder as Connie Hidalgo?" Sarah asked.

"Not exactly. But I have been able to ascertain that her weight loss occurred about four and one-half years ago—the same approximate time as Connie's. And the pages covering that time have been torn from *her* MCB chart as well."

"And you haven't told anyone about this?"

Rosa shook her head.

"After what happened in San Francisco, it's not even easy for me to share this information with you," she said. "But I know how much you've suffered. And although I hardly consider myself an expert on the subject of who to trust, I *do* trust you."

"Thank you," Sarah said. "Oh, God, thank you so much."

Blankenship was right. A break was imminent.

"There's more," Rosa said as if reading her thoughts. "Much more."

"Lisa?"

"Exactly. I haven't spoken to her directly, but I did make several visits to her Boston home. Her housemates were most suspicious of me, especially in view of the lawsuit against you. But finally they came around. Here are some pictures they gave me of her. The top few are from when she first moved into the group house. The last couple are more recent."

"She must be fifty pounds lighter in these later photos!"

"Seventy, actually," Rosa said. "Only one of the people in the house was there four and a half years ago when she lost the weight, but he's sure she did it with a powder of some sort. The same time, probably the same powder. Sarah, we are not dealing with coincidence here. I promise you we're not."

"Did you check Lisa's hospital record for missing pages?"

"There's no physical evidence that pages were removed, but that means nothing. There are no pages from that whole year."

"Rosa, this *is* a breakthrough. Do you have any idea who this Dr. S. might be?"

"Some. The clues provided in Constanza Hidalgo's diary suggested a male, possibly foreign. I added to that equation the time frame over which this fascinating powder was dispensed, and the initial 'S.' Then I checked through the records at personnel." She searched through her portfolio and withdrew a spiral bound notebook. "Assuming the parameters I chose are all correct, there are three good candidates. I wasn't quite certain what to do with her impression that the man was foreign. She did not seem that sure. The first name of the three is still on the staff at MCB. The other two haven't been for several years."

She passed the notebook over to Sarah.

"Gilberto Santiago, M.D. . . . Sun Soon, M.D., Ph.D. . . . Pramod Singh, D.Med. (Ayurv.)," Sarah read. "No bells for any of them. Not even Santiago."

"What does that mean?" Rosa asked. "That last man's degree?"

"Probably Doctor of Ayurvedic Medicine. It's an ancient Indian healing system—" Her voice fell away.

"What is it, Sarah? You look like you've just seen a ghost."

Slowly Sarah's eyes came up to meet hers. "What I may have just seen, Rosa, is the truth. I need to make a call."

"Use that phone right there. If the call is long distance, just use this credit card. I'll be long retired before anyone realizes that a woman on sick leave in Atlanta made this call from Boston."

The best Sarah could do to reach Annalee Ettinger was to leave an urgent message with the operator at

Xanadu. She gave Rosa's name rather than her own and stressed several times the importance of the situation.

"Now," Rosa said after Sarah had hung up, "it seems that it is your turn for explanations."

Sarah shared what little she knew of Pramod Singh and the Ayurvedic Herbal Weight Loss System. She had sketched Peter Ettinger as fairly as she could, but Rosa quickly picked up on the tension the man brought to her voice.

"He sounds to me like a textbook megalomaniac," Rosa observed.

"I always knew he was prideful. But I considered him very much a visionary."

"My experience is that both are often stepping-stones on the road to megalomania."

When the phone rang Sarah reached instantly for the receiver.

"Dr. Rosa Suarez, please?"

Sarah recognized Annalee's rich alto. "Annalee, it's Sarah. How are you doing?"

"Hey, what a nice surprise. We are doing beautifully, thank you. The baby's getting cranked up for the big plunge."

"How much longer?"

"Six, seven weeks. For my money, tomorrow would be fine. Peter's got two midwives from Mali hovering around me all the time. Since I've had no problems whatsoever, they spend all their time cooking and cleaning and bumping into one another."

"Annalee, I'm so excited for you."

"Yeah. Peter's really come through this time. So, what's this urgent stuff? And who's Rosa Suarez?"

"There really is a Dr. Suarez. In fact, she's right here. She's—she's been studying weight loss programs for the government. I told her about Peter's program and about Dr. Singh."

"Those two are really raking it in," Annalee said. "Peter's added a whole new shipping area to this place.

Twenty or so employees just packing it up an' shipping it out. It seems half of America is overweight and watching late-night TV. And every one of them is looking to walk the high road to slimness, as Peter puts it."

"Annalee, do you have any idea how we can get in touch with Dr. Singh?"

"None. He comes by every few weeks with a new supply of the vitamin caps that go with each order. But I almost never see him. I can try asking Peter without telling him it's for you. He's furious that your lawyer has subpoenaed him to testify."

"Tough," Sarah murmured. "Listen, Annalee. Don't get yourself in any trouble over this. But it would be a huge help to us to speak with Dr. Singh."

"I'll see what I can do. Is that it?"

"Could you send me out some of that powder?"

"You mean you don't want to pay forty-nine ninety-five by check or major credit card, and allow three to six weeks for delivery, sorry no CODs? Well, I think I can handle that."

Sarah gave Annalee Rosa's address, thanked her, and again begged her not to get into any conflict with her father. Then she sat staring out at the rich autumn afternoon.

"Rosa, you really believe this weight loss powder might be connected with the DIC cases?" she asked.

"Assuming the facts as we have them are true," Rosa replied, "it is certainly as likely a cause as your prenatal supplement."

"It makes no sense."

"That's because the facts as we have them are clearly *not* all the facts. I'd like to see one of those infomercials you told me about."

"I'll get to work on that. My lawyer has some connections in TV. I'll see if he can get hold of a tape of one for tomorrow night's progress meeting. By the way, are you coming?"

"I wasn't planning on it. But now that I'm officially

off the case, I think I will. Especially if one of the feature attractions is that tape. Besides, with what you told me, and what I heard over the phone just now, I think the stakes might have just been raised."

"I don't understand."

"Your friend Annalee took that diet powder, yes?"

"Yes."

"And she's due to go into labor in just a few weeks, yes?"

"I didn't even think of that."

"With all you've had to process this past hour, that's understandable. Besides, there's time. Not a whole lot of time, but some. I'll see you tomorrow evening at your lawyer's office."

Sarah hugged Rosa long and lovingly, and promised not to share what they had learned with anyone. Then she hurried down the stairs and back to MCB. The roller coaster was cranking upward again. And she was feeling more excited and energized than at any time in weeks.

Alone in her room, seated cross-legged on her bed, Rosa Suarez tried to incorporate the new information with what she already knew. Sarah was right. Blaming the DIC cases on the short-term ingestion of an herbal powder years before made no real sense . . . yet. It also did not connect in any obvious way with the missing hospital chart pages. Scratching lines and drawing arrows on her pad, Rosa strained to put all of the facts in order until she felt her concentration begin to evaporate. Exhausted, she sank down onto the pillow. Nothing was solid. *Nothing.* It was like trying to link up puzzle pieces made of Jell-O. She wanted desperately just to close it all off and go to sleep. Instead, she called Ken Mulholland in the CDC lab.

"Hey, Rosa, how's your back?" he asked.

Just hearing his voice brought a smile. Of all those at work, only Ken knew where she was and how she had gotten the time off.

"Worse every day, thank goodness," she said. "Have you got anything for me?"

"Yes and no. I don't know what it is with you and your boss, but a memo has come down that your investigation is officially closed. No one in our department is to be devoting time to it. My section chief followed up the notice with a visit to me. He knows I've been helping you. I . . . um . . . I've been firmly instructed."

"You mean warned. My chief really wants to be sure I fail this one. I'm sorry, Ken. Listen, don't take any chances. But I really need your help."

"And you've got it. You aren't the only person around here with sick time coming, you know. If I have to, I'll just get the flu and work with you up there. You did say you had access to equipment."

"Not like yours, but yes. A whole lab, complete with technician. Now, what have you got?"

"We've got enough to say your girl had some sort of DNA virus in her blood at the time it was drawn last July. But we don't have enough growth to classify or type it. And we're not going to, either. Our last specimen burned out yesterday. If you want us to go further, we're going to need more serum."

"Then we'll just have to find a way to get you some."

"And I'll need the name and number of your technician up there. I may have to have him do the cultures."

"Anything you want that's within my power, you get."

"That important, huh?"

"I'm sitting on Vesuvius here, Ken. I swear I am. And soon, very soon, I think it's going to blow."

Chapter 28

OCTOBER 10

THIS IS JOHNNY NORMAN SPEAKING TO YOU FROM Television City, asking you, our live studio audience, and you, our millions of home viewers: Are you ready to change your lives for the better?"

"Yes!"

"Are you ready to catch the brass ring and finally hold on to it?"

"Yes!"

"Are you ready to walk the High Road to Slimness and Health?"

"Yes!"

"A little louder, please. I didn't quite hear you."

"YES!"

"Well, all right, then. You've come to the right place, so let's get started. It's time once again to say hello to your guide on the High Road—the man who coached his club to two Super Bowls but couldn't quite coach himself away from the ice cream bowl. Let's have a big, Herbal Weight Loss greeting for Coach Tom 'Bear' Griswold!"

Tall, granite jawed, and slender as a sapling, Coach Tom Griswold bounded onto the stage, clapping his hands the way he might have following one of his fabled half-time harangues. Packed into the waiting room of Matt's office, the viewers watched the taped infomercial in almost morbid fascination as Griswold recited his life story, accompanied by startling pictures of his expanding career, reputation, and waistline.

"I had more money in the bank than I'd ever want to spend, a family that loved me, a great career in broadcasting, and at almost three hundred pounds, a life expectancy that my doctors were measuring in months! At first they calmly advised me to lose weight. Then they got more threatening. They told me that unless I did lose that weight, I might as well stop buying green bananas. . . ." *Burst of laughter.* "Well, look at me now!"

He spun around in a graceless pirouette, to the accompaniment of screaming cheers from the adoring studio audience.

"Amazing," Glenn Paris murmured in awe.

"No, *America*," Eli Blankenship said. "The country where you can't be too rich or too thin."

"And now, Johnny," the coach went on, "before we meet the man responsible for bringing this remarkable discovery to America, give us the grand total to date."

A huge, garishly lit tote board filled the screen, its blank spaces awaiting Johnny Norman's grand announcement.

"Okay, Coach. Here we go. To date, the number of people around the country and around the world who have joined us on the High Road to Slimness and Health is: FIVE HUNDRED AND SEVENTY-ONE THOUSAND, SIX HUNDRED AND NINETEEN!" *Exuberant applause.*

"At forty-nine ninety-five apiece," attorney Arnold Hayden added. "Most incredible. And how long have they been marketing this stuff?"

"About six months," Matt said.

"But don't forget, Arnold," Colin Smith reminded. "From all indications, *this stuff* really works. Truthfully, now. Wouldn't you pay fifty bucks to get rid of that Michelin of yours—especially if you didn't have to knock yourself out dieting?"

"Thank you, Johnny Norman," Coach Griswold was saying. "Now I want to introduce you all to the man who has put years back into my life, to say nothing of what he has done for my tennis game and—my beautiful wife Sherry will be quick to tell you—for my love life as well." A few titillated oohs followed. "But first, let's hear a song from one of the true daughters of the Ayurvedic Herbal Weight Loss System. Betty Wilson was a Broadway star at two hundred and thirty pounds. But she'll be the first to tell you how much she hated looking in the mirror. Today she's still a star. But just look at what she sees in that mirror now." *Whistles and cheers for the singer, whose blue-sequined gown seemed painted on her perfectly proportioned, size-six body.* "Ladies and gentlemen, singing the title song from her new Broadway show, Miss Betty Wilson."

Matt fast-forwarded through the song while the others in the waiting room muttered phrases of disbelief or of grudging admiration. Then the coach, after a syrupy ninety-second introduction, brought Peter Ettinger onstage to a standing ovation from the studio audience. At the sight of him, Sarah felt the muscles of her jaws harden. But even she had to admit that the man, who looked and seemed larger than life in most circumstances, was even more imposing on TV.

Striding from one side of the sound stage to the other with the graceful elegance of a giraffe, Peter recited the meticulously documented tale of his discovery of Dr. Pramod Singh of New Delhi, India, and the man's remarkable Herbal Weight Loss System. Next came a series of testimonials from various carefully selected clients, all of whom were failures on other programs. Their moving tributes were interwoven with a step-by-step introduction to Ayurvedic medicine, tracing its development over thousands of years, from the earliest recorded history, through various periods of abandonment and acceptance, to an incredible resurgence in the 1980s and '90s.

And finally, against a backdrop that was clearly India, came a taped message from Pramod Singh himself. The secret herbs included in the Ayurvedic Herbal Weight Loss System were only part of the story, he stated. Although to be sure, a most major part.

"Use our powder properly, eat in moderation, avoid the five forbidden foods," he advised in a musical accent, "and you will lose the weight you wish no matter what else you do. Meditate five minutes each day, and follow the other basic principles of Ayurveda explained in your manual, and you will know many new freedoms beyond simply being thin. You will know freedom of the spirit. I am sorry I cannot be with you all in person, but I am here supervising the harvesting of the twelve crucial, natural components of our powder. I look forward to seeing you all in a few weeks. And now, back to Dr. Peter Ettinger."

"Doctor of what?" Matt asked, switching off the tape.

"Peter Ettinger has a number of degrees from a number of institutes," Sarah said. "But I honestly don't know if any of them is a Ph.D. from a traditional university."

"You don't sound as if you like the man much," Colin Smith said.

"He's a pompous ass if you ask me," Glenn Paris said.

Sarah smiled inwardly at the notion that almost certainly Peter would have chosen the exact same words to describe the hospital CEO.

"Well," Matt said, "I think we ought to get started. I've already said my piece by reasserting that the account of the nightmarish night Sarah and I survived in Chinatown is quite factual, and that rumors or no rumors, body or no body, Andrew Truscott is quite dead. The police have turned up nothing new. Neither did a private detective I hired—a very good one. We haven't given up trying to prove our story, but we're also at a loss about where to go from here. Any suggestions? . . . Well, then, unless there are any questions, I propose we move on.

"So far in this business, Jeremy Mallon's been scoring all the points, and we have been very much on the defensive. Tomorrow, with the formal deposition of Peter Ettinger, I hope that status will change. Before I ran the video, Mrs. Suarez gave you all some idea of what sort of things we'll be trying to pin him down on. I hope she'll go into more detail in just a bit. First, though, I'd like to hear from Dr. Snyder and Dr. Blankenship. Any order will be fine."

Sarah caught Matt's eye for the briefest moment. He was self-assured and very much in control of the meeting. How far he had come since that first session in the Milsap Room at MCB. Silently she longed for the day when she could be with him openly as his friend and lover—the day when Willis Grayson, his anger *and* his lawyers, would be a thing of their past.

"Suppose I go first, Eli," Randall Snyder offered. "What I have to say won't take very long." He cleared his throat. "I've had the American College of OB/Gyn send letters of inquiry to the heads of every obstetrics department in the country, looking for any unexplained cases of DIC in pregnancy or labor. So far there hasn't been one where there wasn't at least some predisposing thing going on—*abruptio placentae*, infection, toxemia, sickle cell disease, *in utero* fetal demise. Not one. I must say, Sarah, having sent the letters and made the dozens of follow-up calls, the lack of any DIC patient who did not take your prenatal supplement remains most disturbing and, if I may say so, most incriminating."

"Thank you," Matt said coolly. "You may say anything you wish. Someone has gone to a great deal of trouble, and caused a great deal of pain, to make Sarah's prenatal supplement appear responsible for those cases.

That fact, more than any other, suggests to me that it is not. Dr. Blankenship?"

The chief of medicine tapped a pencil thoughtfully against his palm before picking up the sheaf of notes he had set on the floor beside his seat.

"Well," he said finally, "my assignment was to become one of the world's leading experts on disseminated intravascular coagulopathy. It turns out that this was not nearly the humbling task it first seemed it would be. I have discovered that everyone in the clotting world knows *when* DIC occurs but absolutely nobody knows *why*. The more common name for this condition is consumptive coagulopathy, because while it is going on, all of the body's coagulation factors get *consumed*—used up in those tiny, abnormal clots. In its worst form, DIC is almost universally fatal. This fact makes the accomplishment of Defendant Sarah in saving the life of Plaintiff Lisa all the more remarkable. People who have DIC as badly as the plaintiff simply don't make it.

"Would I testify to that on the witness stand, Mr. Daniels? You betcha I would." His manner and tone, which had been quite matter-of-fact, intensified dramatically. "I would do anything I honestly could to help. I am quite disturbed about this case and the lack of overwhelming support Sarah has received from our institution. We made a promise to her and to ourselves months ago when we first met that we would present a unified front, and that Sarah would be considered innocent until proven—*proven*—otherwise. Randall, Glenn, I've spoken with Rob McCormick about this letter he sent out requesting Sarah's replacement as chief OB resident next year. He says he'll be happy to retract it for the time being if you two are in agreement to do so."

"Eli," Paris said, "this is hardly the place or time to—"

"Glenn, please. I don't want to start a war here or embarrass Sarah. But if we're going to present the unified front we agreed to, then we've got to get McCormick to back off. Yes?"

Paris's annoyance was apparent. Whether or not he agreed with Blankenship's request, he was uncomfortable with being told what to do.

Finally, after a long pause during which he regained his composure, he grinned and nodded.

"Right you are, Eli. I don't know where Rob got the idea to do what he did, but I'll call him tomorrow and set him straight."

"Excellent. Randall?"

"No problem," Snyder responded unenthusiastically.

"In that case, on with the show," Blankenship said. "There's one last category of causes of DIC I thought I might mention, and that's poisons. The injection of the naturally occurring clotting agent, thrombin, can cause a DIC-type picture, as can certain snake venoms. The toxin found in at least five different species of crotalids can cause lethal DIC."

"Crotalids?" Matt asked.

"Sorry, Matt. Rattlesnakes."

"But I don't believe the poisons you describe are effective by mouth," Sarah said. "And Lisa was at home when her DIC began. I can't imagine she could have received an injection of any sort."

"Or been bitten by a diamondback." Arnold Hayden guffawed.

No one else laughed.

"As I said," Blankenship replied, "I only included the poison possibility for completeness. There may be an oral toxin we don't know about that can cause DIC. Maybe someone has such a substance and is on a vendetta against our hospital or the obstetrics department. At this point, who knows?"

"That's all we need," Glenn Paris groaned. "A psycho."

"Any questions for Eli?" Matt asked. "Okay, then. Rosa, you've kindly shared some significant developments in your work. Can you sum up what your conclusions are at this point?"

Earlier in the day, Sarah had spoken with Rosa for over an hour. The epidemiologist felt torn between the desperate need for all concerned to share information and ideas and her deep-seated bias against disclosing research still in progress. Until her results were checked, double-checked, and locked away, she felt uncomfortable trusting anyone with the details of her work. In the end, nothing was really resolved between them except that Rosa would attend the meeting and disclose as much data and theory as she felt comfortable in doing. No more.

"I must first stress what Dr. Snyder has already brought up," Rosa began. "The connection, whether significant or not, between the three DIC cases and the ingestion of Sarah's prenatal supplement is quite firmly established. I should add, however, that my laboratory work and research does not suggest a direct toxic relationship between DIC and the ingestion of any herb. An allergy of some sort to one of the components, or perhaps contamination with a toxin, would be much better bets. But I have serious doubts about either of those possibilities as well. As has also been mentioned, discovery of a labor patient with DIC who has never taken herbal prenatal vitamins would effectively absolve Dr. Baldwin of any responsibility."

"What do you make of this Herbal Weight Loss product?" Paris asked.

"I was hoping you'd be able to help us there, Mr. Paris," Rosa said. "This Pramod Singh, what can you tell us about him?"

"Not very much, really. Six years ago, when I came to MCB, I made the decision to incorporate various aspects of what is called holistic medicine into our hospital. I was looking for an identity for MCB—something that would make the public want to come to us.

"Pramod Singh was a highly respected Ayurvedic

physician who heard about what we were trying to do and contacted me. I put him on salary, and he worked in our outpatient department for almost two years. Then he just quit. No notice. Not even a letter of explanation. Just a one-sentence note. The next time I heard about him was when I saw him on one of these dumb programs.

"I had originally hoped Singh might be part of a larger holistic department at the hospital. But until our McGrath Foundation grant, we've been on such thin financial ice that I couldn't guarantee anything. By the way, as long as I'm on the subject, I hope you'll all be my guests at the demolition of the Chilton Building the end of the month. It will kick off the largest construction project in MCB history. We'll be having a champagne reception just before the big bang. I also hope some of you will buy chances in the raffle we're running to be the one to actually push the button. A once-in-a-lifetime opportunity, if I do say so myself."

"Did any of you know Dr. Singh was using this weight loss powder when he was at MCB?" Rosa asked, pointedly ignoring Paris's bombast. "Well, you might ask around."

"Do you really think this product and the DIC cases are connected?" Snyder asked.

"Remember, Dr. Snyder," Rosa said. "My stock in trade is probabilities. The more times a connection happens, the more likely it is to be significant. Now, to the many other commonalities I have uncovered among our three cases, we can most probably add the exposure four or five years ago to Dr. Singh and his product. But remember, as Mr. Paris just explained, he purposely established a unique facility where products like Singh's powder or Sarah's prenatal supplement might exist. So in the end, our three women's choosing to be cared for at the Medical Center of Boston may prove to be the most significant commonality of all."

"God, that's all we need!" Paris exclaimed. "Rosa,

you're not planning to speak to the press about this, are you?"

Rosa smiled at the notion.

"It was like pulling teeth for Dr. Baldwin just to get me to speak to you at all," she said. "I'm not inclined to trust any wider audience with my findings, at least not yet."

"Okay, everyone," Matt said. "If there's no other business, we'll call it quits and I'll finish preparing for our first offensive. Arnold, the Ettinger deposition's going to be taken at eleven at Mallon's office. You're welcome to attend."

"I just might," the lawyer responded.

"Give 'em hell, Daniels," Paris said.

One by one the MCB group filed out, until only Matt, Sarah, and Rosa remained.

"I thought the session went very well, Matt," Sarah said.

"Come on. We got almost no place, and you know it." He paced to the window, his fists clenched in frustration. "Parts of hospital charts missing; Chinese tongs getting paid to frame you and a helpless old man; some nervous, little, stuttering weirdo following you. Somebody, someplace knows what in the hell is going on around here. And I'm getting sick and tired of it not being me."

"I might be able to help a little bit," Rosa said softly.

"What are you saying?" Matt stopped pacing.

"There's something I know that I haven't spoken about at all. I've decided to share it with you two but, for now at least, with no one else. Please don't speak of this to anyone."

Matt glanced over at Sarah.

"You have our word," he said.

"Okay. Lisa Grayson had some sort of DNA virus in her bloodstream at the time she had her crisis. My lab person doesn't know exactly what it is, but he does know it's not usual. He wants some more serum from Lisa."

"Even though she has no DIC symptoms?" Sarah asked.

"He'll take what he can get. If nothing grows, he'll look for antibodies and see if he can back his way into an identification. He's very good at what he does. One of the best. But I'm afraid we can't get to Lisa without going through this attorney of hers."

"In that case, maybe we should ask him before we begin to dissect Ettinger," Matt said.

"It's very important," Rosa said. "I don't believe either the herbal weight loss powder or Sarah's vitamins are solely responsible for what's happened. They may both be playing a role, but an infection of some sort makes more sense. I have a terrible, terrible feeling that unless we get to the bottom of things soon, more women are going to die."

Fifty miles to the west, Annalee Ettinger lay on her canopied bed, nestled in the arms of her fiancé, Taylor.

"Tay," she said. "It's happening again. Here, feel right here. I swear I'm having some contractions."

Chapter 29

OCTOBER 11

THERE WERE NO POLITE INTRODUCTIONS; NO CIVIL shaking of hands. Once the combatants were present and seated at the massive conference table in Jeremy Mallon's law firm library, once the stenographer had readied her machine and loosened her fingers, the battle simply began. With no judge present, Sarah wondered just how ugly it might get.

"State your full name please," Matt said, after dictating the time, date, location, list of those present, and the purpose of the session.

"Peter David Ettinger."

"Your occupation?"

"I am an anthropologist and a healer."

"Your education?"

"I have a bachelor's degree from Reed College and a master's from the University of Michigan, both in anthropology, and both with honors."

"On the television ads for your weight loss product, you are often referred to as 'Doctor.' Have you a degree at that level?"

"I hold an honorary doctorate in herbal sciences from

the Holbrook College of Chiropractic, and several other honorary doctorates as well."

"Do you have a Ph.D.?"

"No."

"An M.D.?"

"Certainly not."

"And what is your current occupation?"

"I am the executive director of the Xanadu Holistic Health Community and president of the Xanadu Corporation."

"And exactly what does the Xanadu Corporation do?"

"We formulate and distribute the Ayurvedic Herbal Weight Loss System."

The key to a successful deposition, Matt had explained to Sarah, was the same as that for a successful courtroom cross-examination—never ask a question to which you do not already know the answer. Unfortunately, he was quick to add, the only significant questions he would be asking Peter Ettinger today *were* those to which they had no answer.

Sarah stared down at her hands, folded tightly on the table in front of her. She hoped Peter could not tell *how* tightly. When she had first returned to Boston, she had actually entertained notions of reestablishing some sort of professional or platonic relationship with the man. Now she could barely stand to look at him. She had never done anything more virulent than to move her life along in directions that did not include him. No public condemnations; no nasty letters; no tell-all articles; no demands for palimony. Yet here he was, helping to orchestrate a legal case against her that could well put her in professional purgatory, if not in prison.

"You mentioned you were a healer, Mr. Ettinger—oh, excuse me, do you prefer to be addressed as *Mister* or *Doctor*?"

"Either way. Mister will be fine."

"Don't badger this man, counselor," Jeremy Mallon

warned matter-of-factly. "Either in your words or your tone. You do, and this deposition may be over a lot sooner than you expect."

"Mr. Mallon, please don't threaten me," Matt countered. It seemed to Sarah he was purposely exaggerating his Mississippi drawl. "You saddled this mule months ago in the shop of a sick old man. Now you and your stable of experts had better be ready to ride it yourselves."

In the corner of the room, the stenographer dispassionately whispered into the hooded microphone of a tape recorder at the same time she was tapping out the exchange on her machine. Arnold Hayden, seated to Matt's right, nodded that Matt's response was appropriate and necessary. Across from Hayden, Jeremy Mallon's associate countered by whispering something in Mallon's ear. Sarah managed a furtive glance across at Peter, but saw only an emotionless mask. Circles within circles within circles. The whole affair would have been incredibly fascinating to her, had not her livelihood and way of life been at stake.

The morning had begun contentiously an hour before the actual deposition. Mallon flatly refused to allow his client, Lisa Grayson, to have her blood drawn or, in fact, to be contacted by Matt, Sarah, Rosa Suarez, or anyone else who did not clear such contact with him. Matt had kept his cool and had stopped short of indicting the Ayurvedic Herbal Weight Loss System. But it was clear to Sarah that before this session was through, Peter's remarkable gold mine would come under attack.

Arnold Hayden had been with them from the outset of the day. Sarah was pleasantly surprised to realize that her initial impression of the man as being far more legal form than substance was way off base. He had a practical and theoretical acumen that Matt clearly found useful, and a calming manner that helped keep her inside her skin. Now, in combat, his presence and bearing seemed to add credibility and force to Matt's examination.

There was also the matter of Hayden's helping out should Matt's compromised objectivity become manifest in any way. Unwilling to give up either Sarah or her case, Matt had asked for his assistance with that in mind. And although he had not spelled out to Hayden the extent of his and Sarah's evolving relationship, she suspected the hospital attorney had some idea.

"Okay, now, Mr. Ettinger," Matt said, "getting back to the issue at hand. Would you mind telling us your definition of what a healer is?"

For almost an hour and a half, Matt asked, rephrased, and asked again questions designed more to fill in blanks and set tone than to get at any major legal point. The strategy he, Sarah, and Hayden had agreed upon was to try to get Peter to acknowledge that Sarah's method of prescribing and dispensing herbs was, in fact, no different from his own. Once made, the point would essentially transform Peter into an expert witness *for them.* They would then begin to dissect the connection between Ettinger, the Xanadu Ayurvedic Weight Loss System, and Pramod Singh.

"When I get to that point," Matt said, "I'm just going to wing it." He dangled his Egyptian amulet. "I mean, what chance does he have against two thousand years of black magic?"

At the ninety-minute mark, they took a break, during which Mallon had one of his secretaries serve coffee.

"Hey, Matt, maybe you should switch cups with Jeremy," Sarah whispered. "There's no telling what he might have put in yours."

"Nonsense," Matt drawled. "He's about as intimidated by me as a hungry mountain lion would be by the Easter bunny. The last thing he'd want to do at this point is to bump me off. I'm too much fun to play with. But right about now I'm going to start tightening the screws on his expert. The measure of how effective I am will be how loudly and how often Mallon objects to my questions. Arnold, do you have any suggestions?"

"None, really," Hayden said. "Except that I think it's time to pin down some things about this Dr. Singh. So far, I'm impressed by the way you've handled matters."

"Thanks. That's kind of you to say—especially considering that I haven't done any damage whatsoever."

"What you've been throwing are body blows," the older lawyer replied. "No one really pays much attention to them, but they set up the head shots. You're doing just fine." He patted Matt encouragingly on the shoulder as the session resumed.

"Okay, Mr. Ettinger," Matt began, "I'd like to spend some time talking about this Ayurvedic Herbal Weight Loss System of yours."

"Why?" Mallon asked.

"You're the one who brought this man in as an expert," Matt said. "I'm just trying to document his qualifications."

"Peter, I don't see where this line of questioning is relevant. If you don't care to answer the questions, I don't see any reason why you should."

"Offhand I can think of two reasons, Mr. Ettinger," Matt said with calm force. "First of all, if you refuse, I promise you that I'll be in front of a judge before this day is done, bringing a motion to compel you to answer. And second"—he looked first at Sarah and then at Mallon, before deliberately leveling his gaze again on Peter—"*second*, I have good reason to believe—hell no, *I have proof*—that just as Lisa Grayson took Sarah Baldwin's herbal preparation before her ill-fated delivery, so did she take your Herbal Weight Loss product as well!"

"But—"

"I said *proof*."

"Wait!" Mallon snapped. "Peter, hold it. Don't respond. Mr. Daniels, I don't intend to bite at that worm. But since what you are alleging is news to me, I would like to speak with Mr. Ettinger in private before we continue."

"Take your time," Matt said.

Arnold Hayden turned his face away from Mallon and brought his fist up to the side of his jaw. Matt's timing and delivery had been perfect. His first head shot had landed squarely.

Sarah watched as her former lover unfolded his reedy six-and-a-half-foot frame. He glanced over at her, his expression pinched and angry. For a moment, it seemed as if he was about to make an obscene gesture.

Grow up, she mouthed.

She was gratefully uncertain of his reply.

"Okay," Mallon said upon their return. "Not only do I approve of Mr. Ettinger's answering this line of questions, I encourage it." His expression was smug, his manner once again self-assured—too self-assured.

Sarah strained to understand why.

"Mr. Ettinger, how did you first meet Pramod Singh?" Matt went on.

"We had done a series of seminars together some years ago when he was on the staff of the Medical Center of Boston. He told me about a set of ancient Ayurvedic dietary rules and herbs that he had been using on his patients for weight loss with remarkable success."

"Was Lisa Summer one of those patients?"

"I don't know."

"Constanza Hidalgo?"

"I don't—"

"Stop, Peter!" Mallon snapped. "Mr. Daniels, stick to the issue and the patient at hand."

"Mr. Ettinger, did Pramod Singh want to market his product to the general public?"

"He did."

"With you as the spokesman—the figurehead?"

"Among other things."

"And so you two Ayurvedic entrepreneurs struck up a deal of some sort?"

"Object to the antagonistic form of the question," Mallon cut in. "Don't answer it, Peter."

"Mr. Ettinger, exactly what is in this product of yours?"

"A number of herbs, plants, and roots. Twelve to be exact. Dr. Singh obtains them in India and elsewhere in the Far East, and ships them to me. We have a production facility where the naturally occurring substances are combined with a protein powder to form a combination balanced nutritional replacement and appetite suppressant."

"But you have no *scientific verification* of the product's composition, do you?"

Ettinger glanced over at Jeremy Mallon. When he turned back to Matt, he was grinning confidently.

"As a matter of fact," he said, "unlike Dr. Baldwin's preparation, we have absolute scientific verification—FDA analysis *and* approval of the product. I demanded those before ever allowing the Xanadu name to be used, and we insist upon retesting on an ongoing basis."

Another head shot. But this time, from the plaintiff's side of the table. Matt fussed with his notes. Sarah could feel him struggling to maintain composure as he searched carefully for the next question.

"This production and packaging facility," he asked finally, "is it out there on the grounds of the Xanadu Community?"

"It is."

"Shipping, too?"

"In a separate building, but yes. Shipping is done at Xanadu also."

"Mr. Ettinger, just how much money are you two raking in off this powder?"

"Objection!" Mallon cried out. "Peter, don't answer. Mr. Daniels, the form and content of that question are amateurish—in the baseball terms you might better understand, strictly bush league. Until now I have made a number of allowances for the fact that, aside from a misplaced molar or whatever, this is your first malpractice case. But I draw the line at questions like this."

Crimson rushed to Matt's cheeks. Beneath the table, Sarah patted him gently on the thigh.

"Easy does it," she whispered.

Matt calmed himself with a slow, deep breath. "Mr. Ettinger, go over briefly what happens at this production plant of yours."

"It's quite simple, really," Ettinger said, as if he were speaking to a third grader. "The raw plants and roots come in, get thoroughly washed, inspected, and sterilized by heat or U.V. light. Next they're ground or pulverized, proportioned out according to the ancient Ayurvedic menu we're using, and combined with the commercially prepared protein base. Finally, the mixture is sterilized again and packaged."

"And then just like that it's shipped?"

"The final, shipped product includes four months' worth of powder, a manual on Ayurveda and Ayurvedic dietary principles, and a supply of vitamins."

"Vitamins?"

Matt visibly perked up at the word.

"Yes."

"Herbal vitamins? Like Dr. Baldwin's?"

Again Peter grinned smugly.

"Hardly." His delivery was pure vinegar. "Dr. Baldwin's supplements are, well, Dr. Baldwin's. Ours are pure vitamins—standard, FDA-approved multivitamins, manufactured for us by Huron Pharmaceuticals."

Matt's eagerness deflated.

"Pills?" he asked.

"Actually, they're gelatin capsules. One is dissolved in each daily weight loss shake."

Jeremy Mallon feigned a yawn.

"Mr. Daniels, please," he said. "Your fishing expedition has run aground, and you know it. Mr. Ettinger has been much more patient with you than need be. Certainly more tolerant than I would have been in his position."

"Mr. Ettinger, are you and Dr. Singh partners?" Matt asked, ignoring Mallon's protest.

"We are."

"How would I go about locating this man, this Ayurvedic Herbal partner of yours?"

"Enough!" Mallon barked.

"That's okay," Ettinger said. "The truth is, Pramod spends most of his time in India now. And mostly he's traveling. I reach him through an American Express office in New Delhi. If you want that address, I'll be happy to have my secretary send it to you."

"Now, enough," Mallon said. "Find another line of questioning, or it's over and out."

"Actually, I'm done. But I have something to say to both you and Mr. Ettinger. Strictly off the record."

"Evelyn, we're finished. Thank you." Mallon chatted in whispers with his associate until the stenographer had cleared out. "Okay, go ahead," he said then.

"Even though we haven't mentioned them, and I intend to see that they are not part of this case, we all know with certainty that two other women beside Lisa Grayson have had this DIC."

"So?"

"I said before that we had proof that Lisa Grayson was treated by Dr. Singh some years ago with what I assume was the Ayurvedic Herbal Weight Loss System. Well, we also have proof that the other two DIC cases lost large amounts of weight with him as well."

"What!" Ettinger exclaimed.

Anticipating Matt's revelation, Sarah had her attention fixed on the man across the table from her. His surprise seemed genuine. However, she reminded herself, she had misread Peter Ettinger before.

"Easy, Peter," Mallon said. "This man's been playing losing cards all morning. I see this as just a bluff to rattle us."

"It's no bluff," Sarah said.

"I want to see your so-called proof," Mallon said.

"And we want to see a blood sample from Lisa Grayson," Sarah countered angrily.

"That's it, we're done," Mallon declared.

He threw his papers into his briefcase and as much as pulled Peter Ettinger to his feet and toward the door.

"This is no game," Matt said. "This is people's lives. Don't you care?"

"Fuck you," replied Mallon.

"Peter," Sarah tried, "this is very important. Remember, Annalee took your powder, too."

"But she didn't take those bogus herbs of yours. You just stay away from her and she'll do just fine."

His vitriol nearly brought her hurtling over the table and into his face.

"Peter?" she said sweetly instead.

"Yes."

"Don't tell me what to do."

Chapter 30

OCTOBER 17

AUTUMN ON LONG ISLAND WAS PROFOUNDLY BEAUTIful. Dressed in an aqua running suit, Lisa Grayson loped through a tunnel of shimmering foliage, up the mile-long hill of Kennesaw Road, and onto the flat, gravelly stretch that led back to Stony Hill. She was perspiring, but not excessively so—especially considering that when she reached home, she would have completed her first halfmarathon ever. *Fantastic!* she thought. Thirteen miles by a woman who not too long ago considered a brisk walk to the corner convenience store to be her physical limit.

"Too darn much. . . . Too darn much. . . ."

She sang the words nursery-rhyme style, in sync with her strides. The Boston Marathon was in mid-April, and she might well be ready. Her physical therapist knew the organizers of the race. If Lisa could do the twenty-six plus miles in anything under four and a half hours, he would see to it that the documented marathon time necessary to receive an official entry and number was waived.

"See how she runs. . . . See how she runs. . . ."

Some sweat dripped from her forehead into her eyes.

Slowing just a little, Lisa reached her right hand into her jacket pocket.

Fist, she thought intently. *Fist.*

The Otto Boch myo-electric hand was truly incredible, but it had no sensory input. She had to rely on other messages to tell her the prosthesis was doing what she wanted it to. First she sensed the now-familiar tension around her elbow. The electrodes had been implanted there, in what remained of her forearm flexor muscles. Next she felt the firmness of the closed fist, pressing against her side from within the jacket pocket.

"Come on, fake hand," she said, panting in cadence. "Do your stuff."

She pulled her arm free of the pocket and sensed without looking that the lifelike fingers were clutching her balled-up handkerchief.

"Way to go, hand," she said, mopping her brow without breaking stride. "Way to go."

Over the two months since receiving the limb, she had made remarkable progress. In time, she had been promised by the physical therapist and the prostheticist, she would be able to pick up a cigarette ash without having it crumble. She would also be able to latch onto an object and dare anyone—*anyone*—to pull it away from her. *The Bionic Woman!* There were limits, to be sure. She had chosen the less obtrusive "cosmetic" skin over the more functional and more easily maintained metal pincers. In general though, the hand far exceeded her projections of what being an amputee would be like. And focusing on learning to use it had done worlds for her depression.

She still missed her baby terribly and thought many times each day about how life would have been with him. But she also knew that somehow, all she had been through had become a passage for her. In facing her tragedy, in working to overcome the pain and grief, she was growing up in areas that had not changed since the day she ran away from home.

And then, of course, there was her father. The transformation in Willis Grayson over the months since her return to Stony Hill was, if anything, even more striking than her own. He was mellower than she could ever remember—far less controlling and more willing to listen. And he went out of his way to spend time with her. She had never really believed the man was capable of change, but change he had.

She passed over the one-lane bridge at the base of the long dirt and gravel drive leading up to the house. The video-monitored security gate was closed, but the narrow pass-through alongside it was not. Four-tenths of a mile to go. The muscles in her legs were beginning to tighten up, but she could make it. She knew she could.

"Miss Grayson," a man's voice called out from behind her.

Lisa stopped and turned, still running in place. A young man in a gray uniform and hat stepped from behind a tree. He carried a Federal Express envelope beneath his arm.

"Meet me at the house," she said with a pant, keeping her distance and wondering where his truck was. "I want to finish this run."

"I can't," he said urgently. "I'm being paid to give this to you personally. This is the third day I've tried to meet up with you. Your father's security patrol will hurt me if they catch me again, and they'll be back here again any minute. We've got to hurry."

Bewildered, Lisa glanced at her watch, debated, and then stopped running.

"Okay, what is it?" she asked, still keeping a good twenty yards between her and the man.

"I don't know. I'm being paid to find a way to deliver this to you. That's all. Please, I hear a car now."

"Set it down right there," she ordered. "And then get away."

The young man hesitated and then placed the envelope on the grass by the road.

"Don't let them take this from you," he said. Then he whirled and sprinted off.

Through the still morning air Lisa could, in fact, hear a car approaching from the direction of the house. She snatched up the envelope and dashed back down the road until she found a copse dense enough to conceal her. Hidden there, gasping for air, she watched two of her father's security people cruise slowly past. By the time the motor noise had faded, she had recovered enough to tear open the Federal Express envelope. The enclosed, unembossed, white envelope had her name written on the outside in a meticulous, woman's hand. The note within was typed.

DEAR LISA,

The man who delivered this is not with Federal Express. I hired him in hopes that he might find a way to get this letter to you. My name is Rosa Suarez. Perhaps you remember me. I am the epidemiologist assigned by the Centers for Disease Control to study the three cases of DIC at the Medical Center of Boston. I need your help, but have been unable to reach you by phone or mail. After leaving several phone messages for you, I called to find that your home phone number has been changed, and that the new number is unavailable—at least to me. Two certified letters from me were reported as delivered and signed for by you. It is possible you received them, but I have my doubts. I do not believe your lawyer or your father want you to hear what I have to say—and what I must ask of you. . . .

"Mr. Daniels?"

"Yes."

"Phelps here, Roger Phelps. I'm glad I caught you in."

I'm not, Matt thought. The claims adjuster for the

MMPO may have been responsible for assigning him to Sarah's case, but there was something about the little man—something in his speech, perhaps, or in his eyes—that made Matt uncomfortable.

"Yes, Mr. Phelps. What can I do for you?"

Matt's desk was piled high with research volumes, law tomes, and Xeroxed hospital records. In the next two weeks, he would be taking depositions from two of Mallon's expert witnesses, as well as from Lisa Grayson herself. On the plaintiff's side, Mallon would be getting a crack at Sarah and at Kwong Tian-Wen. There had been no feedback from the man following the intense ending to Peter Ettinger's deposition. Not one word. Matt had half hoped that his opponent might at least suggest putting things on hold until the allegations about Ettinger's weight loss product could be evaluated. But nothing. It appeared that regardless of what facts and revelations cropped up, Mallon was not intimidated.

"Mr. Daniels," Phelps said, "first of all, I want to thank you for keeping me abreast of the developments in the Baldwin case. It's made it a good deal easier for us to evaluate things and come up with a decision of how to proceed."

"Decision?"

"Yes, Mr. Daniels. After carefully weighing all the aspects and prospects of this case, we've decided to settle."

"What?"

"You've done an excellent job, and I can assure you that in the future you'll be called upon many—"

"Mr. Phelps, excuse me, but I don't understand."

"Don't understand what, Mr. Daniels? We looked at the costs of continuing, the potential magnitude of a jury award, and the possibility of losing. Then we made the decision to try to settle, came up with a figure, presented it to Mallon, and on behalf of his client, he accepted. Of course, the settlement will include no admission of any guilt on Dr. Baldwin's part."

Matt stared in disbelief at the phone.

"Mr. Phelps," he said as evenly as he could manage, "Sarah Baldwin is not guilty of any malpractice. There have been developments—significant developments. We are going to win the case."

"Ah, the Chinese tong story. I'm sorry, Mr. Daniels, but we considered that, too. As things stand, all a jury has to listen to is that poor old man and—"

"How much did you settle for?"

"Mr. Daniels, there's no need to get testy about this."

"How much?"

"Two hundred thousand."

"And Willis Grayson accepted that?"

"Apparently."

"Mr. Phelps, Willis Grayson keeps that kind of money in his cookie jar. He wanted Dr. Baldwin behind bars. Her hide, that's what he's after. Why in the hell would he agree to settle if he thought they had a case?"

"Mr. Daniels, please. I did not call to start an argument. The decision has been made."

"And the other two women? What happens when their families get wind of this?"

"We'll deal with that when it happens. Now, if you have no further questions—"

"Dr. Baldwin can refuse to drop the case."

"She would then be personally responsible for all legal fees and any jury award. Why on earth would she want to do that?"

"Because she's innocent, that's why, dammit."

"Mr. Daniels, I know about your relationship with Dr. Baldwin. If you talk her into continuing with this case and collect any legal fees at all, I would consider that a serious breach of ethics."

"What do you know about legal ethics?"

"I'm an attorney and a member of the bar, sir. That's what. Now, I hope I have made our position clear. As far as the Mutual Medical Protective Organization is concerned, this case is closed."

Over her twenty-three years as a government epidemiologist, Rosa had met cabinet secretaries, governors, and two vice presidents. She had faced up to a boss who wanted to crucify her and stared down the barrel of the congressional subcommittee investigating her BART allegations. But never had she felt quite as intimidated, measured her words quite as carefully, as tonight with Willis Grayson.

The WNG Corporation helicopter had picked her up on the roof of the surgical building of the Medical Center of Boston and had then made one gratuitous sweep over the glittering downtown area before heading southwest toward Long Island. The aircraft was more opulent and far quieter than Rosa had imagined it would be. The pilot and a second man were separated from the rear cabin by a glass slider that was essentially soundproof. The only other passenger in the plush compartment beside Rosa was Grayson. His chilly manner and persistent glower made it quite clear that flying her from Boston to New York and back merely to draw his daughter's blood was not his idea. He had nodded a greeting to her as his man assisted her into the cabin, and then had motioned for her to fasten her seat belt. But they were over Providence before he actually spoke to her.

"I don't understand why you insisted on drawing Lisa's blood yourself when we have any number of people who could have done it," he said after some small talk.

"In situations that are critical to my work, I have learned that nothing can be completely trusted unless I have done it myself."

Grayson's smile was ironic. "That understanding puts you well ahead of ninety percent of my executives. You don't seem very comfortable. Are you afraid of flying?"

"No."

"Of me?"

She shrugged. "You're very wealthy, and very powerful, and not at all a reassuring person."

"I'm not accustomed to being told what to do, Mrs. Suarez. Now, because of your letter and that stunt with that bogus Federal Express man, my daughter is issuing me orders like a five-star general. I have no choice but to do what she asks, or I risk losing her again."

"Mr. Grayson, *your* actions left *me* no choice. You signed for mail addressed to Lisa. You had your phone number changed to keep me from reaching her."

"Well, now I have given you the new number, as well as my promise to cooperate with you in any way you ask."

"I'm sure Lisa appreciates the significance of those actions."

"I hope so. Do you have children, Mrs. Suarez?"

"Three daughters."

"If someone hurt one of those girls, you would punish them if you could, yes?"

"I would do what I could through legal channels to see they were appropriately punished, if that's what you mean."

"Sometimes my methods are more direct," Grayson said. "Today my attorney called and recommended that I accept an offer from the insurance company to settle our case against Dr. Baldwin without a finding. In view of the revelations regarding Lisa and this diet product, my lawyer feels we might not be able to convince a jury of Dr. Baldwin's guilt. I, however, remain convinced she is responsible for the maiming of my daughter and the death of my grandson."

"You are certainly entitled to that opinion, sir."

"My daughter is not as certain as I am."

"Based on what we know to this point, I don't believe she should be—or you either, for that matter."

"Mrs. Suarez, exactly what *do* you know?"

It was Rosa's turn to smile. She gazed down at the lights gliding past two thousand feet below.

"Mr. Grayson," she said, "I have learned from bitter experience that it is unwise to discuss the findings of an ongoing investigation with anyone unless it is absolutely unavoidable."

"Ah yes, your debacle in San Francisco."

Rosa spun to face him. "You, sir, are exactly the sort of person from whom I have learned to protect myself. I don't like being checked up on, Mr. Grayson. The mere fact of your doing so could already have jeopardized my work."

"I assure you, my people excel at keeping their inquiries discreet. They've had a good deal of practice."

"I'm sure they have. Well, if they are that good, you must understand me well enough to know that there is no point in pursuing this discussion."

"What I know is that your department chief would be upset to learn you had recovered from your ruptured disk so miraculously but had neglected to inform him."

Rosa glared at him, her cheeks burning.

"Mr. Grayson," she said, "I can see that your reputation has been earned. Well, sir, if you want to bring the force of your massive corporate empire crashing down on the head of a sixty-year-old lady, go right ahead. I assure you, there is precious little trouble you could cause me that others have not already. But just remember, there are some problems I can cause you as well."

Willis Grayson studied her for a time. Then suddenly he laughed roundly, reached across, and patted her on the arm.

"Perhaps, Mrs. Suarez," he said, "after you complete this investigation and retire from government service, you'll consider coming to work for me."

Chapter 31

OCTOBER 25

T WAS EIGHT-FIFTEEN IN THE MORNING WHEN SARAH MA-neuvered the borrowed maroon Accord into one of the outbound lanes and inched down into the William Callahan Tunnel.

"*Ovejas*," Rosa said, gesturing at the grim-faced drivers jockeying for their spots in the procession. "Sheep."

"It's especially impressive considering the rush-hour traffic is coming the other way," Sarah said.

She and Rosa were heading to Logan Airport to pick up Ken Mulholland. The CDC virologist, who had been working on Lisa Grayson's serum, had come up with something. But the pressure had intensified on him to turn over any information on the Boston cases to Rosa Suarez's department head and *not* to assist her in any further way.

"There are just too many egos involved," Rosa had explained. "My chief will go to his grave believing that I ruined his career. I honestly feel he would rather see this mystery go unsolved than to have me come up with the answer. Ken is pretty immune to being squeezed by his superiors, but I really don't want him to get in any trouble. He has a wife and two little ones depending on him. That's why I begged him to let us do as much of the work as possible up here. He was involved in a portion of the BART investigation with me. Some of the culture reports that were altered came from his department. Since then he's had as little trust for the politics of the place as I do. So he's taking a personal day off to fly up to Boston. He's arranged things with a friend at a terminal someplace in Atlanta. They'll plug in by modem to the data banks and electronics in his lab. Ken will be working on his department's computers, but he'll be doing it *in absentia* twice removed."

"And all he wants from us is an empty room with an IBM compatible terminal?"

"And a modem."

"In that case, we're all set," Sarah said. "Glenn Paris has provided us an office in the data processing unit."

"No questions asked?"

"No questions asked. Rosa, do you think this is something significant?"

"I have believed all along that infection of some sort was the most likely—though certainly not the only—explanation for the DIC cases. So yes, I believe this day could prove most interesting and eventful."

The week just past had been most eventful as well. It began with the surprise decision by claims adjuster Roger Phelps of the Mutual Medical Protective Organization to settle Sarah's case. Then there was Rosa's flight to Long Island to draw Lisa Grayson's blood. And finally, just a day ago, there was the letter from Sarah to Phelps—formal notification that she had opted to reject the MMPO's no-guilt-admitted, $200,000 settlement. She would either have the case against her dropped entirely, or go to trial at her own expense.

There would be no settlement.

Sarah swung onto the exit ramp leading out to the airport. The early-morning overcast was beginning to burn off. The day, with temperatures predicted in the sixties, promised to be near perfect. Sarah had some clinic responsibilities and some library work she needed to do. But she had no surgery scheduled, and planned to spend as much time as possible with Rosa and her virologist.

"Five whole minutes to spare," Sarah said, pulling up in front of the Delta terminal departure level. "I'll wait here. I don't imagine he'll have to go through baggage claim."

"I should think not. He's booked on the three-fifty flight back to Atlanta."

Rosa hurried into the terminal. She emerged a short time later, arm in arm with a cheery, ruddy-cheeked fellow who was taller than average by any measure, but positively gargantuan next to her. He had a curved meerschaum pipe bobbing from the corner of his mouth and looked more like the *Burgermeister* of some Bavarian village than a scientist. By the time they had passed through the Sumner Tunnel and back into the city, though, Sarah knew why Rosa spoke of Ken Mulholland's dedication with admiration that bordered on awe.

"There ain't much of our little viral friend in your lady's blood," Mulholland said with something of a midwestern twang. "But he's there, alive and kicking. For now, until we've got something a bit more scientific, we're calling him George. Although we could just as easily have made him a Georgia. The first evidence we got was indirect—an antiviral antibody that didn't match any of the ones we know about. Now we have some actual electron microscope pictures of the little guy. Handsome. A veritable matinee idol. Might be in the adenovirus class. We're going to be working today on completing the chemical dissection of his DNA. But as far as we've gone, he's a perfect match with the DNA sequence from the previous sample you sent us from Lisa Grayson. How much time before we get to your hospital, Dr. Baldwin?"

"Ten minutes. Less actually. Listen, though. I'm

afraid that when I'm being addressed by someone to whom I already owe a great deal of gratitude, I'll have to insist on 'Sarah.' "

"Well, then, Sarah—and you, too, Rosa—supposing I use the drive time we have left to give you both a little background of what we're up against, and what we're going to try to do today. I'm glad I decided to conduct this business up here. It'll be much easier for me to operate without looking over my shoulder every other minute. I've disconnected the screen on the terminal in our lab. The modem's hidden beneath a pile of papers. My department head—or yours, Rosa—could be standing three feet away, and he'd have no idea that data's pouring out of the place."

"Thank you for going to all this trouble," Sarah said.

"Just being cautious. This woman here's a star. It's time some people down there besides me know it. Now, then. There's no question your Miss Grayson has a low-grade viral infection of some sort."

"And not a commonly known virus?" Rosa asked.

Mulholland shook his head. "Hardly. We're going to finish mapping out George's DNA as soon as we get your computer booted up. But even at this point, I can say that whatever George is, he ain't in the books I've checked. He could still be something natural that we just don't know about yet. But I doubt that. A much better bet is something man-made. With luck, we'll know for certain by lunchtime."

"Then what?" Sarah asked.

"Well, assuming we finish our DNA sequencing and still suspect George is a product of man rather than a production of God, I think it will be time for a crash legal course on *Diamond versus Chakrabarty*."

"What's that all about?"

The virologist nodded respectfully toward Rosa Suarez.

"Well," he said, "it's about these hungry little bacterial beasties that eat oil slicks. I suspect that when we get to that point, Dr. Rosa, here, will tell you all about it, since she's the one responsible for introducing it to our unit. Before we can do anything with *Diamond versus Chakrabarty*, though, we have to get a more detailed biochemical picture of George."

Sarah pulled up to the security gate at the MCB campus.

"We're just going in to drop some things off, Joe," she lied. "We'll be out in half an hour. Probably less."

Finding parking within the enclosed campus was never any great problem. But getting past the security guard often demanded inspired guile and panache. This morning Sarah had both. She found an empty slot directly behind the Thayer Building.

"Welcome to the Medical Center of Boston, Dr. Mulholland," she said.

On the far side of the campus, workmen were setting up barriers around the antiquated, decaying Chilton Building.

"Is that the building they're going to blow up?" Rosa asked.

"Blow down, from what I understand," Sarah said. "An implosion. Next Saturday. The hospital press release said that the expert doing the demolition is the best in the world. He claims there won't be so much as a brick outside of the barriers."

"Should be quite a show," Mulholland said.

"Almost everything that happens around here is quite a show. Glenn Paris, the president of the hospital who's providing your computer today, is the one primarily responsible for that atmosphere. This time he's actually having grandstands put up. He's also raising money by raffling off the chance to be the one who actually presses the button. I bought five chances myself."

"Sounds exciting," Rosa said. "Well, if I'm still around here, perhaps I'll join you."

• • •

By noon they were getting close to identifying the man-made recombinant DNA virus that Ken Mulholland had named George. With the exception of a five-minute break to stretch and plod to the men's room, the virologist had not moved from in front of the screen. Seated to his right, equally immersed in the evolving puzzle, Rosa Suarez determined various probabilities with a calculator and took notes on a yellow legal pad. Sarah, feeling at times like a fifth wheel, came and went, seeing her patients in the clinic, and trying to do some reading for an article she was writing. She returned to the small office each time with coffee or Coke and Danish—always politely refused by Rosa and inevitably wolfed down by Mulholland, who seldom took his eyes off the screen to see what he was eating.

He was younger than Rosa by two decades or so, but it was clear the two of them delighted in working with one another. *Three hundred IQ points between them,* Sarah estimated. *Probably more.* She felt a spark of anger at those who had the audacity, arrogance, and self-serving immorality to have tampered with their BART investigation results.

"Okay," Mulholland said, still transfixed on the screen, "this is the next sequence. A-T, A-T, C-G, A-T."

A-T: adenine and thymine; C-G: cytosine and guanine. The paired deoxyribose bases that were the building blocks of life. From medical school courses, Sarah knew the rudiments of DNA structure, function, and replication. But these two, working with Mulholland's biochemist in Atlanta, were operating in the stratosphere of the subject. At the Atlanta end of the modem connection, the chemist—a woman named Molly—had used specific enzymes to chop the viral DNA into small segments. Those segments had been identified and now were being sequenced by computer to re-create the complex, three-dimensional, DNA double helix that was, in essence, the virus. Mulholland and Rosa were pausing with each new set of data to extend the model they were building on the screen, and to compare it to an extensive library of knowns.

Sarah watched Ken Mulholland down a pastrami sandwich as he recited the latest sequence of phosphates and deoxyribose units to Rosa.

```
That's all she wrote, Ken. What you
have is what George is. I'm finished
         . . . and famished.
            Good Luck.
             Molly
```

The message appeared on the screen, and was followed by a Gary Larson Far Side cartoon in which two geeky scientists, peering intently into their microscopes, were themselves beneath someone's huge microscope lens. Rosa took a turn at the keyboard, running the final piece of structural information against the library of known viruses. In just a few minutes she shook her head.

"Not here," she said.

Rubbing his eyes, Mulholland swung his chair around to Sarah.

"George is some sort of adenovirus, but he's had parts added," he said.

"He's bioengineered," Rosa said. "*No es de Díos*. Not of God. The questions now to be answered are: *By whom?* and *Does George have anything to do with DIC?*"

"*Diamond versus—*" Sarah was going to attempt the other name in the case, but Mulholland spared her the effort.

"Chakrabarty," he said. "Rosa, do you want to explain?"

"No, no. You go ahead, please."

"She's too modest," Mulholland said. "Okay. *D. versus C.* is the landmark case for patenting new life forms. Ananda Chakrabarty was a microbiologist working for

General Electric. Back in the early seventies, he genetically altered the naturally occurring bacterium
Pseudomonas aeruginosa. The resultant bioengineered
germ could digest a number of the hydrocarbons found
in crude oil, breaking chemical bonds, and in effect turning a disastrous slick into fish food. The discovery was
potentially worth hundreds of millions. But the U.S.
patent office refused to allow him to patent the beastie.
In 1980, the U.S. Supreme Court reversed the decision,
saying in effect that there was no difference between
building a better mousetrap and building a better mu-
tant."

"How does that help us now?" Sarah asked.

"Well, it might not help us at all," Mulholland responded. "But then again, it might. That's where Rosa,
here, came in. With bioengineering companies popping
up from sea to shining sea like corks, the possibility of
an outbreak of disease caused by a new life form seemed
more than possible. The Andromeda Strain in the novel
was from outer space. In truth, we no longer have to go
nearly that far for trouble. So Rosa made a deal with the
U.S. patent office to share their data with us. Whenever a
new life form is patented, we get a description."

"By law," Rosa explained, "the patent description
must be detailed enough so that the life form could be
identified and reproduced by an expert in the field. Now
a majority of genetic engineering firms cooperate with
us directly by submitting descriptions of their new mi-
crobes, and often even their work in progress, for inclu-
sion in our data banks."

"Amazing," Sarah said. "So now you can tap into
your data banks in Atlanta and see if you can come up
with a match. Do you have that many new life forms on
file?"

"You don't want to know how many," Mulholland
said.

"Do you want to take a break before you start that

process?" Sarah asked. "We should allow at least an hour to get you back to the airport."

"In that case, I'll have lunch on the plane," the virologist said. "Or have I already had it? No matter. This part shouldn't take too long, thanks to the miracle of how much money we convinced Uncle Sam to spend on our mainframe. Rosa, why don't you do the honors?"

"*Seria mi placer,*" Rosa replied. "What we'll do, Sarah, is start with the largest commonality, in this case the type of virus initially used." She typed

Adenovirus

onto the screen and entered it. "Then we work our way down. If we get a no match at any point, the game is over. The truth is, the computer could probably do the whole process itself, but I like the adventure."

"She likes the adventure," Mulholland echoed reverently.

Piece by piece, Rosa entered George's DNA sequence and asked the Atlanta mainframe to search for a match. Sarah was astounded at how many recombinant viruses there were. *And the field of genetic engineering is only in its infancy!* Rapidly, though, the number of matches to their virus got smaller and smaller.

"Okay," Rosa said. "This next piece of data should separate the man from the boys."

She entered another of George's sequences, and a second or so later

No Match

appeared on the screen.

"Damn," Rosa whispered.

The word was barely spoken when the screen flashed another message:

Typo suspected - Check for data entry error or repeat inquiry

"We'll have to find that programmer and give her a raise," Mulholland said.

"I never could type," Rosa muttered, studying her notes, then again entering the sequence. "Next time I *will* let the computer do it."

In just seconds, data began to appear on the screen.

Unknown matched to access number ACX9934452; probability of confluence - 100% - Please type access number and your security code to continue.

"Bingo," Rosa said.

She did as the mainframe requested. And almost instantly, George had a new name . . . and a home.

CRV113 - BIO-Vir Corporation, 4256 New Park, Cambridge, MA 02141; (617) 445-1500; U.S. Patent # 5,665,297; RDV332,210 (1984). Adenovirus spliced with thrombin-thromboplastin producing genes; potential application: rapid wound healing, hemostasis. No further information available.

Rosa turned to Sarah. The epidemiologist's expression was, at once, triumphant and grim.

"Thrombin," she said. "Unless I am mistaken, it is also *factor two* in the biological cascade of blood clotting."

"And thromboplastin is a clotting factor, too," Sarah said excitedly. "Rosa, this is it. I just know it is."

Rosa was already dialing the BIO-Vir number.

"Well, that was easy enough," she said, after a brief conversation. "I have an appointment tomorrow morning at ten with Dr. Dimitri Athanoulos, president of the BIO-Vir Corporation."

"I wish I could go with you," Sarah said. "But I have a case, and I'm on call."

"Fortunately, I have no such obligations," Mulholland said. "My wife and kids could use a little vacation from me. And I wouldn't miss this for the world. Does that landlady of yours have any spare rooms?"

"If she doesn't," Rosa said with a wink, "I have a double bed."

Chapter 32

BLACK CAT DANIELS WAS TREADING ON THIN PROFES-
sional ice, and he knew it. Sarah had rejected the
decision by MMPO claims adjuster Roger Phelps
to settle her case. All charges against her would
be dropped, she insisted, and no settlement paid,
or she would go to trial at her own expense. And
despite the love relationship that was deepening
each day between him and his client, Matt had chosen to
continue representing her.

The truth was, he admitted now, he wished it was
over. Deep down, he wished she had simply said "Pay
the man. Pay the man the two hundred thousand and
close the book. I want to spend some time getting to
know this lover of mine without having this suit hanging
over our heads."

The plastic, fortune-telling eight-ball on his desk dou-
bled as a paperweight. It was a gift from Harry several
Father's Days ago. Matt knew in the most sensible, practical parts of his intellect that it was a toy—molded
plastic, filled with water, enclosing a floating octahe-
dron, or whatever. It had been manufactured and sold
for decades now . . . by the millions. And certainly

this particular one had no more predictive ability than any of the others.

"Are we going to win this thing?" he asked, hefting the eight-ball in his hand.

If anyone knew the number of major life decisions he had made after consulting the plastic sphere, he would probably be disbarred, he thought.

Ask again later, the ball replied.

As expected, Roger Phelps was furious that despite his offer to settle, Sarah had elected to continue fighting the malpractice suit against her. Her obstinacy, Matt knew, left doubt at the MMPO about the $200,000 Phelps had instructed them to give away. That doubt would linger for however many months—or years—it took for the case to come to trial. Then, if Sarah lost for a big jury reward, Phelps would be Hero for a Day. But if she won, Phelps would have approximately $200,000 worth of egg on his face. Even for someone without Phelps's arrogance, that was the fixin's for a big league omelette.

But Matt also knew that he had no less at stake in this game than Phelps. For starters, he would have to bill Sarah to maintain appearances should his motives and ethics be called into question. A loss in court, and he could be accused of convincing Sarah to continue the case in order to keep his billable hours going as well; a win, and the best he personally could hope to come away with was some positive publicity. To all intents, he had earned his last dollar from *Grayson v. Baldwin*.

And in addition, Matt knew that lose or win, he had also seen his last malpractice case from the MMPO, by far the largest medical liability carrier in the state. Thanks to Phelps's insistence on settling, what had started as a huge break for him, with unlimited potential, was now doomed. He snatched up his glove and ball and began to pace. With his credit cards maxed out and much of his time to be spent on Sarah's case, flying Harry east for Thanksgiving or Christmas was going to be the longest financial stretch yet. Left alone, he quite possibly could have won Sarah's case while he continued to have a decent income for his work. *Why in the hell couldn't Phelps have just let him be?* His fees to defend Sarah would have stayed well below $200,000. And bit by bit, Mallon's case was beginning to crumble. *Why hadn't Phelps been able to see that?*

Something wasn't right about this whole business, he began to think, something he already knew but simply could not put a finger on. *How could Phelps not believe that the families of Alethea Worthington and Constanza Hidalgo would go after similar settlements?* It stood to reason they would. The cost of his move wasn't $200,000, it was *$600,000*. With the case Matt was beginning to build, and with the possibilities raised by Rosa Suarez's discoveries, a $600,000 giveaway was a hell of a vote of no confidence.

Something wasn't right.

For five minutes he paced, snapping the old ball into his mitt. The source of his concern remained vague—a hazy mist, swirling in his mind. He thought about Peter Ettinger's deposition. He had spent much of the day—most of the past week, in fact—reading and rereading the two-inch-thick document. Much of it he knew by heart. Perhaps what was troubling him wasn't Roger Phelps, but something Ettinger had said. *Something.* . . .

The pops of ball against leather were like rifle shots now. Beneath the paper-thin pocket of the glove, Matt's palm was beginning to sting. His problem-solving ritual was threatening to break a bone in his hand. But stopping wasn't an option. Black Cat Daniels never gave up on a ritual until it absolutely let him down. He had to stuff a sponge in there, as he did when playing catch with Ricky and the boys. Or better still, he thought, he might get a grip on himself and snap the ball in a bit more gently. What was bothering him so? Some strange wording in one of Ettinger's answers? Some odd reference? *Something.* . . .

The intercom from the waiting room crackled on.

"Mr. Daniels," Ruth said. "I'm leaving now. You do remember I said I had to leave early?"

"I don't remember, no, Ruth. But that's okay. I'm sure you told me. Have a good time."

Ruth was another problem he would have to face, he thought. She had been with him since day one, and he did feel loyal to her. But she had made no effort to curb her chattering to clients about anything and everything. The feedback from several of them was downright embarrassing. Besides, the way things were going, it might be coming down to her paycheck versus a plane ticket for Harry. *Damn you, Phelps!*

"Mr. Daniels, what do you mean, 'Have a good time'? I told you I had a dentist's appointment. No one has a good time at the—"

"Ruth, that's it!"

"What?"

"The dentist. That's it. That's what was eating at me. Put yourself in for a raise. . . . On second thought, better make that an extra day off."

The secretary muttered a bewildered thanks, but Matt did not hear her. He had dropped his glove and ball on a chair, and was skimming through the deposition once again. But this time, it wasn't a response by Peter Ettinger for which he was searching. It was something said by Jeremy Mallon. It took about twenty minutes, but he found it. He knew he would.

D: *Shipping, too?*
E: *In a separate building, but yes. Shipping is done at Xanadu also.*
D: *Mr. Ettinger, just how much money are you two raking in off this powder?*
M: *Objection. Peter, don't answer. Mr. Daniels, the form and content of that question are amateurish. In the baseball terms you might better understand, strictly bush league. Until now I have made*

*a number of allowances for the fact that aside from
a misplaced molar or whatever, this is your first
malpractice case . . .*

Matt took a yellow marker from his desk and high-
lighted Mallon's words. How could his opponent have
known about his only other malpractice case? There was
one answer to that question that made sense—but only
one.

Matt snatched up the phone and dialed the Mutual
Medical Protective Organization.

"Mr. Phelps, please. Attorney Matt Daniels here. . . .
Phelps, listen. I've spoken with Sarah Baldwin, and I
think she's willing to reverse her position on this settlement thing. How about you and me meeting to talk out
the details first thing tomorrow? Eight o'clock, my office? . . . Perfect, Roger. That's great. It'll be a relief to
finally get some of this business cleared up." He set the
receiver back in its cradle and then added, "Beginning
with why in the hell you hired me in the first place."

Matt hefted the plastic eight-ball once again.

"Am I the turkey of the decade for not seeing what
they were doing to me?" he asked out loud.

The answer is most definitely yes.

. . . .

*CRV113 in Lisa Grayson's bloodstream at the time of
her DIC and three and a half months later.* Seated at the
nurses' station on the obstetrics floor, Sarah scratched
out the characters "CRV113" on a progress notepad.
*CRV113—a man-made virus, constructed years before
by a lab in Cambridge.* She had rounds to make, and a
number of notes to write, but the remarkable discovery
of the virus was making it next to impossible to concentrate. As had been the case for months now, most of the
nurses were keeping their physical and emotional distance from her. Sarah was quite conscious of their coolness. She always was. But this afternoon, it did not affect

her as much as usual. The pieces were finally coming together. The end of the nightmare was drawing closer. *CRV113—created to speed the clotting of blood.* How could infection with such a microbe *not* be somehow responsible for Lisa's DIC?

"Dr. Baldwin."

The nurse speaking to her, Joanne Delbanco, was about Sarah's age. At one time they had gotten along quite well and had even gone out once for dinner. Now there was never any extraneous conversation between them. Another casualty of CRV113.

"Oh, hi, Joanne," Sarah said with exaggerated cheer.

"Dr. Baldwin, you have a visitor. A woman. She's very anxious to see you, and she's very upset. I put her in your call room. She won't tell me what the problem is."

"Thank"—the nurse turned and headed off—"you."

The obstetricians' on-call room was at the far end of the hallway. As she hurried there, Sarah ticked through a quick mental list of women who might be waiting for her. The list did not include Annalee Ettinger.

"Oh, God, I'm so glad you're here," Annalee said.

She was lying on her back on the narrow bed, dressed in a nightgown and quilted housecoat. Her knees were drawn up. Tracks of tears glistened on her cheeks. Sarah sat beside her and instinctively laid her hand on Annalee's gravid abdomen. Even through the housecoat, she could feel the solid, irregular mass of a uterine contraction.

"Just squeeze my hands until it's over," Sarah said. "Don't be frightened, Annalee. Everything's going to be all right."

Nearly a minute passed before the tightness in Annalee's womb began to abate. During that time, Sarah calculated from their conversation following the July 5 press conference, trying to determine how far along her pregnancy had come. Thirty-three weeks, perhaps thirty-four, she guessed.

"How often are your contractions coming?"

"Every eight or nine minutes," Annalee said. "I've been having them off and on for weeks. But it's been like this for about twelve straight hours."

"Your water break?"

"No."

"Fever, chills?"

"No."

"Bleeding of any kind?"

"No."

"Where's Taylor?"

"Believe it or not, he's in East Africa. The band's touring for two more weeks. I have no idea exactly where they are right now. He wanted to cancel the tour and stay home because I was having those off-and-on contractions. But I told him to go. How stupid of me."

"Easy does it, Annalee. Don't be so hard on yourself. You did the right thing. And what about Peter?"

"He—he doesn't know where I am. He refused to take me to a hospital, even though I told him it was too early for me to be delivering. I ended up calling a friend and then climbing out through my bedroom window. She picked me up on the road and took me here. Sarah, Peter's crazy." Her eyes filled with tears. "He has those two midwives he flew in from Mali at the house. They've been giving me some sort of tea that they say will stop my labor. I mentioned your name once, just once, and he exploded. He said if I saw you for any reason, I needn't bother coming home."

Sarah took the sobbing, frightened woman in her arms.

"Annalee, don't even think about Peter or anything else. Let's just think about your baby. You're definitely in labor, and you're still six or seven weeks early. Delivering now is a concern, but it's not a crisis. Ideally, we'd like to see the baby stay where it is for a couple more weeks."

"What can I do? Can you stop labor? I—I don't have

any health insurance. Peter's been paying for. . . . Sarah, I think another one's coming."

"Okay, easy does it, Annalee," Sarah whispered again, stroking her forehead. "One contraction at a time and one question at a time."

She glanced at the clock. Six and a half minutes since the last contraction. This time, responding perhaps to Sarah's reassurance, Annalee closed her eyes and quietly breathed her way through the contraction.

"Annalee, don't worry about the insurance," Sarah said. "Don't worry about anything. I'm going to get you admitted here, and I'm going to get one of our staff obstetricians to care for you. In fact, I think I can get the chief of the service. His name's Dr. Snyder."

"What will he do?"

"Well, my guess is he'll put you on an IV and give you some medication to try to stop these contractions and prolong your pregnancy. That depends, though. There are ways we have for finding out not only how far along you are, but how far along the baby is in terms of its lung development. The status of the lungs is the key to when a woman in premature labor should be allowed to deliver."

"You can measure the baby's lungs before its born?"

"We can," Sarah said. "Actually, we're pretty good at it."

Annalee pushed herself up and threw her arms around Sarah's neck.

"I knew I did the right thing in coming to you," she said. "I knew it."

Sarah called the hospital operator and put in a page for Randall Snyder. Then she called admissions and asked to have someone sent up to the obstetrics unit. Finally she took a fetoscope from a hook on the door and listened to Annalee's belly.

"The baby's doing great," she said after half a minute or so. "Just great."

"That's wonderful. I can feel it kicking. Listen, Sarah, please don't call Peter."

"Hey, kid, I work for you. That means you give the orders. You may want to find a way to call and let him know you're okay, though. You don't have to say where you are. I know he really loves you a lot. It's me he can't stand."

"Well, that's his problem. You know, while you were on the phone, I was looking at you and thinking about the incredible things you can do. And I was remembering what you were like when you first came to live with us."

"And?"

"Let's just say you've come a long way, baby. A hell of a long way."

Sarah hugged the woman once again. Save for her moderately prominent abdomen and engorged breasts, there was virtually no bulge on her body—no loose skin; no fat whatsoever.

"You're a member of the Long Way Club, too, Annalee," she said, taking pains to mask her concern. "One more thing. When did you take that weight loss powder of Peter's, and for how long?"

"About four years ago, and for about three months. Dr. Singh had already tested the powder someplace on a number of people. But before Peter would allow himself to be associated with it, he arranged for ten or twelve people he knew to take it. Altogether, we lost about a half a ton. Why? Is there something wrong with it?"

"No, no. I was just wondering. Nothing's wrong with it. Nothing at all."

"Well, I hope not," Annalee said. "Because according to the last figures I saw, since they began marketing the powder about seven months ago, a few hundred thousand people have done exactly the same thing."

"I know," Sarah said, flashing on a stainless steel surgical pan and the dusky, severed arm of a young woman. "I know."

Chapter 33

OCTOBER 26

MATT ARRIVED AT HIS OFFICE AT 7:15 A.M. FEELING the sort of nervous energy he had once associated with game day. Earlier in the morning, he had run three miles—part of the fitness regimen he had instituted after being so badly outclassed by Sarah in Chinatown. He had also read several sections of the *Globe* and the sports section in the *Herald*, and spent fifteen minutes of intense practice on Nintendo baseball—the impressively realistic game at which he was determined, at least once in his lifetime, to beat Harry.

After four arduous, confusing months, pieces in the bewildering puzzle of *Grayson* v. *Baldwin* were beginning to come together. Rosa Suarez and a virologist from the CDC had identified the genetically altered virus circulating in Lisa Grayson's bloodstream and had traced it to a company across the river in Cambridge. The virus, labeled CRV113 by the BIO-Vir Corporation, had been developed to enhance the clotting of blood and the healing of wounds. Later that morning, Rosa and Ken Mulholland would be meeting with the director of the lab. The BIO-Vir bug still might prove to be a red herring in terms of Lisa Grayson's DIC. But given the purpose of its creation, that possibility seemed remote.

And with any luck, before the hour was out, yet another piece of the jigsaw would be set in place. Matt had done what homework he had time for and had rehearsed the scenario in his mind. Now it was showtime. Unless he was way off base, Roger Phelps had two Achilles' heels—arrogance and greed. The trick was to expose one or both of them without alerting the man. Failing to accomplish that, there was always Plan B—the frontal assault approach he had used with such mastery against Tommy Sze-to. His groin ached at the memory. He was reaching nervously for his glove and ball when, with a soft knock, Phelps entered the outer office.

"Daniels?"

"In here, Roger. Come on in."

The claims adjuster, wearing a three-piece suit, tapped playfully on Matt's office door and then entered. Despite his dandyish appearance, Matt knew he was calculating and intelligent—a man to be dealt with carefully. Matt offered him coffee and then motioned him to the seat across the desk from his.

"So," Phelps said, settling in, "it's a change of heart we've had, is it?"

"Dr. Baldwin's getting cold feet about going to court."

"You can call her Sarah. I've heard rumors that the two of you know each other on—um—shall we say a first-name basis."

"Now, Roger, what in the hell am I supposed to say in response to that remark?"

"Nothing. She's very attractive—in a tomboy sort of way. I really wouldn't blame you if you were carrying on with her."

Right away an assertion of power and control, Matt thought. *The man is good. Damn good.*

"To tell you the truth, Roger, the thought *has* crossed

my mind. But believe me, nothing's going to happen on that front until this case is resolved."

"Smart. Is that perhaps a reason you want to settle?"

"Perhaps. I told you that I honestly think we can win."

"Well, obviously we're not as sure of that as you are. A pretty young girl with a dead baby and a stump for an arm makes a damn persuasive argument to a jury. And when juries decide for plaintiffs, they tend to decide big."

"I understand."

"I'm glad. So, then, what's your pitch?"

"On behalf of my client, I'm prepared to agree to your offer of a settlement with no admission of guilt. But I'm a bit concerned about my reputation in this whole business. *Grayson versus Baldwin* has been a high-visibility case. If I go to trial and win, I'm probably set for business for years to come—if not from the MMPO, then either from the other malpractice carrier or even from plaintiffs. Goodness knows there's a pile more money to be made from suing doctors than from defending them."

"So?"

"So, I'd like some guarantee of referrals from you. Perhaps a retainer of some sort."

"Mr. Daniels, you know we don't do that."

"There's always a first time. Believe me, for the right amount, I can be as good or as bad as you want me to be."

Matt could see that his remark, delivered more or less offhandedly, struck a nerve. Phelps paled visibly, but then just as quickly regained his composure.

"I think you'd best stop right there," he said.

Matt pushed back from behind his desk and rubbed wearily at his eyes.

"Roger, please. I need your help," he said. "I'm nervous as hell talking to you like this, but I'm in financial trouble—pretty deep financial trouble."

"I thought you were a big baseball star."

"Never that big, believe me. A few years ago, I got talked into this can't-miss real estate deal and, well, it missed. You know how it is. Right now I'm staying afloat, but just barely. So like I said, I really need your help."

"Sorry. No can do. No retainer. But I will keep you in mind as cases come in."

Matt could see the suspicion in the man's eyes. He was not going to be at all easy to trip up.

"You know," Matt said, "there's this question I've been asking myself over and over. *'Why did Roger Phelps hire me for this case in the first place?'* Especially when I was being opposed by Jeremy Mallon, the Michael Jordan of malpractice litigation. *'Why?'* Finally, when the answer just wouldn't come, but the question just wouldn't go away, I started doing some checking. Did you know that Jeremy Mallon goes to trial more than any other malpractice lawyer in Boston? It's like the man doesn't know the meaning of the word 'settle.' "

"But he's settling here," Phelps said.

"You know what else I learned?" Matt went on as if the statement hadn't been made. He was hoping that if he kept talking fast enough, and with enough authority, Phelps would fail to consider that he might be winging it. "I learned that not one of the lawyers opposing Mallon in those trials had much more experience in malpractice cases than I did. Lambs to the lion—every one of us. *Now* do you see what I mean about being as bad as you want me to be? Roger, I don't need a cut of the jury awards or anything like that. I'm not greedy. A retainer will do just fine. Some guarantee that this business will continue rolling my way."

"Daniels, I don't take kindly to this sort of innuendo. Besides, what you're saying is utter nonsense. Like I said before, Mallon is settling in this very case."

"That's because he's *going to lose*," Matt responded

with icy calm. "He knows it, and you know it. Roger, get it through your head. I'm not out to crucify you. I want to work with you. I *need* to work with you."

Phelps eyed him for a time, clearly weighing all the variables, and then said, "Go to hell."

Damn you, Matt thought. He was getting closer by the moment to Plan B. He stood, slipped on his glove, and began gently flipping the scuffed ball into its pocket.

"The proof is out there, Roger," he said. "Any board of bar overseers with half a brain will be able to add one and one together and come up with you." He began snapping the ball with more force. "How much of a cut of the jury awards does Mallon kick back to you? Fifteen percent?"

"Daniels, you're crazy."

"Twenty? Twenty-five? Mallon knew about the dentist, Rog—my one other malpractice case. I mentioned it to a couple of the people at the hospital, but they hate Mallon with a passion. There's no way they would have told him. It was you, Rog. Mallon needed another patsy to win a big jury settlement against, and you fed him me."

Matt turned his back on the claims adjuster. He was totally improvising now, but it really didn't matter.

"You have no damn proof of that. Not a bit of—"

Matt whirled and, without so much as a flicker of hesitation, gunned the ball at Phelps's head. There was no time at all for the man to react. The pitch tore past him, perhaps two inches from his ear, and shattered the protective glass on a huge print of the Boston skyline at night. The ball was already bouncing back toward Matt by the time Phelps threw himself onto the carpet.

"Jesus!" he screamed. "You really are crazy!"

"But fortunately, I am also very accurate."

Matt scooped up the rolling hardball with his bare hand and whipped it sidearm at the chair Phelps had just vacated. The cherrywood back of the chair exploded like balsa.

"Now tell me, Roger. What does Mallon pay you?"

Phelps tried to get to his feet, but Matt easily pushed him back onto the floor. He picked up the ball once again and backed across the office. The claims adjuster was cowering against the desk.

"I'm very accurate with this, Rog," he said. "Only one point nine walks per nine innings pitched. But I promise you, I'm going to keep at it until I miss—or I run out of furniture. You've tried to make me just another one of the patsies. But unfortunately for you, it didn't work this time. Now I want in. I want to be part of this little scam you and Mallon are running."

"Go to hell!" Phelps shouted again.

"Okay. I think I'm going to do this one off a full windup. We relief pitchers never get to use full windups very much. I need the practice. And I don't need that paperweight right there by your head."

"You're crazy!"

"Here we go. . . . It's a tie game, fans. Bottom of the ninth. The bases are loaded, there are two outs. Here's Daniels's windup . . ."

"Wait. Don't!"

"Stay right there, Rog," Matt said, freezing his arms with the glove and ball at shoulder height. "Just talk."

"Okay, okay. You're right. Mallon and I have an agreement. He lets me know when he gets a good case, and I assign a . . . um . . ."

"Go ahead. Say it, Rog. A loser."

"An *inexperienced attorney* to oppose him."

"And then you refuse to settle and insist on going for a jury award. Oh, you are beautiful, Rog. Just beautiful. Has Mallon ever lost one of those cases?"

"Never."

"Until now. How much do you get?"

"That's none of your business. Now let me up."

"The tension's so thick, baseball fans, you can cut it with a knife," Matt said, adopting his announcer's voice again. "A walk means a run. . . . A hit batsman means a run. . . . The runners are leading off. . . . Daniels is going into the windup—"

"A third of Mallon's forty percent," Phelps said quickly.

Matt lowered his glove. "That can add up."

Phelps scrambled to his feet, carefully brushing slivers of wood and glass from his suit.

"Listen," he said, still hyperventilating, "you want in, you'll have in. Just give me a few days to work out the details."

Matt slipped his hand from his glove. "Do I have your word on that?"

"Yeah, yeah. You have my word. You are really crazy, do you know that?"

"I want to hear from you within the week, Rog."

"Just be cool about this."

"I will. I will."

Phelps backed toward the door.

"I mean it," he said. "Just be cool."

"Roger, why don't you think about starting me off with a little portion of this settlement? You're offering two hundred K. Chances are Mallon will represent the other two families and get the same settlement. How about I get half of your third of Mallon's forty percent? That would be . . . let's see . . . forty thousand. Not bad math for a dumb jock, eh?"

"Okay, okay. After all three cases are settled. Just let me the hell out of here."

"Go ahead," Matt said simply.

"Just like that?"

"Just like that. I trust that if you say we've got a deal, we've got a deal." Matt waited until Phelps had opened the office door, then added, "Of course, I will have to charge you an additional two dollars and ninety-eight cents for your souvenir copy of the tape."

Smiling broadly, he opened his suit coat. The miniature tape recorder was strapped to his belt—right next to a rabbit's foot and a small, blue ribbon.

• • •

Dr. Dimitri Athanoulos, the president of BIO-Vir, welcomed Rosa Suarez and Ken Mulholland cordially. His
office was on the fourth floor, river side of a somewhat
dated building, typical of the glass and brick high-tech
showpieces of the early 1980s. He was in his late fifties,
Rosa estimated, handsome and urbane. His thick, wavy
hair was the color of his lab coat.

"So, you are both with the Centers for Disease Control?"

"Yes," Rosa said. "I'm a field epidemiologist. Ken is a
microbiologist."

"A virologist, if I'm not mistaken."

"Some would say so."

"From Duke."

"That was twelve years ago," Mulholland said, quite
obviously impressed.

"If I recall correctly, you did some wonderful work
on tobacco virus phage infection."

"Cater to my ego and I am yours," Mulholland said.

"Well, I am a DNA biochemist, primarily," Athanoulos said. "But I have always had an interest in viruses . . . and in bacteriophage. In the three years since
I left academia to become director here, my interest in
both has become more intense and, how should I say,
more proprietary."

Rosa, seeing how quickly the two men connected,
sensed that the BIO-Vir chief, urbane or not, tended to
take men more seriously than women. Ken's decision to
stay overnight was turning out to be yet another break
in the investigation. She sat patiently through five more
minutes of scientific small talk and do-you-knows? then
shifted in her seat and cleared her throat. Athanoulos
immediately picked up on the cue.

"So now," he said, "what can BIO-Vir do for our
friends in Atlanta?"

"I've been in Boston for most of four months now,"

Rosa said, "investigating three unusual obstetrics cases at the Medical Center of Boston."

"The young resident who gave toxic herbs of some sort to her patients, yes?"

Rosa sighed.

"*La potencia de las prensa,*" she said. "The power of the press. Dr. Athanoulos, despite what you and a million or so others have read, it does not appear that those herbs are playing a major role in this drama. Although I should add that the possibility remains. Ken, do you want to review your studies thus far?"

"Dimitri," Mulholland said, "Rosa here is far too modest to admit it, but she has done a damn thorough job of evaluating these cases. For many years she's been the best field person at the CDC."

"Go on."

"She sent me some serum from one of the victims of this DIC bleeding problem—the one of the three who survived. We've gotten viral growth and identified an antibody indicative of a smoldering infection. Yesterday we finished sequencing the DNA of the bug. Its composition matched a virus created in your lab."

Athanoulos's thick white brows rose a fraction. Mulholland passed over the printout describing CRV113, and the lab director scanned it.

"Come," he said, standing abruptly. "Let us take a walk to our primate unit. I know absolutely nothing of CRV113. The date of its patenting precedes my arrival here. And assuming we once were, we are no longer involved with such a virus. Of that I am certain. Since I took over, we have focused on building viruses that make gamma globulin and viruses that make certain hormones. But nothing like this. Cletus Collins has been in charge of the primates we use since BIO-Vir opened in '80. If anyone would know about this CRV113, it is he."

They took the elevator to the subbasement. Even before the doors opened, Rosa could smell the animals. The nearly silent corridor outside the elevator was lined with glass, which was quite obviously thick. For behind the glass wall were three long tiers of cages, virtually every one of them occupied by an active monkey. A stoop-shouldered old man was swabbing the floor in front of the cages. Athanoulos rapped on the glass.

"Where's Clete?" he said.

The old man, lip-reading, strained to understand the question. Then he smiled. He pointed down the corridor and mouthed what seemed to Rosa to be "the rec room." Athanoulos opened a door at the end of the corridor, and the three of them stepped into a glass cage, five feet square and perhaps ten feet high. Surrounding the cage was a huge room, rising two stories, and packed with toys, ropes, tree limbs, and climbing bars. At the center of the room, with one good-size chimpanzee riding on him piggyback and another, smaller one clinging to his leg, was Cletus Collins. Rosa noted the man could almost have passed for one of his charges, with his simian features and posture. Ken Mulholland had clearly made the same observation.

"Remarkable," he murmured.

"Yes, isn't it," Athanoulos said.

"I'm surprised you let him commune with the primates like that."

"You mean because of the viruses the animals carry? I assure you, Kenneth, after all these years, any virus *they* have, *he* has."

"Clete, can we see you for a moment?" he said into a speaker on one wall.

The primate keeper freed himself from the monkeys, came over, and accepted the introduction to the visitors from Atlanta. Concern darkened his striking face.

"We exercise these animals good, real good," he said in a midwestern twang that was several times more defined than Mulholland's. "Every day. I take care of them like they was kin. I promise you that."

"Mr. Collins, we're not with any animal rights group," Rosa said. "We're trying to learn about some research that was done here a few years ago on a virus named CRV113. It was related to—"

"Clots. I know the work you mean."

"Are there any records of it?" Athanoulos asked.

"Who knows? There should be. At least the animal records. Probably in the old metal cabinets in the storage closet next to the boiler room."

"I did not even know that room or such files existed."

"Abandoned projects, mostly. No one's ever been much interested in them."

"*I* am interested. Would you please take us there, Clete?"

"Sure. You wait in the outer corridor while I get these fellows back in their cages. They'd just as soon bite and scratch your face off as look at you. Everyone except me 'n' old Stan the cage man out there, that is."

The trio of scientists watched from behind the protective glass as he returned the two animals to their cages. Rosa could have sworn that just before one of them let go of Collins's neck, it kissed him on the cheek.

"I sort of liked Fezler," Collins said as he led the three to the storage closet. "But I hated what his damn experiments did to my monkeys. You sure you're not with one of them animal groups? Believe me, I take good care of these guys. Real good care. It's hard on me when they . . . you know, when they don't make it."

"You have nothing to worry about," Rosa said. "Who's Fezler?"

Collins searched out the storage closet key from a belt ring that might have been holding a hundred. He connected on the second try.

"*Warren* Fezler. CRV113 was one of his projects. He had about a dozen of 'em, it seemed. Not a damn one worked out right as far as I know. Too bad his job wasn't to come up with a way to kill monkeys. He'd a been a big success then."

Collins's mucusy laugh was cut short by a spasm of coughing. Rosa instinctively backed away from him a step. She wondered how many job-related diseases he might have contracted over the years. He flipped on the light, revealing a small, concrete room, barren save for half a dozen file cabinets.

"Fezler wasn't the best record keeper in the world," he said. "But he was one hell of a worker. Weekends. Two in the morning. Holidays. It didn't matter none to ol' Warren."

"I'm only the director here," Athanoulos mumbled, clearly dismayed. "Why should I know this room exists? Or that we once employed a monkey-killer named Fezler?"

"What happened to the monkeys?" Rosa asked as Collins used one of his keys to unlock a cabinet.

"Just got sick 'n' died. Fezler would put them under with anesthesia, then cut them with a scalpel in some weird way and draw some blood. Then he'd measure how quickly and how well their wounds healed." He flipped through one drawer with no success, and went to the next. "You sure you're not from one of those wacko animal groups?"

"Positive," Rosa said.

"Well, I can't really tell you what happened to the monkeys. They just kinda shriveled up 'n' died. It wasn't on purpose, though. I can tell you that much." He skimmed through the files in that drawer and went to the next. "Fezler liked the monkeys. They liked him, too. He was the only one besides me and Stan that they ever took to like that. He always wore the protective suits when he was in the rec room with them. But suit or no suit, they never bit him that I recall. Not once. They played with him just like they do with me. They liked bouncing on his belly. And believe you, me, he had a whopper. Maybe it was sort of like one of them Moon-walks for the chimps. You know, like at the carnival."

Again, his laugh became a choking cough.

"What's the problem?" Athanoulos asked, still irritated and now a bit impatient as well.

"The files ain't here. It says right here on the top that they're supposed to be. In my handwriting, too."

"Could they be somewhere else?"

"If you think that, you don't know me. I'll look—it'll take some time, but I'll look."

"Do that, please," Athanoulos said. "I'll check with some of the other scientists and lab techs about this Fezler."

"And also with personnel," Rosa said. "Clete, do you know when and why Warren Fezler left BIO-Vir?"

"I'd say it was six years ago at least. Maybe more. I'm not really sure why. Except I think he got sick."

"Why do you say that?"

"I don't know for sure." He rubbed at his chin in a way that any one of his charges might have done. "He went from being this roly-poly guy to being not much but skin and bones. I guess that's why. The chimps stopped bouncing on him because to tell ya the truth, there was nothing much left to bounce on."

Rosa and Mulholland exchanged quick glances. The previous evening, she had shared with him the contents of Constanza Hidalgo's diary and the discovery that Hidalgo, Alethea Worthington, and Lisa Grayson had all lost massive amounts of weight.

"I shall learn what I can about this incredible shrinking man and his work," Athanoulos said as they left the storage room and headed down the hall. "And I shall get back to you as soon as possible."

"That's much appreciated," Rosa said absently.

Behind her wide glasses, Rosa's brown eyes narrowed as she worked at connecting some thoughts. They had reached the elevator when she stopped short, whirled, and called back to Cletus Collins.

"Clete, tell me something. Do you remember anything else about Warren Fezler? Anything unusual at all?"

"I don't understand what you. . . ." The animal keeper suddenly broke into a broad grin. "Oh, yeah," he said. "I think I know what you're getting at. It was the way he talked. He couldn't get his words out—especially when he was upset or something. He . . . I can't think of the word for it, but you know—"

"I *do* know, Clete," she said intently. "He stuttered, didn't he?"

"Yeah, that's it," Cletus Collins said. "He stuttered. He stuttered like goddamn Porky Pig."

Chapter 34

OCTOBER 27

O KAY NOW," SARAH SAID, "THIS IS ONE OF THE two delivery rooms on our unit. For those women who want it, and have no risks or complications, we also have a birthing room that's quite a bit less formal. I'll show you that later."

The three third-year medical students shifted nervously as they stared about at the monitoring equipment, the gleaming anesthesia apparatus, and the delivery table. Before their ten-week clerkship in OB/Gyn was over, each would perform an unassisted delivery from start to finish—possibly a number of them. The MCB rotation offered more responsibility and clinical opportunities than was customary at other hospitals, and therefore was very much in demand. One of Sarah's duties as the next chief resident was supervision of the med students.

"Are there any questions so far?" she asked.

"Do you do any home births?" one student asked.

"Two of us residents do home births with a staff person along just in case of problems."

There was no point in adding that she had been asked

by her chief resident not to do any further home deliveries until the charges against her had been resolved.

"I've heard of you," a second said. "I have an interest in alternative therapies. Do you teach acupuncture?"

"I'm afraid I haven't time for any formal classes. But feel free to join me at the pain clinic. I'll give you my schedule later. Anything else before we move on to the outpatient department?"

"Yes," said the third student, motioning down the corridor. "The man who just came out of that room. Isn't he the Herbal Weight Loss guy from television?"

Sarah whirled. Peter Ettinger had just left Annalee's room and was stalking toward her. His fists were balled at his side. His face was crimson, and so taut with anger that he actually looked to be snarling. The medical students stepped back a pace. Sarah forced herself to hold her ground.

"Why didn't you call me?" Ettinger snapped. "Why did I have to search all over the city before I found my daughter?"

"If you'd like to speak with me, I think we should do so in the office," Sarah said.

"There's no need to do any speaking. I want my daughter released immediately from this . . . this poor excuse for a hospital. What in the hell are you putting into her body anyway?"

"Peter, please. Let's go someplace where we can sit down and talk about this like adults."

Ettinger glanced over at the students, whose name tags identified them all as M.S. III.

"What's the matter?" he said. "Are you worried these virginal medical minds will be soiled by learning what you do to patients? Tell them what's going on. Tell them exactly what it is you're dripping into my daughter's body. Go ahead, tell them. I'll just listen in."

Sarah bit at her lower lip and tried to think of some way out of the situation. She was no match for Peter's intensity, anger, and charisma. With his loathing for western medicine, he had honed his arguments through countless presentations and organized debates. Now he had her in a corner.

A few yards away, two nurses stopped to watch. Perhaps either recognizing Peter or sensing Sarah's discomfiture, neither made any move to intervene. Sarah took a deep, calming breath and turned to the students.

You want it, Peter? You got it.

"Mr. Ettinger's daughter, Annalee, is a twenty-three-year-old para one, gravida zero," she said evenly. "That means this is her first pregnancy. The date of her L.M.P.—last menstrual period—is uncertain. But by ultrasound and other studies, she appears to be in her thirty-fourth week. The fetus is female, approximately twenty-four hundred grams. That's about five and a half pounds. Annalee was admitted to our unit the day before yesterday in premature labor, with contractions varying from fifteen minutes apart to seven minutes. Her membranes are intact, her cervix is closed, and she is nontoxic—that is, without evidence of infection. An amniocentesis, done yesterday, has disclosed fetal surfactant levels that are slightly below normal. That means that the baby's lungs should be all right if she is delivered now. But each day we can keep the child *in utero* gives her that much better of a chance." She now turned a bit toward Peter, grateful that he had allowed her to get this far uninterrupted.

"Dr. Snyder, her private physician, is the chief of OB/Gyn," she continued. "He is attempting to arrest her labor with terbutaline, a beta adrenergic agonist. So far, she has responded somewhat to treatment, although she continues to have some regular uterine contractions. Now, Mr. Ettinger, if you'll excuse us, we have a visit to make to the outpatient department. Dr. Snyder is in the hospital. If you have any further questions, I suggest you contact him."

"I've called an ambulance," Ettinger said. "I have discussed the situation with my daughter. She wishes to leave this hospital immediately. I'm making arrangements for her to be evaluated at White Memorial prior to returning home with me."

Sarah was stunned. "I don't believe she would agree to that."

"Ask her yourself if you wish," Ettinger said snidely. "Beta adrenergic agonists, indeed." He looked at the three medical students with withering scorn. "The answers are not in your *Physicians' Desk References*, or your fancy tests, or your beta adrenergic agonists," he said. "They are in the minds and spirits of your patients. Keep *your* minds open to that, and as your careers progress, you will come to understand what I mean. And someday, when one of your superiors tells you to give a patient some drug or other that a pharmaceutical salesman has convinced him to use, you will turn to him and simply say 'Why?' "

"Mr. Ettinger, I'm sure these students are pleased to be exposed to your views on their profession," Sarah said, battling her exasperation. "Now, please excuse me. I'm going to speak with Annalee. Alone. If you refuse to allow me to do that, I'll call security."

"Go right ahead," Ettinger said smugly. "I doubt you'll turn her head again. After you've satisfied yourself that she wishes to leave this place, I want her discharge orders written."

The medical students exchanged bewildered, uncomfortable glances. Sarah herself was surprised that Ettinger exuded such confidence. She wondered what he had said to Annalee—what he must have promised—to get her to agree to leave MCB. It had to have been plenty. Otherwise, there was no way—

At that moment, Annalee Ettinger began to scream.

"Oh, my God! Help! Oh, God, please help! Please help me!"

The two nurses, Sarah, and Ettinger dashed toward the room as a pack, with the three medical students close behind. Annalee's piercing screeches of pain filled the corridor.

Sarah was the first through the door. Annalee was on her side, kicking her feet and wailing piteously. Her intravenous catheter had pulled out. Blood, flowing briskly from the site, was saturating the sheet in a widening circle of crimson.

"My hands!" she cried. "My hands are killing me. Both of them."

"Page Dr. Snyder," Sarah immediately ordered.

She gloved quickly, grabbed a towel, and put pressure on the IV site, taking pains to keep Annalee propped on her side, so the heavy, fluid-filled uterus would not be compressing the main artery and veins in her abdomen.

"Susie, go ahead and get another IV ready, please," Sarah said with forced calm. "Ringer's lactate. Large-bore cannula."

"What's going on here?" Peter asked. "What's the matter with her hands?"

"My hands . . . my hands," the woman kept moaning.

Sarah could see that the flesh beneath Annalee's nails —the nail beds—were dusky. Her fingers still had motion, but she was splinting them in a protective, claw position. Sarah checked for radial artery pulses and felt them, though faintly, at each wrist.

"Dr. Snyder just called," the nurse said breathlessly. "He's on his way. So is the lab. Here's fifty of Demerol and fifty of Vistaril. He said to give them IM if she's not actively bleeding. Thirty-five of Demerol IV if she is. They're getting the fetal monitor now."

A thin trickle of blood began flowing from one nostril.

"Let's get that line in right now," Sarah said grimly. "Also a temp. She feels hot to me. Very hot."

"I demand to know what's going on here," Peter said.

Sarah glared at him. "She's sick. Even you can see that. Peter, you were just in with her. Didn't you see that anything was wrong?"

"I . . . she . . . um . . . she said she was having a headache and her arms were feeling heavy."

"Oh, is that all?" Sarah said irritably. "Peter, please wait in the hall and let us do our work."

"I want her private doctor in here."

"Susie, will you please call security and—"

"Okay. Okay. I'm going. But I'll be right outside. And I'll be listening."

"I'm sorry to be a crybaby," Annalee sobbed. "But it hurts. . . . It hurts so much."

Over the minutes that followed, the tension continued to escalate. First the fetal monitor and a third nurse arrived, next the nursing shift supervisor, then the phlebotomist. One of the nurses called out that a rectal temperature was over 103. Annalee's wailing was unnerving—a hundred new pieces of chalk screeching at once across a hundred slates. The urgency in the room was electric. Not only was there the realization that something terrible was happening to the woman and quite likely to her unborn child as well, but there was the still-fresh memory of the other virtually identical cases.

Sarah and the nurses were unable to keep Annalee from writhing about, but with composure, teamwork, and skill, they were able to slip a wide-bore intravenous cannula into place. Before attaching the Ringer's lactate infusion, Sarah used the cannula to draw out a large syringeful of blood for the laboratory. One less venapuncture site to worry about—one less bleeding point. The sedating, painkilling Demerol injection had just been given when Randall Snyder raced into the room. He quickly took in the scene.

"Oh, no," he whispered, though not softly enough to go unheard.

"I saw her forty-five minutes ago, and she was fine," Sarah said. "Her father's here. He's in the hall right now."

"I know. I saw him."

"He was in with her fifteen minutes ago. She was complaining of a headache and heaviness in her arms. Then suddenly she started screaming. Labs are off. I've ordered four units crossmatched."

"Let's make it eight. Gosh, she's burning up." There was undisguised and uncharacteristic panic in his voice.

"She's one-oh-three point five rectally," Sarah said. "We just took it."

"I called Dr. Blankenship. He should be here any moment."

"Good. Annalee, listen. Just hang on. We just gave you something for the pain. You'll be feeling better in a moment."

Sarah once again toweled off her forehead and wiped the trickle of blood from her face. Immediately it began again.

"I'm sorry I'm being such a baby." Annalee sobbed again. "But my hands are killing me. Now my feet are starting to hurt. What's happening to me?"

"I don't know yet," Sarah said. "And stop apologizing. You're being incredibly tough. An internist is on his way right now to help us."

"Sarah," Snyder asked, "did she take your prenatal vitamins at all?"

Sarah shook her head.

"But she did take what I wrote about in her admission history," she answered softly. "Four years ago."

Annalee had begun to breathe easier. She eased over onto her back. Her constricted pupils said the Demerol was starting to work.

"This is what happened to those other women, isn't it?" she said. "The ones who died."

"We don't know that," Snyder replied. "Annalee,

we're doing everything we can to stop what's happening to you. We're also watching the baby. If there's any sign of trouble, we're prepared to take her out by cesarean." He glanced over at the fetal monitor. "Would somebody please call Dr. Blankenship again?"

Within seconds Eli Blankenship entered the room.

"What's Ettinger doing out there?" he asked.

"Annalee is his daughter," Sarah said. "Annalee, this is Dr. Blankenship, the chief of medicine."

"We've met," Blankenship said. "In fact, I saw her just a little while ago. Annalee is part of the study we've instituted to draw blood daily on every obstetrics admission. Is Barnes your married name?"

Annalee shook her head.

"We picked that name because her father doesn't approve of hospitals," Sarah said. "Especially ours. Annalee didn't want him to be able to track her down. Somehow, though, he did."

"And I'm paying close attention to what goes on in here," Peter called out from the doorway.

"Well, just stay out of our way," Blankenship snapped as he began his examination.

"Peter, please," Annalee begged. "Do what he says. The medicine's starting to work. My hands feel a little better."

"Thanks for telling him that," Blankenship said. "I promise I'll go out and speak with him as soon as I finish figuring out what's going on."

Blood had now begun to trickle from both of her nostrils.

"Damn," Snyder whispered. "Eli?"

"Rectal Tylenol, run the IV wide open, be sure the lab is running everything stat," Blankenship rattled off. "Check her pressure and her radial pulse every minute, get us two units as soon as possible and ten units of platelets. I don't want to fall behind. Also, find out who's on for hematology."

He motioned a nurse to take Sarah's place at the bedside, and then led her and Snyder over to one side of the room. A few feet away, the three wide-eyed medical students were like statues flattened against the wall. Sarah made no attempt either to involve them or to ask them to leave.

"She's not in as active labor as the others," Blankenship said, "but she's progressing faster than any of them did."

"I don't recall any of the others having fever," Sarah said.

"They didn't."

"Even so, it sure looks like DIC."

"Agreed."

"You know, Sarah," Snyder said, "assuming the lab confirms it, we have the case Rosa Suarez was talking about. The case that finally takes you off the hook in all this."

Sarah narrowly kept from criticizing her chief for the inappropriate timing of his remark. But she reminded herself that Annalee had not been *his* friend, and that the accusations against his next chief resident had severely disrupted his department.

"I'd be lying if I said that point hadn't occurred to me," she said instead. "But what concerns me most now is Annalee. I think we have to section her quickly. Remember how rapidly Lisa began recovering after she was delivered?"

"What do you think, Randall?" Blankenship asked.

"As things stand, she's too unstable for us to go in. The fetal monitor is holding for now. I think with a six-and-a-half-week preemie in there, and her labor slowing down as it has been, we should try to get her bleeding and clotting under control."

"I agree," Blankenship said.

Sarah knew that in a medical discussion with two full professors, her opinion mattered, but only as long as it jibed with theirs. In this instance, it most certainly did not. The cesarean section, for whatever reason, had all but cured Lisa Summer. She excused herself and returned to the bedside. The Demerol injection had calmed Annalee considerably, but she was drenched in perspiration, and the bleeding from her nose and her original intravenous site was intensifying. Her fingernail and toenail beds were at least as dark as Lisa's had been. Still, as Sarah conducted her examination, she could not shake the feeling that the two cases were different in some basic way. First there was the fever. Neither Lisa nor the other hospitalized case had experienced a rise in temperature, although it certainly could accompany DIC. Then there was the frightening speed with which Annalee's symptoms were developing. And finally, there were unsettling weaknesses in her acupuncture pulses. Sarah tried to attribute the strange pattern she was feeling to altered blood flow. But her instincts told her she was picking up on something significant. Whatever it was—possibly some sort of systemic toxin—seemed to be affecting every organ in the woman's body.

She returned to the two department chiefs and shrugged.

"Have you anything to offer her?" Snyder asked.

"I don't know. I can try some of the things I did with Lisa. But no guarantees."

Snyder glanced over at the fetal monitor. "Eli, I've got the anesthesiologist and the pediatrician standing by. But I want to exhaust every possibility before we go ahead with a section."

A unit clerk raced in and handed Eli a computer printout.

"These clotting studies look remarkably like Lisa Summer's did," he said. "They make DIC pretty much a certainty. We've got to get her on heparin. Sarah, if you want, I'll give you ten minutes—fifteen if she gets no worse."

"I can't promise anything, but I'll do what I can," Sarah said. "Someone please talk to her father and tell him what's going on."

Her thoughts swirling, she raced past Peter, and off the labor and delivery floor. For months she had hoped Rosa was wrong about their seeing just the tip of the iceberg; prayed that they had encountered the last tragedy from the macabre, malignant complication of childbirth. Now the lives of Annalee Ettinger and her daughter were on the line. But having studied the previous cases so intensively, Sarah had questions. *Why the high fever? Why the unusual pattern in her twelve acupuncture pulses? Why the rapid evolution of symptoms?*

She took the tunnel to the Thayer Building, bypassed the elevator, and raced up the five flights to her locker.

"Two spins to the right, then stop at three . . . left to forty . . ."

As always, Sarah murmured the combination to herself as she dialed it. Halfway to the forty, the dial caught momentarily. In freeing it, Sarah spun well past the number. She cursed out loud. Even in the most trying OR situations, her hands had always been her most supple, dependable allies. Now, with Annalee in such trouble, they were stiff as cold taffy. She was about to spin through the combination again when she noticed the scratches in the metal door, just beside the lock. Instead of redoing the combination, she tugged on the dial. Her pulse was throbbing in her ears as the door swung open. Her lacquered mahogany box of acupuncture needles was gone, as was the electrostimulator she occasionally attached to them. In their place was an unopened Federal Express box addressed to her care of MCB. On top of the box was a small brown paper bag.

Her hands trembling, Sarah reached into the bag and withdrew a glass vial and a receipt. The vial was empty, but its label made all too clear what was going on. It also answered the gnawing questions about Annalee's clinical picture.

CROTALID (MIXED RATTLESNAKE) VENOM -
FOR RESEARCH
PURPOSES ONLY
CAUTION: HIGHLY POISONOUS
HAVE ANTIVENIN AVAILABLE,
AND REVIEW USAGE

The receipt, from a mail order laboratory supply house in Houston, was made out to her. Sarah dropped the vial into her clinic coat pocket and carefully tore open the FedEx package. There was no doubt in her mind what it contained. *Polyvalent Crotaline Antivenin* —twenty vials in all.

Badly shaken, Sarah stood alone by her open locker on the dimly lit fourth-floor corridor of the Thayer Building. In her pocket was quite likely the cause of Annalee's hellish, imminently lethal situation. In her hands was the cure. No one was likely to believe her story that both the empty poison vial and the packaged antidote had been placed in her locker by whoever had actually administered the venom to Annalee.

If her account of Andrew's death had strained her credibility around MCB, this latest tale would snap it.

It made much more sense to believe that Sarah had infused the rattlesnake poison in order to create a case of labor-induced DIC that was unrelated to her herbal supplement. That Annalee was supposedly her friend would impress no one—especially after Peter got through telling whatever version of their history he concocted. Why, then, had Sarah produced the antidote? Perhaps, some people would reason, she had intended to create a dramatic though sublethal condition, but had missed. Only when things were clearly on a downhill slide for Annalee had she come up with the antivenin—and the farfetched explanation that it had just shown up in her locker. Perhaps, others would claim, she had not initially cared whether the case was sublethal or lethal. But seeing Annalee's extreme distress had brought about a sudden change of heart.

The two groups might argue over nuances. But clearly, there was one and only one logical explanation for Sarah's miraculous, eleventh-hour discovery of both the cause and cure of Annalee's DIC. Sarah herself had to have administered the toxin in the first place. No one with half a brain would believe otherwise.

For a moment, the notion flickered through her mind simply to dispose of the empty vial and the antivenin. She could say that her locker had been pried open and her acupuncture needles stolen. No one except the person who had set her up would ever be the wiser. With luck and aggressive treatment, Annalee and her child— or at least one of them—might possibly survive. And as Randall Snyder had said, with a case of DIC unrelated to Sarah's herbal supplements, she would at last be off the hook. By the time Sarah was even aware of having that notion, she was bounding, three at a time, down the stairs to the tunnel, the precious FedEx box tucked beneath her arm like a football.

The scene in Annalee's room was much as it had been when Sarah sprinted off, except that hematologist Helen Stoddard was now conferring with Eli and Randall Snyder. Sarah groaned at the sight of her. Since their conflict over Lisa Grayson, they had passed in the halls and sat near each other at conferences, and not one word had been exchanged between them.

Well, Dr. Stoddard, Sarah thought as she approached the three treating physicians, *if you thought I was a quack before, you're going to think I'm a positive lunatic now. And a homicidal lunatic at that!*

"I need to speak with you all over here," Sarah whispered, motioning toward the only unoccupied corner of the room. "It's very important."

"Not again." Helen Stoddard moaned. "Eli, I thought you promised—"

"Helen, either shut up or leave," Eli snapped with

uncharacteristic impatience. "This girl is in big trouble. We've got to do whatever we can to save her."

"What's going on?" Snyder asked. "Are you all going to give her the heparin or not?"

"Yes," Helen Stoddard said, quickly and definitively.

"I think you'd best hear what I have to say first," Sarah countered.

She briefly described what she found at her locker and showed the three physicians the contents of the FedEx package.

"I was concerned about Annalee's high temperature, the speed with which her symptoms were developing, and also the pattern of her twelve acupuncture pulses. Crotalid poisoning would explain all that."

"You're absolutely mad," Helen Stoddard said. "Someone purposely placed this in your locker? How on earth can you possibly expect us to swallow—"

"Dammit, Helen," Eli cut her off. "Would you just listen for once?"

The woman glared at him, then at Sarah. Then she whirled and stormed from the room. A moment later Peter Ettinger stormed in.

"What in the hell is going on here? Why did the hematologist leave that way?" he demanded.

Eli moved to confront him, but Sarah stopped the professor with a raised hand.

"Wait, Dr. Blankenship," she said. "Please. I know how important Annalee is to Peter, and I know how worried he is about what's going on. Let me talk to her for a second." She whispered a few words in Annalee's ear and then returned to the group. "Annalee says it's all right with her if he stays."

"Okay," Blankenship growled. "But one disruptive word, Ettinger, and you're out."

"Peter, Annalee has been poisoned," Sarah said. "Someone has injected crotalid venom either into her IV line or into the IV bag. I don't know enough about crotalid venom to know which or when it was done. But

I am absolutely certain of what I'm saying. It is essential that we get this antivenin into her as soon as possible."

"This is insane," Ettinger said.

"How do we know the antivenin is what is in those vials?" Randall Snyder asked.

"Well, for one thing, they're sealed. For another, if this was anything *but* antivenin, there would be no sense in someone placing it in my possession."

"Assuming someone did," Peter said.

"Dr. Blankenship," Sarah asked, ignoring Ettinger, "do you know if there are any side effects to the antivenin?"

"An allergic reaction to the horse serum it's made in, I would think," Blankenship said. "Nothing else comes to mind."

"We can handle that."

"Here, let me see the package insert."

Randall Snyder glanced once again at the fetal monitor. "Eli, there's been a slight drop in the baby's pulse. You've got to decide."

"Crotalid poisoning," Peter said. "Sarah, you are really crazy."

"Ettinger, this issue has been decided," Eli warned, glaring at the taller man from beneath his massive brow. "Either go stand on the other side of the bed or get the hell out."

Peter hesitated and then rather meekly did as he was ordered. Eli quickly scanned the instructions and drew the contents of ten of the vials into a large syringe. Sarah explained the situation to Annalee. There was complete silence in the room as Eli slid the needle into the rubber port of the IV tubing and slowly discharged the cloudy liquid into her bloodstream.

The response to the antivenin was dramatic.

In less than five minutes, Annalee reported that the intense pain in her extremities had begun to abate. Twenty-six minutes after the injection, the bleeding from her nose and needle stick sites stopped completely.

By early afternoon, her fever was gone and nearly all of her clotting studies and other laboratory tests were normal.

Six hours after the administration of the antivenin, Glenn Paris convened an emergency session of the executive committees of the hospital trustees and medical staff. After hearing the accounts of Randall Snyder, Eli Blankenship, Helen Stoddard, and the labor and delivery nurses, the participants voted unanimously to place Sarah Baldwin on immediate, indefinite, paid leave from the hospital and from her residency until the details of her involvement in Annalee's case became known with certainty.

.   .   .

The body had been in the morgue at the state medical examiner's office for three days before a definitive identification was made. Actually, *body* was not so apt a description of the remains as *skeleton*. A week before, the crew of a trawler, fishing seventy-five miles off the Massachusetts coast, had hauled it aboard along with several hundred pounds of haddock.

The skeleton had not a shred of clothing or tissue left on it, except for some cartilage on the ribs and in several of its joints. Still, the medical examiner was able to place the time of death within the past six months. He also had no problem classifying the death as a homicide. There were fracture/dislocations of two cervical vertebrae. The nature of the bony fragments strongly suggested blunt force. The ropes and diver's weights, still tied around the skeleton's extremities and what was once its midsection, removed what doubt remained.

Now, the ME inspected the dental X rays obtained from the Boston police. His dental forensics expert had just matched them with certainty to those films taken of the skeleton. He dictated his findings into a hand-held recorder and then called the BPD detective who had sent the X rays over.

"I think you can contact the missing man's family and tell them he is no longer missing," the medical examiner said. "Unfortunately, it would seem that your Dr. Truscott has done his last operation."

Chapter 35

IT WAS EARLY AFTERNOON WHEN MRS. ANNIE FRU-
manian knocked on Rosa's door.

"It's that charming Mr. Mulholland calling from
Atlanta," she twittered.

Mulholland, who had flown home shortly after
the visit to BIO-Vir, had spent his one night in Boston at her bed and breakfast. He was an almost
legendary insomniac, and had made inestimable points
with Mrs. Frumanian by staying up until well past midnight listening to stories of her life. He later told Rosa
that no prescription sleeping pill had ever worked as
well on him.

"Ken, have you got anything?" Rosa asked, once she
was certain the landlady had hung up the extension.

"An address from three years ago is the best we've
been able to do so far," the virologist said. "If you find
our Mr. Fezler, maybe you should let him know that,
assuming the social security number we used is the right
one, we have inadvertently alerted the IRS that he hasn't
filed a tax return in four years."

Fezler, the creator of the CRV113 virus, was almost
certainly the skittish, stuttering little man who had tried

to make contact with Sarah. However, although the old-timers at BIO-Vir remembered him as having been there for at least five years, none of them knew anything about his personal life, and there was no record in personnel that he had ever worked for the lab. From what little their inquiry around BIO-Vir turned up, Rosa and Ken had formed a picture of Fezler as an extremely solitary, very bright, and strikingly overweight man, perhaps in his late forties or early fifties. While in BIO-Vir's employ, he lost an enormous amount of weight. He also lost an enormous number of monkeys. And much to the dismay of animal supervisor Cletus Collins, the record of those primates, like Fezler's personnel file, had vanished.

It was Mulholland's idea to use FASTFIND to locate him. The FASTFIND computer network had been implemented in 1981 by a commission secretly appointed by the President. Its purpose, purely and simply, was to track down individuals for the government. It cost over $12 million to install, but in its first year of operation, the tax evaders alone that it located more than paid that bill. It functioned by rapidly integrating data from the IRS, FBI, military, police, social security administration, passport office, immigration and naturalization service, credit bureaus, unemployment offices, motor vehicle licensing offices, and a dozen national mailing lists. Rosa's department had used the system a number of times to locate people who had been exposed to infectious processes and dangerous toxins.

"The address I got for Fezler is in a place called Brookline," Mulholland said.

"I know where Brookline is."

"Three thirty-one Beech; apartment two-F."

Rosa wrote down the address and then located it on her street map.

"I found it," she said. "Another cab ride. I don't know which frightens me the most with all these taxis

I've been taking: the fares or the drivers. Maybe it's time to think about renting a car."

"Or borrowing one. Remember, you're on sick leave. No charging rentals to Uncle. Rosa, listen, there's one more thing of interest. While I was in Boston, one of my people here was sneaking in some more tests on Lisa's serum. We're getting a little above normal blip in her level of interferon."

"Interferon?"

Rosa took some time to process the development. Interferon, a naturally produced antiviral protein, was well known and extensively studied, but still little understood. In high doses, it had definite anticancer effects. In the lower amounts produced by the human body, it almost certainly played a role in keeping chronic viral infections like herpes and chicken pox in check.

"Ken," she said finally, "walk me through your thoughts on this."

"Well, the way I see it right now, Lisa's got a subclinical, no-symptoms infection with CRV113. The growth of the virus is held in check by her own interferon, antibodies, or more likely both. Sort of a biological Mexican standoff. I suspect we all have dozens of different viral infections smoldering in our bodies like that. Some of them may even be ones that cause certain forms of cancers. Anyhow, here's this smoldering CRV113 infection, not getting any worse, not getting any better. Then some specific stress comes along to upset the delicate balance . . ."

"Like labor."

". . . And bam! The virus gets the upper hand."

"And begins doing more and more of whatever thing its DNA tells it to do. In our cases, inappropriate activation of the clotting pathway."

"Exactly. Then the stress is removed and the body summons up more interferon and more antibodies until balance is restored."

"But are there ever any knockouts? I mean of the virus."

"Maybe some," Mulholland said. "Maybe lots. But the herpes simplex model—the one we know the most about—suggests that there are lots of draws. Anyone who has ever had cold sores or sun blisters pop out over and over again can attest to that. The whole field of chronic viral infections is still too new to know precisely how it all works."

"Ken, this is beginning to come together."

"Perhaps. There's still a load of questions."

"Only now we know who probably has the answers."

"013-32-0885."

"013-32-0885," Rosa echoed.

. . .

"Matt Daniels to see Mr. Mallon," Matt said.

He glanced past the receptionist, through the glass-enclosed library, and out at Boston Harbor. Several years before, he had actually sent in a résumé to the firm of Wasserman and Mallon. He had been granted an interview with a junior partner, who produced a ball for Matt to autograph and asked, perhaps, one or two questions unrelated to sports during their twenty-minute session. The man, whose name Matt could not remember, had not even bothered to suggest that his application would get serious consideration.

It had not been necessary for Matt to explain to Jeremy Mallon his reason for wanting a meeting. Roger Phelps had laid the necessary groundwork. Given the choice of sites, Matt had opted for Mallon's office, perhaps in some sort of grand, ironic gesture to that sanctimonious junior partner. There was also, of course, the more practical matter of his not yet having cleaned up the glass and shattered furniture from his own office.

"Mr. Mallon will see you now," the receptionist announced in a pronounced British accent.

"Will he now," Matt muttered to himself, wondering

if the accent had been a requirement in the original job description.

The Jeremy Mallon who met Matt at his office door was clearly the worse for wear. His face was drawn and pale, his slightly bloodshot eyes enveloped in gray hollows. The odor of mouthwash hung heavily about him, and Matt suspected he had spent a goodly portion of the previous night in his cups.

"You wired for sound this time?" Mallon asked after closing the door.

"Why should I bother with that? I have the tape I need."

"You threatened Phelps to get that tape. You threw a baseball at his head."

"Jeremy, at six or seven feet, if I was throwing at his head, Roger would have been awarded first base and a bed in intensive care."

"How do I know the wire actually worked? How do I know there's anything at all on that tape?"

Matt grinned ruefully.

"Always the lawyer," he said. "Well, first of all, Jeremy, it makes no difference if I have that tape or not. Once a bar overseers investigator is pointed in the right direction, he won't have to be any rocket scientist to figure out what's been going on. And second, I didn't come over here to blackmail you. I came over to get the case against my client discharged once and for all."

"Done," Mallon interjected quickly.

"Are you speaking for the Graysons?"

"You may assume that."

"I also want to know exactly what changed to prompt you to instruct Phelps to settle in the first place."

"I *might* be able to tell you that. First, though, I'd like it if we could come to some sort of an understanding."

"Like what?"

"Like we have a position open in this firm. You want it, it's yours. Junior partner for two years, then full. Guaranteed one fifty a year to start."

"Thousand?"

"Of course." He withdrew a document from his desk. "I've had the contract drawn up. The guarantee is spelled out in it. I've already signed it. Just sign it at the bottom, and your name's on the door."

Matt glanced at the two pages. They were titled simply: *AGREEMENT*. They might just as well have been titled: *SET FOR LIFE*. He thought about Harry and what income like this, at this stage of the game, would mean to them both.

"You don't have much of a poker face," Mallon said.

Matt folded the agreement and slipped it into his inside jacket pocket.

"I'll have to study this," he said. "Now, I want to know why you offered to quit the Baldwin case."

"Because you were starting to win. That's why."

"That's bullshit." Matt stood to leave.

"Wait. Wait. Will you just cool your jets?"

Matt stayed where he was. He did not sit back down.

"Okay, okay," Mallon said. "I grant you the case is still a tossup. But you *were* coming on strong. Too strong. And I realized that I made a mistake in preparing the case."

"Namely?"

"Will you sit back down, for chrissakes? Thank you. *Namely*, I should never have gotten involved with that egomaniac Ettinger. It was an accident that I called the bastard to begin with. He was on TV so much, I figured he was a giant in the field of holistic healing."

"He is."

"No, Matt. What he is, is a liar. And a vindictive liar at that. It wasn't until *after* we went to that Chinese guy's shop that Ettinger admitted he and your client had been lovers for three years. He says he didn't think it was that important. *Not important?* I mean, *give me a break*. My take is that he wanted desperately to get even with her, so he insisted on being part of the team. Who cares that his past relationship to the defendant makes him about as useful to me as a pair of cement running shoes? Then he conveniently neglects to tell me that his fucking diet powder was invented by some guy who just happened to be working at the Medical Center of Boston."

"You mean Pramod Singh?"

"Yes, I mean Pramod Singh. Oh, this Ettinger is beautiful, Matt. Just beautiful."

"What do you know about the powder?"

"I don't understand what you're driving at. I don't know anything about the powder."

Again Matt stood to leave.

"Okay, okay," Mallon said, waving Daniels back to his seat. "Where in the hell did Phelps find you anyhow? In some South Chicago junkyard?"

"He underestimated me."

"I'll say. Well, the only thing I know about Ettinger's powder—and that's the truth—is that something very screwy is going on with the money all those chubby people are sending in."

"Go on."

"After you brought up the diet powder thing at Ettinger's deposition, I asked him to tell me everything about it. He didn't, of course, but I really didn't expect him to. Goddamn egomaniac. So I started to do some checking. I put a couple of my sharpest people on it. According to the charts on Ettinger's office wall and the quantity of product rolling out of his shipping operation each day, that powder is taking off like a space shuttle. Ten thousand orders a week now, and rising. Four million bucks a month."

"So?"

"So we can't find the money."

"What?"

"Those TV shows of his are being aired all over the country. But the addresses to send checks to and the phone numbers to call in orders to are different for different areas. There are at least eight of them. L.A., Chicago, Florida, New York. Somehow the *orders* find their way to Ettinger's place in Hillsborough—you know, Xanadu. But the money's going every which way."

"Explain."

"I'm assuming you're going to accept that partnership offer, Matt."

"It's a safe assumption. Tell me about the money."

"It moves around faster than the pea in a shell game. There's an office in each area—at least eight of 'em. Maybe more. The money gets deposited in one area bank. Then it gets wire-transferred to another. Eventually it ends up in banks in the Caribbean and Europe—maybe a dozen of them. Then it begins to work its way back to Ettinger. But from what we can tell so far, the amount that comes back to him isn't close to the amount that goes out. It's like he's a junior partner in all this. We don't have enough money ourselves to bribe all the bankers we'd have to to sort out how Ettinger or Singh or whoever it is set up this laundry, or where the rest of the money is. But one thing has come to light that has big potential for us. I mean *big*. In addition to Ettinger's paychecks, the Xanadu Foundation has received extensive support from someone named T.J. McGrath. Maybe a million bucks' worth so far."

"And?"

"And Crunchy Granola General—you know, MCB —has been saved from bankruptcy by a huge grant from something called the McGrath Foundation. Until last week, goddamn Paris guarded the name of that foundation like it was the combination to his family safe. Saturday he's blowing up a building on the hospital grounds and starting construction on a new research facility. He's paying for the whole extravaganza with McGrath Foundation money. Is this coincidence?"

"Doesn't seem like it."

"Ettinger's making money off this powder, and so is the Medical Center of Boston. Plus the powder was initially developed and tested by a doctor who worked there. I think that once we know what in the hell is really going on, we may be able to put Glenn Paris and his motley crew out of business for good. Do you know what kind of bonus is waiting for us if we can pull this off for Everwell? Can you spell *yacht*?"

Matt grinned.

"I always was very good at spelling," he said. "Is that all you know about the powder?"

"So far. My people are still working on it. When can I expect to get that signed agreement back?"

"Within the day. I promise."

"Excellent. We're all looking forward to having you on board."

"A most appropriate figure of speech." Matt tried unsuccessfully to think of a way to avoid shaking hands with the man.

"Cheerio," he said to the receptionist as he headed through the art gallery and out to the elevators.

He left the plush office building and had not walked half a block when he came to a grizzled old man pushing a shopping cart full of bulging plastic bags, empty bottles, and other junk.

"G'day," Matt said, handing over a five-dollar bill. "How're you doing?"

"Can't complain, Bucko. Can't complain," the old man said with a broad grin.

He wore a red bandana around his tangled gray hair and had a rolled-up green plastic bag looped around his neck. The bag was tied in a four-in-hand knot that was actually quite passable. In addition to, perhaps, a new tie, he also needed dental care in the worst way.

"What's your name?" Matt asked.

"Siggins," the man said. "Alfie Siggins."

"Well, Mr. Siggins, I have good news for you." He took out Mallon's agreement, crossed off his own name, wrote in Alfie's, and helped him sign it. "See that building over there? Number one hundred? Go on up to the twenty-ninth floor, show the receptionist this contract, and tell her that you are Mr. Mallon's new partner. If the security guard tries to stop you, just show that to him. Sell it back to them if you want. But don't sell it cheap."

"What do I have to lose, Bucko?" Alfie Siggins said.

"You got nothing to lose, Alfie," Matt replied. "Nothing at all. Here, take this ol' rabbit's foot for luck. It's on a roll."

Matt watched until the man and his shopping cart disappeared into number 100 Federal Plaza. Then he headed for the lot where he kept his car. Phelps's tape would be in the hands of the Board of Bar Overseers within a day. Now it was time to let Sarah know that thanks to the plaintiff's expert witness, she was no longer the defendant in a malpractice suit. Then, provided she was not on call, he would beg her to celebrate their victory by going for a walk together, boldly and unabashedly holding hands in public.

. . .

Sarah was summoned to Glenn Paris's office, where she was informed that, until further notice, she was no longer a resident physician on the staff of the Medical Center of Boston. The joint executive committee decision did not come as much of a surprise, and she took the news with little emotion. In truth, she was drained almost beyond feeling—beaten by an unknown adversary who had systematically, methodically destroyed her. What few believers she still had at MCB could hardly be expected to stand by her after this latest movement in her carefully orchestrated decimation. Now there was really nowhere for her to go but home. Later she would call Matt. He would understand she had been set up once again. . . . At least he might.

Before going up to clean out her locker, Sarah stopped by the labor and delivery floor to see Annalee. A uniformed private security guard, posted by her door, firmly and not too politely refused to allow her in. She returned to the nurses' station and wrote a note to Annalee reaffirming her innocence, and explaining as best she could what had been done to both of them. She had just finished the note and was searching for an envelope, when one of the nurses handed her one. She was about to thank the woman for the envelope when she realized that DR. SARAH BALDWIN was typed on the front of it.

"A pink lady just dropped this off for you," the nurse said, referring to one of the salmon-jacketed volunteers. She turned and left before Sarah could voice any acknowledgment.

IF YOU ARE INTERESTED IN LEARNING ABOUT RATTLESNAKE POISONING, GO TO ROOM 512 THAYER. I WILL CALL YOU THERE AT EXACTLY SIX P.M. TELL NO ONE ABOUT THIS UNTIL YOU HEAR WHAT I HAVE TO SAY. YOU WERE FRAMED.

The note was neatly typed and unsigned.

Sarah glanced at her watch. Five fifty-five. She folded the note and the one she had written to Annalee, and thrust them both into her pocket. Then she raced through the tunnel to the Thayer Building and took the elevator to the fifth floor. Room 512 was at the very end. It was exactly six when she reached the door. Inside, the phone was ringing. Without knocking, Sarah hurried into the dark room and across to the bedside phone. As she reached it, the door slammed shut behind her. The blackness was immediate and total. Before she could react, a blanket was thrown around her from behind, and she was thrown facefirst onto the bed. She cried out and tried to resist, but the blanket and the weight of her assailant made movement almost impossible.

"Please, no!" she cried.

The man on top of her thrust his pelvis tightly onto her buttocks. Then he grabbed her hair in his fist and forced her face into the pillow. An instant later she felt a sharp, needle-stick pain in the back of her scalp.

"Please!" she cried again. "Please, no!"

Her voice was muffled in the soft, feather pillow. Seconds later, a tidal wave of dizziness and nausea washed over her. Her arms and legs began to shake violently. Her breathing grew heavy. The man remained on top of her, although he no longer had to work to hold her down. She was helpless and fighting a rapidly losing battle to maintain consciousness—a losing battle to remain alive.

"Please," she whimpered. "Please."

This time there was no sound. No sound at all. Her thoughts quickly dispersed, and the darkness grew even more oppressive. For a few seconds she could hear the gurgle of air being sucked desperately into her lungs. Then that sound, too, disappeared. Relentlessly the oppressive darkness consumed her. Then suddenly, mercifully, her terror vanished.

Chapter 36

T WAS NEARING SIX WHEN ROSA ARRIVED BACK AT THE Brookline apartment building that had, until about two years before, been the home of Warren Fezler. She had interviewed as many of the building's residents as would answer their doorbells and had then returned to BIO-Vir to see if there was anyone they might have missed who could add to what little she had learned of the man. By and large, her efforts had been fruitless.

According to the few neighbors with whom Rosa had been able to speak, Fezler had been a quiet, most unobtrusive tenant until one day he simply did not return home. His furniture had been put in storage and eventually auctioned off. The secretary at the rental agency swore that no rental application was ever thrown out for at least five years after a tenant moved away. But apparently Warren Fezler's was an exception. Rosa glanced up at the apartment building. It was dinnertime. *Perhaps people were home now at some of the no-answers.* Perhaps one of those she had interviewed had remembered something. Suarez-type thoroughness demanded one more crack at the neighbors. And before she quit for the day, she knew she would do it. But reluctant to start ringing doorbells again, she wandered off through the gathering evening, searching for some other move that made sense.

Details, she thought, as she headed absently down the street. *Think about the man. . . . Think about Warren Fezler.* She had already passed by the smallish, upscale market when she stopped. The air outside the market was rich with the aroma of fresh breads, cut flowers, and bins of fruits. *Food!* Judging from the descriptions of Fezler, prior to his remarkable transformation he had been 230 pounds or more. Food would quite possibly have been at the epicenter of his life. And if so, a gourmet market not a block from his home would have been the equivalent of a hangout.

Rosa started with the cashiers and worked her way through the employees in the store. With the fourth person she questioned, an older man working behind the meat counter, she hit pay dirt.

"Course I know Warren," the butcher said. "He was about the nicest guy who ever came in this place. A real sweetheart. Never talked much—he had that speech thing, you know. But he'd give you the shirt off his back."

"Has he been in recently?"

"Not for a while. A few months, maybe. Probably not since sometime this past summer."

A few months. Fezler had left his apartment two years ago, yet he continued coming to this little market.

"Any idea why he stopped shopping here, or where I might find him?" Rosa asked.

"Nope. But I'll bet Mrs. Richardson knows. She's a sweet old lady. Can't see much, and can't walk too well neither. I don't think she has anyone. Warren used to bring her groceries to her to save her a little money. Since he stopped coming around, we've had to deliver. Poor old gal. Three dollars a bag hurts someone like her."

"Bull's-eye!" Rosa said.

Fifteen minutes later, she was brewing tea and straightening out the kitchen of Elsie Richardson. The spinster, who certainly was ninety and very possibly much older than that, lived in a cluttered two-room basement apartment with three cats, none of whom seemed any younger than she did. She moved with excruciating slowness on swollen feet and ankles, and had only enough vision to make it about her place. But she seemed somehow to be managing. And her mental clarity was spiced with surprising wit.

"It's *Miss*, not Mrs.," she had corrected Rosa. "I kept waiting to marry a man who was smarter than I was, and he never came along . . . at least not until Mr. Fezler.

"It's so nice to hear Mr. Fezler's all right," she said now. "He hasn't called in weeks."

"I don't know if he's all right or not, Miss Richardson. I'm trying to find him."

"I take a little lemon and sugar, dear. The lemon's on the bottom shelf of the refrigerator. Left-hand side. I know where *that* is, but I don't know where Mr. Fezler is. He never said. Such a kind man. Do you know how we met? I fell, that's how. Right in front of the market. He helped me up and brushed me off. And that was the last time I had to go out to the store. Six dollars a week. That's what he saved me. To say nothing of the money he *gave* me. I tried to refuse, but he just left it anyway."

"He sounds like quite a guy," Rosa said, flashing on the horrible descriptions of the women who died of DIC. "Miss Richardson, is there any place he might have gone if—if he was in some trouble? Any friends or relatives?"

"None that I can . . . wait. He has a sister. Her name is . . . Mary. No, no, not Mary. Martha. 'My sister Martha.' He talked about her all the time like that. I can't believe that I didn't remember. Oh, I'm so sorry."

"You're doing wonderfully, Miss Richardson," Rosa

said, setting a tea biscuit on the woman's saucer. "Was Martha's last name Fezler, do you know?"

"No. I'm afraid I—" She suddenly brightened. "The calendar," she said.

"Calendar?"

"Mr. Fezler said it was from his sister's place. He gave it to me because the numbers are big. He hung it up for me, too. But I'm afraid I never look at it. It's in there, dear."

She pointed through her bedroom door. The calendar, hanging on a side wall, had a photo of a huge-breasted, platinum blond model on the top half. She was scantily clad in skin-tight overall shorts and was holding a gasoline can. Printed on the calendar was:

FEZLER MARINE AND AUTOMOTIVE REPAIR SHOP
MARTHA FEZLER, PROP.
MERCRUISER SPECIALISTS

The address of the shop, printed at the very bottom, was in Gloucester, a city Rosa knew was thirty or so miles north of Boston. She wrote it and the phone number down. Then she straightened up the bedroom as best she could, gave Elsie Richardson a hug and twenty dollars, and headed back to her rooming house. If Martha Fezler was not actually hiding her brother, she knew where he was. Every ounce of intuition was telling her so.

Rosa walked to the closest thoroughfare and flagged a cab. She felt elated. Soon, very soon, her career as an epidemiologist would be over. But not before the ghost of BART was at last laid to rest.

. . .

"Ruth, hi, it's Matt. I'm sorry to call you at home."

"That's all right. How did your session with Mr. Mallon go?"

"They're dropping the Baldwin suit."

"Oh, that's wonderful. Just wonderful. Congratulations."

"Thanks. Ruth, listen. I'm at the Medical Center of Boston and I can't find Sarah. Have you heard from her?"

"Yes. She called just before I left, an hour or so ago. I put the message on your desk. She said she's not going to be on duty tonight. She's staying at the hospital until six or so and will be home after that. She sounded upset."

"From what I've been able to learn, she has reason to be. Thanks, Ruth. I'll see you tomorrow. And thanks for getting my office cleaned up."

"Is there anything else I can do?"

"No. You switched the phone over to the answering machine?"

"I *always* do that, Mr. Daniels."

"I know, I know. Good night, Ruth. I'll see you tomorrow."

Matt set down the pay phone receiver and glanced about the busy lobby area. It was six-thirty. Sarah said she would be leaving the hospital at six. But her new bicycle was still chained outside. She had not answered her Motorola page, nor had she responded to two separate voice pages by the hospital operator. A call to her apartment had gotten only her answering machine, and there were no messages from her on the one at his home.

Something significant and unpleasant had occurred involving Sarah and a patient. Matt had learned that much, although no one around MCB seemed anxious to share details. Apparently, she was being asked to take a leave from the hospital. Glenn Paris, to whom Matt had been referred for details, had been tied up in some sort of emergency meeting. Now, feeling more anxious and uncomfortable by the moment, Matt again sought the CEO out in his Thayer Building office.

"I'm sorry, Mr. Paris is tied up on a call," his harried secretary said.

"Break in. Tell him it's Matt Daniels, and that it's an emergency."

"But—"

"Do it, please. Or I'll do it myself."

Less than a minute later, he was ushered into Paris's inner office.

"You can't possibly think she would do such a thing," Matt exclaimed, after Paris recounted the events surrounding Annalee Ettinger. "Mallon and the Graysons have dropped the malpractice suit against her completely. Doesn't that tell you something?"

"Look, all I know is that this hospital has received more negative publicity in the last six months than in the previous six years. And your client is involved in virtually every bit of it. We had to put her on leave until the dust settles and we can sort out what's happened."

"Isn't it clear what's happened? Somebody's tried to frame her."

"For Sarah's sake, I hope that's true. I like her, Daniels. I really do. But as things stand, we have to take action that's in the best interest of the Medical Center of Boston and our patients. There are a good number of people on our medical staff and board of trustees who think that she is a very sick and dangerous person."

"That's utter nonsense."

"I hope so. But at this point, there's nothing I can, or want to, do."

"Listen, Sarah hasn't answered her page for the past hour. Do you have any idea where she might be now?"

"No."

"You've made a mistake," Matt said.

"As I said, I hope so," Paris responded.

Matt was already heading out the door. He made another pass through his office and home answering machines, and left another message on hers. Then he called the hospital operator, who again attempted to reach Sarah by her beeper and the hospital-wide loudspeaker system.

"Tell me," Matt asked, "when you can't get hold of residents who are supposed to be on duty, what's usually going on?"

"That doesn't happen very often," the woman said.

"But when it does."

"Our Motorolas have a display window, but they also can be voice activated. Usually, if a resident is on call and doesn't respond, their page unit is defective, and they're asleep in the house officers' quarters. They wouldn't be able to hear me on the overhead. There is none there. We use the room phones."

"Where are those rooms? Can you call them?"

"Thayer Building. Fourth and fifth floor. But I can't call every room. There are about twenty or twenty-five of them."

"Look," Matt said. "Just in case, could you please keep paging Dr. Baldwin over her beeper every couple of minutes. Use the voice mode. It's very, very important. You've got my name in case she calls in. I'll check back with you shortly. And thank you. . . . Thank you very much."

She's gone for a walk, or else she's sleeping in one of the on-call rooms, Matt told himself as he headed up to Thayer Four. *Either possibility makes perfect sense. She's upset over what's happened. A nap or a long walk. I'd do one or the other. . . . So would she. . . .*

He began going from room to room, knocking on each door, then trying the knob. Most of the small on-call quarters were open and empty. Two rooms were locked, but in both, a sleepy voice responded to his knock. A third, though unlocked, was also occupied. The resident within, fully dressed, lying facedown, spread-eagle on the narrow bed, was so deeply asleep that he barely stirred when Matt knocked and entered.

You've got to really want it, Matt thought, gazing down at the exhausted young physician. He closed the door with unnecessary care and headed up to the fifth floor. The sixth or seventh door he tried was locked. He knocked and waited for the expected sleepy response. There was none. He knocked again, this time a bit louder. Only visions of the spread-eagle man on the fourth floor kept him from kicking at the door. He decided to check the rest of the floor before knocking any more forcefully. But then, just as he was about to turn away, he heard a woman's voice broadcasted from within the room.

"Dr. Baldwin. Dr. Sarah Baldwin. Please call the operator. . . . Dr. Baldwin. Dr. Sarah Baldwin, the operator please."

"Sarah!" Matt cried out, kicking the base of the oak door with force. The retort, piercing as a gunshot, echoed down the empty corridor. "Sarah!"

Matt stepped back and rammed the sole of his shoe into the center of the door with all his strength. The wood split. A second kick opened a hole large enough for him to peer into the dimly lit room. Sarah was lying peacefully and motionless on the bed. Beside her, on a portable IV pole, a plastic intravenous bag was draining its solution into her arm. Matt reached through the hole and unlocked the door from within. Sarah was warm, but her color was poor. And she was not breathing.

He found a shut-off valve on the intravenous tubing and shut the infusion off. He hollered her name and checked her neck and wrist for a pulse. There was none that he could feel. He tilted her head back, pinched her nose closed, and tried several mouth-to-mouth breaths. After the third one, he thought he felt her jaw move. Again he cried out her name. Then, impulsively, he slapped her sharply across the face. She responded with a single, gurgling breath. He slapped her again. Again she took a breath.

Battling dread unlike any he had ever known, Matt snatched up the phone and dialed the operator.

"I found Dr. Baldwin," he said breathlessly. "She's in cardiac arrest. Fifth floor. Thayer Building. Please get a team up here now!"

Chapter 37

OCTOBER 28

IT WAS A NIGHTMARE WITHIN A NIGHTMARE. AT SOME level of her mind, Sarah struggled to believe that—to remember that as a teen she had always awakened, always been safe and in her bed. But there was nothing she could do with her thoughts, and *absolutely* nothing she could do with her body, to stem the helplessness, the pain, and the unremitting terror. As they had during countless dreams in her early life, rough hands pinned her on her back, then tied her down. She fought to free herself until her arms and legs burned. But the bonds were like steel.

Then thick, powerful fingers began forcing a wadded cloth between her teeth. She pushed against the cloth with her tongue. She shook her head violently from side to side. But the gag was thrust deeper and deeper into her mouth, clogging the back of her throat and choking her. She strained to pull in air through swollen, narrowed nostrils. Her efforts grew weaker. She prayed for unconsciousness or even death. But always there was just enough air to keep going, just enough to prolong the agony.

Please let me die! Please just let me go to sleep and die. . . .

"Sarah. . . . Honey, listen to me. It's Matt. . . . Try to hold still and listen. . . . Better. That's better. You can keep your eyes closed, but please listen. . . . Sarah, you're on a ventilator. There's a tube down your nose and one down your throat and into your lungs helping you breathe. And they've got you strapped down. Squeeze my hand if you understand all that. . . . Good. Good. Just try and keep calm, honey. I'm going to tell the nurse you're waking up."

Sarah felt Matt's huge, comfortable hand squeeze hers and then vanish. She strained to separate nightmare from nightmare. Bit by bit she remembered.

As her consciousness and awareness grew, so did the indescribable discomfort of the endotracheal breathing tube and the fearsome sensation of air hunger. She could hear the ventilator bucking and whirring as it fought against her own attempts to breathe. Clearly, it was set on automatic rather than assist. It was set to breathe for her, not necessarily with her.

Slow down, she begged herself. *Don't fight it. . . . Remember what you tell patients on vents. . . . Easy now. . . . Go with it. . . . Relax and go with it. . . . Meditate. . . . Find the swan. . . . Find your spirit. . . . Find it and just watch it fly. . . .*

"Sarah, can you hear me? Sarah, open your eyes. It's Alma. Alma Young. . . . There, that's it. . . ."

Sarah blinked against the blurriness and the sting of light. Gradually her vision cleared. The SICU nurse was looking down at her with concern.

"They were full in the medical ICU," she said. "We all wanted you in here anyway, and Dr. Blankenship said okay. One of the other nurses called to tell me what had happened, and I came back in to 'special' you. Do you understand all that? . . . Good. I'm going to undo the restraints on your wrists. Please don't touch the tube. Understand? . . . Good."

Sarah waited patiently as the broad leather straps were loosened and then removed. Her pounding headache was subsiding. She was fully awake now and rapidly regaining control. *Someone had tried to kill her!* Someone had injected her beneath her scalp with something rapidly acting and incredibly potent. Now she was on a vent. All those school psychologists and university psychiatrists had been wrong. The recurring dreams that had once so plagued and disrupted her life had never been a distorted reenactment of some terrible event hidden in her past. Rather, they were a prophesy, just as Louis Han's Thai healer had intimated they might be. *This* was the struggle for which the dreams were preparing her. *This* was the battle of her life. And she had survived—first in Chinatown and now in the SICU. Thanks in some way to the horrible nightmares, she was continuing to endure against whatever evil was trying to crush her.

To everything there is a season, and a time to every purpose . . .

Sarah flexed some circulation into her hand, and then reached up and pointed to the endotracheal tube.

"I know. I know," Alma said. "As soon as we get your blood gas results, I'm going to call anesthesia and Dr. Blankenship, and see if we can get that tube out. Are you okay for now? . . . Good. I've switched your vent to demand, so you can breathe any way you want. You sure you're okay? Sarah, I just want to say that whatever's going on will pass if you let it. There's never the need to do what you thought you had to. But listen, we can talk about all that later. I'm just glad you're all right."

A respiratory therapist came in and drew a sample of blood from the line in Sarah's radial artery. During the interminable half hour that followed, Matt stayed beside her, doing what he could to keep her calm, and filling her in on the events surrounding her resuscitation.

"It was morphine in the IV bag," he said. "The empty

vials were on the floor. Dr. Blankenship says we got to you just in time. Whatever the emergency team gave you worked incredibly well. You've actually been awake for most of the night. But the nurses have been giving you stuff so that they could keep you on the ventilator. The box of acupuncture needles that you reported as stolen was on the desk in that room, along with an unopened vial of the rattlesnake venom and a scribbled, unsigned note on a prescription blank, that just said 'I'm sorry.' The door to the room was bolted from the inside. Right now I'm about the only one in this hospital who doesn't believe you tried to kill yourself. . . . Am I right?"

Sarah squeezed his hand and nodded as vigorously as she could manage.

"I knew it," Matt whispered. "It's been at least, oh, three or four months since any woman who was *my* lover tried to kill herself. . . . Squeeze my hand if you think that was funny. . . . Oh, I see. . . . Listen, there have been some wild things going on in this Ayurvedic powder business—not the least of which is that Mallon is going to tell the Graysons to drop their suit against you. Not settle, *drop*. I'll tell you all the details later.

"Rosa told you she found out who engineered that virus, right? The guy who stutters. But she wouldn't tell you or anyone else his name, right? Well, now she thinks she knows where he is. She tried calling you at home and at the hospital to bring you up to date. Finally, one of the nurses told her what had happened and exactly where you were, and she showed up here around eleven last night. She came in again at two this morning. She really cares about you. I'd be surprised if she's slept any more than I have. She won't say where this virus guy is, but she's driving there today to try to find him. Eli's arranging for her to use a hospital car for the day, no questions asked. . . .

"Hey, hang on now, pal. Alma's coming, and I think the anesthesiologist is with her."

The news from the laboratory was excellent. Sarah's

blood gases—her pH, oxygen, and carbon dioxide levels —were all good enough for her to come off of assisted ventilation. The sensation of having her trachea suctioned out, and then the endotracheal tube pulled, was one Sarah hoped never to experience again. She sputtered and gagged, and coughed spasmodically. But again, Matt was there for her, steadying her through the coughing jag, stroking her arm, even kissing her on the forehead.

"Careful you don't get disbarred," she rasped, when the cough had finally subsided.

"I told you, they're dropping the case. I won't be your attorney anymore. We can go public. In fact, I've rented a sound truck for later today just to cruise the streets and tell the people of Boston that I love you and that we're going to get to the bottom of this."

"I love you, too, Matt. I really do. Hey, what time is it, anyhow?"

"Six. A little after."

"God, twelve hours of my life, gone just like that."

"It could have been *all* of it," Matt reminded her.

Sarah's response was cut short by the sound of a throat being politely cleared. Standing at the foot of the bed was a rumpled, graying man wearing a red clip-on bow tie. He held Sarah's loose-leaf SICU record cradled open in one arm and peered down at it through Ben Franklin spectacles. Although she had never met or even seen the man, Sarah correctly guessed his specialty before he introduced himself.

"I'm Dr. Goldschmidt," he said. "I'm a psychiatrist. Sir, if you'll excuse us for a few minutes . . ."

"This is Matt Daniels," Sarah said quickly. "He's my —my lawyer."

Goldschmidt eyed Matt for a few seconds.

"Perhaps he should stay, then," he said. "If it's all right with you."

"Please," she said hoarsely.

"Very well, then. I know you've been through a lot

and that they just took your breathing tube out. So I'll be as brief as I can." He moistened his thin, bluish lips with his tongue. "Tell me, Dr. Baldwin. Have you ever tried to hurt yourself before last night?"

Sarah's eyes flashed. She glanced over at Matt, who motioned for her to keep calm.

"The answer is no. But I did not try to hurt myself last night either, Dr. Goldschmidt. Someone tried to kill me and make it look like suicide."

"I see," Goldschmidt said, scratching something down in her chart. "But how do you explain the door being bolted from inside?"

"Someone had a key."

"Perhaps. But from what I've been told, even housekeeping and maintenance don't have keys to those rooms."

"I didn't try to kill myself."

"Dr. Baldwin, I just want to help you."

"Then let me go home."

"You know I can't do that."

"Why?" Matt asked.

"I have been assigned Dr. Baldwin's case by Dr. Blankenship because it is hospital policy for every attempted suicide to have a psychiatrist, and I am on call for my department today. Her current diagnosis is"—he read from her chart—"*narcotic overdose, suicide attempt.* I have both the power and the obligation to hospitalize her on a secured mental health unit until I am convinced she is neither a danger to herself nor to others. Surely you as a lawyer can appreciate the importance of my doing just that."

"I do, yes," Matt said.

He thought about all he wanted to accomplish that day to clarify the connection linking Peter Ettinger, the McGrath Foundation, and the Medical Center of Boston. What safer place could Sarah be for the moment than on a locked, closely controlled ward?

"Sarah," he said, "I think you've got to go along with whatever he says. At least for the time being."

If the psychiatrist appreciated the support, it did not show on his face, which looked tense. He was about to speak when Eli Blankenship strode up beside him.

"Thanks for coming in so promptly, Mel," Blankenship said. "Sarah, are you okay?"

"I'm feeling better every second. Dr. Blankenship, please tell Dr. Goldschmidt that I'm not crazy and I didn't try to kill myself."

"No one ever said you were crazy."

"Listen, someone injected me with something right here under my hair, and tried to make it look like I killed myself."

Blankenship studied her scalp with a penlight and then shook his head. "Nothing."

"It was a tiny needle. A twenty-nine gauge or smaller. Shave my hair off if you need to," Sarah pleaded. "You'll find it."

"Sarah, please. Just be patient with us and let us do our jobs. Alma says that your lungs are clear and your vital signs are stable. Within an hour or two, when we're sure your larynx isn't going to go into spasm, I'd like you transferred out of here to Dr. Goldschmidt's service. Apparently, they're going to be very tight on beds here when the surgical schedule starts."

"Where am I going?"

"The only place you can go and stay in this hospital is Underwood Six."

"Matt, please. That's a locked ward. Don't let them do this."

"Sarah, it won't be for long. Besides, with what happened last night, I'd worry if you were anywhere else. I've got things to do and people to see today to try and sort out this powder business. Just go for today, and then we'll see what we can do."

"I'm telling you, there's a needle puncture mark

someplace under my hair where the man who tried to kill me injected something."

"Please, Dr. Baldwin," Goldschmidt said, "I'm sorry if you have something against psychiatrists, or don't trust me in particular. I *do* want to help you. But it's six-thirty in the morning. I've been up most of the night, and I have a full day of patients and consultations ahead of me. Try not to make this situation any more difficult than it is."

"Sarah, listen," Blankenship said, "my gut tells me that you're okay, and that you're telling the truth. But there really is nothing else we can do right now. I'll tell you what. Twenty-four hours of observation and I'll do everything in my power to convince Dr. Goldschmidt and the staff to send you home. I promise."

Sarah studied the determined expressions on the three men's faces and then reluctantly agreed to the transfer. The psychiatrist wrote a brief note in her chart and promised to be by to see her on Underwood Six as soon as he had a break in his schedule. One of the psych residents would be by to do her intake history and physical.

"I can hardly wait," Sarah said.

The yellow vinyl police ribbons across the doorway of room 512 on Thayer Five were not unlike those that had been used on Kwong Tian-Wen's shop. The door itself, with its shattered center panel, was shut. Matt checked to be sure he was unobserved, then loosened the ribbon and slipped inside. The IV pole was still there, but the infusion bag was gone, as was Sarah's lacquered box. There was no evidence that the room had been dusted for fingerprints. There was no closet, and no room for concealment except under the bed. Someone had found a way to get out and lock the door behind him.

Matt inspected the lock, which seemed no different from others on the floor. Certainly whoever it was could have called in a locksmith and had a key made. But for the killer to purposely create such a witness hardly seemed likely. He walked to the only windowed wall. The two ancient double-hung windows were nearly opaque with months, if not years, of outside grime. Through them, he could see the next building, some hundred or hundred and fifty feet away. Screw holes told him that at one time in the remote past the windows had had latches. Replacing them had undoubtedly been a low item on the MCB maintenance list. At five stories above the ground, there was hardly any need for outside security. Then Matt glanced down.

Not three feet below the sill, running the length of the building, was the tattered slate roof of some sort of porch on the fourth floor. The slight pitch of the roof was, to all intents, negligible. Matt opened the window and carefully stepped outside. Forcing himself not to look down, he eased his way along, peering into the other rooms on the fifth floor until he saw one that was empty. The window, like the one in room 512, was not latched. Moments later he was standing in the deserted hall once again.

"So much for that mystery," he muttered.

It was possible that his discovery, coupled with Sarah's protestations, would be enough to get her discharged. But Matt knew that it was in her best interests to spend at least this one day someplace safe. And this was hardly the day he wanted to be worrying about her. He still had few answers to the mystery of the Ayurvedic Herbal Weight Loss System. But at least now, he had the questions. And he had a short list of those he felt could fill in the blanks—beginning with hospital comptroller Colin Smith.

He closed the door behind the yellow ribbons and hurried down the hall.

Chapter 38

SARAH, YOU'RE SURE PARIS TOLD YOU ABOUT THE McGrath Foundation?" Matt asked.

"I'm positive. He's known about a possible grant from the foundation for a year or more. He told me that himself. He said he was counting on the money to help get MCB out of the hole. In fact, I think Colin Smith mentioned it, too. If that much money is coming in, it seems to me the chief financial officer's got to know about it. Maybe he and Glenn and Peter are in it together somehow. Maybe he's skimming off the top before the hospital gets its share."

"I'll ask him. He's *numero uno* on my list for today."

"Matt, please listen to me. I'm fine and I can take care of myself. I don't want to get shipped off to the damn nut ward. Besides, Peter's in all of this right up to his righteous, self-centered eyebrows, and I want to help nail him."

It was nearly nine-thirty in the morning. Sarah had just been notified that transportation—and security—were on their way to transfer her from the surgical intensive care unit to the locked psychiatric ward on Underwood Six.

"Sarah, I know this isn't what you want," Matt said, "but the truth is, you've been through hell. You're just a couple of hours off a ventilator, and I've never seen you look so tired. If you don't go to the psych service freely, Goldschmidt's going to have you committed. As long as he believes you tried to commit suicide, he doesn't really have much choice. And there's something else we shouldn't forget. Since we both know you didn't try to commit suicide, we also know that someone out there tried to kill you."

"Correction," Sarah said, her voice still quite hoarse. "Someone out there tried to make it look like *I killed myself*. That's what administering that venom to Annalee was all about, Matt. Don't you see? It had to look like I attempted suicide because I was guilty of causing those other DIC cases as well as trying to create one in her. Killing me in any other way would have said just the opposite. We're hitting somebody's raw nerve. Maybe Peter, maybe Glenn, maybe this Dr. Singh. Maybe some combination of those. I don't know. But we're getting close to the truth. Trying to set me up was a very desperate move. We've got to get to the bottom of this before whoever did it tries something else. I can help, Matt. Really I can."

"I know. But please, there isn't anything I can do. I hate the idea of your being on a locked ward as much as you do. But for the next day we've got to go along with it. Even if we could somehow get you discharged, which we can't, I'd be worried about you every minute we weren't together. I talked to Rosa and Eli before I went to your apartment to get your things. We're going to be working like hell to find out who's behind all this. And today we've got a lot of moving around to do. Hang in there for just this one day. Then I promise we'll do whatever we have to to get you sprung."

The brief meeting with Blankenship had been fruitful. Matt had shared the details of his encounter with Jeremy Mallon, and Mallon's belief that Peter Ettinger and

Glenn Paris were somehow connected through the Mc-
Grath Foundation and the Ayurvedic Weight Loss System.

Blankenship knew the McGrath Foundation was
based in New York City and that the heads of the philanthropic organization had made initial contact with
Glenn Paris and Colin Smith some four or five years
before. He had never seen the application Paris had sub-
mitted to the agency, nor the actual terms of the grant.
But he did know that millions of dollars were involved.
He took on the job of trying to locate and penetrate the
foundation. He also would arrange for the car he had
promised Rosa.

The epidemiologist, playing her cards close to the vest
as always, would say very little of where she was going,
or even whom she was after, other than that she was still
not at all certain of his whereabouts.

The strategy they decided upon for Matt was to speak
with Colin Smith, then Peter Ettinger, and finally Glenn
Paris. Smith seemed to Blankenship the likeliest of the
three to crack. If he did, they could play one off against
another. And of course, Matt added, if that approach did
not work, there was always good old Plan B—some sort
of spontaneous frontal attack.

"Transport's here," the charge nurse called over.

Matt pulled the curtain closed and waited outside it
while Sarah changed into the jeans and sweatshirt he had
brought from her apartment.

"Okay, I'm ready as I'll ever be," she said.

The security guard kept a respectful, perhaps embarrassed, distance as the transportation worker pushed his
wheelchair to Sarah's bedside.

"The visitors' hours on Underwood Six are six to
eight in the evening," Matt said. "I checked."

"That's it? Just two hours?"

Matt took her hand in his.

"It takes younger men days to accomplish what us

older, more experienced guys can do in two hours," he said. "Just be strong, okay?"

Reluctantly Sarah slid off the bed and into the wheelchair.

"Oh, don't worry about me. I'll be fine," she said. "As long as you don't let them keep me more than a day. Besides, the cuisine on the psych ward is world famous. They serve soup to nuts." She pointed toward the SICU exit. "Home, Jeeves."

The locked ward on Underwood Six was newly painted and furnished. Each room contained two single beds. The exception was the room next to the nurses' station, which had no furniture at all except for uncovered mattresses on the floor and walls that made it literally a padded cell. Sarah had been on the ward for two hours before she noticed that the heavy screens were on the inside of the windows and the inside door handles were not there at all.

Except for a brief physical exam by a male psych resident, who used his stethoscope, penlight, and ophthalmoscope, but seemed loath to touch any part of her body with his hands, she was left pretty much alone. The second bed in her room was, for the moment at least, unassigned. For a time, she lay on her bed trying to read an obstetrics journal; then, failing at that, a Sue Grafton mystery. Finally, when she could not even concentrate on *Good Housekeeping*, she wandered out of the room and joined the eight or nine people who were hanging out in the lounge.

"Group in fifteen minutes, everybody," a woman called out in a cheerful singsong. "Right here in the lounge. Attendance mandatory."

Sarah gazed absently out of one of the windows. She was on the side of the building facing the MCB campus. Streaming through the pane, free of any breeze, the autumn sun felt hot enough to bake bread. Far below, to one end of the broad, grassy mall, workmen were completing construction of a temporary grandstand—perhaps ten tiers high, with a platform and podium at the top. Loudspeakers were mounted on poles to either side of the stands. Sarah was wondering about the setup when she looked across the campus. The Chilton Building, on the side farthest away from Underwood, was the site of intense activity.

It was Friday, the twenty-eighth, she suddenly realized. Demolition Day minus one. The huge old eyesore had been boarded up for as long as Sarah had been at MCB, the grass around it noticeably less well maintained than the rest of the mall. Tomorrow, in just a few spectacular seconds, the decaying structure would cease to exist. The view of the extravaganza from Underwood Six would be astounding—perhaps the one real perk of being a patient on the locked ward!

Resting on the window ledge was a scratched, ancient pair of binoculars, whose optics turned out to be surprisingly good. The Chilton Building was cordoned off by two concentric rings of blue sawhorses. Huge canvas dust shields had been strung together and draped over the nearby parking garages. A small group of men in shining metal hard hats were talking and gesturing up at the condemned structure. But most of the workmen seemed to be packing up their gear. Apparently, the preparation of the building and the laying of charges was complete. Sarah wondered if any of the officials from the McGrath Foundation would be at the next morning's festivities. Just then she noticed a white panel truck pull away from the deserted side of the building. Slowly and unobtrusively it eased through a small opening in the barriers and headed off. Through the binocs, it was not difficult to make out the bright red block lettering on the truck: HURON PHARMACEUTICALS. The printing was repeated, in smaller letters, across the truck's rear doors.

The name struck a chord of some sort . . . *but why?*

"Okay, *group,* everybody," the singsong voice announced. "Attendance mandatory. No excuses. Let's get going."

Huron Pharmaceuticals, Sarah mulled as she took the seat that seemed the least conspicuous. Where in the hell had she run into that before? *Where?*

"Okay, everyone," the group leader said to the twenty or so patients on the locked ward. "We've got two new people with us today, so I think it's appropriate to go around the group for first-name introductions. I'm Cecily, one of the group facilitators on Underwood Six."

"Marvin," the worn-out looking black man next to her said.

"Lynn."

"I'm Nancy. Don't ever call me Nan."

"Pete . . ."

Peter! Sarah did not hear any of the succeeding names and had to be prompted to say hers when her turn came. She had suddenly remembered why Huron Pharmaceuticals had seemed so familiar.

"Ours are standard, FDA-approved multivitamins, manufactured for us by Huron Pharmaceuticals."

Peter Ettinger had spoken those words at his deposition. Sarah was absolutely certain of it. She heard them now in his voice and in her mind's eye saw his smug expression as he delivered them. First the McGrath Foundation and now Huron Pharmaceuticals. Two direct connections between Peter Ettinger, the Ayurvedic Herbal Weight Loss System, and the Medical Center of Boston.

Coincidence?

Sarah's fists clenched tightly in her lap.

No fucking way! she thought.

"Very well, Sarah," Cecily said. "If you don't want to share today, we all certainly understand. But I also must tell you that we frown on profanity during group. . . ."

Chapter 39

I T WAS NEARING NOON. TRAFFIC SOUTHBOUND ON THE central artery, leading out of the city, was light. Nevertheless, Matt was well aware of the vindictive nature of Boston drivers, and stayed in the middle lane, intent on offending no one. Colin Smith was out of the hospital for the remainder of the day, his secretary reported. An avid sailor, he spent every Friday afternoon from mid-April to early November aboard his boat. However, she added, a meeting had run late, and he had left the office not twenty minutes ago. If Matt's business with him was important, he might try calling the South Boston Yacht Club.

Instead of calling, Matt had decided to show up at the dock unannounced. He knew the way, having been there several times during his Red Sox years. And Colin Smith, very much the CPA, seemed like someone who might not do well with surprises.

Before calling Smith, Matt had stopped by Eli Blankenship's office. The medical chief had tried New York information in an attempt to reach the McGrath Foundation. They were not surprised that there was no such listing. The foundation had undoubtedly been established some years before, with no purpose other than to prepare for the laundering of the huge profits projected from the sales of the Ayurvedic Herbal Weight Loss System. Whoever had set up the operation had remarkable foresight, as well as keen insight into weight-conscious, do-it-the-easy-way America. Properly marketed, a no-diet slimming product with or without any proven effectiveness was a virtual gold mine. And the Ayurvedic Herbal Weight Loss System was not only well marketed, but actually seemed to work.

The way Matt saw it, the herbal product had been introduced and possibly developed at MCB by the mysterious Indian Ayurvedic physician, Pramod Singh. About four and a half years ago, the powder was tested by Singh, and quite successfully so, on at least three people—Alethea Worthington, Constanza Hidalgo, and Lisa Summer. There were probably more test subjects, but fortunately, none of the others had become pregnant and gone into labor.

Eventually Singh joined forces with Peter Ettinger, and then with a marketing agency that had an understanding of the power of infomercial television. King Midas himself could not have done a more efficient job of turning their herbs and protein into gold. A portion of the profits from the sale of the product was now finding its way into the coffers of the hospital, perhaps in payment for the early work done there. Some other monies were at work fostering the establishment of Xanadu and Ettinger's holistic healing empire.

But the rest?

According to Jeremy Mallon's operatives, the sums funneled to Xanadu and the Medical Center of Boston were still only fractions of what the marketing blitz was actually generating. It was quite possible that Colin Smith did not have the whole picture of what was going on. But he had to know something.

The South Boston Yacht Club, for many decades a landmark for boaters, was a rambling, three-story, clapboard affair, built on pilings. Easily visible from the expressway and from the harbor, it was harder to get admitted into than a Celtics playoff game. A network of floating docks fanned out from the old building like spokes. During the summer, not one slip of the several hundred along the docks was unaccounted for. And even this late in the season, there were still a good number of boats in the water. The dirt-and-gravel parking lot adjacent to the club was fenced off, with access restricted by a guard house. Matt slipped a ten across to the attendant in exchange for allowing him unannounced to surprise his old college classmate, Colin Smith.

Following the attendant's directions, Matt parked just behind the club and made his way down a stony slope onto the docks. Colin Smith's boat, the *Red Ink,* was at the far end of spoke 5. A thirty-foot, crimson-hulled catboat, the attendant said. The prettiest boat in the club. Smith was neatening some lines at the stern and was apparently alone. His expression upon seeing Matt approaching was not one of pleasure.

"Daniels," he said, dusting his hands off on his tan jeans and eyeing Matt suspiciously. "What brings you down here?"

"Business," Matt said simply.

"With me?"

"Mind if we sit down for a couple of minutes?"

"No longer, though." He motioned Matt into the cockpit. "This is the nicest day in weeks. I'm late as it is, and I want to get out there."

"You can sail her alone?"

"Blindfolded."

"I'm impressed. Listen, Colin. Have you seen this morning's paper?"

"You mean about their finding Andrew Truscott's body?"

"What was left of it."

"What has that got to do with me?"

"Maybe a lot. Sarah Baldwin and I have been telling

people all along that Truscott was murdered. No one believed us. Now they will. From the day Sarah was sued by Willis Grayson, someone has been doing his damndest to make sure she appeared guilty of causing those DIC cases. Truscott was murdered trying to prove she was being framed. Then, last night, someone tried to murder her and make it look like she had killed herself. To be perfectly frank, Colin, I think you're involved."

"You're crazy."

"I think you either did it, or you know who did it."

Smith stood up and began to uncleat one of his stern lines.

"Go chase an ambulance," he said.

"Colin, what's with the McGrath Foundation? Why is it sending money to your hospital at the same time it's sending money to Peter Ettinger's operation? Who started it? Who's the one that's really getting rich?"

The money man finished uncleating the line and started loosening another. Matt looked for anger in his face, but saw only fear and confusion—hardly the expression of a man who was a willing participant in murder.

"I'm heading out now, Daniels," he said. "If you have accusations to make, I think you should be talking to the police or to a lawyer. Not to me."

Shit, not Plan B again. Matt sighed. He grabbed Smith by the front of his shirt and yanked him upright. The spark of fear in the man's eyes intensified.

"Listen to me and listen good," Matt said through nearly clenched teeth. He hoisted the smaller man up until he was on his tiptoes. "That fucking powder that everyone is getting rich off of is killing people. *Dead!* Young women and babies and God only knows who else. You may not know that, but somebody you're connected with does. And that somebody doesn't give a damn whether people die or not, as long as the bucks keep pouring in. Do you understand?"

Smith's weathered face was chalk. "Let me go," he said hoarsely.

Matt loosened his grip, then slowly released it. "Every second you keep your mouth shut, you're getting dirtier and dirtier. I don't think you're behind all those people dying, Colin. I wondered about you while I was driving out here, but I can see now that you're not. I actually think you might be a decent guy."

"I am. Now get off."

Matt handed over his business card.

"It's Paris, isn't it?" he said. "Glenn-the-Showman Paris and that Dr. Singh."

"Get off."

"You may not have known before today that people were dying," Matt said, stepping up onto the dock, "but you do now. So I'm holding you responsible for whatever happens from here on out. You hold out . . . women and babies die . . . your fault. Get that? . . . Call me when you change your mind about sharing what you know. . . . And have a real nice sail."

Without waiting for a reply, Matt turned and stormed off. He was twenty yards down the dock when the *Red Ink*'s engine rumbled to life. Matt slowed but continued walking, his eyes straight ahead, his concentration riveted on the man behind him.

Come on, he urged, certain he had gotten to Smith, but not at all certain how deeply. *Call out to me, Colin. Call me back.*

"Daniels, wait!"

"Yes!" Matt said.

He whirled around and had taken a single step back toward the *Red Ink* when it exploded. It was a fierce, molten, petroleum-driven explosion—one that no living thing could have survived. Reflexively Matt dove belly first onto the coarse planking. Fiery debris clattered about him and hissed in the water. Seconds later the cabin cruiser in the slip adjacent to Smith's catboat exploded in sympathy, taking with it what remained of the seaward thirty feet of dock.

Accident? Something rigged to the ignition? Something detonated by radio?

Matt scrambled to his feet and brushed himself off. He stepped to the smoldering edge of the dock and assured himself that there was no sign of Colin Smith. Then he spun back toward the clubhouse. Six or seven people were racing frantically onto the dock. He scanned upward, beyond the men to the parking lot, just as a jade-green Jaguar XJS backed up and sped away, spitting sand and gravel. Matt had no chance to make out the driver.

"I'll be right back!" he lied to the men as he dashed past them.

Head down, he sprinted up the slope to the parking lot. His Legacy, only a year old, was damn quick. But the Jaguar had quickness, power, *and* a huge head start. If it reached the expressway unseen, there would be no way of knowing whether it had turned north or south. And that, for all intents, would be that. Matt cursed his habit of always activating his Z-loc security system. He deactivated it and then lost several more precious seconds fumbling with the ignition key. Spraying a rooster tail of dust and gravel, he shot past the bewildered attendant, out of the lot, and down the access road. The Jaguar was nowhere in sight. Immediately the guessing game began. The first choice was no contest. *Left at the paved road and head toward the expressway.*

Matt skidded around the first corner, then cut the next one by speeding across a lawn. The Subaru's engine, usually remarkably silent, was screeching—first gear to fifth, then to first, then back to fifth. Still no Jag. Another intersection. More possibilities. *Right. Keep heading toward the expressway.* To his left, above the trees, Matt could see the expanding cloud of black smoke, carried up and outward by an offshore breeze—the breeze that Colin Smith, just a few minutes before, was expecting to fill his sails.

"Oh, God," Matt whispered as the horror of what he had just witnessed sank in.

The expressway was just ahead, and the chase just that close to being finished. Then, far to the right, Matt saw the Jag. It was already up on the elevated highway, speeding north toward the city. But by the time Matt had cut off half a dozen cars and a tractor trailer and darted out to the left-hand lane of the expressway, the XJS was gone again. He flashed past one off-ramp, then another. There was nothing he could do now but keep heading north and pray they were still both on the same highway. The traffic slowed as he approached the Mass. Ave. exit, and beyond it, the South Station tunnel. The distance between cars quickly narrowed. A vintage midday central artery tie-up. The chase was over. Matt slammed his fist against the wheel. He would have to find some way to backtrack from the distinctive Jag to its owner. *Difficult, perhaps,* he thought, *but certainly not impossi—*

Then, once again, Matt spotted the car. It was a hundred or so yards ahead, and three bumper-to-bumper lanes over. But even worse, it had just pulled away from the jam and was now starting on the long circular drive leading down to the Massachusetts Turnpike. Matt leaned on his horn and began screaming *"Emergency!"* at anyone who looked over at him. Many did not. Inch by inch, he took first one lane, then another, receiving along the way a number of obscene gestures, several of which he had never seen before. Tires screeching, he rode the very edge of control around the sweeping entry ramp and was going nearly sixty by the time he hit the turnpike. The Jag was gone again. But this time Matt was more relaxed. The Back Bay exit was less than a mile ahead. If the driver took it, there was nothing Matt could do. But if not, the Cambridge/Allston tolls would almost certainly bring them close. In fact, Matt was several miles beyond Allston, almost to the Newton tolls at Route 128, before he spotted his quarry.

I guess it was just meant to be. He settled back in the seat, slowed down, and rolled through the automated ticket dispenser nine or ten cars behind the Jag. The trick now was to follow the driver to his—or her—destination without being seen. For a year, he had debated putting a phone in the Subaru. Now, a day late as usual, he decided he would do it. A call to the State Police would have given them a crack at the radio control that had triggered the bomb aboard the *Red Ink*. As things stood, Matt still had a chance at recovering it—provided the driver felt home free and not pressed to dispose of it.

The Jag left the turnpike east of Worcester. Moving now with no apparent urgency, it headed into the beautiful, rolling countryside of north-central Massachusetts. Matt, still keeping well back, had yet to catch a glimpse of the driver. But with each passing mile, it became less necessary for him to do so. Just a dozen or so miles ahead was Hillsborough, the home of Xanadu and the Ayurvedic Herbal Weight Loss System. And unless Matt was absurdly off base, the man in the jade motorcar in front of him was six feet four, with thick silver hair and an ego the size of Greenland.

XANADU
ENTRANCE ONE MILE AHEAD
AN EXCLUSIVE RESIDENTIAL COMMUNITY
BASED ON THE HEALING PRINCIPLES OF AYURVEDA
LIVE SPIRITUALLY . . . LIVE LONGER . . . LIVE HERE
HOMES STARTING AT $450,000

The huge billboard—elegant lettering, overlaid upon a Himalayan sunrise—also included a number to call for an introductory tour and interview. Matt stopped by the sign as the man he assumed was Peter Ettinger drove on down the deserted, newly paved road toward the entrance. Across the street, two endless stretches of seven-foot chain-link fence converged in what was probably one corner of Xanadu.

Xanadu. Matt knew the name came from a mystical, magical land in some poem—one that he had once been forced to study and, it seemed, even memorize.

> *In Xanadu did Kubla Khan*
> *A stately pleasure dome decree . . .*

His mind's eye saw the words printed in an even hand on some teacher's blackboard. *Milton? Wordsworth? Maybe Coleridge.* He simply could not remember the author. Nor could he remember anything else of the poem. The image, though, of Peter Ettinger as Kubla Khan was not a hard one to conjure.

Matt was sorting out his options when he heard a car approaching—the same direction from which he and Ettinger had just come. He ducked behind the Subaru and inspected its right front tire just as a white panel truck flashed past, continuing on along the road perpendicular to the one Ettinger had taken. Having read Ettinger's deposition almost to the point of memorization, Matt immediately honed in on the name painted on the truck. Huron Pharmaceuticals produced the vitamin capsules that were included with the Ayurvedic Weight Loss powder. Assuming the truck was making a delivery, and the billboard was pointing toward the main entrance, there had to be some back way into Xanadu. Matt scrambled into the Legacy and followed the truck.

After half a mile, another newly paved road cut off to the right, as did the chain-link fence. Keeping a safe distance, Matt continued following the Huron truck until it made a right turn onto a dirt road that apparently cut through the fence and into the sprawling compound. He found a little-used path off the opposite side of the paved road, left the Subaru in a concealed spot, and hurried across to where the truck had turned in. The gate in the fence was about a hundred feet up the dirt track. Not surprisingly, it was unlocked. The Huron delivery man clearly anticipated a quick turn-around. Matt glanced about. Then he slipped through the gate and headed into Xanadu.

For about a hundred yards, the dirt road snaked through dense woods. The trees and bushes were well past fall peak, but autumn had been unusually mild, and they were still far from barren. The forest ended suddenly at expansive acreage that had been carved out of the rolling woodland. Straight ahead of where Matt crouched was an impressively large lake, newly landscaped, and probably man-made. Spaced along the far bank were new, sumptuous homes. Merely within his line of sight, Matt could see several that appeared completed and several more that were under construction. *In Xanadu did Kubla Khan* . . .

The Huron Pharmaceutical truck was parked behind a complex of low, whitewashed buildings, set in a densely wooded grove a short distance to Matt's left. To his right, perhaps two hundred yards, was a large, two-story farmhouse, also white, with a single-story wing jutting toward the spot where Matt was hiding. Parked on the drive by the farmhouse was the XJS.

There was the hum of machinery coming from the buildings that Matt assumed housed the Herbal Weight Loss factory. But there was no one in sight, either there or at the farmhouse. From the woods to the wing of the farmhouse was no more than twenty feet, and from there to the Jag fifteen more. It seemed quite possible to reach the car unseen. If it was unlocked, he would take a crack at finding the radio detonation device. Failing that, he would take as much of a look around as he could manage and then slip back out the way he had come. Even if he failed to uncover anything to connect Ettinger with the death of Colin Smith, there was always the chance that the attendant at the yacht club parking lot would have seen and remembered the Jaguar, or possibly even Ettinger himself.

Staying low and just within the tree line, he crept to the rear of the farmhouse and flattened himself against the wall. Next he worked his way to the corner of the building and was gauging the distance to the Jag when he heard sirens approaching from the direction of the main entrance. He pushed back into the shadows. Not thirty seconds later two cruisers, their sirens now cut, sped up to the farmhouse and stopped on either side of Ettinger's car. Two officers stayed by the Jag, while two others raced to the front door of the farmhouse. One of them had withdrawn his service revolver. Matt inched back into the woods and nestled into concealment in a shallow swale. Several minutes passed. Matt tried desperately to imagine what might be happening inside the farmhouse. He strained to make out the exchange between the two remaining policemen. They were close enough to him, but with one seated in the cruiser, and the other facing away, their conversation was muffled.

Finally the door to the farmhouse opened, and the two officers emerged, one on either side of a clearly agitated Peter Ettinger. Ettinger's hands were manacled behind him.

"I was there. I admit that," Matt heard Ettinger protest. "But dammit, I didn't do anything! Colin Smith called and told me to meet him at the yacht club. At least he said he was Smith. . . ."

"Remember, Mr. Ettinger," one of the officers said. "Like I told you inside. Anything you say may be used against you in court. Now, is this the car you were driving?"

"Yes, of course it is."

"And these are the keys you just gave me?"

"Yes, yes. Now go ahead and open it, dammit. There's nothing in there."

Totally bewildered, Matt scrunched even deeper into the leaf-covered gully. *How could the police have gotten here so quickly?* Ettinger *was* a national celebrity, and the Jag hardly an inconspicuous car. Perhaps the lot attendant or someone else at the club had recognized him.

"Got it," the officer searching the car said after just a minute or so. "Under the front seat." He held up by its edges what was clearly a radio control box. "Someone get me an evidence bag, will you? Mr. Ettinger, do you really think we're that dumb?"

Ettinger, suddenly stoop-shouldered and almost limp, gazed from the policeman to the control box and back. Even at some distance, Matt could see the filmy confusion in his eyes.

"I want to call my lawyer," he said.

"From the station, Mr. Ettinger."

Ettinger was helped into the screen-enclosed back of one of the cruisers. The slam of the door echoed in the still afternoon. Matt waited until well after the cruisers had disappeared before he worked his way over to the factory. He assumed there were security people about someplace. But without Ettinger around to identify him, he could be a bit more brazen. Some sort of inspector, perhaps. *Yes*, he thought as he backed against the wall of the smallest of the factory buildings. Better not to get caught. But if he did, a health inspector story should work.

There was a small anteroom near where the Huron truck was parked. Matt glanced around for the driver, and then rolled along the wall and peered in the window. The space was empty save for two freezers, both top-opening. Each had *Huron Pharmaceuticals* painted across the front, in letters identical to those on the truck. Neither appeared locked.

A final check around him, and Matt slipped inside. The half-glassed door from the anteroom to the main building was closed. Through it, Matt could see twenty or more women, each at a work station, filling shipping boxes with what he assumed were the components of the Ayurvedic Herbal Weight Loss System. He backed

away from the door and moved to the freezer that was
out of the line of sight of any of the women. *KEEP
VITAMINS FROZEN UNTIL SHIPMENT* was sten-
ciled on the lid. Carefully he twisted the handle to one
side and eased up the heavy lid. The fitted rack, containing sheets of vitamin capsules, completely filled the
space just beneath the lid. Matt studied the sheets for a
moment. They were identical to those Sarah had received from Annalee Ettinger. Each contained ninety
capsules—a three-month supply. He was about to lower
the freezer lid when, for no particular reason, he lifted
one of the racks.

The body beneath it, a man's, lay serenely on its back.
Eyes open, it was staring sightlessly up at Matt. It was
dressed in a dark business suit and red silk tie, and fit
into the freezer with no more than an inch or two to
spare at each end. Its hands and bronze, mustached face
were covered by a thin film of rime. But Matt had no
difficulty recognizing the man. He had seen him a number of times on videotape and had wondered about him
often over recent weeks.

Pramod Singh, the X-factor in the Ayurvedic puzzle,
was a factor no more.

Suddenly queasy, Matt lowered the freezer lid and
wiped off the handle with his jacket. Then he slipped out
the back door and braced himself against the building,
breathing deeply and deliberately, fighting the vision
and the nausea. Sarah nearly murdered. Colin Smith and
Pramod Singh dead. Peter Ettinger either guilty of killing them or, more likely, set up to look guilty. Someone
was tying up loose ends in a hurry. Someone was pan-
icking.

Relax, Matt said to himself. *Just get the hell out of
here and back to Sarah*.

He sensed the presence behind him an instant before
he saw the shadow on the wall—the shadow of an arm,
slashing downward toward his head. He began to react,

but way, way too late. An object, heavy and unyielding, slammed onto a spot just behind his right ear. His teeth snapped together as paralyzing pain exploded through his head and into his neck. The last thing he saw was the ground, careening up toward his face.

Chapter 40

ROSA SUAREZ HAD JUST PASSED THE GLOUCESTER ROtary at the end of Route 128 when the Medical Center's ancient Chevy wagon began handling strangely. She sped up, wondering if perhaps she had snagged a branch. But the problem only worsened. Cursing softly in Spanish, she pulled over. As things were, she had gotten off to a much later start than she had wanted. If Martha Fezler closed her shop early for any reason, the day, and possibly the whole weekend, would be lost. She carefully folded the map that was spread open on the passenger seat and slid across. Chastising herself for not renting instead of borrowing the wagon, she stepped out onto the soft shoulder and into the hazy midafternoon glare. The problem, it was immediately apparent, was the right rear tire, which was shredded and hanging off the rim in spots.

Rosa had never in her life changed a tire. She opened the rear door and located the jack and the spare. Then she retrieved the owner's manual from beneath a stack of repair receipts in the glove compartment. If the procedure seemed clear to her, she decided, she would give it a try. If not, she would risk flagging someone down.

She returned to the rear of the wagon, engrossed in the instruction manual.

"Hi."

The man's greeting startled her so, she dropped the instruction book.

He was standing a few feet away, arms folded, grinning kindly. He was in his late twenties, Rosa guessed, with a fine, handsome face and wire-rimmed glasses. He wore a woolen seaman's cap and a dark windbreaker. His car was parked twenty or so feet behind hers, its hazard lights flashing.

"Sorry if I frightened you," he said. "I just stopped to see if you needed a hand."

Rosa took a calming breath, assured herself that her heart was still beating, and retrieved the manual.

"Oh, my," she said, patting her chest. "You did startle me, yes. But I thank you for stopping. It's very kind of you. As a matter of fact, if I change this tire myself, it will be a first for me."

"I'd be happy to do it for you."

The man came forward and pulled out the jack and spare. He walked with a fairly marked limp, caused by his left leg, which seemed not to bend at the knee at all. She hoped the problem was nothing permanent.

"An old college football injury," he said, setting the jack in place. "I often wish I could have that moment back."

"Oh, I'm terribly sorry. I didn't mean to be staring."

"You weren't, really. It's just that I notice things. Except that I didn't notice that linebacker. If I had dodged to the left instead of to the right, who knows where my life might have gone? You heading into Gloucester?"

"As a matter of fact, I am. Are you from there?"

"Temporarily. I'm a biologist with the Department of Marine Fisheries. We're doing a lobster project up here."

"How interesting. I'm a scientist with the government, too. An epidemiologist at the Centers for Disease Control."

"Atlanta's a nice place," he said. "Although a little hot for my taste. One hint in changing a tire is always to loosen the lugs before you jack up the car. It makes everything much easier and safer. Where're you headed in Gloucester?"

"A place called Fezler Marine."

"Never heard of it."

The man took off his cap and wiped his brow with the back of his hand. His hair was the color of the sun. He had all the physical attributes of a movie star or a model, Rosa noted. Yet here he was, a highly educated scientist. She was impressed.

"It's on Breen Street," she added.

"Never heard of that either," he said, jiggling the spare into place and spinning the lugs back on. "Maybe I should pay more attention to where I'm living."

"I suspect you have more important things on your mind. I'd like to pay you for helping me. I'm very—"

"Nonsense. I could use a cup of coffee, though, if you'd like."

"I'm sorry. I would very much like to learn about your work. But I really must get going. I'm terribly late."

"Hey, no problem. My name's Darryl. It's been a pleasure."

"Rosa," she said. "Thank you so much."

The man smiled warmly, shook her hand, and then hobbled back to his car and drove off. Rosa glanced at her watch. Fifteen minutes was all it had taken.

"*Díos hace las cosas,*" she said as she slid back behind the wheel, and headed into Gloucester. *God provides.*

Two sets of service station directions and two missed turns later, Rosa found Breen Street. It was tucked among a tangle of narrow waterfront byways that were paved, but were probably still laid out exactly as they were when the Revolutionary War began. Fezler's Marine Railway and Automotive was a huge, decaying, shingled barn, flanked by two equally dilapidated wooden warehouses. The whole area seemed like a tinderbox—a conflagration just waiting to happen. Rosa drove nearly two blocks away before she found a street wide enough for parking.

Both of the large street-side doors, and a smaller entrance just around the corner of the building, were closed. Rosa knocked once, waited, knocked again, waited, and finally entered, shutting the door behind her. It was as if she had taken a step back in time.

The inside of Fezler's Marine Railway was as cluttered and dimly lit as it was spacious. Tools, some fairly modern, many antique, filled the barnside walls. Lines and chains and hauling blocks of various sizes hung everywhere. The atmosphere was heavy with the pungent odor of oil, grease, and gasoline. To one side of the shop was a large rolltop desk, cluttered with invoices, magazines, and catalogs. Above the rolltop was the same calendar Rosa had seen in Elsie Richardson's bedroom. From somewhere on the far side of the shop, classical music was playing. *Almost certainly Mozart,* Rosa thought.

"Hello?" she called out.

No one responded. There was an enclosed loft on the water side, accessed by an open staircase that climbed up one wall. Rosa glanced upward at the moment someone closed the door at the top of the stairs.

"Hello," she called again. "Is anyone here?"

"In the back," a gravelly voice hollered.

Rosa followed the voice toward the music and the water. The huge doors at the rear of the building were open to the harbor. A set of steel rails rose up from the water, cut through an opening in a narrow platform, and leveled off on the floor of the shop. Two feet above the tracks hung a large marine engine. It was suspended perhaps thirty feet from the ceiling by a complicated series of pulleys and lines. Standing beside the engine, working on it, was a woman. She was not impressively tall, but she was physically imposing in almost every other respect. *Big* was the only word that came to Rosa's mind. Not fat. Not even heavy—although she most certainly was that. Just *big*. Her broad shoulders and back splayed the straps of her grease-stained bib overalls. The sleeves of her black T-shirt were stretched to the limit by her arms. Her hair, beneath a Mobil cap, was tied back in a short ponytail.

"Welcome," she said. She glanced up at Rosa just long enough to size her up and then returned her attention to the engine.

"I'm looking for Martha Fezler," Rosa said.

"You found her." She loosened several bolts and dropped them into a coffee can half filled with an acrid-smelling liquid. "Fezler's famous degreaser," she explained. "Gasoline, boric acid, and just the right amount of saliva." She looked up at Rosa again, smiled mischievously, and winked. "The boom box is over there by the stairs. Feel free to turn it down if you want me to hear what you have to say."

Rosa did as the woman requested. When she returned, Martha Fezler had taken hold of a heavy, oil-stained line and was hoisting the massive engine up over her head.

"How heavy is that?" Rosa asked.

"Without the reverse gear? Oh, two-fifty, three hundred maybe."

"I'm very impressed."

"No need to be. With the block and fall setup I have here, I could lift two of these at once if I ever really wanted to or had to. . . . At least I think I could."

She wrapped the greasy line just a single time around a cleat on the wall and tucked a loop under to secure it. Rosa could not believe what she was witnessing.

"Just that one loop will hold it up there?" Rosa asked as the woman reached overhead and loosened the oil pan.

"Will if no one messes with it," Martha said. "And since I work alone here, no one does."

Her moonish face was unlined and open. And although her manner was brusque and her voice like sandpaper, there was an appealing quality to her. Rosa introduced herself.

"Miss Fezler, I need your help," she said.

"It's Martha. And unless you've got car or boat trouble, I don't see how I can—"

"Martha, I need to find your brother Warren. It's very, very urgent."

Martha lowered her hands and wiped them with a towel that seemed incapable of absorbing any more grease. For just a moment, Rosa thought she was going to deny having a brother and demand that she leave. Then, just as quickly, the woman's expression changed.

"Maybe we ought to go sit down," she said. "Would you like some coffee?"

The small, metal-top table overlooked the placid harbor from a spot just to one side of the rails. Seated across from Martha Fezler, Rosa traced her involvement in the DIC cases from her arrival at the Medical Center of Boston, through her discovery of Constanza Hidalgo's diary, and finally to Ken Mulholland, and their efforts to pin down the source of the virus CRV113.

"I believe that somehow the women I have been investigating became infected with the virus that your brother created," she concluded. "It is quite possible that some component of this diet powder they all were taking was contaminated. I don't know. I hope Warren does. Once the virus got into the women, their natural defenses battled back, but never completely eliminated it. It remained in balance with their bodies, until the stress of labor upset that balance."

"How many women have died from this?"

"Two that we know of. And their babies. A third woman—the one we cultured the virus from—lost her baby and almost died. I fear she is not going to be the last case, Martha. That's why I need to find your brother."

Martha Fezler stared out at the water and the lengthening afternoon shadows. Finally she handed a pencil and notepad to Rosa.

"Write down your name, where you come from, the name of the virus, and the name of that disease," she said. She waited until Rosa had complied, then tore off the sheet and slipped it into her overall pocket. "Wait here," she said.

She lumbered up the staircase and disappeared through the door to the loft. Rosa doodled absently on the pad as she watched a pair of gulls do strident battle over a mussel. Only when she glanced down did she realize that she was shading in the carefully blocked letters BART.

Five minutes passed. Once Rosa swore she heard Martha Fezler shouting. The gulls resolved their dispute and glided off across the harbor. Finally the loft door opened and Warren Fezler emerged, followed by his sister. He was even slighter than Rosa remembered from the time he dashed past her on the MCB campus. Compared to him, Martha looked positively hulking. He approached Rosa and smiled sheepishly.

"S-sorry I've given you s-such a hard time," he said. "I've been v-very frightened."

He took the seat opposite Rosa. Martha brought over another folding chair and settled onto it, facing the tracks.

"Warren says it's okay if I stay for this," she said.

"That's fine," Rosa replied. "Believe me, Warren, coming forward is the right thing to do."

"Even if I g-get k-killed?"

"We'll have to see to it that doesn't happen. When my department head finds out what's going on, you'll get all the protection you need. If I'm right, Warren, others have already died from this virus. There's a good chance that by coming forward, you may save a lot of lives."

"I honestly d-didn't know it was hurting anyone. He said that D-Dr. B-Baldwin caused their problem. N-not the virus."

"Who's *he*, Warren?"

Warren Fezler rubbed at his eyes, which looked flat and tired. He turned to Martha, who gave an encouraging nod.

"Blankenship," he said, suddenly. "Eli B-Blankenship."

Rosa stared at him incredulously. *Blankenship!* The one person aside from Sarah and Matt Daniels whom she had trusted with all her information. She felt a sick, empty churning beginning in her gut.

"Explain," she said.

"I s-stutter a lot. I'm s-sorry."

"There's nothing to apologize for, Warren. Don't even think about it. Just tell me about CRV113 and Eli Blankenship."

"If I sp-speak slowly, it's not as bad."

"You're doing fine."

Fezler took a calming breath. In fact, when he did begin to speak again, he seemed more composed and fluent.

"The CRV s-stands for coagulation-related virus. I stumbled on its weight loss p-property by accident. I th-think it's due to some sort of gene that's closely linked on the chromosome to one of the ones I w-was working on. The linked gene interferes with the digestion and cellular storage of fat by blocking a specific enzyme. In isolating my clotting genes from their chromosomes, I apparently cut away the genes that provide the checks and balances on the fat-inhibiting one. My m-monkeys began losing weight. A lot of them died. After I realized what was happening with them, I p-played around with the inoculum size and some other stuff. They stopped dying, and just lost weight—right down to dry weight. F-finally I ingested the virus myself. It w-worked perfectly. I l-lost a hundred pounds in just a f-few months with no p-problem and absolutely no side effects."

"But Cletus Collins said all your monkeys died."

"I—I'm ashamed to say it, but I k-killed them m-myself to protect the secret. It was B-Blankenship's idea. We were classmates in graduate school. He has an M.D. I have b-both an M.D. and Ph.D. I s-swear I n-never thought anyone would get hurt. You've g-got to believe that."

"She does, Warren," Martha said sadly. "Just go on."

"I t-told Eli about the virus and what I h-had found. He said we could get very rich from it. There were two p-problems, though."

Already, for Rosa, the final pieces had dropped into place.

"The patent," she said.

"Exactly. B-BIO-Vir owns the virus."

"And I guess the second would be the FDA."

"You're very s-smart," Fezler said.

Rosa thought about how much she had shared with Eli Blankenship—especially over the past two days.

"Not so smart," she said. "So, Blankenship concocted the Herbal Weight Loss powder to avoid any lengthy research protocol with the FDA."

"Which they w-would n-never have approved of any-how. Eli set up the whole thing. He's incredibly b-brilliant. But he's a demon. He's a liar, and he's v-very, very secretive. No one involved ever knew w-what anyone else was doing. N-not Singh, not Ettinger, not Paris, n-not even me."

"None of them knew about the virus?"

"Just me . . . and Eli."

"But it's in the diet powder."

"N-no. Not in the powder. In the vitamins. One of the vitamin capsules—n-number nine—is different f-from the rest. I made them myself in a lab Eli s-set up for me. At first I believed him about D-Dr. Baldwin being responsible for those women. Then I b-began to have doubts. I got f-frightened about what we w-were doing. Especially with s-so many people buying the p-powder."

"So Blankenship tried to kill you?"

"Not Blankenship. A m-man he hired. Tall and b-blond with—"

"No!"

Rosa was about to say the word herself when Martha Fezler screamed it. Her eyes were wide with terror. At that instant a soft pop came from Rosa's right. Martha cried out and flew over backward as if she had been hit by a wrecking ball. Warren and Rosa dropped to where she lay. She was grunting for breath. Her eyes were glazed.

"Oh, God!" Warren said, touching the dime-size hole in her overall bib, which was already soaking through with blood. "She's been shot."

"Excellent deduction, Warren."

They spun to the voice, which Rosa had recognized even before she saw the man. Darryl was leaning comfortably against a support beam, grinning at her the way he first had on the highway. The silenced revolver, held comfortably in his hand, was pointed at a spot somewhere between her and Warren.

"H-he's the m-man," Fezler said from his knees. "B-Blankenship's man. Why d-did you sh-shoot my s-sister, you f-fucker? Why?"

"It's just business, Warren," he said, taking a step toward them. "I'm sure Rosa there understands that. She doesn't hold it against me that I shot out that tire of hers. She knows it was just business. Just a way to find out exactly where she was headed. I don't hold it against you that my knee got blown apart the last time we were together and that I'm going to be a fucking gimp cripple for the rest of my life. Occupational hazard is the way I look at it. Business. Now, though, it's your turn."

"You s-son of a bitch!" Fezler whined.

"Get up! Now!"

Numbly the scientist did as he was asked. He looked like a man resigned to death.

Darryl's gun came up. Rosa could see Fezler had no intention of moving. She dove at him from the side and pushed him as hard as she could. He stumbled, tripped, and then toppled off the rear platform between the rails and the building. The gunman's reflex shot splintered the floor where Fezler had been standing.

"Run, Warren, run!" Rosa screamed.

Darryl turned to her and smiling in a calm, twisted way, shot her in the chest. In grotesque ballet, Rosa spun nearly full around, her arms flapping like a rag doll's, her glasses flying off. She fell heavily to the floor, not two feet from where Martha lay. Pain exploded through to her back from a spot just above her right breast. She cried out, but was not aware that she had made a sound. Drawing even a shallow breath sent daggers through her chest, and up into her shoulder and jaw.

Darryl, now ignoring her completely, had moved to the spot where Warren had fallen from the platform. He held the obscene, silenced revolver loosely as he stared out toward the water. Lying on her side, gasping for air, Rosa prayed that Fezler had overcome his cowardice and kept his head enough to try to escape.

"P-please d-don't sh-shoot," she suddenly heard him beg.

"Up," Darryl said. "Slowly now. On your feet."

Silently Rosa cursed both men. Moving through pain unlike any she had ever known, she pulled herself toward them.

"Now, Warren, this way. Come on. . . . Come on, boy."

Rosa felt herself move, then move again, first on her belly, then on her hands and knees. Her lung had collapsed. Of that she was sure. She tasted blood and sensed it welling up from her chest. She felt dizzy. Her vision blurred. Then, as she wondered if she could move even one more foot, her hand brushed against Martha Fezler's coffee can. Hearing the soft scrape, Darryl turned. With all her strength, Rosa splashed the solvent into his face. He staggered backward, screaming, pawing frantically at his eyes with his free hand and firing the revolver wildly with the other.

A bullet tore through the flesh of Rosa's arm, but she barely noticed. She had pulled herself up by a line and stumbled over to the wall.

"Warren, help!" she cried hoarsely.

Darryl, now writhing on the floor by the tracks, fired instinctively at her voice. The bullet shattered the barn-side just inches from her face.

"Please help me!"

Again a bullet slammed into the wall by her face. The blood gurgling in her throat was beginning to suffocate her. Her cough was futilely weak, her consciousness beginning to go. The room swirled mercilessly as she slipped toward the floor. Suddenly, through the unrelenting haze, she heard a crash, followed instantly by Darryl's dreadful wail. Then, just as suddenly, there was silence.

Rosa lay by the wall, conscious, but barely so. Her hand was inches from her eyes. Still, it took some time before she realized that she was clutching the safety line Martha had so loosely tied. She peered across through a deepening gloom. Twenty feet away, Blankenship's hired killer lay facedown and very still. The huge marine inboard engine rested squarely on his back.

"Warren?" Rosa whimpered, almost soundlessly. "Please come."

There was no response. Rosa battled the encroaching darkness. But slowly her eyes closed.

"Rosa?" Fezler meekly whispered her name, as he touched her shoulder. "C-can you hear me?"

Rosa nodded but could not speak. She felt blood oozing from her mouth.

"Hang on. I'll c-call an ambulance."

"Wait," she gasped.

"W-what?"

"Pad . . . pencil . . . over there."

Bewildered, Fezler retrieved the pad and then lifted her head and rested it on his lap. Painfully, slowly, she dictated a phone number to him.

"Call . . . now," she managed. "Explain . . . to . . . him. . . . Sarah . . . is . . . at . . M . . C . . . B . . . . This . . . man . . . will . . . help."

"I'll g-get an ambulance," Warren said. "Rosa? Dammit, Rosa, no!"

The muscles in her face relaxed. Her lips curled up in a thin smile.

"Go," she said.

Chapter 41

OCTOBER 29

EACH HOUR OF SARAH'S INCARCERATION ON THE locked ward of Underwood Six was more traumatic and unpleasant than the last. The staff seemed determined that she should neither expect nor get any special treatment merely because she was a physician. And some of them clearly enjoyed having power and control over an M.D. Every request she made, however minor, was prohibited or modified by some sort of unit rule. Her primary antagonists were the mental health workers—mostly recent college graduates who majored in psychology or sociology, and who all seemed to have taken the job as a stopgap while they tried to decide what to do with their lives.

"My doctor hasn't been by to see me all day. It's very important that I talk to him. Could you please call him?"

"I'm sorry. We never call doctors unless it's an emergency or a problem with medication. He'll be here later tonight or in the morning, just like all the other doctors."

"Hi, I hate to bother you, but I'd like to see the nurses' *Physicians' Desk Reference*, please. I'm trying to

check on a drug company named Huron Pharmaceuticals."

"I'm sorry. No staff books can be lent out to patients."

"Well, could you check on Huron for me?"

"Perhaps later, after group, if there's time."

Eventually, a surprise letup in the line waiting to use
the one pay phone had allowed Sarah to call a friend in
the hospital pharmacy. There was, he told her, absolutely no such company as Huron Pharmaceuticals. Not
local, not regional, not national, not foreign. Nowhere.
That information sent Sarah marching once again into
battle against the mental health workers.

"I was certain my lawyer was coming during visitors'
hours. Now they're over and he hasn't shown up. Can I
see him just for a minute if he comes late? It's very
important."

"I'm sorry. That's not possible."

"If he happens to call the nurses' station, could you
put him through to me?"

"Outside calls can only come through the patients'
pay phone."

"But the pay phone was tied up all evening. And then
it got shut off at ten. No one told me that was going to
happen. Could I please use the nurses' station phone to
try to reach him?"

"Everything will be just the same tomorrow morning,
Sarah. You may not believe that, but it will. Now, why
don't you take the medication Dr. Goldschmidt ordered, read for a while, and get some sleep?"

After learning that the pay phone had been shut off at
ten, Sarah gave up on hearing from Matt before morning. But with each passing hour, her concern for him
grew. *Why would he not at least have called?* She calmed
herself only by reasoning that he had inadvertently
missed the narrow, two-hour visitors' window and then
had become the victim of a constant busy signal on the
pay phone. Perhaps he had come to the ward late and

had been turned away by one of the mental health workers.

The hours on Underwood Six had dragged past a minute at a time. Now it was half-past two in the morning. Sarah sat in a worn leather chair by the lounge window, grateful that no one had produced a rule prohibiting that specific behavior. The one redeeming thing about being a patient on a locked psych ward, she was realizing, was that one could act crazy and have no one take much notice.

Her throat was still raspy from the endotracheal tube, and in addition to feeling tired and weak, she had a rather nasty cough. But she also felt committed to staying up all night if necessary. If and when the Huron Pharmaceuticals truck returned to the Chilton Building, she wanted to know it. In less than seven hours, the building was going to blow. And secrets were either going to be buried beneath the rubble or were being hauled away before the blast made their removal impossible. The Huron people might have already finished their business within the condemned building. But maybe, just maybe, they hadn't. One lucky shaft of light, one good look at the driver of the truck, might pull everything together.

"How're you doing?"

Sarah, perhaps drifting off, was startled by the voice. "Oh, hi," she said.

The man, Wes, was a mental health aide. He and an RN were the graveyard shift staff on Underwood Six. At forty or so, he was older than the day and evening shift mental health workers, but Sarah assumed that his role on the floor had more to do with security than therapy. He had the lean, muscular frame of a gymnast or weight lifter, and a tattoo of a skull and dagger on one deltoid that he seemed determined to show off. Sarah's impression was that he was quite taken with himself. She also doubted seriously that his formal education extended much beyond high school. Since his arrival at eleven, this was his third trip over to talk with her.

"You watching anything interesting?"

"Not really. That building over there's going to be blown up tomorrow."

"I know. I'm going to stay to watch it. These'll be the best seats anyplace. You ever work in there?"

He had made it clear in their earlier conversations that he had learned a great deal about her from the evening shift report and from reading her chart. The notion of that infuriated her.

"What? Oh, no. It's never been open since I've been here. I'm just curious about it, that's all."

Sarah continued staring across the campus, thinking about Matt. Logic told her he was fine. But a heavy, unpleasant, totally illogical sensation in her gut told her something had gone wrong.

"So, are you dating anyone?" Wes said, scanning her unabashedly.

Oh, no! Sarah thought. "Yes. Yes, I'm engaged," she said quickly.

The mental health aide coming on to her. *Just what she needed.* She flashed on how valuable it would be if every prospective doctor was required to spend time as a patient. They could call the course Helplessness 101.

"Hey, that doesn't matter to me if it doesn't matter to you," Wes said, adjusting the sleeve of his T-shirt to fully expose the skull. "There are a lot of rules here. I can help you get around some of them."

Sarah thought for a moment he was going to reach over and touch her. The prospect nauseated her. But if she rebuffed him too harshly, almost anything might happen to her. The Sealy Posturepedic Suite, as the patients called the padded room, was occupied primarily by those who lashed out in some way against the authority of the staff.

"Look, um, Wes. I really appreciate your coming over

to talk to me. But I just need to take things slowly . . . if you know what I mean."

The man's face lit up.

"Oh. Oh, yeah. I know what you mean. You want anything right now? A cold drink? Something sweet? Maybe something white and powdery? You have no roommate and the room next to yours is empty."

Sarah's nausea intensified. If this nightmare ever was over for her, she vowed to return to Underwood Six as a physician. And in the name of all those women who would ever be incarcerated there, she would hang this sleaze out to dry.

If . . .

She begged off any favors from him for the time being, told him it was fine for him to stop by later provided she was still awake, and continued staring intently across the campus. With each passing minute, she felt more and more determined, before the big blast, to find a way off Underwood Six and into the Chilton Building.

Now that idea, she acknowledged with a half smile, *was crazy.*

By three-thirty, she was beginning to lose her battle with exhaustion. She knew she was nodding off between stints with the binoculars. But she was totally unwilling to quit, and kept prodding herself awake. Rosa, Matt, and Eli had spent most of their day unraveling various threads of the CRV113 mystery. She had spent her day in group and her night fending off a mental health aide who was more disturbed than most of the patients. The impotence of her situation was intolerable. Somehow, she was going to make a contribution, she insisted to herself. Somehow, she was going to find a way to—

Sarah shook her head to clear it and wiped her face with the damp washcloth that had been her only ally through the long night's vigil. There was movement on the far side of the Chilton Building. She cut the overhead fluorescent lights, took up the binoculars, and braced her elbows firmly between the sill and the window.

Lighting immediately around the Chilton Building was nonexistent. But the moon, though setting, was nearly full; and the campus walkway lights were numerous enough to further soften the gloom. Sarah waited for her eyes to adjust to the darkness, but she felt certain already of what she was seeing.

The Huron truck was back.

. . .

Black Cat Daniels knew that he was going to die. And at times over the brutal hours he had spent as Eli Blankenship's captive, he had prayed that he would. Some time after being knocked unconscious, he had come to lying facedown in the back of what he assumed was the Huron Pharmaceuticals van. His hands were bound tightly behind him with thin wire, and his ankles were lashed to one wall. His head throbbed mercilessly, and his debilitating dizziness and nausea refused to ebb.

The van was parked inside a darkened structure of some sort, possibly a garage. There was some street noise—an occasional passing automobile—but no voices. The position Matt had been left in was horribly uncomfortable. But even his slightest movement sent pain screaming up his arms from where the wire cut into his wrists.

Blankenship made his first visit to the van long after Matt had regained consciousness. There was some surprise at seeing that it was he, but in truth, not all that much.

"I should have known," Matt said.

"Yes. Yes, I suppose you should have."

"You killed Colin Smith."

"I had to."

"And Pramod Singh."

"Had to."

"And you set up Ettinger to take the blame."

"Now, *that* I wanted to do. So, then. I've answered your questions. Suppose you answer a few of mine. I

need to know if there are any other, shall we say, loose
ends I need to tie up. Is there anyone else I should be
concerned about? Anyone else you've spoken with? Jeremy Mallon? Paris? What did they say to you?"

Matt did his best to turn away, but Blankenship
merely shook his elbow. Matt screamed with the pain.

"I don't know anything," he cried. "I don't know
anything else."

Blankenship pulled his head up by the hair.

"I hope you're telling the truth," he said. "We'll see."

He let go suddenly. Matt's face slammed onto the
metal floor. The next time he came, he brought a drug—
some sort of injection. Matt nearly passed out from the
pain of merely having his arm moved about for the needle. Then, moments later, the pain vanished. For a
stretch that might have been minutes—or days—he
heard only isolated words and phrases, first in Blankenship's voice, then his own, floating through his mind like
feathers. Finally darkness and silence swept down and
enveloped him.

When he regained consciousness, he was sitting on the
floor of a damp, totally darkened room, his legs extended, his ankles tied together. His hands were lashed
behind him to a metal pipe. The air was dusty, and
smelled of concrete and mold. His face felt battered and
swollen. One tooth was broken off. The only positive
thought he had was that he was still alive. But he knew
that condition would not be lasting too much longer.
Minutes later, now fully awake, he learned precisely
how long.

The voice, a man's, came over loudspeakers that were
mounted somewhere in the blackness.

"Attention, attention please," it said. "This building
will be demolished by explosion in three hours. No one
should be inside the structure, or within the blue protective barriers. Repeat. This building will be demolished . . ."

"Help!" Matt hollered. "Please help!"

His voice echoed weakly about him. There was no chance anyone would hear him. No chance at all. Silently he cursed Eli Blankenship and his own carelessness. Then he lowered his chin to his chest and waited.

Chapter 42

AT SIX-THIRTY, WHEN A SET OF CHIMES ANNOUNCED wake-up, Sarah had showered and changed and was back in the patients' lounge, drinking coffee. If all went according to her still-evolving plan, she would be inside the Chilton Building within the hour. The clock was still ticking toward the 9 A.M. demolition, but the stakes had risen considerably. For hidden somewhere within the building, probably in the basement or subbasement, was a body.

· The Huron Pharmaceuticals truck had remained by the building for half an hour. The driver, a large, strong man from what Sarah could make out, had pulled the body from the back of the van, swung it up over his shoulder, and hauled it down into the basement. Through the binoculars, Sarah had gotten a clear, unmistakable look at the arms of the victim, dangling down the driver's back. Thirty minutes later, the man returned to his van empty-handed and drove off.

A few minutes after that, Sarah approached Wes. Charming the aide was easy. Charming him without having him touch her was not. She flirted as she had not for many, many years and pandered to his ego in every way she could. She made thinly veiled promises that had the man's fantasies exploding like Independence Day fireworks. She ran her lips over the rim of her coffee cup as if it held vintage Dom Perignon. By dawn, she had learned how mealtimes were organized on Underwood Six. Group A—one of two classifications—were the least stable patients on the unit. They went down for meals in the cafeteria, but with no more than two patients per staff member. However, the evening shift staff had determined that Sarah was not predictable enough even for Group A. Her breakfast was to be sent up to the unit. The day shift could decide about lunch. Now, some flattery, some promises, and a few come-hither smiles had bought her a promotion. Wes had moved a patient to Group B and added her name to the Group A list. She would be dining in the cafeteria from six forty-five to seven-fifteen.

A none-too-subtle allusion to the anatomical secrets known only to M.D.'s, and Wes also allowed her to use the phone in the staff office, although that deal almost fell through when she begged off sitting on his lap while doing so. Before Wes signaled that the shift nurse had finished preparing meds and Sarah needed to vacate the staff office, she had managed to make two calls. The first was to Matt's home; she felt sick when she heard his answering machine come on. The second was to the hospital page operator, who functioned as the answering service for Eli Blankenship. Sarah had written out the message she wanted the operator to give him. However, after a minute on hold, to Sarah's surprise, the medical chief himself came on the line. He had spent the night in the hospital, he said, and was napping on the couch in his office.

"Sarah, are you all right?" he asked as soon as he heard her voice. "How did you get to a phone at this hour?"

"I'll tell you that one when I see you, Dr. Blanken-

ship. And no, I'm not all right. I need to get off this
ward, and quickly."

"Sarah, Dr. Goldschmidt is the only one who can
discharge you from a locked ward. I'm sorry, but that's
the—"

"Please, Dr. Blankenship. I don't have much time on
this phone. You said yesterday you believed me in your
gut. And that was even before everyone found out I was
telling the truth about Andrew. You've got to believe me
now. Something terrible is going on in this hospital. It
involves a company called Huron Pharmaceuticals—the
company that supplies vitamins to Peter Ettinger's
weight loss company. I can prove it."

"How?"

"I'm going to be in the cafeteria for breakfast at six
forty-five. Can you be there?"

"Yes, but—"

"Just keep an eye on me. You'll know what to do."

"You said proof."

"Can you get us into the Chilton Building?"

"I . . . yes. Yes, I can."

"The proof is there. Dr. Blankenship, I've got to go.
Please trust me. Please be there for me."

"Count on it," Eli Blankenship said.

One of the mental health workers called out the list of
those in Group A. Sarah shuffled over to where they
were convening by the electronically controlled door.
After a brief discussion among the staff—Sarah sensed
that it dealt with her—the door was buzzed open, and
the procession of six patients and three overseers made
its way off the locked ward. Standing off to one side,
Wes gave her a wink and a thumbs-up sign.

The MCB cafeteria was modestly busy, primarily
with residents and nurses. Sarah felt herself under scru-
tiny as she queued with her group. But after nearly six
months of the hell she had already endured, she barely
noticed.

Keep staring, everyone, she thought. *In just a few minutes, you're going to get a real eyeful.*

She selected items with no intention of eating them, and kept searching for Eli Blankenship. The mental health workers assigned each patient to one of two tables. Sarah positioned herself to get as wide a view of the cafeteria as possible. It was then that she noticed the delivery floor nurse, Joanne Delbanco, having coffee at the next table over.

"Joanne," she said in a half whisper.

"Oh, hello, Sarah."

The nurse looked away quickly, but not before Sarah saw the expression of distaste on her face. Sarah knew the keepers were watching her. One sign that she was annoying the hospital staff, and she might find herself on the way back to Underwood Six. Still, she had to try.

"Joanne, just tell me how Annalee is doing. Is she all right?"

The nurse hesitated for an interminable few seconds and then made a partial turn back, almost speaking over her shoulder.

"If you must know," she said coolly, "she's in active labor. She'll probably deliver sometime this morning or early this afternoon."

Sarah was horrified.

"What about the terbutaline?" she asked.

Sarah could see the two keepers at her table exchanging glances. She was operating right on the edge of their tolerance now, and Blankenship still hadn't appeared.

"Dr. Snyder stopped all her medications," Joanne replied. "He felt that the stress you—the stress she's been through was enough. The baby's big enough, and the surfactant level is—"

"Joanne," Sarah cut in excitedly, "you've got to find Dr. Snyder. He's got to do a section on her before it's too late."

"I've got to what?"

"Sarah, I think that's enough," one of the keepers said.

"Joanne, please. It's—"

"Sarah, if you don't stop right now, we're going back up to the unit early. Everyone in the group will be punished for your actions."

Sarah barely heard the man. The huge, bald pate and massive physique of Eli Blankenship had just appeared in the doorway farthest across the cafeteria from them.

Thank God. Sarah sighed. The news from Joanne Delbanco had changed everything. She was no longer fixed on getting into the Chilton Building. Now the only thing that really mattered was to explain the situation to Blankenship and get him up to the labor and delivery floor. With his influence, and perhaps Rosa Suarez's as well, they might be able to convince Snyder to perform a cesarean on Annalee before disaster struck.

If, in addition, they could stop the demolition of the Chilton Building, so much the better. But Annalee and her baby were far higher priorities than anything—or anyone—that might be buried beneath the rubble.

Okay, everyone, Sarah thought. *It's showtime.*

"I don't feel well," she whimpered.

"What's the matter?"

"I—I don't know. I'm dizzy and—and I keep seeing these little flashing dots of light."

"Has this ever happened before? . . . Sarah, I asked you if this has ever happened before?"

Sarah began by snapping her hands rhythmically at her wrists. Then she jerked her head up and down. Her eyelids flickered, and beneath them her eyes rolled up until only the whites showed.

"Sarah!" someone cried out.

At that instant, affecting a dreadful, gurgling moan, she threw herself backward, twisting just enough to avoid smashing her head against the linoleum.

"She's having a seizure!" she heard the mental health

worker exclaim. "Back off, everyone! Back away! Just
let her be!"

You ass, Sarah thought. *Get me on my side!*

"Out of the way!" she heard Eli Blankenship's voice
boom. "Get her on her side quickly, before she aspi-
rates!"

He worked his beefy hand beneath her head to cush-
ion it, moved her on to her side, and then slipped his
billfold between her teeth. Sarah bit down on the wallet,
continued her seizure activity for another half a minute,
and then allowed herself to slow down. Next would be a
lapse into "unconsciousness."

"I'm her medical doctor," Blankenship explained
with calm authority. "She has a past history of epi-
lepsy. There's nothing to worry about. Absolutely nothing. Everything's going to be all right. That's it, Sarah.
You're doing fine. I think just in case, we ought to get
her over to the ER. Would someone please call transportation and have a litter sent down?"

One of the mental health workers rushed off to do as
he requested.

"What should *we* do about her?" another keeper
asked.

"Just notify Dr. Goldschmidt of what has happened.
Tell him that for the time being, we'll transfer Dr. Baldwin back to the medical service. I'm Dr. Blankenship."

"Yes, Doctor. I know."

Sarah sensed the gaggle of onlookers begin to disperse. Blankenship bent over and whispered in her ear
that she was doing great, and to keep her eyes closed
until he told her all was clear. She moaned. A minute or
so later transportation arrived, and she was lifted up
onto the litter.

"Okay, everyone, she's doing fine," Blankenship said.

Sarah kept her head lolling from side to side as she
was wheeled from the cafeteria, then down the hall and
into the elevator. Although the cafeteria was on the
basement level, Sarah felt the car go down. She tried to

picture where they were as she was wheeled out and down another fairly long corridor.

"Okay, you can sit up and open your eyes now, my friend," Blankenship said. "That was an Academy Award performance."

Sarah pushed herself up, blinked her vision into focus, and looked around. She and the medical chief were alone in the subbasement tunnel. They were outside a steel security gate, draped with canvas on the far side. It bore a large sign warning of the time and date of the demolition, and requiring that anyone entering the Chilton Building prior to the 29th of October be accompanied by hospital security. There was a wall phone by the gate. Taped above it, a printed card gave the number of the demolition company and the extension of the hospital security office.

"Where's the transportation guy?" she asked.

"Abe left us at the elevator," Blankenship said, unlocking the gate. "I got him his job about a million years ago, and I take care of his family. He does favors for me when he can."

"Dr. Blankenship, it's all true. There's a connection between Peter Ettinger's diet product and those DIC cases. It's a virus of some sort. Rosa Suarez went out yesterday to speak with the man who created it."

"I know. I got her the car she used."

"Well, now Annalee is in labor. Her terbutaline's been stopped. Dr. Blankenship, Peter tested that diet powder on her several years ago. If she's not sectioned soon, she's going to go into DIC like the others. I'm sure of it. We've got to get up to the L and D floor and speak with him."

"Hey, slow down, slow down," Blankenship said. "You just had a grand mal seizure, remember?"

"Dr. Blankenship, this is serious."

"Well, what about that pharmaceutical truck you told me about? The proof."

"This is more important. Can you get them to hold off on the demolition?"

"Maybe, provided I can come up with a damn good reason. The mayor, the governor, and dozens of high rollers are going to be up there in the grandstand. This is the biggest day of Paris's career. But listen, Sarah. We used the Chilton Building for storage. That's how I have the keys to these gates. I was in there just a week or so ago, helping to move the last of our stuff out. There's a lot of debris and rubble. That's all."

"Well, there's a body inside now. I guarantee it. That's reason enough to delay things, isn't it? But please. Annalee took that weight loss powder. The farther she gets into labor, the more danger she's in. We've got to help her."

Sarah was still seated on the litter. Moving too quickly for her to react, Blankenship opened the security gate, shoved the stretcher inside, and slammed the gate behind them. Instantly they were in near-total darkness.

"What are you doing?" Sarah cried as Blankenship reached through and resecured the padlock.

But in that moment, she knew. The broad hand supporting her head in the cafeteria . . . the distinct, unpleasant blend of body odor and cologne. She had experienced both before. *He was the man—the assailant in room 512.*

"Help!" she screamed. "Help!"

He pulled her roughly off the litter and shoved her down the darkened corridor.

"Yell all you want," he said. "It's therapeutic. There's no one within a few hundred yards of this place."

He twisted her wrist to keep her still and flicked on a powerful flashlight. They were at a second security gate, almost identical to the first.

"The canvas is for dust protection during the big blow," Blankenship said, withdrawing the ring of keys from his clinic coat pocket. "The last thing we want is dust in our hospital, right?"

Sarah's intense fear was quickly displaced by anger. She swung a fist at his face and actually connected a glancing blow. But he merely twisted her wrist a bit more and forced her down to one knee.

"They know I'm with you," she said. "Everyone knows."

"You broke free, took off, and disappeared," he said simply.

"Eli, that girl's dying."

"Everyone dies."

He dragged her through the second security gate and again locked it behind them. His grip on her wrist kept her in check. The corridor was strewn with rubble—chunks of concrete and pieces of glass and plumbing. He flicked off the flashlight, giving her a sense of the oppressive, total darkness. Then, from somewhere down the hallway, a loudspeaker announced that there were ninety minutes to demolition and that absolutely no one should be in or around the Chilton Building.

"I guess I'd do well not to lose these keys," Blankenship said. He switched on his beam. "Now, then, let's go find that body you're so damn curious about."

Chapter 43

ELI, PLEASE," SARAH BEGGED AS HE PULLED HER into the subbasement of the Chilton Building. "You've been such a wonderful physician and teacher. You've got to stop this before Annalee and a lot of others die."

"Do you know that nine days after the first infomercial hit the airways, I made more money than I had in twenty years as a wonderful physician and teacher? Everyone thinks we just get our M.D. degrees and step into the Cadillacs and country clubs. If you want to get angry at someone, get angry at them for setting up those expectations in us. You know, I didn't even have a damn retirement fund. Well, I do now."

"Eli, please don't let this happen to all those women."

"Oh, don't be so dramatic. Science will figure out a way to overcome their problem. It always does. Besides, do you know how many man-years of life have already been saved by all of that blubber-melting we've accomplished? If the Nobel committee ever did *that* arithmetic, I'd be a shoo-in for the prize. Now look, we don't have much time. Do you want to see this or not?"

Sarah kicked his shin as hard as she could.

"Stop it!" he ordered, tightening his grip.
"Good. . . . That's much better. Now, let's take a brief
tour of our facility. Then I promise I'll set you up with
that body you're so intent on finding."

"Who is it?" she asked, frightened by the man's imposing size and strength, but not nearly so much as by
the total lack of feeling in his words. Perhaps the most
brilliant man she had ever known, and he was absolutely
mad.

"Who is it? Well, who do you think?" he asked, half
shoving, half dragging her down the coal-black corridor.

"Oh, God. Eli, where is he?"

"Now, behind this door was our virology lab. The
nerve center of the Ayurvedic Weight Loss System, if
you will."

He kicked the door open and panned the light about a
large, fully equipped laboratory.

"Where is he?"

"Dr. Baldwin, are you going to pay attention? It took
almost two years to get this operation going. No one but
my virologist—make that my *late* virologist—and I have
ever *seen* this room, until this morning. Do you realize
how difficult that was to pull off?"

"Damn it, where's Matt? What did you do to him?"

"Can you believe Singh and that fop Ettinger actually
believed the herbs I concocted were causing people to
lose weight? I spent a week in the library and came up
with an Ayurvedic mix that I must admit the Maharishi
himself would have been proud of. But a week. That's
all. I made the whole thing up. Every herb. I told Singh a
friend had brought the mixture back from India, and I
needed to test it out. The minute he heard the word
Ayurvedic, he adopted it as his own. No questions
asked. Now, isn't that something? Later on, after the
first group lost so much weight, I suggested that Singh
ask your ex-lover to be the spokesman for the whole
thing in exchange for a modest share of the profits. And
Ettinger bit hook, line, and sinker. Why shouldn't he,

though, right? It was alternative medicine, and he loved that. And it was going to make him rich, and he loved that even more. Do I know human nature or what?"

He kicked open another door, shined his light into the room, and snapped Sarah's head around, making her look inside. "Here's the little suite where my late virologist lived while he was putting together our product," he went on. "Home, home in the hospital, and no one ever knew he was here. Now isn't that just something?"

"Where's Matt?"

"All in good time."

"Attention, attention please. This building will be demolished by explosion in seventy-five minutes. No one should be inside the structure or within the blue protective barriers. Repeat . . ."

"Right on time," Blankenship said. "That asshole Paris runs a tight ship."

In spite of herself, Sarah began to cry.

"You bastard. You crazy bastard," she whimpered.

"Now just shut up," he rasped, his voice reverberating down the corridor. "If you don't have the decency to listen and appreciate what I've been able to accomplish, then just keep your mouth shut. I've already helped half a million people lose weight, live longer, and feel better about themselves, and I've banked almost twenty-one million dollars in just eight months. If you're not impressed, then you're not listening."

"Where's Matt?"

"Oh, I am just sick and tired of you," he said. "I expected more from a woman of your breadth and worldliness." He dragged her a few more feet down the corridor. "I give you your knight in shining armor," he announced. "Unfortunately, he is at this moment a tad the worse for wear."

He cast his light down at Matt, who was seated on the floor, a broad adhesive tape gag across his mouth. His hands were secured behind him to a vertical sewage pipe, and his face showed the ravages of a fearsome beating. But he was alive.

"He's been waiting here patiently just in case my clean-up campaign hit any last-minute snags. But except for your unfortunate recovery from your suicide attempt the other night, there really haven't been any."

Blankenship loosened his hold on her. Sarah rushed to Matt and gently peeled off the tape. He breathed in the stale, dusty air hungrily. She stroked his face and kissed the dark swelling about his eyes.

"Matt, I'm sorry. I'm so sorry" was all she could say.

"I love you," he managed. "I was praying he wouldn't hurt you any more."

"They'll find us, Eli," Sarah said angrily. "They'll dig this place out, they'll find us, and they'll get you. You're really not as smart as you think. There are too many loose ends."

"There are none," he said. "At least none that I can't deal with, especially with Peter Ettinger around to absorb the blame for absolutely anything. The dupe from heaven, that's what I call him. In jail and absolutely clueless. Now, if you'll be so kind as to put your hands together behind your back, I have just enough wire left over."

Sarah stayed where she was, her arms around Matt's shoulders. Blankenship was reaching again for her when Matt lashed his feet out. In one motion, he knocked the light free and continued upward until he made solid contact with Blankenship's chin.

"Run, Sarah!" he shouted as Blankenship reeled several steps backward. "Run!"

Matt cried out as Blankenship hit him. But Sarah was already through the doorway. The subbasement corridor was pitch-black. She slammed into the wall, stumbled momentarily, and then dragged her hand along it, moving as fast as she could in the direction away from the tunnel and the locked security gates. The windows and doors from the first floor on up were boarded over.

If she could somehow get to one of those and kick the boards out, there was a chance. Behind her, she heard Blankenship laugh.

"What a flashlight," he said. "First chance I get, I'm writing a letter of endorsement to the manufacturer. Sarah, give it up!"

Sarah continued working her way along the wall as the powerful flashlight beam began sweeping the corridor, searching her out. At the moment it found her, she glimpsed the stairs, just a few feet ahead and to her left. She raced upward as fast as she could, hitting the wall at the landing, bouncing off it, and then sprinting upward to the basement level. Behind her she could see the bobbing light and hear Blankenship's heavy footsteps. The debris was a problem now. Huge pieces of concrete and planking tripped her once, and then again, as she picked her way up to the first floor.

"Give it up, Sarah," Blankenship called out once more.

If she could only put some distance between them, Sarah thought—just find a place to hide until he *had* to leave the building—she had a chance. Every story meant more possibilities Blankenship had to consider before he could confidently move on. Every turn that presented her with new options presented him with new problems. She fell again but scrambled up and, as quietly as she could manage, worked her way to the second floor. This was where she would stop, she decided. This was where she would hide.

She dragged her hand along the wall as she made her way over the rubble and through the oppressive darkness, searching for a room of some sort. Up ahead, through what she felt must be a boarded window, she saw the faintest sliver of light. Behind her, Blankenship's footsteps and labored breathing were getting closer. Suddenly the floor beneath her left foot vanished. At almost the same instant her left hand slipped from the wall into nothingness. She felt herself falling. Reflexively she pushed off her right foot and dove forward. She fell heavily to the floor, pieces of concrete gashing her chin and knee. Then, helplessly, she toppled off into what she realized at that instant was the elevator shaft. She was beginning to free-fall when first her right hand, then her left, found the edge of something metal. Her fingers closed on it. Her arms snapped to full extension, but her grips held. And suddenly she was dangling over a black abyss.

Desperately she tried to comprehend her situation. She was clinging to the metal frame that had once held the elevator doors. The concrete had broken away from the frame, leaving a gap several inches wide between it and the remaining floor. Through the darkness, she could hear Blankenship leave the first floor, following the sound of her fall to the second. The metal was cutting into her fingers. She had only seconds to make a decision. She either had to try and haul herself up . . . or drop. Three stories to the subbasement, she figured. Twenty-five feet, maybe. Would she have any chance at all dropping through the impenetrable blackness to a concrete floor? The answer was clear.

Planting the sole of her sneaker against the wall of the shaft and pulling with strength she would never have believed she possessed, she kicked one foot up to the doorway and over the metal frame. The gap beyond the frame was quite wide, actually—eight or nine inches. With her heel set in the space, she had just enough purchase to haul herself up.

"Attention. Attention, please. This building will be demolished by explosion in sixty minutes . . ."

Shielded by the noise of the loudspeaker's warning, Sarah scrambled on her hands and knees across the corridor. She was cowering against the wall, in a small alcove opposite the shaft, when Blankenship's light knifed through the darkness from the stairway landing.

"Come on, Sarah," he called, inching his way along. "We'll talk. . . . Maybe work out a deal. . . . I'm not leaving until there's only a minute or two left. . . . You don't have a prayer without me. Neither does Daniels. He's hurt, you know. . . . Hurt pretty bad. You can help him. . . ."

There was one chance, Sarah realized as he approached. Only one. She braced herself against the wall. If he spotted her before he reached the open shaft, it was over for her. But if not. . . .

Ten feet away . . . five . . . still the beam had not found her. Three. . . . *One more step,* she urged. *Just one, and—*

At the moment the light hit her, she sprang forward, hurling her body against Blankenship's chest with all her strength. It was as if she had leapt against a slab of granite. Before she even realized how totally she had failed, the man's arms were around her, crushing her.

"Not a chance," he said, laughing out loud and intensifying his grip. "Not a—"

Sarah felt his bulk suddenly shift and his hold on her lessen. He had taken a single step backward. She knew that. But then something had happened. He was off balance, falling backward and to his left . . . falling into the shaft. Still clutching Sarah too tightly for her to break away, Blankenship began to scream.

"My leg! . . . Jesus, my leg! . . ."

He howled, again and again, bellowing as he toppled backward in what seemed to Sarah to be slow motion. She was frantically trying to sort out what was going on, what action she might take, when Blankenship's two lower leg bones snapped. The moment she heard the crunch and his hideous wail, Sarah understood. He had stepped into the space between the metal frame and the concrete floor. What little force she had provided against his chest was just enough to keep him from recovering his balance. He swung backward rapidly now, his leg bending at a newly created joint several inches above his ankle.

Still conscious and screeching in agony, he hung upside down in the pitch-black shaft, clinging to Sarah's right wrist, dangling her beneath him. Then, wailing piteously, he let her go.

. . .

Sarah had the briefest warning before Blankenship's grasp on her wrist released. In that second, countless thoughts and bits of advice on how to fall and land flashed through her mind. *Roll . . . relax . . . land on your feet . . . land on your butt . . . land on your side . . . push off when you hit . . . flatten out. . . .* So desperate was she to do something to keep from dying that she was completely unprepared for the actual impact, which came after a free fall that lasted only moments, and covered less than six feet. She landed heavily on the steep slope of a mountain of rubble that extended upward into the shaft almost two stories from the subbasement.

Clawing at the chunks of concrete and other debris, she stopped herself from tumbling downward. For half a minute she lay there, gasping for breath. She hurt badly in spots, but none of the injuries seemed incapacitating. Above her, enveloped in the intense darkness, Blankenship continued to moan. He had not passed out, she realized, because he was suspended upside down. There was no reflex blood vessel dilation, no drop in blood flow to his head. No merciful lapse into unconsciousness.

She peered through the gloom. Her vision now adjusted to the circumstance, she could see the slight changes in the shaft above and below her at what must have been the doorways at the first floor and basement. She was inching her way downward when she suddenly remembered the keys. Blankenship had slipped them into his clinic coat. Of that she was almost certain. Without them she had no option but to find a window and try to break through the boards.

Fifty minutes to go. Perhaps less now. With Blankenship suspended the way he was, could she possibly reach his pocket? She turned and began picking her way back up the slope of shattered concrete. She would work on obtaining the key until there was half an hour to go, she decided. And then she would try the first-story windows.

"Eli," she called out. "Eli, listen to me. I'm just below you. I need the keys. Can you work your clinic coat off and let it drop?"

The soft, whining moan from above continued. Sarah pushed herself up the rubble another foot. She was opposite the very top of the first-floor opening now. But the slope had ended. She was as high as she could go. Blankenship was close. Just a few feet above her at the most. She tried to picture his down-stretched arms and imagine how his clinic coat might be hanging. If she leapt up and out, could she reach it? Could she hang on to it enough to pull it free? What if the keys had already fallen out? She stood at the very top of the slope, her back pressed against the rear wall of the shaft. Blankenship's heavy breathing seemed almost within arm's reach. Still, she could see nothing.

One try. One try and that would be it.

Expecting to connect with nothing but air, she braced her foot against the wall behind her and threw herself up and out. Blankenship screamed as her outstretched arms, flailing for his coat, collided with him. She hurtled on through the blackness, landing heavily on the unyielding slope and tumbling over and over toward the basement doorway. At the bottom of the slope she dropped out of the shaft, falling several feet from the rubble onto the basement floor. Air exploded from her lungs at the impact. She lay there, battered and sobbing, struggling to catch her breath, to regain her composure, to will herself to move. Suddenly she realized that she was clutching Blankenship's clinic coat.

The key ring was in the right-hand pocket.

Painfully she limped to the stairway and then made

her way down to the subbasement. She called out Matt's name, and followed his voice to the room that had so nearly become their tomb. The darkness was suffocating.

"It's over," she whispered, touching his face with her fingertips. "I've got Blankenship's keys. Now we've got to get you out of here, and I've got to get to Annalee."

She kissed him, and then reached behind to where he was bound to the pipe.

"It's wire of some sort," he said. "It's cutting my wrists to shreds. I'm not sure you can do anything back there in this dark without pliers."

"Let me try."

"Sarah, Blankenship's a demon. He had Rosa and Warren Fezler killed. He wired explosives to the ignition on Colin Smith's boat, and then arranged for Ettinger to be arrested for it. He's engineered everything—*everything.* . . . Singh is dead, too. Blankenship shot him and set it up to look like Ettinger did that one as well. He was just about home free. You were the last loose end and—ouch! Careful, that really hurts."

"Sorry. Matt, I can't do this. The wire's too tight. . . ."

"Well, we've got forty minutes or so. Get hold of Paris. Have him stop the countdown and get some people down here. Is Blankenship dead?"

"Maybe. I don't know. Listen, there's a phone just outside the outer gate in the tunnel. I'll be right back."

"You'd better be," he said. "I don't like it here too much. I think it's a very unlucky spot."

She kissed his forehead, then moved as quickly as she could down the corridor and through the two security gates. Until she picked up the receiver, she hadn't considered that the house phone outside the second gate might be disconnected. The dial tone was a hymn.

"I need to reach Mr. Paris," she told the operator. "This is Dr. Baldwin. It's an emergency."

"He's in his office," she said: "I just put a call through to him. In fact, he's still talking."

"Break in," Sarah said.

In seconds, Glenn Paris came on the line. The moment she heard his voice, Sarah knew the nightmare was truly over. The last problem—the Chilton Building countdown—was under control. She gave him the briefest summary of what had transpired and asked him to send someone down to the Chilton subbasement with flashlights and a wire cutter.

"We'll also need a stretcher for Dr. Blankenship," she said. "And maybe one for Matt as well. I'm not sure he'll be able to walk. And I think we'll need an orthopedist. I don't know how we're going to get Eli up from where he is."

"Don't worry," Paris said. "I'll take care of everything. Just stay right where you are by the security gate. I'll stop the countdown, and I'll be down in a minute with help."

"Thank you."

"And Sarah—"

"Yes?"

"You've done a hell of a job."

"Thank you, sir. Please hurry. There's another problem going on right now with Annalee Ettinger. And to overcome it, I may need your help with Dr. Snyder."

"We'll be right there."

Sarah sighed and sank to the floor. Her jeans and shirt were torn. Her face, legs, and arms were bleeding from dozens of scrapes and cuts. But far more painful to her than any of her injuries was Matt's news about Rosa Suarez. Rosa had wanted so badly to have everything turn out all right.

Within minutes, Sarah heard footsteps hurrying toward her down the connecting tunnel. Moments later, Glenn Paris entered the Chilton cutoff. He smiled and waved the flashlights he had brought.

"Everything's on hold up above," he said breathlessly. "Thank goodness you reached me. I was about to go out to the ceremonies."

"Well, I was prepared to run across to the grandstand if I had to."

Paris led her back into the stygian blackness of the Chilton subbasement.

"I guess you haven't heard about Colin Smith's death yesterday," he said, panning his light about. "I was just sitting in my office thinking about him."

"Matt just told me. He said Blankenship killed him and framed Peter Ettinger."

"That son of a bitch."

"Matt's right up here on the left," Sarah said. "Matt, honey, we're coming."

"I hear you."

Paris stopped at the doorway of the room and shined his light in from there.

"Maintenance is on the way with wire cutters, Matt," he said. "They should be here in a minute. Meanwhile, if you can hang on, I'd like Sarah to take me to Blankenship."

Sarah hesitated.

"Go ahead," Matt said. "I've been here like this for hours. I'll be okay."

She took a flashlight and led Paris up to the elevator shaft opening on the basement level.

"He's hanging from the doorway on the second—"

Sarah stopped in midsentence, directed the light onto her forearm, and gasped. She had been spattered by several thick drops of blood. She leaned into the shaft and directed the beam up at the second floor. The lower third of Blankenship's leg remained wedged as it had been. But the medical chief was gone.

"He's not th—"

Snarling in pain and rage, Blankenship came tumbling out of the darkness, down the slope of rubble. He slammed into Sarah, sending her sprawling out of the shaft and onto the concrete. Sarah cried out as Blankenship grabbed her ankle. Paris quickly stepped forward and put a foot down on his wrist. He held it there until she scrambled free. Then he aimed his flashlight beam straight into Blankenship's face. The medical chief was an apparition, smeared with gore, yet ghostly pale, and clearly more dead than alive.

"Is a medical team on the way?" Sarah asked.

Paris did not answer. Instead, he kicked Blankenship viciously in the mouth.

"You ruined me, you son of a bitch," he said. "I invested every cent my hospital could beg or borrow in that diet shit of yours because you swore there were no problems with it. You never said anything about there being a goddamn virus in it, you bastard. Nothing!"

"You knew?" Sarah said, stunned.

"Yes, I knew. I'm not stupid. But by the time I realized what that powder was doing to women, it was too late. We were in it too deep. I know about all the money, too, Eli. Colin's been checking up on you and your bogus foundation since day one. And that goddamn lab in there—I found that months ago. We've already gotten into two of your accounts. As soon as I get back to the office, I'm cleaning them out. Then I'll decide if I need to bail out of here or not. I was set to leave because of what this whole thing was going to do to me. My career and reputation down the drain; everyone blaming me for those women. But now, from what Sarah tells me, it seems that everyone who could connect me to you and that goddamn powder is dead. That is what you said, isn't it, Sarah?"

He loosed another short, choppy kick—this time to Blankenship's chest. Before Sarah could react, he whirled around and grabbed her hair.

"I'm sorry about this," he said, ignoring her cries of pain. "I really am." He reached into her pocket and pulled out Blankenship's keys. "I'm sorry about not stopping that countdown, too," he added. "I ordinarily don't lie about things that important."

He produced a length of rope from his jacket pocket, forced Sarah onto her belly, and tied her hands behind her. Then he dragged her to her feet and back to the stairs to the subbasement.

"I've changed my mind about a research building on this spot," he said. "I think instead we're going to fill it all in and go for a parking lot . . . or perhaps some tennis courts. I assume you'd rather be downstairs with your lawyer than up here with that monster."

"Please, Glenn," Sarah pleaded as he forced her down the stairs. "Please don't. I beg you. I know you didn't actually hurt anybody. I can tell everyone that."

"Sorry. I really have no choice. And I promise you won't feel a thing."

He pushed her back into the space that, once again, was to become a tomb. Ignoring Matt's pleas and Sarah's attempts at reason, he lashed her to an exposed girder, across the room from Matt, and secured her ankles.

Then, without a backward glance, he left them in the darkness and hurried from the Chilton Building.

An instant later, the overhead speakers announced that there were fifteen minutes left before demolition.

Chapter 44

". . . It is our hope, our dream, that this new Institute for Medical and Healing Studies will form a golden bridge between our rapidly advancing medical technology and the more mystical healing arts from across the centuries and around the world. . . ."

Glenn Paris proudly accepted another round of applause from the two hundred or so dignitaries and other ticket holders seated in the grandstand. The morning was sparkling, clear, and nearly windless—perfect conditions for the spectacle at hand. All around the campus, patients, staff, and visitors watched from rooftops and windows. On the far side of the mall, the Chilton Building stood alone, a deposed queen, facing the crowd with what little grace she could muster as she awaited the guillotine.

". . . Now, before the winner of our drawing steps up to thrill us all, I would like to pause for a moment of silence in honor of Mr. Colin Smith, the chief financial officer of this hospital, who perished yesterday in a most tragic boating accident. . . . I intend to recommend that our board of directors name a wing of this new institute after Colin. He will certainly be missed. . . .

And now, Governor, Mr. Mayor, esteemed colleagues, and all of you who have been so faithful over the years to the Medical Center of Boston—it gives me great pleasure to announce the winner of our raffle. Thanks to the devoted efforts of our raffle ticket sellers and canvassers, this contest has netted almost thirty-three thousand dollars for the new institute. . . . Thank you, thank you. The winner is here with me, and she is—" He glanced down at a three-by-five card. "—Mrs. Gladys Robertson of West Roxbury."

To the accompaniment of polite applause, a nervously smiling middle-aged woman in a floral-print dress stepped up to Paris and whispered in his ear.

"Oh, my apologies," Paris said into the microphone. "Our winner is *Miss* Gladys *Robinson*. I'm not actually a doctor, but obviously I write like one." Paris milked the ensuing laughter as long as he could. "So, then, Miss Gladys Robinson of West Roxbury," he said finally, "this is your moment. Here's the plunger that will set off the charges placed by our team of world-renowned specialists and give you your place in history. Mr. Crocker, do we have the green light? . . . Excellent. Miss Robinson, if you'll just allow us to get in a little drumroll. . . ."

Paris pointed to his right. From among the spectators, five men stood up with snare drums slung in front of them. The surprise brought a murmur of approval from the crowd. The drumroll began softly and then crescendoed. Paris waited . . . and waited, until the tension in the air was almost palpable.

"Now!" he shouted.

A thousand pairs of eyes were fixed on the Chilton Building as Miss Gladys Robinson depressed the plunger that had been set on the podium. For a suspended moment, there was only silence. Then, heralded by puffs of smoke from around the base of the foundation and up the brick walls, a dull rumble began and quickly expanded. The ground shook as the noise increased. A huge, thick cloud of gray dust erupted, enveloping the first two floors. Then, with a wondrous roar, the walls of the building dropped straight down into the billowing gray abyss.

Seconds later, there was silence once again.

The crowd watched in awe as the dense, concrete cloud floated upward and began to slowly disperse on the higher thermals. Then there was applause . . . and cheers . . . and whistles and pats on the back. Glenn Paris accepted them all with the confidence and aplomb of a man accustomed to successes. The governor shook his hand, and then the mayor.

Proudly, jaw thrust forward, Paris turned to survey his hospital. Suddenly he paled. His smile vanished. Two men and a woman, none of whom he expected to see, were approaching the grandstand across the grassy campus. Behind them walked two more men. Both of those men were tall and broad-shouldered, and carried themselves like the bodyguards Paris knew they were.

"Great job, Glenn, great," someone said, slapping him on the back.

But Paris, fixed on the approaching quintet, did not respond. The group had reached the base of the grandstand when Willis Grayson, his arm around his daughter's shoulders, beckoned him to come down. Flanking Lisa Grayson on the other side, limping, though not badly, was Matt Daniels. He was filthy and disheveled, his face swollen and discolored. But he squinted up at the man who had left him to die, and through cracked, bloodied lips, he forced a smile.

"You blew it, Glenn," he said hoarsely. "You blew it big time."

"I'm disappointed in you, Mr. Paris," Willis called up. "Very disappointed."

Paris glanced frantically about for an escape route.

"Don't even think about it," Grayson warned. "Either of my men could run backward and still catch you. Five minutes, Paris. That's all the time that remained when we arrived in the basement of that building. Five minutes. You left Dr. Baldwin and Mr. Daniels, here, tied up and helpless. You just turned and walked away, and left them to die! You're a very crude man, Paris."

The group around Glenn Paris peeled back and stared down at the new arrivals. Clearly, a number of them recognized the man known as the Ross Perot of the Northeast. The governor, who had reached the bottom of the grandstand, crossed to Grayson, spoke briefly with him and Matt, and then looked up at the hospital CEO.

"I think you'd best come down here," he said sharply.

Glenn Paris, his face pinched and ashen, hesitated. Then his shoulders and his gaze dropped, and he trudged slowly down the red-carpeted stairs.

. . .

"Obviously, if we had kn-known th-the trouble you and your f-friend were in, we would have t-tried to get here sooner," Warren Fezler said.

He and Sarah were hurrying as best she could manage through the tunnels toward the labor and delivery floor.

"I'm just glad you made it when you did," Sarah replied. "You're sure Rosa's okay?"

"She s-spent six hours in the operating room. But when we all left to fly d-down here, they told us she was stable."

"Thank God."

"After Rosa was sh-shot, j-just before she l-lost consciousness, she wrote down Mr. G-Grayson's home number. As soon as I explained what was going on, he f-flew right up in his ch-chopper. Rosa s-saved my life. I w-wish she could have s-saved my sister."

"That's very sad. I'm sorry. But I'm very angry, too—at Blankenship, at all of you."

"I understand. I d-don't know what I can do."

"Just help me now, and then try to set some things straight with that damn virus of yours."

Sarah wanted to take the stairs up to L and D, but her battered body dictated she use the elevator.

"Warren, how did you manage to find us?" she asked as they waited for the car.

"N-not that hard f-for a man like Grayson. He knows how to m-move people like no one I've ever s-seen." He thought for a moment and then added, "Except maybe f-for Eli. We started at th-the ICU and then went to the psych w-ward. Some man there—Wes something—said you had had a seizure at breakfast and w-were in the ER. He also said you had s-spent the whole n-night watching th-the Chilton Building through binoculars. Next w-we found out you were wheeled away by Eli and someone from transportation. And then when we f-found you had never arrived at the ER, we began to suspect where you were. Mr. G-Grayson latched onto the man from transportation. Then we kn-knew we were right."

"So you went into the basement of the building through the back door."

"I h-had the keys. That was once my home away from home, remember? Mr. G-Grayson decided to look for you rather than to t-try and s-stop the explosion."

They pushed through the doors of the labor and delivery floor, and were immediately confronted by a sound Sarah had heard before. Annalee Ettinger was screaming in pain. Mindless of the nursing staff, Sarah grabbed Warren's hand and pulled him down the hall to Annalee's room. The uniformed guard was gone—discharged, Sarah assumed, when the evil Dr. Baldwin was locked up on Underwood Six. Randall Snyder, quite obviously agitated and on the razor's edge of panic, was checking the pulses at Annalee's wrists.

"Would one of you please page Dr. Blankenship again," he was saying to the nurses assisting him.

"You can page him all you want," Sarah cut in, "but I guarantee you he won't be answering. Not now, not ever. Annalee, will you let me talk to you, please? It's very important."

"They said you tried to hurt me."

"They were wrong. Will you talk with me?"

"Can you help this pain in my arms and my feet?"

"I can make it go away."

Huddled to one side of the obstetrics family room, Willis Grayson, Lisa, Matt, and Warren Fezler watched the monitor screen intently. Glenn Paris had installed the video system as part of his overhaul of the OB/Gyn service. The cesarean camera was mounted directly above the operating table. The field it projected now consisted of two pairs of hands—Randall Snyder's and Sarah's—and Annalee Ettinger's smooth, gravid belly.

"Okay, is the blood up and running?" they heard Snyder ask.

"Up and running," a nurse's voice replied.

"Signs stable?"

"All systems are go," said the anesthesiologist.

"Ready, Sarah?"

"Ready."

Lisa Grayson gave Matt a teasing nudge.

"Okay, then," Snyder said. "It's your case, Doctor. I'll assist."

"But—"

"Quickly!"

"All right. All right."

The four viewers watched as Sarah and Randall Snyder vanished from the screen, and then reappeared, having changed places at the table.

Sarah flexed her gloved hands once, then again.

"Okay, everyone, let's do it," she said. "Scalpel, please."

Epilogue

OCTOBER 30

SARAH ETTINGER WEST, MEET YOUR NEW GOD-mother."

Radiant in her hospital bed, Annalee held the infant away from her breast long enough for Sarah to see.

"You make a great kid," Sarah said. "I'm honored to be her godmother."

After a beginning that was considerably rockier for mother than daughter, both were now doing fine. As Sarah had predicted, the cesarean section delivery essentially cured Annalee's DIC. First Lisa, now Annalee. Two cases sectioned, two cases cured. At least they had a place to start in dealing with the virus.

"How many women do you suppose are facing this?" Annalee asked, as if reading her mind.

"People are checking on that now. But I can tell you, it's going to be a lot. Blankenship just didn't care. He didn't care at all. I still don't understand it."

"Crazy doesn't require any understanding. It just is."

"I guess. Fortunately, it appears your father kept decent records of who received the powder and vitamins."

"He always was the decent record sort."

"The product's been on the market for almost eight months now. That means the first cases of infected women going into labor could happen any time."

"I can give you the list of people Peter tested the stuff on at the time he gave it to me."

"Great. That will leave only the rest of Singh's group from the clinic here—the original set of guinea pigs. With Singh dead, we have to rely on finding Blankenship's records of his work. I think he must have a list— that's how he knew right away that the first women who got the powder were starting to get into trouble. If we can't find his records, we'll have to rely on publicity to bring them in."

"And all for money."

"All for money," Sarah echoed sadly. "Plus whatever thrill Blankenship got from using his intellect to maneuver and control people."

"Speaking of which—"

Sarah knew what was coming next.

"What's the situation?" she asked.

"Peter's still in jail. His lawyer called a little while ago. There's some sort of hearing scheduled later today. He says that if you came and spoke to the judge, Peter would probably at least be able to post bail and get out. If you don't tell them that Blankenship admitted killing that man on the boat, Peter might have to stay."

"A thought that is not entirely unappealing."

The two women exchanged conspiratorial smiles.

"He's the grandfather of your godchild, remember."

"I know, I know. I just wonder how much of a dent this whole thing has made on his cast-iron ego. Blankenship played him like a violin."

"And Peter went right along with it, no questions asked."

"All for money," Sarah said.

"Xanadu was in trouble. I think it was as much pride and ego as profit."

"Well, I'm going to insist that whatever money we can

retrieve from this whole mess be used to find some sort of definitive cure. And that includes whatever Peter has."

"I agree."

"The six-foot four-inch violin. Boy, I'll bet he really loved the publicity of those damned infomercials."

"He did that," Annalee said, lifting Sarah E. West and gently bringing the infant over to her other breast.

"Maybe another week or so in jail might—okay, okay. I'll give his lawyer a call and see what I can do."

"Thanks, Doc."

Sarah stood to go.

"Annalee, do me one favor, though," she said.

"Anything."

Sarah bent down and kissed first mother, then daughter. "Don't ever let him forget it."

●   ●   ●

TAKE IT OR LEAVE IT

by Axel Devlin

July 3

Yesterday I had an appointment with my acupuncturist. Her name is Dr. Sarah Baldwin-Daniels. When my back goes out, which it tends to do when I engage in any activity more strenuous than clicking my channel changer, my acupuncturist tells me to relax, sticks a few of her special stainless steel needles in me, and takes the pain away.

Helping folks like me with her acupuncture is sort of a hobby for Dr. B-D. Her real job is being a surgeon. In fact, as of two days ago, she is the new chief resident in Obstetrics and Gynecology at the Medical Center of Boston. For those of you new to my column, i.e., those who have been living on Mars for the last ten years, let me say that for much of the past year, I was not a supporter of my acupuncturist or her hospital. I thought she was a quack.

She is not a quack. She sticks her special needles in me and my back feels better. And as far as this layman goes, that's all I care to know. Make me feel better without some horrible side effect that's worse than my illness was, and you are okay in my book.

So I was wrong. This is my column, and I get to use it any way I want. And today, a year after Dr. B-D and the diet powder nightmare first lit up my word processor screen, I'm using it to say I was wrong.

Because of you, Doc, performing cesarean sections before active labor has saved countless lives. And now we hear there's a blood test and treatment coming for the dreaded weight loss virus. God willing, maybe soon all those cesareans won't be necessary.

So yesterday I saw my acupuncturist. I went to her six months ago to do an interview and to get the full story on the Herbal Weight Loss horror. And I happened, just happened, to mention my lousy back. That was when Dr. Baldwin-Daniels stepped forward.

"I might be able to help you," she said. "I might be able to do something for the pain."

So yesterday afternoon, just hours after my former enemy stuck a few of her special needles in me, I broke 90 at my club for the first time.

Quack!